Kid Glove Charlie

Charlie Peace—burglar, murderer, clown and womanizer—a North Country imp who scandalised Victorian sensibilities. His tale here as a novel, but based on facts and contemporary fictions. Perhaps the most bizarre of 19th century rogues, Peace's acts of derring-do made headlines in his time— placed him on equal footing with such stalwarts as Claude Duval and Robin Hood. Victorian propriety, however, excluded him from the Dictionary of National Biography. But the scoundrel is not totally forgotten: not in the Industrial North, nor at Madame Tussaud's—where he sits forlornly by a gallows, waiting for Marwood to stretch his scrawny neck. This novel attempts to re-advertise Peace's ironic name and dubious dealings.

Kid Glove Charlie

A Ballad of Charlie Peace

(1832–1879)

John Cashman

ROBERT HALE · LONDON

ISBN 0 7091 7868 9

Robert Hale Limited
Clerkenwell House
Clerkenwell Green
London, EC1R 0HT

WEST LANCASHIRE

Much nonsense for Suzy

18008005

032 113544

ST6196

Printed by Billing & Sons Limited
Guildford, London and Worcester

Contents

	Foreword	vii
1.	Blue O'Clock in the Morning	1
2.	Ferrae Naturae	15
3.	The Wrestling Man of God	25
4.	The Fabergé Gewgaw	43
5.	Whitsing	54
6.	Parke's Law	74
7.	Manchester Rick-Rack	82
8.	Nathaniel Down Below	93
9.	Every Bullet Has Its Billet	105
10.	Cutting Quick Sticks	112
11.	In the Marsh	120
12.	"Down ta Lunnan"	131
13.	At the House of Nobs	153
14.	Rozzer Robinson's Rumble	169
15.	Traitress Sue	177
16.	Little White Lies	193
17.	Death Only Wars on the Quick	218
18.	The Harrowing of Hell	240
	Addendum	277
	Glossary	279

Foreword

This story is based on facts, legends, and half-truths. Probably more of the latter were told about Charles Peace than any other English criminal since Robin Hood. Shortly after his own lifetime, Peace almost became a folk hero on the lines of Dick Turpin and Jack Shepherd, but this was checked by the Victorian sense of propriety and he was eventually just branded a scoundrel. Yet his name still endures—even in a modern children's comic book —as an example of good-natured villainy and a "real peacer" means a dashing murderer. In fact though, there was little dashing about the real Peace: his life was a series of eccentric bungles. He was an incompetent burglar and may have died on the gallows for mere manslaughter, but certain things do make him remarkable. He was self-educated, and an accomplished musician, craftsman, and actor; had he tried the stage, his career might have been different. He was both incredibly ugly and exceptionally strong—it was said he could carry a twenty-score pig on his back for a mile (an odd thing to have said, to be sure). He had a passion for large ladies, and certainly two of them, in turn, found him fascinating, although they both proved to be his undoing. He was a "great boaster," but some of his boasts were true, and he was not entirely responsible for all the myths that sprang up about him—the newspapers were mostly to blame. And once he was captured for murder, the press published any old story concerning him, whatever the source. When he was under sentence of death, *The Times* had this, inter alia, to say of him.

Charles Peace may claim a remarkable place among the great criminals of modern days. Seldom has there been a person so typical of the criminal class which tends more and more to organise its war against society and elevate law-breaking to the rank of a profession. In Peace, the qualities of a criminal inspire wonder as well as disgust by their enormity. A cold and cynical depravity and an undisguised subservience to coarse and vulgar forms of pleasure were conjoined in this man with extraordinary courage, with self-reliance and self-possession, with cunning and daring, with reticence, and, above all, with an iron, a resistless force of will. Fortunately it is not often that these dangerous qualities are to be discovered in high perfection among those who devote themselves, as Peace certainly did, to a life of crime. Before justice laid her grasp upon him, the iron had already entered into his soul.

These rather fanciful notions were proclaimed in a lead editorial sharing a page with articles on the French cabinet, education, industry, and import duties. Peace would have been flattered and chuckled merrily at such nonsense for he mocked the world. His most engaging characteristics were his impudence, joie de vivre, and ability to laugh at himself. This tale attempts to show what he *might* have been like.

More comments are contained in the Addendum, together with a Glossary of contemporary terms and West Riding dialect. Peace himself spoke as if he had a mouth full of plums.

1

Blue O'Clock in the Morning

Heeley Hall was part of the Norfolk Estate on the outskirts of Sheffield. The estate itself was managed on behalf of the absentee Duke of Norfolk by one Marcus Smith, steward. He collected the rents and dues, governing the tenants with an iron discipline, and was generally hated by the colliers and foundrymen who made up the estate's lessees. By way of reward for his management, he was permitted by His Grace to occupy the Hall.

The latter, a Queen Anne house, was set back from a lane behind high walls. Within those walls were lawns and lebanons running down to an ornamental lake. Few outsiders entered the grounds for Marcus Smith was fond of his privacy. Nor did the locals even venture very often down the road outside. They preferred to stick to the high road because there were mastiffs guarding the big house. And today, on the last day of October, 1875, the only traveler upon the lane was an old woman leading a pony and cart.

It was dusk when she first came into sight, and dark when she reached the Hall gates. Here she stopped, ostensibly to sit by a ditch and rest her feet. Her pony also came to a noiseless halt, as did the cart—the wheels of which, oddly enough, had been bound round with tape. But more than the cart was unusual: the old woman sported a beard hidden under her shawl, and, after easing her feet, she replaced her clogs with a pair of rubber-soled shoes. Then she got up, rather nimbly for her age, and crossed the road to peep through the gates, after which she returned to her pony. "Come, Dziggitae," she said gruffly, and escorted the beast half a mile down the road where she hitched it to a tree on the fringe of a wood and blinkered it. The woman then took off her long Irish shawl and at once was revealed as a man—small and bow backed, with the gait of a jockey—who delved under the tarpaulin covering his cart and extracted a bag and a sack. Then he pulled a woolly hat over his gray cropped hair, patted the pony's neck, muttered endearments to it, and started off back to the Hall. Somewhere in the woods an owl hooted, and the man uncannily answered its call, absolutely.

The man was Charlie Peace and he didn't break into the mansion immediately, but scouted the grounds, located the kennels, and examined every downstairs window. The dogs he found were locked up, but he took the precaution of scattering "pudden"— balls of drugged meat—outside their kennels. The house itself was quiet; lights showed only in the servants' quarters; and Peace assumed the Smiths to be away. But then a sliver of moon lit the grounds, so he retired to hide by the gates. As he crouched, he considered his mission. It was not his custom to hit houses around Sheffield—so close to family and home, but Marcus Smith had been described as a "rum cove," as well as very rich, and Charlie was in need of money this month for his wife Hannah had found them a house in Darnall, his brother required the price of a publican's license, and their mother was hard up as usual. So Marcus Smith had been chosen to ease the financial strain. Charlie likened himself to the Pinner of Wakefield, robbing Peter to pay Paul, with a medieval concept of justice. Anyway, that's how silly Willie, his stepson, would see it. . . .

At three o'clock, Charlie finally went into action. He climbed

into the Hall through a rear window and found himself in a
pantry. The room was in darkness, but he had a small spotlight
with him and saw that a servant was asleep in a chair—a mere
kitchen boy, who had supposedly been guarding some silver.
Charlie stole nothing from his custody—he didn't want the lad
dismissed for failing his duty—and he quickly moved on into the
body of the house. He found the drawing room and went inside,
shutting the door and screwing it fast to its frame, which experience had taught him was safer than just locking a door. Then he
extinguished his spotlight, lit a larger lamp, and systematically
began searching the room. He took mostly little things, of sterling or gold, including a metal bird on a stick. There was a grand
piano draped with a cloth and covered with miniatures, of which
he stole several, and by the piano stool he found some musical
instruments, including an American guitar which was too large
for his bag, but he squeezed in a fine concertina. It pained him
that Marcus Smith might be a musical man; Peace had been
expecting a room full of bad taste and hunting crops. When he
finished this room he decided to try the upstairs in his quest, for
hard cash and jewelry, which was the most dangerous part of the
night's operation. Then a sound from outside made him freeze.
Someone was trying the door handle and wood creaked under
pressure. He blew out his light and put it down, retreating in the
dark to the piano and crawling underneath it. And he was barely
in time—a shoulder rammed the drawing room door, forcing it
open, and a man with a bull's-eye lantern blundered into the
room. A servant, thought Charlie; only bobbies and flunkeys
carried bull's-eyes. The man bent down and then gasped with
pain; he'd touched Charlie's hot lamp. Charlie grinned and drew
a revolver from his belt, leapt out from under the piano, gun in
one hand, sack and bag in the other. He faced the servant, a fat
man in a nightshirt, and raised his revolver. The pepperbox
flashed twice, filling the room with its roar, but Charlie had fired

high, well over the man's head, and merely pocked the wall with buckshot, though the servant cried out, dropping his lantern as he flung himself flat on the floor. Charlie jumped over him, with a "Move, and I'll blow thy head off!" Then he was out the door, down the hall, and back in the pantry, where the kitchen lad was on his feet, poker in hand. "Don't try it!" Charlie warned, waving his pistol, and the lad dropped the iron bar like a snake, as Charlie flew past him and dived headlong out the open window.

He hit the lawn with a shoulder roll and came to his feet all in one, running fast as a hare for the garden wall, tucking away his gun but listening for dogs. He was over the wall and off down the road before any pursuit had even left the house. Then he could hear the dogs barking, and soon humans were shouting. He trusted the hue and cry would be confined to the grounds, with men and mastiffs chasing each other, until he got clear of the neighborhood. Nevertheless, he sprinted the half-mile back to his cart, unveiled his pony, and whipped her up into a trot. His hat, sack, and bag went under the tarpaulin, and out came the old woman's shawl. Charlie felt safer; but he conceded he'd been careless—two men could have been shot—and he cursed himself for an incompetent fool.

II

Jacob Bradbury, of the Highfield Division, was put in charge of the inquiry about the intruder.

"We're under pressure, Sergeant," the chief constable told Bradbury, for Marcus Smith considered a burglary of his property nigh on High Treason.

Bradbury started by searching records at the Water Lane Police Station, assisted by a young constable named Pearson, who was to cover all areas east of the city. But both officers soon drew a blank: every known criminal was possessed of an alibi. So they broadened the investigation to include those ex-convicts who now purported to lead honest lives, looking through their files, some of them yellow with age, others mysteriously missing, all of them pretty useless.

"Shall us go back ta t'60s, sir?" Constable Pearson asked after a two-hour spell in the sergeant's office.

Bradbury nodded wearily, and Pearson heaved out a stack of dusty folders from the back of the old tin safe. The two men divided the pile and scanned the dossiers in silence.

"Here's summat!" Pearson said suddenly. "A Ticket o' Leave on a fella named Parker—number 9170. He did a sixer for housebreaking, starting August, 1859."

"Release date?" Bradbury asked.

"June, 1864. From Millbank pen, Lunnan."

"London! Nay, lad—yon villain probably stopped south. Now find us summat more recent!" And Parker was abandoned for a more likely suspect.

III

Otto Senf was due to meet Charlie Peace at the Riding Academy in Hamburg at nine. The district of St. Pauli was full of sailors that night, and Senf was careful to dodge their boisterous groups. Someone might try to rob him, and he was carrying a large amount of cash in his money belt. He hoped that Charlie had brought something worthwhile from across the German Sea. He also wished Charlie had chosen somewhere more discreet than the Academy for their rendezvous. But the Academy, a dance hall, was a lively place, and the Englishman liked rowdy forms of entertainment.

As it was, Senf reached the hall just as two drunks were being ejected by the doorman. He was given a nod of recognition by the latter as he passed through the swing doors. The Academy wasn't fussy about its clientele, provided they paid for their drinks.

It was a blaze of lights inside. Gilt mirrors lined red-papered walls, the tables were marble and the floor mosaic, and the room was packed. Trawlermen rubbed shoulders with ferrymen and "jig-jiggi" girls in frilly short skirts. Two such girls were with the man Senf sought, one sitting on his knee, the second filling glasses with kümmel. Charlie was at a table under a high stage at the end of the hall. He was dressed as a seaman and smoking an Albert Ross.

"Vi gehts?" said Senf, in his worst plaat-deutsch.

Charlie came to his feet, shook Senf's hand, and drew up a chair for the German. "This is Mr. Mustard, girlies," he introduced him. "Mr. Mustard, meet Frisky and Whiskey."

Senf nodded to the girls. He assumed Charlie would send them away now that he'd arrived, but Charlie merely called upon a waiter for an extra glass. Senf studied him as he paid for the drink. Charlie's gargoyle features were grotesque, with a pugilist nose and protuberant jaw. His eyes were both hazel, but one was distinctly darker than the other. Senf also noticed that Charlie wore just one kid glove as he usually did. "Cheerio," he said, raising his glass. Charlie returned the toast, and then reached under the table to produce a corduroy bag. "Bits 'n' bobs, Mr. Mustard," he said, opening the bag.

"Not in here!" Senf protested.

Charlie laughed. "Nivver fret, Mr. Mustard; we be safe as mice in a mill." He took packages out of the bag, spreading them out on the table, removing the wrappings to reveal articles ranging from brooches to plate. Some of the silver was crushed, as if deliberately bent to reduce its size, which was commonplace damage in the case of stolen dishes. Senf leaned forward to inspect the haul, while the girls cooed over some of the rings.

"Not a good catch," Charlie admitted. Before him lay the proceeds of seven burglaries between Heeley Hall and Doncaster.

Senf completed his valuation. "Four hundert marks," he offered.

Charlie raised his hand with a groan. "I wants more than that, Mr. Mustard. I ran fearsome risks for that lot. Why, the Ridings be adder stung with bobbies these days!" And he shut his eyes as if to blot out some dreadful memory.

"Five hundert?" Senf tried.

Charlie's eyes opened. "Seven—when I add this little gem." He went into his bag and produced a square shape wrapped in oilskin. He unveiled it—a picture. "Pretty as pins, eh?" Senf studied the miniature, that of a woman in white with curly brown hair. "Mary Smart," Charlie told him, "painted by hubby John in '06. She was his third missus—dirty old bugger!"

"Where did you get it?" Senf asked with wonder; Smart was an important miniaturist.

But Charlie tapped the side of his nose. "Now, what dost thou say? Seven hundred?"

Senf knew that Charlie was aware of the worth of the Smart. Senf would get five hundred for the picture alone down in Bremen. "As you will," he agreed.

"Right-O!" cried Charlie. Business was over. Now he and Senf could relax and enjoy the pleasures of Hamburg. And as if in recognition of the good moment, the stage above them came to life. Gas footlights came on and the band struck up a Sneiderdeern song. The maître d'hall came onstage, dressed like a ringmaster, flourishing a whip, and announced the next attraction. Five Northern beauties, he said, would now try to ride a Wild Ass of the Carpathians. A trumpet sounded and five women skipped onto the boards, grossly fat and clad in togas of flimsy gold lamé. The maître introduced them by name. "Who dares deny their beauty?" he challenged the crowd.

"Bloody 'ell," Charlie said quietly.

"Have they not the charms of Diana?" said the maître.

"As painted by Rubens!" Charlie called to him.

The maître spied Charlie. "Do I hear a note of contradiction, meinherr?"

"Nay; just a cry from a simple heart!"

"But where is your *heart*, meinherr?"

" 'Twixt my bloody legs, Dutchman, and that's why 'tis crying!"

This exchange brought cheers from the crowd. The maître shook his whip at Charlie with apparent good humor, but Senf noted that his eyes were far from benevolent. Hamburgers did not like to be called Dutchmen. But now the ass was led onstage by a youth with a halter. It was not a wild ass, just a gray donkey dyed brown, and the animal was plainly terrified. Charlie's grin faded. One of the plump showgirls mounted the donkey's back. The animal bucked and swirled, trying to unseat her, and the youth smacked its muzzle with the end of the halter.

"This is villainy," Charlie said to Senf. "Yon bag o' lard wilt break that beast's back. I do not care for it at all." And he rose from his chair.

"Be seated, please," Senf urged him.

But Charlie's nutcracker jaw was set and his bushy brows frowned. The scene up above was getting worse by the moment, with the donkey braying, lashed by the youth.

"Nay, I'll not see it done!" Charlie cried, and he swung himself onto the stage.

Most people thought Charlie part of the act, but the maître, who knew better, stepped forward. Charlie ignored him, looking at the donkey and stout showgirl. Then as the youth struck the animal again Charlie rushed at the group, seized the halter, and flung the youth to the floor. Without pausing, he spun the rope in an arc, lassoed the girl on the donkey, and hauled her off. She landed on the boards with an undignified bump, her shrieks lost in a howl of pleasure from the crowd. The maître was red with rage and brandishing his whip; with luck, a good brawl lay ahead. But Charlie didn't notice the maître; he was calming the donkey with comforting words of Romanish. Only when he felt the sting of the whip across his shoulders did he turn. He caught the whip as it fell again, twisted the lash around his wrist, and janked the maître toward him. Charlie's bare fist struck him hard on the jaw, and he sprawled on the ground as if poleaxed. Then Charlie stepped calmly over the stunned man and helped the showgirl to her feet. He dodged her slaps and gave her five marks for her bruised bottom. Then he went to the youth in charge of the ass.

"Remember this, you young bugger," he admonished him, "the Saviour rode one of yon fussacks on Palm Sunday. They may be stupid, but they once bore the bum of Our Christ!" He handed the boy money—"Take this brass and go find a more menseful h'occupation"—pocketed his wallet, and went to get off the stage. But the maître's reinforcements had arrived from the wings—two bully-boys a match for most men. "Oh dear, what a mess," Charlie muttered, facing them. He considered the gun in his belt, but decided against it. He looked down at Senf. "Get my bag and thysen out of here, Mr. Mustard!" he called, and watched the German head for the exit with the girls. Then he turned to the bully-boys with a smile. The maître was behind them, giving directions in German: Charlie was to be relieved of his purse and thrown out of the place. One tough drew a black cosh and came at Charlie, who put his arm in a "come-with-me," and spun the tough off the stage. He landed on a table of seamen, who immediately set about him, which distracted the second bully. Charlie avoided his wild swings and countered them with a few accurate jabs to the face. The young thug pitched back into the donkey, which panicked, and pandemonium broke out on the stage. Free-for-alls were also under way among customers, and Charlie took the opportunity to jump from the boards and leave.

He found Otto Senf and the girls on the Reeperbahn, hiding down an alley. He laughed and patted the frightened German's shoulder. "Another pub I be banned from," he said, taking his bag. He led Senf and the girls toward David-strasse, chatting merrily. "I h'abominate violence—'tis the failure of civilization," he told them. "But 'twas bad to see a poor dumb beast frightened." He put his arms round the girls' waists. "Nuff said about that. . . . Now then, take old Charlie to h'another drum with good ale. I'm minded to festivate!"

IV

Charlie sailed back to Hull on *The Labor in Vain,* an old tug of a whaler battered by ice floes. Her skipper was Olsen, a Norsker, who asked no questions of passengers. Charlie himself was afraid of the sea and tended to stick to his cabin, reading tracts on the Testaments. But he came up on deck as dawn broke over the slate-gray waves. The night before, the ship had been lashed by a gale, but now all was calm, and Charlie could make out the Spurn Head peninsula; two lighthouses which rang mournful bells at regular intervals. Charlie admired their construction. "Ocellum pronsontorium," he announced to a sailor mending tackle nearby.

The sailor stared up from the deck. "Howsay, mister?"

"Latin, lad. Hull was a portant place in Roman times. Don't they larn thee nowt at school nowadays? Aye, Hull's full o' history, my boy. Romans, Vikings, and h'Icelandics." He noted the sailor's red hair. " 'Appen you're the downthrow of some Daneclagh thysen! Where you from, lad?" The sailor had the singsong accent, typical of Hull trawlermen, known as North Sea Chinese.

"Patrington, mister," the sailor replied. "And you, mister?"

"I'm from all over. But I was born in h'Ethiopia."

The sailor didn't know whether to believe him, but grinned. He finished repairing his nets and stood up to heave a bucket over the side, drawing water to wash. He had stripped off his vest and when he turned his back Charlie saw that the skin was criss-crossed by a network of scars, some slight, several deep.

"I h'observe you've enjoyed a spot of air and h'exercise," he said.

The sailor jumped as if touched by a ghost. "Mister?"

"Which cat scratched your back?" Charlie asked. "Army—Navy—or plain Queen's Castle?" He winked and lit his pipe. "But you should be proud of those claw marks," he added. "For mysen, I didn't feel owt after the third cut."

"You too?"

Charlie nodded. "And they crossed the cuts in my case, lad."

The sailor was impressed. "Then I'll not envy you your time, mister. Where was it—while serving Brown Bess?"

He'd put Charlie in the Army, and the little man saw no reason to disillusion him. "One hour before Inkerman. When you were a nipper."

The other shook his head with awe and started to sponge himself. Eventually he went below while Charlie stared out to sea. The ship had entered the Humber estuary, but Charlie's mind was still on the sailor's back. Charlie hadn't been as tough as that man when he'd received his two dozen lashes at Chatham Gaol; the force of the cat had knocked the breath from his body and excelled any punishment he'd received in the ring. He remembered the bewhiskered Visiting Magistrates who'd ordered his flogging, the blue-coated warder who wielded the cat. Where had it all started? With a conviction at Manchester for burglary: six years' hard labor in June '59. He'd begun his sentence at Portland, high on the cliffs, overlooking the Bill, where he'd broken rocks for the breakwater with a nine-pound hammer. Manual labor, however mindless, he'd endured, but then they'd sent him to Chatham. Picking oakum made anyone fractious and the convicts there had mutinied. Charlie had been George Parker in those days—with a reputation for locks, and he'd unlocked three inner doors at one prison but had been caught at the fourth. The mutiny had been quickly put down and the twenty participants flogged with a two-pound "cat"—a relic from the wars against Boney. Then they'd been transported to the Rock of Gibraltar . . .

Charlie took out his pipe and spat in the sea—at his memories. He stopped glowering and crossed the decks to go midships and thence to his cabin.

When the ship docked at Corporation Pier Charlie took his leave of *The Labor in Vain* and walked toward the town center on his way to visit his aged mother. The waterfront was a maze of masts and spars and doubtful people; and the whole area stank of fish. He passed by some sheds; faces peered out at him— Russian and Polish faces, refugees from pogroms bound for either London or New York. Charlie saluted them with an upturned thumb; he pitied their lot; Hull was as much a market for unhappy mankind as for timber and fish.

Mrs. John Peace lived in Paragon Square, an acreage of pawnbrokers and slop shops. Charlie wanted her out of Hull and with the rest of the family in Sheffield, but she was a woman with a mind of her own.

Her house stood in the crumbling terrace. A seaman was spewing out his heart in the gutter as Charlie came up.

"Drink is the bane of mankind," Charlie cautioned, giving him a shilling. "Go eat summat for the liquor to work on."

Mrs. Peace answered her son's special knock and they embraced. His mother was eighty, but almost as alert as when she'd married his late father, a manager of Wombwell's Wild Beast Show. She took Charlie into the kitchen, sat him down, and began to make him breakfast.

"How was Germany?" she asked from the range.

"Full o' bloody Dutchmen."

"That'll be tuppence for the Swear Box!" Mrs. Peace no more approved of her son's bad language than she did of his life of crime—which was something they no longer discussed. "How long are you stopping in Hull?" she said.

"I must away on the midday train," Charlie told her. "We move to Darnall on Sat'day and there's much to be done."

"And how are Hannah and family?"

" 'Annah's the same," Charlie laughed. "But Janey's bloomed like a rose, and Willie's a strapping fine lad."

Mrs. Peace nodded. Janey was Charlie's favorite, of course, his own daughter by Hannah. His own John had died of consumption aged eleven. Charlie had been on Dartmoor at the time, and his grief had been terrible. Willie was just Hannah's by a man named Ward; she'd been carrying the boy when Charlie had married her. Not that Charlie treated him as less than his own flesh and blood. Mrs. Peace looked across her kitchen. Framed on a shelf was a small memorium; she couldn't read it but she knew the words off by heart.

> Farewell my dear son, by us all beloved,
> Thou art gone to dwell in the Mansions above,
> In the bosom of Jesus, who sits on the Throne.
> Thou art anxiously awaiting to welcome us Home.

Charlie's words—in memory of his boy.

Willie Ward, slow and stupid, was no compensation for bright little John, but Charlie gave his best to his stepson. "I'm glad you've kept Willie at home," Mrs. Peace said, bringing over fried gulls' eggs.

"I've tried to keep him away from the metalyards," Charlie agreed, tucking into his breakfast, "but the lad's got no h'aptitude for book larning. He can scarcely manage a readamadeasy."

Mrs. Peace grunted. "Well, just so long as he doesn't follow your line of business," she murmured.

"Nivver that!" Charlie promised her. He put down his fork, took out his purse, and handed his mother two hundred marks. "For thysen." He paused because he'd now have to lie to her. "And come by honest, I swear it!"

His mother took the notes gingerly and slipped them into her apron. Her face gave no indication of what she believed. But she'd only Charlie to look to financially; he'd been supporting her since the death of his father. That's why he wanted her in Sheffield, near other Peaces who could keep an eye on her should anything happen to him.

Charlie finished his breakfast and rose from the table. "Well, I must be off!" he said, consulting his hunter. "I'll send thee a postcard once we're settled." He came round and kissed the top of his mother's head. She smelled of lavender. "God bless, little Queen!" He hurried his departure. He hated leaving his mother, unsure whether he'd ever see her again, and their goodbyes were quick.

Alone in her kitchen, Mrs. Peace sat down in a rocker. She had a cup of tea and looked for omens among the tea leaves. Her life had been dogged by misfortune ever since she ran off with John Peace and lost her own family. Her husband had not been a bad man—certainly never a criminal—but life with the fairs was hard. Mrs. Peace's gaze rose from her cup to the dresser. Beside the memorium was another card, also made by Charlie, when his father had died: "In Peace he lived. In Peace he died. Life was our desire. But God denied." Charlie's terrible poetry! Mrs. Peace smiled to herself.

2

Ferrae Naturae

Darnall was four miles from Sheffield, on the railway. It suited Arthur Dyson, a civil engineer with the railroad, for he often had to travel to York. But being out in the countryside did not please his wife; she longed for the bustle of town. The Dysons, who had been living in Ohio, had returned to England and had rented a house in Victoria Place, one of a row of forty small cottages in Britannia Road, not far from Holy Trinity Church. It was also near several public houses, the Halfway House in particular, to which Mrs. Dyson, thirty, tied down by a five-year-old son, would repair on the sly. Her husband, who was nearly double her age, six and a half feet tall, and as precise as one of his calculators, bored her. He'd officially retired at fifty, but an indolent life was not to his liking, and he soon took an appointment with the Yorkshire railways. Kate Dyson would even have preferred to remain in America. She found English countryside life dull.

So when the Peaces moved into 40 Victoria Place, Mrs. Dyson's interest was easily aroused. The Peace family, of four, came in with the vans at the weekend, setting up house next door but one to the Dysons. They brought with them an impressive range of furniture, which was hefted into the villa, followed by cases and boxes, a piano, and coops for the backyard. Mrs. Dyson watched from her front window, through a discreet gap in the curtains. In charge of operations, she saw a small man with bandy legs and a sharp-featured, angular woman, obviously his wife. Very *com-*

15

mon sort of people, she thought, typical of the environs of Sheffield.

Her husband came up behind her, looming like the mast of a ship. "We've gotten some new neighbors," she explained, in an Irish-American twang.

"No need to stare 'em scared," said Dyson, with much the same accent.

"Shall we offer them tea?" asked his wife.

Dyson inspected the couple for himself. "I've never took in a stray in my life," he said, "and I don't aim to start now." He drew his wife away from the window and closed the curtain. "But I'll own it's high time for tea, so maybe you'll fix me some?" Mrs. Dyson knew that her husband expected people to do his bidding immediately, and that she was no exception to his rule. This high-handedness often infuriated her—had driven her to rebel in the past, when her Irish temper cut loose—and then she would throw around crockery or take to the bottle. A drop's what I need at the moment, she said to herself, as she started preparing her husband's tea. But there was nothing to drink in the larder or even scones and cake; most of the shelves were bare. Her housekeeping allowance was strictly limited and she spent most of it on gin. She blamed her husband for penny-pinching. "Miser!" she muttered aloud, in the brogue of her Maynooth forefathers.

Charlie was pleased with Number 40. The house had a cellar and attic for his tools, and the yard a shed for his menagerie of pigeons and parrots, ferrets and songbirds, and Chimarosa, an old boar badger.

The next day was Sunday and the Peaces breakfasted on blood-worms and porridge. Charlie had a taste for the latter, sweetened with molasses, and Hannah's black sausage was famous. They all sat round the fire in the small kitchen, Janey dressed for church in a very pretty Sunday frock. Hannah, a keen churchgoer from

Methodist stock, was also dressed for church. She sent Willie upstairs to put on his best suit once he'd eaten, but Charlie still loafed about in his jerkin.

"Not coming?" Hannah looked down her long nose at him.

"Not today, woman. I've my beasties to tend to."

Hannah sniffed, but said nothing. She put on a flowerpot bonnet, which obliterated a side view of her face, save for the long nose, which stuck out like a duck's bill. Charlie grinned at his wife. Hannah's clothes always amused him; they'd gone out of fashion before he was born. Janey, on the other hand, dressed well—leaning toward pinks—and Charlie complimented his daughter on her Dolly Varden dress. When Willie reappeared, in a shapeless crinkled old suit, Charlie handed out various sums of money to his family for the plate, and saw them off from the front door.

Once Hannah and the children had gone, Charlie went through the house to the backyard where he fed the animals and cleaned their pens. Chimarosa was poorly, and stared at Charlie mournfully from his cot. Charlie ran a hand over the badger's back, searching for lumps, but was soon reassured. "Tha's a coat like an Ikey's immensikoff," he told the animal. He'd keep him another winter and set him free when he'd diagnosed the badger's malaise. Charlie turned his attention to his birds, and decided to take them outside to enjoy the morning sun. It was a warm day for November and he ranged the cages along the front of the house, facing south. He was feeding a bullfinch a grub, when the slight rattle of a stone in Britannia Road made him look up. By the garden gate stood a small boy of five or six, with dark curly hair, his brown eyes glued to the birds.

"Like 'em, does ye?" Charlie asked gently.

The boy extracted a thumb from his mouth and nodded.

Charlie held the bullfinch up on a forefinger. "This is His Imperial Highness, the King Maximilian of Mexico. He looks pretty stauled since he lost his Queen Carlotta—flew off and forsook him, she did—but I daresay if *you* were to feed him he'd feel better."

The boy was quick to come into the garden. Charlie carefully put the bird on the boy's wrist. "He's tame—but keep still," he advised, and the boy fed the bullfinch the rest of the grub. Then Charlie put the bird back in its cage and rummaged in his jerkin for a piece of peppermint. It was covered with fluff, but the boy accepted it happily. "Life is sweet," Charlie observed, "as the flea said when it tummeld into treacle." The boy laughed, but at that moment their game was interrupted.

"Will Henry! Will Henry!" called a woman coming down the road.

It was Mrs. Dyson seemingly in search of her son. She stopped short by the gate and Charlie saw a tall, attractive woman with rosy cheeks and very dark hair. He quickly raised his cap. "Good mornin', ma'am."

"Good day, sir! I've been wonderin' where my boy has got to!" Mrs. Dyson smiled—a lovely smile, thought Charlie. "I beg pardon if he's been troubling you, sir."

"Not at all! Not nivver! The lad's more than welcome. Bin showing him Max—one of my feathered folk. Your lad's a nice way with small creatures!"

Mrs. Dyson treated him to another smile. "You're very gracious," she said.

Charlie rushed over to open the gate for her and she came in. She was taller than he. She showed interest in the birds, clapping her hands at the sight of a green parrot. "What beautiful colors! Mr. — er . . . ?"

"Peace, ma'am. Charles Peace, at they service."

"Katherine Dyson, Mr. Peace." She held out her hand. Charlie shook it briefly; he admired her eyes, which were a soft smoky violet. "You must be the gentleman who moved in yesterday?" she went on, avoiding his gaze. "I trust everything has gone satisfactorily?"

"Very nicely, ma'am. Very nice of you to h'inquire! My missus be at service right now, else I'd have her out for h'introductions!" Charlie beamed at her, but then fell silent. He desperately wanted to say something clever but his tongue was frozen.

"Well, I guess I best leave you in peace, Mr.—er—Peace," Mrs. Dyson said at last, and then laughed. The ice was broken.

"Your lad can come anytime," Charlie said. "I've plentiful creatures to show him."

"That's very neighborly, Mr. Peace." Mrs. Dyson bowed, steered her boy through the gate, gave Charlie a small wave, and walked sedately back to her house.

Charlie saw she lived at Number 36. Interesting woman, he thought. Was her speech American? He knew he could soon find out about her at the local public house, the social and gossip center of any Northern village. He returned to his birds, tickling the chest of a cockatoo. The bird's crest rose with pleasure. "Very pretty," Charlie told it, "nearly as pretty as yon Mistress Dyson."

When Hannah got back from church she discovered Charlie had been to work in the parlor, placing clean antimacassars on chairs and lighting a fire in the grate. This was unlike her husband.

"What's up then? 'Spectin' visitors?"

" 'Appen," he replied, busy with furniture polish, "whilst thou was at worship, I met with the folk as be our neighbors. Thought we might ask 'em over."

Hannah wasn't surprised by this proposal. Charlie liked to sound out everyone who lived near him—as a simple matter of safety—and he'd invite anyone into his house, bishop or tramp, if they took his fancy. These neighbors must be from Number 36, Hannah guessed, since next door was empty. "What's they called?" she asked.

"Mrs. Dyson."

Ah! thought Hannah, so Charlie had encountered the *lady* of the house. A small warning bell rang in her mind.

Charlie immediately sent Janey round to Number 36 with his invitation and when she returned she told her parents, "They're coming!" "She's a lovely lady, Mum! And he's that tall man as we saw at church!"

"*That* you saw in church," Charlie corrected his daughter. "Which tall man?" he asked Hannah.

"Proper beanstalk up to'front," he was told. "Sang like a foghorn."

The Dysons arrived at four. It was getting dark, lamps were lit, and the parlor was cozy and warm. Hannah answered their knock while Charlie waited by the parlor fire, hands behind his back and legs akimbo, like a proper country gentleman in his rough tweed suit. He heard voices from the hall, followed by a sharp thud and a cry of pain. He quickly ran to see what was amiss. It appeared that the enormous Dyson had cracked his head in the doorway but with Hannah's help, Charlie guided the stricken man into the parlor and onto the sofa while Mrs. Dyson hovered anxiously and her small son stood by grinning. "Take the lad out back and feed him some parkins," Charlie directed Janey and Willie. Dyson was moaning now, but Charlie thought he was shamming. "A nasty whack!" he said, gravely inspecting the small red mark on Dyson's brow. "Look to him, Hannah love, while I fetch summat to ease the swellin'." He retired to the pantry, where he found beef and horsemeat. He chose the horsemeat—big ninnies like Dyson didn't qualify for good beef. Back in the parlor, Dyson was still playing the Dying Gaul, his head now resting on the arm of the settle, eyes closed and breathing stentoriously. Charlie put the strip of meat on his brow. "He'll make do." He winked at Mrs. Dyson. "He hasn't burst the crust." He looked at Hannah. "Tea up, Mother?"

Hannah poured tea and cut a cake while Charlie talked of various ways of treating bruises until Mr. Dyson slowly sat up, apparently recovered.

"Sure ain't to one's advantage, Peace, to stand as high as I do," he said. Charlie put the meat poultice on the trolley and sat down in a chair next to Mrs. Dyson. "My wife tells me you moved in yesterday," Dyson continued. He looked around the parlor, leisurely inspecting the chaos of furniture and musical instruments.

"That's so, sir," Charlie answered politely, handing him a cup of tea. Then he offered the man a slice of oatmeal cake, but Dyson waved it aside.

" 'Parkins' ain't supposed to be eat till Guy Fawkes' Night," he observed. "I'm afraid I'm a stickler for tradition, Peace!"

And you're a long streak of misery, thought Charlie. "I h'understand you're back from foreign climes, sir?"

Dyson laughed—a nasally snort. "We've bin back some time. Back from Ohio and Missourah—they're in the United States of America, Peace. I guess that's why my wife talks funny. I never picked up that silly accent myself; avoided that weakness. But I figure Kate's stuck with it, ha-ha! She's from Paddyland, you see? Natural-born mimics, the Irish; got no proper language of their own, ha-ha!"

Charlie smiled grimly; he believed Dyson was deliberately trying to embarrass his wife, and his initial contempt for the man began to turn into dislike. He glanced at Kate Dyson, who was smiling brightly. A woman with gumption, he thought. But Dyson was speaking again.

"Kate's also a Roman," he said. "That's why she wasn't at Trinity Church this morn'." He paused to frown. "Come to think of it, I didn't see you there either, Peace?"

"That's how us come to meet thy charming wife, sir."

Dyson grunted. "What line of business you in, Mr. Peace?"

"I mend things, sir."

"*Mend things?* What sort of things?"

"Picture frames and whatnots."

Dyson shook his head. "I'm a professional man myself. Railroad engineer. Tunnel construction on the Sheffield-Lincoln line."

"They built Arthur a special desk to accommodate his legs," Kate Dyson put in.

"Back in the States," her husband continued, ignoring her, "I was with Sir Samuel Morton Peto. We did some pretty fair bridging for the Atlantic line."

"Even across the Mississippi!" Kate Dyson said.

"That weren't with 'Atlantic'!" Dyson corrected her angrily. "Sir Samuel and I were much acclaimed for our work," he told Charlie. "I reckon I'll be remembered for my bridges much as Samuel is for Nelson's column. Sort of makes my throat lump to think what we done for mankind."

Charlie nodded. "Like a prophet cuttin' a way through the wilderness," he murmured.

"What's that? Yes, just that! Not a bad similitude, Peace!" Dyson had missed the sarcasm, but his wife hadn't—and she was giggling into her teacup. "And a wilderness it was, Mr. Peace," Dyson ground on, "what with forests full of wolves and bears and renegades . . ."

"I like bears," Charlie interrupted. "My daddy had a dancing h'Ebenezer from Spain onetime . . ."

"A dancing bear!" cried Kate Dyson with delight. "A real dancing bear?"

"Oh, aye; play the fiddle and he'd dance his pugs sore. We also had lions and tigers with the show, and a h'orang-utang that looked like Old Dizzy . . ."

"Great man, Disraeli," said Dyson in a bored voice. He'd finished his tea and passed the cup to Hannah as if she were a servant. "Well, can't hang about," he added, consulting his watch. "Come on, Kate. Let's get the boy and go."

They all rose to their feet and Hannah fetched Will Henry from the kitchen. Charlie was again staggered by Arthur Dyson's size —the top of his head almost touched the parlor ceiling, while

Charlie's head barely reached Dyson's shoulder.

"Ye've a nice lad there," Charlie said as Will Henry was brought into the room. He ruffled the boy's hair. "Did ye like my wild things, master?"

Will Henry nodded vigorously.

"Then you must come again. Ye can help us clean their cages."

"Is that hygienic?" asked Dyson.

"I keep my beasts sweet, sir!" Charlie protested.

"I'm sure you do, Mr. Peace!" said Kate Dyson quickly. "And I'm sure Will Henry would love to help you!"

Charlie grinned at her, and the party went into the hall, where Charlie helped the Dysons into their coats. Arthur Dyson's struck him as somewhat shabby for such an important person. He opened the front door and goodbyes were said, rather tartly by Dyson. "Mind ye head," Charlie warned him, and was disappointed when Dyson stooped just in time. He watched the couple and their son go down the path. At the gate, Kate Dyson turned to give him a final wave, as did her boy. Charlie closed the door in a happy frame of mind.

He found Hannah in the parlor, stacking the trolley; Willie Ward and Janey had returned to the kitchen. Kicking off his house slippers, Charlie cartwheeled onto the sofa, where he took out his pipe.

"Bloody daft, yon Dyson," he said. He struck a match against the settle, leaving a line on the upholstery.

"How often must I ask tha not ta do that!" Hannah snapped.

Charlie peered at her through smoke; he wasn't even supposed to have a pipe in the parlor. "Give us rest," he grumbled.

" 'Appen I'd like ta give tha a skelping!" said his wife. She was in a bad mood about something, clattering crockery on the trolley. Then it came out. "The way you kept leering at that Dyson woman! Looking proper goats and monkeys!"

Charlie laughed. "Go t'Halifax!"

"I'd go anyroad ta get shot of your ways wi' wimmin!" Hannah went on at him. "You're too old, Charles Peace; tha should have lost the walsh for the lasses!"

"Too old!"

But Hannah sadly shook her head and wheeled the trolley from the room, quietly closing the door behind her. In the hall, she smiled to herself: she had long known how to put her man in his place.

And inside the parlor, a crumpled Charlie was indeed considering her hurtful words. Too old was he? It was Hannah who no longer seemed to desire him, but then *she* was over fifty. Maybe he did sometimes play her false. Not often, and only with bought women in towns as far away as Hull or Hamburg. But even such brief flings were on the wane. Was he indeed too old? Charlie shivered slightly. Hannah's words were partly true—as the mirror told him every time he trimmed his whiskers. He'd been forty-three last birthday—but he looked sixty. The process of rapid aging started early in the industrial North, and his years in prison hadn't helped. Charlie leaned back and shut his eyes, wondering when he'd first begun to age. Probably as long ago as his fourteenth birthday. He'd been working for Millsands Mill that day, on a winch, and a shaft of red-hot steel had impaled his leg just above the knee. He hadn't cried—not even when they'd cranked out the skewer. The pain had been too fine for tears. But he'd lain on a filthy palliasse at Sheffield Infirmary for the next eighteen months —while inner voices told him he'd never walk again. But he had learned to walk, or hobble on his shattered kneecap. Though he lost an inch in height. And the accident had impressed his father enough so that he had never returned him to the factory yards. But Charlie's mind hadn't mended as well as his knee. His childhood had stopped short, and his aging had then commenced.

"Too bloody old, eh?" he mumbled on the sofa. The remark still rankled. But he suddenly regarded Hannah's taunt as a challenge.

3

The Wrestling
Man of God

Challenged, he continued to savor the charms of Mrs. Dyson, and set about fostering her acquaintance. Making friends with her husband he considered too irksome, but he liked Will Henry well enough and so he used her child. He kept his promise about the pets, showing the boy their tricks, and he made Will Henry presents of sweets and small sums of money.

"Nuncle Charlie's got this weasel that bites real hard," Will Henry told his mother. "But he won't bite me none 'cos Charlie's told him not to."

Kate Dyson was content for her child to visit Number 40. She now didn't have to rely only on Mrs. Hutton across the street to mind the boy when she slipped away to drink—which was every day at noon. But, soon enough, she was encountering the kindly Mr. Peace; he'd run into her in the village, he helped her carry shopping, and his cherry manner was a tonic.

"I think he's a dear little man," she said to her husband. "Why, he's even offered to frame those tintypes of your family."

Dyson was weary, following a bad spell in York. "I reckon he's another member of his zoo," he muttered. Nevertheless, he permitted the pictures to be framed but gave no thanks even when this was done for free. It was Kate Dyson who was embarrassed by Charlie's gift and endeavored to avoid him. But he was always on her tail, and he tracked her to the Halfway House on one of her lunchtime visits, sauntering across the Private Bar to where she was sitting.

"Mr. Peace, what a surprise," she said politely.

No surprise at all, mused Charlie; he'd been well informed of the other's habits by Mrs. Norton, the landlady, and he even had a glass of Satin for her in his hand.

"Compliments of an 'umble h'artisan," he said, placing the gin before her. "May I join thee, ma'am?" He sat down with his glass of ale. "And how's Will Henry then?"

"Full of Codcraft, Mr. Peace."

"*Calcraft*," Charlie corrected her. "After our last public 'angman. And Mr. Dyson?"

"At York again. Arthur works very hard." Mrs. Dyson sighed.

Charlie looked at her sharply. "Which drives you to the juniper?" His tone was inoffensive, but Mrs. Dyson blushed.

"I don't know, Mr. Peace." She laughed nervously. "Arthur says it's the Irish in me!" She hesitated. "You won't tell him you saw me here, will you?"

Charlie shook his head. "I nivver saw you . . . But ye must call us Charlie."

Mrs. Dyson sipped some gin. "And you may call me Kate—Charlie." Her smile was enigmatic.

"One more condition for my silence," Charlie added. "You and Will Henry shalt h'accompany my fambly to the Winter Fair on Sat'day?"

"I don't know . . . Arthur doesn't hold with public amusements."

"He'll nivver know," Charlie assured her. "We'll keep it on the Q.T.—'We have the receipt of fernseed; we walk h'invisible.' "

"What's that?" Mrs. Dyson asked.

" 'Enry Four by the Bard. Fernseed means barley, and barley means playing quiet hereabouts."

"You are a funny man!" Mrs. Dyson laughed. She was won over, but she still pretended to dither. "I'll send you a note with my answer."

"Send it by young Kirkham, our milkboy. The lad'll mind his mouth." Charlie took his beer and left her table for the bar. Mrs. Norton was behind the counter, an upright woman with a face as stern as Hannah's. He handed her his empty tankard. "Yon Mrs. Dyson's to have my credit," he told her quietly. "She can ginnify hersel' on strap. I'll pay."

Mrs. Norton looked curiously at Mrs. Dyson but nodded. Business was business, whatever the propriety, and she rather liked the bouncy Mr. Peace. His reputation as a jack-of-all-trades had already spread in Darnall and she remembered a broken concertina hanging by the bar. She took it down. "Cans't tha mend it, Mr. Peace?"

Charlie examined the instrument; the bellows were full of holes. " 'Appen," he said, "but this constant-screamer's had its day." He thought of the one he'd stolen from Heeley Hall. " 'Appen I can let thee have anuther, mistress. I'll drop it round tonight." He'd show her customers how to play it, too; a concertina was one of the many instruments he could play. He gave her back the broken one, and left the bar.

Both ladies watched him go—Mrs. Norton thinking it strange that he'd given Mrs. Dyson unlimited credit, Kate Dyson with conflicting thoughts. She'd divulged her vice to an ugly, coarse little man, yet she didn't care a fig. Something about Charlie eroded her sense of discipline and made her happy. She found herself looking forward to the fair, not just because it might be fun, but because it also involved sneaking behind her husband's back. Worst of all, sneaking behind it with the likes of Charlie Peace.

II

That year the tents for the Winter Fair were pitched at Bramall Lane fields, next to the cricket ground. People poured into the smoky bowl of Sheffield in gigs and carts, but Charlie and family caught a train from Darnall. Kate Dyson and her son joined his party at the station. She wore a flowery hat and a Princess Polonaise, and Charlie was full of compliments. He had Janey and Willie Ward in tow—Hannah didn't care for fairs—and they all arrived at Sheffield in a party spirit. It was a two-penny ride in a four-horse 'bus to Bramall Lane, and Mrs. Dyson sat on top between her son and Willie Ward. Charlie was out of earshot—the clatter of wheels along the gritstone streets drowned most conversation—and she took the opportunity to question Willie.

"He married Ma when I was bun in t'oven," Willie told her. "Clumsy bugger someone."

"But what of his early life?"

"Pretty 'ventful. His dad was a miner who took to circuses, and met Charlie's ma at Rotherham. She run off wi' him like Gypsy Davy; she comes of a menseful fam'ly; Charlie says her dad was a Navy surgeon. Anyroad, she's still alive and stops in Hull."

Mrs. Dyson found these details complex. "And now Charlie's a picture framer?"

Willie regarded her suspiciously. "He's many things, missus. Watchmaker and musician."

"Musician?" Mrs. Dyson recalled the instruments in Charlie's parlor.

"Aye: a proper Rosin on t'fiddle!" Willie became enthusiastic. "Some say he was taught by Saint Nick. He can break a glass with high notes. He used to call hissel' the Modern Paganini."

Kate Dyson was surprised; she'd assumed Charlie's gloved left hand injured. Yet he managed to play the violin. "How old is your stepfather?" she asked.

Willie shrugged. "As old as his tongue, and a mite older than his teeth. Ma says he's not yet fifty, others say he's Methuselah."

Mrs. Dyson had put him at over fifty, yet he moved like a younger man. Charlie intrigued her more and more by the minute. She looked toward him across the 'bus and found him staring at her intently. She gave him the brightest of smiles.

The fairground was flanked by the hideous brick walls of factories, but the sky was clearer than usual and the tents and marquees lent color to the scene. Charlie helped Mrs. Dyson down from the omnibus onto the boggy ground. "Take care, 'tis sanky," he warned, and she hitched up her dress.

They set off for a principal tent, flying a flag marked REFRESHMENTS, where Charlie said they'd meet other Peaces from Sheffield. Then they passed a large steam roundabout piping a waltz and Janey tugged her father's sleeve.

"Oh, Papa! Can we go for a ride?" she begged him, in her best society voice.

"Aye, lass. Take thysen off wi' the boys." Charlie distributed handfuls of pennies and the children vanished in the crowd. "Have a care now!" he shouted after them. "Should summat go amiss, ye'll find us in yon tentafluge!" He turned to Kate Dyson and laughed. "C'mon, Kate, I'll buy thee a drink."

Inside the tent, four bars were busy serving and several voices greeted Charlie's arrival. He led Mrs. Dyson over to a big trestle table, introducing her to a dozen or so people.

"Dan'l Peace, my brother," he said of a man older than himself. "And that's my Aunt Rosie, a flower by name and nature." She was a freckle-faced old dame, already well in her cups. "An yon horror be Josiah Clegg, the h'ugliest publican in West Riding!" This observation was true—Clegg was monstrous to behold, with no lips and only slots for a nose. "Blew away his phizz in a foundry," Charlie explained, pulling a chair out for Mrs. Dyson next to Aunt Rosie. The latter engaged her in conversation, a tirade about encroaching industry ruining good countryside, but her dialect belonged to the Middle Ages and Mrs. Dyson soon gave up listening. Her eyes roamed around the tent. At another table she recognized some folk from Britannia Road—a family called Sykes, a Mrs. Padmore, and Mrs. Hutton gave her a wave.

"Dost yon people know you?" Charlie asked at her elbow.

"Mrs. Hutton sometimes minds Will Henry; and Mrs. Sykes takes in our laundry."

"You should let my Hannah do that." Charlie poured her some beer and a gin chaser. He moved his chair closer, shutting off Aunt Rosie's chatter. "When were you married, Kate?"

"Out in Ohio. I was staying with my sister in Cleveland when I met Arthur. I was very young at the time."

She's making excuses for wedding the fool, thought Charlie. "Tell us about h'America?"

"It was a rough life—we were fairly knocked about. I could take it—I'm pretty tough—but poor Arthur got sick and we quit."

For a boring life in Darnall, thought Charlie, looked at through the bottom of a liquor glass. Kate Dyson's tone seemed to lack sympathy for her ailing husband; not that Charlie could blame her from what he'd seen of the man. "Wilt Arthur be vexed 'bout your coming to the fair?" he asked.

"Very!" Mrs. Dyson drank her chaser rapidly.

"So what if he is? There's nowt he can do 'bout it."

Mrs. Dyson looked at him hard. "Oh, yes he can! You don't know Arthur. He can be darn mean. He never gives me enough money—nor our child a toy! He cares for nothing but railroads!" This outburst was followed by a loud hiccup. Some people at the table laughed, but Charlie saw that Kate Dyson was really upset. She's in gin land, he thought, refilling her shot glass. Very cautiously, he placed his right hand over hers, and she didn't withdraw her hand.

"I'll fashion thy lad a toy," he promised her. "I'll wittle him an 'are pipe." Such traps had been outlawed for five hundred years. "And I'll also find a summat for you." He pressed Mrs. Dyson's hand and, for a second, he thought her about to lean her head on his shoulder. But at that moment Willie Ward came up to the table and she straightened up.

"Where's te baan?" Charlie asked crossly. His stepson was holding Will Henry's hand, but there was no sign of Janey. "Where's Janey?" he demanded.

Willie looked guilty. "Piked off wi' a fella."

"Done what? What fella? Speak up!" Charlie gave his stepson a shake.

"Fella named Bolsover . . . Leggo, you're hurting! They went up t'cricket ground!"

Charlie released Willie's collar. "Show us." He rose from his chair with a thundery face.

"Leave her be, Charlie," Aunt Rosie said drunkenly. "Your Janey's aged sufficient ta hold her own."

Charlie glared at her. "T'aint her own I'm troubled about—'tis her holding someone else's!" Laughter followed, but Charlie didn't share the amusement. His Janey was sacred; the thought of some lout laying hands on her touched upon all that was black in him. Seizing Willie by the coat again, he dragged the boy from the marquee in search of his daughter.

They almost ran to the far end of the fields, well away from the fair and into a sea of mud. The ground was like glue, hampering their progress, and Charlie swore all the while. "I'll not have her tampered with!" he said as they went by a circle of caravans. He was about to call upon the Almighty's hand for the deliverance of Janey when a huddle of people inside the caravans caught his attention. He feared they might be a gruesome crowd gathered round the ravished body of his daughter, but then a spitting sound came from the group, followed by a cheer, and he was reassured. Just gypsies enjoying themselves.

They reached the entrance to the cricket ground, but the gates were locked and there was no one about. Willie looked around in confusion.

"They're not here," he announced.

"I can see that, ye daft bugger!"

But Charlie was much relieved; perhaps Janey had never left the fair for naughty purposes.

They started back, Charlie's heart lighter as he prodded Willie along with pokes of his finger. They came to the gypsy encampment again, and Charlie saw the crowd had dispersed. Only two gypsies remained, a youth and an old man, squatting by a brick kiln. Charlie squelched his way over to them—he recalled the strange noise he'd heard and was curious.

" 'Ello, Ishmael," he greeted the old gypsy. "Got any fiddles for sale?" His manner belied his true feelings toward the Romany race, whom he regarded as thievish pagans.

The gypsy stared back distrustfully; he cared no more for an outsider than did Charlie for him. Go away, said his dark eyes, we have nothing for a *gorgiki*. And Charlie was about to leave these dangerous people when his eye fell upon a line slung between two caravans. Washing flapped in the breeze, but there was something else on the line. At the far end, suspended by their tails, hung two dead tomcats, their bodies torn and dripping blood.

"Bloody 'eck," he whispered. "Kilkenny Catting!"

Willie heard him, wondered what he meant, and saw a terrible expression on his stepfather's face. Charlie strode up to the younger gypsy and struck him savagely in the mouth. The youth fell with a cry, drawing a "livett" from his boot, but Charlie kicked the cudgel out of his hand. The old Romany started shouting in a strange tongue at the caravans for help. Charlie ignored him. He reached under his coat to a revolver pocket and pulled out his pepperbox, leveling the five barrels at the young gypsy.

"On ye feet," he ordered, almost conversationally. "On ye feet and cut 'em down." And he commenced kicking the youth toward the cats. The gypsy rolled and struggled to his feet, full of fury and fear. He slid a shiv from his sleeve, and looked at Charlie defiantly. But the other's pistol was aimed steadily at his head. The gypsy cut the line; dead cats and laundry fell to the earth. More gypsies, men and women, rushed out of the caravans.

"Stand back!" Charlie warned them. He kept his gun on the youth, stepped over the washing, and nudged the cats with his foot. "Pick 'em up!" The gypsy did so, a cat in each hand. "Cut off their tails!" The gypsy looked surprised, but obeyed, using his knife, and the cats hit the ground with a thud. "Now eat 'em!" Charlie barked at him.

The other gypsies, who had been watching in silence, started a great commotion, the men jabbering threats, their womenfolk wailing. Charlie's eyes never left the young gypsy. "Do as I say, or I'll settle for you!" he said, and the hammer of his pepperbox rose. The gypsy quickly started to chew on a tail. Fur and gristle filled his mouth. He was soon retching, but Charlie made him devour most of the tail. Then he waved his gun downwards. "That'll do, you cruel bastard." The gypsy ran off to be sick. Charlie immediately turned his gun on the others. The men stood in a line—some had livetts and knives—while the women hovered behind. Charlie knew they'd gladly kill him, and Willie, given the chance. But they'd be slow to move against a pepperbox. "All right, you drab!" he menaced them. "If any of you want buckshot, come on!" The men fell back, cannoning into their women, and he laughed at them. But it was time to leave. "Start walking, Willie," he called to his stepson, and they backed out of

the camp, Charlie shielding the boy. What he feared was a stone
—the Romanies could throw with lethal accuracy as Charlie knew
well; he'd been taught that trick by the diddiki himself. " 'Urry
lad, else we'll end up like Saint Stephen."

And Charlie maintained a watchful eye and drawn pistol until
they were well clear of the camp. Only then did he tuck away his
gun and risk his back.

"Bad bizniz," he said.

"But what was they doin'?"

"Kilkenny Catting, lad. They take two moggies and ties their
tails together with twine. Then they flip 'em over a line so they
hangs topsy-turvy. The moggs will claw each other h'asunder in
their frantics. The poshrats and diddikis have allus done it, the
brown drabs!"

Willie mulled over this information all the way back to the fair.
When they were outside the refreshment marquee, Charlie
turned to him. "Say nowt of what happened to Mrs. Dyson," he
was cautioned.

When Charlie rejoined his party, Janey was sitting opposite a
strange young man in a collier's coat. She looked unhappy and
the young man frightened, but Charlie's mood had changed for
the better.

"Bolsover, eh?" he said, very friendly. "Where ye from, lad?"

"Darnall, sir."

"Billy's with Pedcocks," Janey explained. "His mama has a
shop in the High Street."

Charlie nodded. Pedcocks was their local colliery and he pitied
any young miner, but he didn't want his daughter courted by a
simple delfman either, and he decided to keep an eye on the
couple. "Billy may call on you at home of a Sunday," he told
Janey. "Otherwise, thou must have your mother's permission to
meet." He smiled at Kate Dyson and took Will Henry onto his
knee. Extracting his watch, he flicked open the back. The inside

was engraved with initials other than Charlie's, and it also played
a jingle, with which he kept the child amused while he talked to
its mother. He kept his voice low. "My hunter says it's past five,
Kate. If we leave now, we can put the brats on a train back to
Darnall. Then I can show thee some highlife in Sheffield. How say
you?"

"But Will Henry . . ."

"Janey can give him his supper and mind for him."

"But Arthur's due back at ten!"

"We'll have you home by then."

Mrs. Dyson had consumed too many tots to argue the issue and
yielded and they decided to bus back to Sheffield Station and
then repair to Cragg's tavern in Russell Street, the Marquis of
Waterford. Charlie gave Janey instructions to which she listened
in silence. It was not for her to question the ways of her father.

More drinks at the Marquis were followed by a visit to the
Norfolk Dining Rooms, where Kate and Charlie were joined by
his brother Dan'l for supper. They drank a great deal of port,
became merry, and then went to the Star Music Hall in Spring
Street. The city was in a boisterous temper following the fair,
with bands in the street and shows on the pavements, and no one
paid any attention to time. The Star combined a picture gallery
with musical turns and there Charlie introduced Kate to Nathan
Goodlad, fence and pianist, and more wine was ordered. Charlie
was in his element. He'd drunk more than his custom, he'd a
pretty woman for company, and the tunes were good at the Star.
He accompanied Goodlad's piano on a borrowed violin, removing his glove and revealing two missing fingers. These injuries he
overcame by extra dexterity, and even the rowdiest customers fell
quiet to hear his Paganini. He tore through prestos, whimpered
out lullabies, and played the filigree trills like a man possessed.

"A 'maestosa,'" he explained to Kate Dyson, on concluding a

difficult study. "Old Niccolo died when I was but eight, but his tunes will go on when I'm dust." He put down the violin and took her hand. Her violet eyes were moist, almost maudlin, with drink. But she's old enough to know her own mind, Charlie argued. He turned to Dan'l. "Me and Kate will be off," he said, clearly meaning his brother should remain at the Star. "One more nightcap at Cragg's and we're home to Darnall."

They lurched back to the Marquis, Kate Dyson crooning a County Clare ballad. Charlie spoke briefly to the hideous Clegg, purchased some claret, and took Mrs. Dyson upstairs to the gaming room. This was empty. He lit a lamp and closed the shutters while Mrs. Dyson flopped down on a large sofa. She was feeling less drunk, but she watched Charlie uncork the wine with a mystical smile. She was thinking about her present situation, of her husband, and she suddenly giggled.

Charlie, on the other hand, was now unsure of himself; Kate Dyson was no waterfront doxy. He handed her a glass of claret and perched himself on the arm of the sofa. His arm rested on the back of the settle, behind Mrs. Dyson. She was hatless and her hair was up in a bun, and he felt the desire to touch her neck. But he didn't—he moved not a muscle, watching her drink. Then she put down her glass and leaned back, fulfilling his desire, and he felt her tremble. She knows she'd best double-off like a hare, he thought, but she likes the excitement and sin of it all. He sat down quietly beside her, drawing her to him until their faces were only inches apart, glad that he'd remembered to clip his whiskers this morning. He was aware that she probably found him ugly, but that didn't trouble him. The lighting was dim and his features seldom seemed to mar his success with women. He was the Beast to their Beauties, and therein lay their thrill. . . .

"Would tha scream if I kissed thee?" he asked roughly.

Kate Dyson said nothing and they kissed for some time. Then he bit her bottom lip.

"Oh, you savage!" Mrs. Dyson cried and pulled him to her. She started to moan when he nibbled her ear. She let him lift her legs on the sofa and helped him rummage into her Princess Polonaise.

"Bloody 'ell, woman!" he protested over the elastics. "Thou art dressed in bloody h'armor!" But Charlie knew what he was about. Soon her skirts were over her head like a tent. "Aye, I can tell tha's bin wasted!" he muttered, climbing atop her, and Mrs. Dyson let out a shriek.

III

The Reverend John Littlewood was a burly man of fifty, with crisp gray hair and hands like hams. He'd been appointed Vicar of Attercliffe-cum-Darnall in October, a welcome change of post. Over the years he'd been treated like a Jesuit in disgrace, condemned to the worst of livings: prison chaplain. But now he was finally free of jails, and even smoky Sheffield evoked his gratitude. He accordingly smiled upon his parishioners this morning as he strolled down Darnall High Street. He'd left the vicarage in search of Bibles, of which Mrs. Bolsover's shop had good supply for Mrs. Littlewood had planned to start a Bible Class for local children. But thoughts of Bibles caused her husband's mind to wander. The Good Book had been a mainstay in prisons. He remembered Wakefield—a House of Correction—and one of his first appointments, in 1855. An unsightly building of gray stone, the prison housed more than four hundred of the North's worst citizens. Most were deemed beyond redemption, yet Chaplain Reynolds, Littlewood's predecessor, had faith.

"Their conduct is much improved," he'd told his young successor. "They are devout in chapel and show gratitude for the opportunities afforded them"—such as enforced settlement in Australia.

Indeed, Littlewood soon had endorsed Reynolds's view. But he discovered one lamentable exception—in the form of a youngster called Parker, lame in the leg but fierce as a terrier. This Parker had not only tried to escape from prison—leaping the roofs, battering his way into medical quarters, and hiding on top of a cupboard—but he even had had the temerity to attempt suicide on recapture. It was then that Littlewood had visited the lad in solitary, Bible in hand.

" 'Tis a grievous sin to destroy yourself!" he'd reproached the convict, holding up the rusty nail with which Charlie had tried to cut his throat and wrists. But Parker had proved obdurate. "Hast thou met with one that's snuffed hissel' and said so?" he'd challenged.

Littlewood had sighed. "Only the age of this nail spared you, Parker."

"Spared us from what! From being bellowsed to Van Dieman's Land? From the crank 'n' Cockchafer? Stow thy nonsense, mister!"

Littlewood had felt a certain sympathy; he knew Parker was "in durance vile" for four years for a burglary at Doncaster. He knew Parker was a mere twenty-three, but that there'd be no remission. He determined to befriend the ruffian with such brilliant eyes. "Read of Job," he said, giving the man his Bible.

And Littlewood had visited Parker throughout his punishment period, and saved him from a birching, and the convict gradually had responded. On his release from solitary, he'd worked hard in the tailoring shop, inventing a device to save labor, and had waxed enthusiastic about the Testaments.

"I believe you can quote the Scriptures better than I," Littlewood soon had to concede.

"Aye, yon Book's full o' luvly tales, sir!" grinned Parker.

Then Parker had become of interest for another, more earthly reason. It transpired that he was a clever wrestler in the Cumberland style, and Littlewood himself was a good catch-amateur. The two men exchanged their skills in secret bouts behind the wash room.

"I believe thy arm hast seven men's strength," Parker complimented the chaplain after a heavy session.

"Who taught you, George?" panted Littlewood for Parker had handled him like a sack of down.

"A man called Survival, sir."

Four years passed and Parker had been released. Littlewood had been sad to see him go. They'd parted at the wicket door in the massive wooden gates and had shaken hands. The sky had been blue against the grimy prison stonework and Parker had gulped the air.

"God go with you, Parker, and be honest," Littlewood had exhorted him.

Parker had nodded. "I'll mind mysen, sir, and keep the peace." He had suddenly smiled, touched his cap, and skipped off down Love Lane, clogs clacking, a gift of Littlewood's Bible under his arm.

Littlewood hadn't seen Parker or that Bible again, he was thinking as he reached Mrs. Bolsover's. He was therefore badly startled when he ran into Charlie outside the shop. They stared at one another in amazement. "Parker? George Parker?" Littlewood finally ventured.

"Charles Frederick Peace, sir." But Charlie saw no doubts in the clergyman's smiling face. He laughed without humor. "At least, that's what I calls mysen nowadays!"

They moved out of the way of some pedestrians, and Charlie took Littlewood down a lane hung with baskets. The weavers had gone off to lunch and the two men were alone. Charlie stopped and shook the other's big hand.

"Sweet Jesus, ye nigh on flayed me to death, sir!" he said.

"No need to be frightened, Parker."

"Peace, sir, not Parker."

"Ah yes, of course. Charles Peace. I understand."

"Visiting are you, sir?" Charles asked hopefully.

"No—this is my parish. By Jove, you must be one of my flock!"

Bloody heck, thought Charlie. "I'm highly h'industrious and menseful now, sir. I have a fambly. 'Twould be an awful mess should my past be got about."

Littlewood shook his head. "Not a word, I promise." He found George Parker much changed, and his dialect less marked—a mixture of several counties now. "You have naught to fear, Peace," he repeated. "But come, walk with me awhile."

They strolled out of the lane and down the High Street toward Trinity Church. The vicar broke the silence as they reached the churchyard. "My living," he announced. "Very humble—but better than Wakefield." They went inside.

"Tha stayed up North?" Charlie asked, his mind on Chatham and other jails.

"So fate had it." Littlewood sat on a tomb. "I was confined to Wakefield and Armley. Jujube?" He proffered a bag of sweets.

"Nivver bin to Leeds," Charlie said, quite truthfully, taking a jujube.

"Of course not—you had the sense to reform. And now you live in Darnall with a family. Tell me, shall I see you all at worship?"

"Aye, sir, I'll rent a pew." Charlie looked at the weed-choked graves and poor state of the Trinity steeple; Littlewood could use the money.

"Good man! And tell me this, is your Bible still good?"

"Aye, there are some things one dost not forget."

"Capital!" Littlewood beamed. It just so happened that his wife was short of teachers for her Sunday Bible Class, and who could teach religion better than a reformed criminal? Littlewood offered his sweets again. "You shall take chocolate with us after service on Sunday. You and Mrs. Peace shall meet my lady wife.

Afterward I shall introduce you to our Bible Class."

Charlie inwardly groaned, but there was no escape. "Hast thou an 'armonium?" he inquired.

"Why, can you play?"

Charlie nodded bleakly. "Aye, sir—makes me feel nearer to my Maker to play them luvly tunes."

Hannah was waiting for Charlie at Mrs. Bolsover's. He'd promised to meet her at noon and Littlewood had made him late. Hannah was glummer than usual since the Winter Fair and she scowled when she spied him sauntering back from the church. She suspected that he'd been with Mrs. Dyson, and strongly censured their meeting in a church. She stepped forward, like an angry frigate in her voluminous dress, to block his path.

"Where wast tha?"

Charlie met her eyes. "Trouble," he said shortly. "Come, woman, I'll buy thee dinner."

He looked so perturbed that Hannah held her tongue. They went into a chop shop across the road, where Charlie found a quiet alcove and pies were ordered. "Ivver thought o' running one of these?" he said of the restaurant. "They make good brass, they does." And he small-talked about chop shops until the waitress went away. But once they were alone, he spoke quick and low. "Recall us speaking of a certain John Littlewood in times gone by? Well, the bugger's here in Darnall—as the bloody curate—and he recognized me of old. I divulged my new nomme, told him I'd gone straight, and mayhap he believed us. 'Appen he'll leave us be; he was a good cove at Wakefield. But I deem it wise to show our bestside. Allus today with the clergy." He smiled grimly. "We be in for a spot of the religiasticks, woman."

Hannah twitched her nose. She well knew her husband's pious airs when times grew fraught, and she hated them. Besides, there was Katherine Dyson now . . .

"This pastry's sour," she commented.

Charlie frowned. "I need thine help, woman!"

"Tha'll get it when tha stops chasing Mrs. Dyson."

"When I what . . . ? Hellfire, woman, there's bin nowt untoward!"

"Some say otherwise."

"Who dost? What villainy is this!" Charlie wondered whether tales had come back from the Marquis. Certainly, there'd been no more sin since the gaming room. "I've met her out of pity," he said. "She's a lonely one, that's all. And she likes a drop. But in the hearing of God, I've not laid dawbs upon her. And would I lie to thee?"

"Ofttimes!" Hannah's eyes glittered.

Charlie pushed away his pie; Hannah was right—the pastry was unpalatable. "But not this time," he grumbled.

Hannah smacked his hand with her fork. "Listen to us!" she snapped. "I've met her likes before. She's a slotch—a drunkard fond of men. She'd stand perpendicular for a Lascar, should he tak' her fancy. She's got thine credit at the Halfway, and strapping thee right full. You ask Mistress Norton! But I cares naught for her ways and nowt for her husband. What I cares about is what happens should she cause thee get took! *I'm* in the workhouse then!"

Quite a speech for Hannah; Charlie was dumbfounded. But he knew what she meant. Her greatest fear was the Sheffield Workhouse, where she could well be sent if he was arrested and all his property forfeited. And, he conceded, as his lawful wife she had a right to worry so. "I'll quit with her," he promised.

Hannah sniffed her disbelief, but eventually she nodded. "Then I'll play your game with Littlewood."

Charlie grinned and patted her. "Good, lass!" He noticed the holes in her dress. She was as scruffy as a rag doll. "Come, woman," he said, "I'll buy thee a new coat—that one's got more patches than a whaleman's shirt."

4

The Fabergé Gewgaw

However, Charlie was under the spell of Mrs. Dyson and she enjoyed his vassalage so they went on meeting at the Halfway and other taverns, where he amused her with witty anecdotes and she drank gills of gin. But nothing was said of what had happened between them at the Marquis—that would be unseemly—though they sometimes exchanged a certain look and laughed.

Then Arthur Dyson began a long Christmas leave. Not only did this vex his wife and Charlie, but such a vacation was so unprecedented that Mrs. Dyson wondered if all was well at work. With Dyson on vacation, Charlie avoided the Dysons, and even shrewd Hannah believed he had mended his ways. Besides, she had other worries: Janey was seeing a great deal of Billy Bolsover without her father's knowledge, and Hannah foresaw an outbreak of silly jealous rage when Charlie eventually learned the truth. But meanwhile Hannah kept her part of her bargain with her husband; in her new, more modish coat she graced the Peace pew in Trinity Church every Sunday, baked cakes for Mrs. Littlewood, and put Charlie forward as an honest carpenter. Charlie, in turn, taught the children at the Bible Class, presenting very much his own version of the Scriptures, enlivening the proceedings from time to time by setting fire to himself with his pipe. On the Sunday prior to Christmas week, he and Hannah took tea at the vicarage.

"I don't hold with Prince h'Albert, God rest his soul," Charlie said on arrival, a long parcel under one arm. "But I dost hold with the Dutchy h'instep of Yuletide." And he handed Mrs. Littlewood the parcel. "For thysen, ma'am!"

Mrs. Littlewood, a podgy lady, tutted over the gift, which was opened in the sitting room, when tea was served. Mrs. Littlewood's cry of joy brought her husband over to look at her present for himself. It was the metal bird on the stick.

" 'Tis French, ye know?" Charlie said from the settee.

"But what is it?" Littlewood was turning the foot-long object over and over, feeling its weight, poking the bird with a finger.

"Twist the end of the stick," Charlie advised.

Mrs. Littlewood snatched the toy from her husband and twisted the stick, which triggered a clockwork spring, and the bird began to raise and lower its wings, opening its beak to warble a tinny "Plaisir d'Amour." Mrs. Littlewood was delighted, winding up the spring when the song had finished, playing the tune over and over again. Her husband looked on benignly.

He thanked Charlie. "A magnificent present, Peace. You're most generous. May I venture to ask how you came by it?"

"Promise ye won't be cross, sir?"

"Of course not!"

"I skelped lucky at dice."

"Aha, you rogue! Still can't keep off the cards, eh? Tobacco and cards were always your particular vices. What was the term used for tobacco, Peace? I've truly forgotten."

Mrs. Littlewood was handing round muffins and Charlie took one before replying; he realized that Littlewood must have told her something of his past. " 'Beef,' sir," he said.

"But of course! 'Beef' . . . Well, if you want to blow a cloud of 'beef' over your tea, pray do so, Peace. I'm afraid you've spoiled her," Littlewood confided to Charlie and Hannah. "*I've* only got her a clock for the school." He pointed to the mantelpiece, on which stood a marble Madeline.

"Nowt wrong with that!" Charlie assured him. He knew a good black Madeline cost in excess of forty shillings.

"Still not as dandy as your bird," the other insisted. "I wonder who made it, and why?"

Charlie had wondered the same; he'd examined the gewgaw one night in his shed, found it painted over with cheap lacquer. A simple assay revealed the metal underneath to be of pure silver and gold, studded with expensive enamels. He suspected the work of Fabergé—in which case the Littlewoods had a treasure on their hands. It amused him to think of these poor people owning such a prize, and he laughed.

"Yes?" Littlewood asked hopefully.

" 'Send me a man cunning to work in gold and in silver,' " Charlie teased.

"What's that?"

"Chronicles, sir. Second Chronicles 2—lest I'm mistaken."

And Littlewood looked very puzzled.

Walking back to Britannia Road, Hannah watched her husband closely, but he seemed preoccupied and she didn't interrupt his thoughts. He was thinking about the Reverend's reference to "beef"—and sour memories were evoked. After the Chatham mutiny, the authorities had transported him to Gibraltar. He'd begged the Governor for another dose of the "Cat" instead, but they'd shipped him aboard the convict ship *Hashemy* in the middle of May, 1862. The Rock was in the hands of the Royal Engineers that summer, supervising gangs of prisoners to cut underground vaults in the mountain. They labored on nine-hour shifts, and the dust had been choking. Charlie—with his knowledge of mining—advised his fellows to give up tobacco. His words led to trouble; the "Beef Baron" of the Rock was one Baccy Conningsby, a merchant of cheap Spanish shag who lived like a prince. He attacked Charlie one night, high on the cliffs, by an aperture cut for naval cannon, and a good thousand feet above the water casements. Their struggle had been short and deadly, and Conningsby had fallen, his tobacco empire broken along with his body. But if the warders knew the truth of his death, they maintained a discreet silence. Conningsby was the only man Charlie had ever killed, and he had convinced himself that Conningsby's death was an accident. . . .

"Where did tha get yon songbird contraption?" Hannah said eventualy.

"Eh? Nivver you heed, lass." She should have known better than to ask such a question.

"Tha should'st not have given it ta a stranger," she persisted. She had visions of the toy being shown about, recognized, and that road to the workhouse again.

"Mistress Littlewood's not a stranger," Charlie replied, but he knew Hannah was right; only a spontaneous desire to please the Littlewoods had prompted him to part with the bird. "H'anyroad, I gives what I chooses, woman!" He elbowed her crossly. "And since thou makes mention o' giving, I h'intend to give a small party at Christmas! We'll h'invite all our neighbors, poor and wealthy, in a true festive spirit. So there!"

Hannah saw he was in a mood and fell quiet. It was probably the weather, which had turned very cold these last few days. His temper tended to worsen once the cold winds came. But she didn't care much for his idea of a party.

"I see Number 38's still vacant," she commented as they arrived at Victoria Place.

II

Snow came for Christmas. It racked Charlie's broken frame and he stayed indoors, helping Janey put up decorations. Being an expert cutout man, he scissored the entire Nativity around the parlor, in which Our Lady looked uncannily like Mrs. Dyson and St. Joseph like himself. One of the sheep in the manger was the image of Arthur Dyson. But what was missing was a Christmas tree, and firs were scarce in Darnall.

" 'Appen I know where to find one," Charlie murmured. He went off into the driving snow and promptly returned with a tree —uprooted from the Sykeses' back garden—which he soon disguised under crepe and baubles.

The party was held on Christmas Day. Alas, the Littlewoods could not attend, but seven local families came, including the Sykeses and the Dysons. The fare was extravagantly generous, the highlight being a roasted swan, poached by Willie Ward armed with one of his stepfather's many pistols. After supper, the children were banished to the nether regions to play games organized by Janey and her darling Billy.

"My Janey loves brats," Charlie cautioned the latter. "That's nice, but don't let her get too broody, lad." He'd seen the young couple holding hands under the table during supper. But today was a time of tolerance.

It was also a day for presents from the Christmas tree—trinkets for the ladies and cigars for the men. Kate Dyson was especially favored with a set of Japanese fans, while her husband was given one of the portraits of his family elegantly framed in silver.

"This must have cost a tidy sum," was his only comment. He never thanked Charlie, just sat in a chair by the fireside, bony and bored, his great legs stretched out across the carpet. Charlie fussed around him, plying him with punch; he was determined to make him smile. He started playing a variety of instruments, sometimes three at a time. Then he stood on his head and juggled Indian clubs with his feet while blowing a bugle. Everyone laughed except Dyson.

"The man's a lunatic," he muttered.

Then Charlie decided Dyson was pining for culture. He conceived a plan to please him. Disappearing upstairs, he ransacked his prodigious wardrobe and returned dressed as Sir John Falstaff, a copy of Shakespeare in hand. His entry was applauded by all save Dyson.

"H'act Two—Scene Four—'Enry Four!" Charlie announced, positioning himself by the tree. "And I don't need the Bard." He put down his Shakespeare. "We be at the Boar's Head tavern in Eastcheap. . . ." And he proceeded to act out the entire scene of the play, taking every part in different voices, exeunting and entering as required from behind the tree.

"He's surely deranged," Dyson whispered to his wife. "We'd best be going."

" 'A goodly, portly man, i'faith and a corpulant,' " Charlie was saying as Falstaff. " 'Of a cheerful look, a pleasing eye, and most noble carriage.' "

Dyson yawned. "I gotta get some sleep, Kate. You know how I need my sleep."

Kate Dyson was embarrassed. "Please, Arthur. Not just now."

"Why not? This is crazy!" Dyson's voice rang across the room.

" 'That stuffed cloak bag of guts—that Manning-tree ox,' " Charlie raged on as Prince Hal. He'd heard Dyson, but was quite unperturbed.

But the other could stand no more. "Let's go!" he shouted to his wife, rising from his chair.

" 'That father ruffian. . . .' " Charlie's diatribe droned off and stopped. A silence followed as he stared at Dyson. Then he grinned. "Sorry, Mr. Dyson. I got carried h'away."

Dyson humphed. "My wife and I must be off," he said stiffly. "I'm obliged to Mrs. Peace for your hospitality." He looked round the room. "Now where's young Will Henry?"

Kate Dyson took the opportunity to leave the room and fetch the boy, glancing at Charlie apologetically as she passed him.

Charlie smiled benevolently and helped Dyson into his greatcoat. But he didn't see the Dysons out into the hall, he left that to Hannah, and he stayed by the tree, an expectant look on his face. An icy draft entered the parlor as the front door was opened. Then came the sound Charlie was awaiting—the thud of a skull against wood and a cry of pain.

" 'Appen he's jowled his head," he observed.

Hannah returned and joined him at the punch bowl.

"I can'st h'abide yon Dyson," he commented, ladling her a drink.

Hannah took her glass. "Nor he thee neither," she said.

Charlie grunted; he didn't like to be unpopular. "Can't think why."

Hannah pulled a face. "P'raps he thinks you're dancing a blanket hornpipe with his wife?"

Charlie's mouth opened like a fish, but his retort was checked by Mrs. Sykes approaching. That lady had been eyeing the Christmas tree all evening: there was something familiar about it.

"I've been admiring yon tree," she said to Hannah. "Where did you get it?"

Charlie poured her some punch. "Compliments of the Duke of Norfolk," he replied.

III

With the New Year, the snows stopped abruptly. The people of Darnall welcomed the good weather, but Charlie held that it boded ill for the future—he could smell an east wind, he said, all the way from the Steppes. Yet he made the most of the warm days. Dyson was off at York again, Hannah had taken a job washing bottles for Mrs. Bolsover, and Kate Dyson was looking more comely than ever.

"Can you lend me a pound?" she asked Charlie at the Halfway. "Arthur has left me short again." A few gins-and-bitters had made her bold.

Charlie gave her a five-pound note, and that was just the beginning. She was soon taking money from him every day, sometimes rewarding him with a peck on the cheek. But Charlie considered himself entitled to greater recompense. Her bill on his credit at the Halfway now stood at twelve guineas and he was filling her larder as well. It was all very nice chatting in public houses, she was a good listener, but he wanted her alone. He took her into Sheffield once or twice, but that was no good, and they could scarcely book into a hotel, he was too well known. Then he remembered that Hannah had said Number 38 Victoria Place was still empty. So one quiet dawn he set to work, filing a key to fit the door and inspecting the premises. Downstairs was chaos and upstairs there were no proper floorboards, but at the top of the house there was a garret—a warm little attic under the eaves of the roof. Charlie dusted and scrubbed the attic floor, tacked boards over the small window, and brought in some makeshift furniture, including a huge pile of bedding. By seven o'clock he had finished; the garret was as clean as a pin. It was hardly palatial, but very cozy by lamplight.

Dyson normally left home at half-past seven to catch his train, so Charlie didn't bother to return to his own house for breakfast. He loitered in the street, wishing the odd "Good day" to passers-by, until he saw Dyson leave and head off toward the station, then he went straight to Number 36 and rang the bell.

When Kate Dyson answered the door, she seemed very agitated. She let him in without a word and they went down to the kitchen, where Will Henry was eating his porridge.

"Put some treacle on it, lad," Charlie advised him. He sat down next to the boy and watched his mother boil an egg. Still not a word passed between them, and he wondered what was amiss. But he waited until she chose to speak.

"Arthur's gone for three nights this time," she said at last. "And as usual, he hasn't left me with a farthing."

"Nivver heed!" Was that the sole cause for her annoyance?

"Last night he found my bottle of gin," she went on. "Threw it out, he did, and called me names in front of the child!"

"Names don't hurt, lass!"

"His did . . . I don't know how I stand him! No money—no love —not a tiddlypush of nothing!" She slapped down an egg cup in front of her son.

"I'll give you brass," Charlie said, thinking he'd indeed called at an opportune moment. He buttered and sliced toast to make Will Henry "soldiers" for his egg. "There's nowt I wouldn't give thee, Kate," he added.

Kate Dyson stopped rampaging around the kitchen. Her temper began to subside. "I know," she smiled with effort. "You're a good man, Charlie. Don't think I'm not grateful." She joined him at the table. "It's just that life sometimes gets on top of me."

Lucky life, thought Charlie. He took hold of her hand. "What you need is an h'outing," he said, "and today's the day for that. Drop wee laddie here at Rosie Sykes's and we'll hop on a train to Mansfield. How say you?"

Kate Dyson didn't need much persuading, and Will Henry was duly delivered to Mrs. Sykes. The journey to Mansfield was short but a joy. The dirty environs of Sheffield, with its inky canals and heaps of slag, gave way to woodland and pastures. Even the sky became less forbidding. For Charlie it was as if a hand on his throat were suddenly relaxed, and Kate Dyson was considerably cheered. They lunched at a coaching inn, one of the best in all Nottinghamshire, and returned to Darnall at five. Kate Dyson was drunk, Will Henry was due to be picked up at seven, and Charlie had his mind on the garret. He led her to Number 36 and they got in it through the rear yard—Mrs. Dyson succumbing to a fit of the giggles—and climbed aloft to the attic. What happened within they were both to remember for the rest of their lives.

Mrs. Dyson lay on her back in the dark, listening to Charlie moving about. He'd insisted on turning the lamp out when he'd undressed, saying she might not like the sight of him naked, and indeed she'd later felt odd holes and bumps on his body. Now the light was extinguished again as he dressed but she didn't care; the little man with the twisted physique had given her something she'd never known could happen, and she stretched herself like a cat.

"Right, you can open ye glims." Charlie turned up the lamp. He was fully dressed, glove on his hand, cap on head, and he grinned at her impishly.

But she just yawned, touched her full breasts, and was suddenly reconsumed with desire. "Come over here, you divil!" she said.

Charlie shook his head. "Nay, lass," he laughed, " 'tis past seven—and I've no more ink in mine pen."

Mrs. Dyson sat up at once. "After seven! Gracious me! Will Henry!" She clambered out of the eiderdowns, her flesh very pink, and started to pull on her dress, cursing difficult buttons.

Charlie helped her. "The boy's arright, my beauty," he assured her. "Likely suppin' his little belly tight at Mother Sykes's." He patted her behind as he finished hooking the forty-eighth button. "At least you're not late for thine hubby."

Kate Dyson turned round. "You should have seen Arthur the night of that fair! Will Henry turned informer, I fear!"

Charlie smiled. "Bless his socks."

"Arthur didn't bless him! He put us both on short rations!"

"Miserable man."

"So he is—a skinflint."

"Not like us, Kate?"

"No, you're skin's like a hag's, Charles Peace."

"One bit harder than flint, none t'less?"

They both laughed; smutty talk in the garret seemed suitable, with the attic's weird shadows and the lisp of a wind in the rafters. The outside world was unimportant; Charlie felt younger, and for Kate Dyson a wicked adventure had started. But it was certainly time to leave—before a chink of light was noticed through the window boards out in Britannia Road.

"Let's fetch Will Henry," Charlie said.

Kate Dyson put on her hat and collected a flask of gin Charlie had bought her in Mansfield. She felt quite giddy after what else he had given her and she now wanted to confess a great secret.

"You love Will Henry, don't you?"

Charlie nodded. "He's part of you, Kate."

"He's no part of Arthur."

Charlie was amazed. "Bloody 'eck! Whose is he?"

"His father was a fella from Milwaukee," she said gaily. "Nor is Arthur really his stepfather."

"How's that?" Charlie's face was a treat and she laughed.

"We're not married, not at all! He won't go near the altar because I'm Papish. But he *thinks* Will Henry's his own—that's why we pretend to be dacently married. Poor fool of a man. But *I'm* not the one to tell him the truth!"

That didn't surprise Charlie; he could well imagine the tall engineer's reaction to such an admission. He shook his head quickly, as if to clear his mind. "Th' art surely a one, Mistress Dyson," he said admiringly. "As dishonest a woman as ivver burnt malt!" He picked up the lamp and gallantly escorted her out of the garret. He liked Kate Dyson all the more for divulging her underhand history, but it occurred to him that the lady was far more ruthless than he thought 'common in womankind.

5

Whitsing

The weather held good until the middle of January, during which weeks Charlie and Kate Dyson sinned frequently up in the garret, throwing discretion to the winds. Everyone in Britannia Road soon knew of their affair—except her husband, who was too busy ruining his health with unnecessary work to notice anything outside his York office.

But Charlie's turn to suffer came presently. Across from the North Riding came the full blast of winter, a mixture of rains, tempests, and frosts. It gripped the west with a terrible hand, killing old and young alike, and driving Charlie cursing to his bed for two months. He rarely ventured downstairs, and when he did he came swaddled like a Laplander, demanding meals at unusual times in front of the hearth, forever asking God to put an end to his lot. He was a very bad patient, but Hannah was used to his winter ways and she made him gruels and massaged his joints with curious ointments.

"See that!" he moaned, pointing to a puffy elbow. "A Mancunian bobbie done that with his rick-rack, the bugger!"

Hannah had a mental map of all his injuries, and applied a dollop of badger fat to the offending part. She was grateful to have Charlie at home, away from next door and the Dyson woman, about whom she had said nothing, though she certainly planned to speak up if the relationship was renewed in the spring.

Kate Dyson, however, was less patient. She was vexed by Charlie's absence, her lack of gin, and her husband's parsimony.

54

Gathering her courage, she called round at Number 40 and inquired after Charlie's health.

"He takes ta his bed and reads t'Bible this time o' year," said
Hannah coldly.

Kate Dyson withdrew. In bed with a Bible? she thought. He
should be in bed with her! But she must at least have his charity:
her teapot of gin was empty, and Dyson took his purse off to work
with him. She went to her husband's escritoire, found a slip of
paper, and scribbled Charlie a note. "Send me a drink," it read.
"I am nearly dead."

The milkboy sworn to secrecy delivered the message to Willie
and it reached the bedridden Charlie.

"Take a shilling outa the jar in the kitchen, buy her some Tom,
and fetch it round to her quiet," he ordered his stepson. And this
was done.

Following the success of the first note, others followed, but
Hannah intercepted the fourth, boxed young Kirkham's ears, and
pulled Willie's hair for such deceit. Then she decided it better to
join in with the game, rather than have it continue behind her
broad back and thus began a series of notes, all of them passed
on to Charlie, answered in one form or another, and preserved
by him like treasure in a cocoa tin under his bed—especially Kate
Dyson's small gift of an American penny.

While such absurdities continued at Victoria Place, other
things happened. Arthur Dyson was given his notice by North-
Western Railway. A good engineer, but a poor manager of men,
his mean ways at home had extended to work, where he forbade
a gang of navvies their quota of beer. Since it was a tradition to
fortify navvies with beef, bread, and beer in any amount, the
gangs protested by rioting. And since it was imperative, in the
railroading world, to conclude a contract on time, precious hours
were lost, and a scapegoat was sought. Dyson was dismissed
without compensation.

And meanwhile Janey still mooned with her Billy and the bedridden Charlie could do nothing to prevent their calf love. They canoodled out of his sight, and soon announced their intent was to marry. And lastly, John Littlewood made a happy discovery: an old friend and fellow cleric, Edgar Newman, had arrived in Sheffield as Rector of Ecclesall. Newman was a scholar, but he found much in common with the prison padre and they spent a long afternoon together in Newman's study.

"I've an ex-Wakefielder as one of my flock," Littlewood confided.

"Really? I trust he's as 'ex' as you say."

"Oh, yes! It is pathetic to see him, so old has he grown with remorse."

Newman smiled. He was a thin bachelor in life and of arts, protected by a housekeeper, and he looked very learned behind his desk, surrounded by books. "Most criminals express remorse," he opined, "especially on apprehension. But how emboldened some become on release!"

Littlewood frowned. "Not so with Peace."

"What an impertinent name for a felon!"

"I have been indiscreet in mentioning his name." Littlewood felt guilty.

"Then let us forget him, John. Now, let me tell you—I've just been reading about some recent diggings in Abyssinia. . . ."

"Ethiopia! That's it!" Littlewood interrupted. "He used to call himself the Ethiopian Wonder!"

"Who did?"

"Peace, of course!"

"Never heard of the fellow. . . . Look, do let me tell you about these hidden treasures! You know they were buried by the late King Theodore at Magdala. . . ."

But Littlewood wasn't much interested in the hoardings of a mad king of kings; his friend's obvious skepticism in the reformation of criminals made him anxious to see Charlie. The latter had not attended church for the past five Sundays. Littlewood looked in on him at Victoria Place on his return to Darnall and was relieved to find him in bed, gray-faced yet happy, consuming some of Hannah's elderflower wine.

"I'm indeed cheered to find you in good spirits, Peace," said Littlewood.

He joined Charlie in a glass and was soon so reassured of Charlie's respectability, that he dismissed Newman's bleak theories as those of a cynic. "We've missed you at Bible Class," he told Charlie. "I'm sorry the weather has incapacitated you so."

Charlie raised his glass. " 'I'm chastened also with pain upon mine bed, and with the multitude of mine bones with strong pain.' Book of Job, sir. But I'll soon be h'up and abaht!"

II

And Charlie's resurrection was quick when it happened. The thaw set in on the last Tuesday of March, over the space of a night, and he woke knowing his torment was over for another year. He leapt from his bed, stripped off his nightshirt, and scrubbed himself all over at the washbasin. Then he slapped the still sleeping Hannah playfully on the rump, and went to the window, drew back the curtains, and flung the window wide. It was after six, the sun was above the horizon, and a small bird sang on the sill. For once the air seemed free of smoke, and Charlie took a deep breath. "And the Lord made an h'Earthly Paradise called Darnall!" he cried, beating his bare chest with his fists. He stretched and yawned, sinews cracking, and then looked down on the street to find Mrs. Sykes staring up at his nakedness in horror. She might well have looked alarmed. He was about to retreat when the humor of the situation got the better of him. He laughed and danced a small jig instead while Mrs. Sykes fled down the road.

Charlie continued to laugh as he pulled on his spring clothes, then he went downstairs without waking Hannah and prepared breakfast for the family. Charlie was trimming his whiskers in front of a hand mirror when they arrived. "I'd have made a good figaro," he said, admiring his beard. Hannah eyed him suspiciously. He was too sparkly for comfort and he was obviously bent on going out. She could guess his destination. She puffed up like a bird, about to protest, but Charlie was talking to Janey.

"How's thy Billy-boy then?" he was asking. "Still seeing owt of him?"

Trouble ahead, thought Hannah. Janey had been out carousing last night; she had black rings under her eyes.

"Well, answer us, lass?" Charlie insisted.

Fear flickered across the girl's face, but she was made of strong stuff. "Billy and I want to get wed."

There followed an awful hush in the kitchen. Janey stared at her father bravely; Willie found it time to fetch some more logs; and Hannah stood by the range. They all expected a terrible scene—Charlie's aspect was purple—but with a great effort, he kept his control. "Well, I'll be buggered," he said huskily. "I'm capt t'know what ye see in him. . . . But 'tis your life not mine, girly. . . . I'll have t'see abaht gettin' thine dowry. . . ."

Janey ran to her father. They hugged and kissed one another while Hannah looked on silently. She was full of misgivings—not about the proposed match of her daughter, but with regard to Charlie's strange conduct. He was acting out of character; everything had been topsy-turvy since he'd met the Dyson woman. Hannah was sure 1876 held the promise of being a most bothersome year.

Dyson came out of his house at nine. He was going into Sheffield and he had kept Charlie away from Number 36 for a full two hours. But once Dyson had disappeared down Britannia Road, Charlie left the shelter of some trees and sounded the doorbell.

When Kate Dyson opened the door he grabbed her in the hallway, trying to kiss her passionately, but she thrust him away.

"Not at this hour, for pity's sake!"

Charlie saw her eyes were rimmed with red—and not from crying. She'd obviously been at the bottle last night. "Well, I'm back, lass," he said. "Sorry 'tis been so long but I be prone to rheumatics and pneumatics. My very blood gets h'icicled." He brightened. "But now I be risen like Lazarus! Let's nip round next door?"

"No!"

Charlie was puzzled. "Will Henry can go to Mother Hutton's?"

"She's working in the village now."

"Then how about Rosie Sykes?"

Kate Dyson shook her head. "She's heavy with child."

Charlie was sorry he'd shocked Mrs. Sykes that morning. "When then?" he pleaded.

"No more in the garret." Mrs. Dyson's manner was cool— Charlie put it down to a hangover; what she needed was a drink.

"Then how about the Halfway?" he suggested.

Kate Dyson hesitated. "Perhaps . . . Call back at midday. I'll see what can be done with the boy."

She opened the front door. Charlie felt summarily dismissed.

It was Dyson's loss of employment and his battered ego that were partly responsible for Kate Dyson's new attitude to Charlie. She no longer desired to consort with a man who could loaf around all day, apparently not working, while her husband suffered the indignity of unemployment.

But she could seldom say no to public houses, so Will Henry was duly parked with another neighbor, Mrs. Padmore, and Charlie was delighted to find Kate Dyson ready in bonnet and cloak at twelve. They set off immediately for the Halfway. Mrs. Norton gave Charlie a nod when he came in and handed him the sum of Mrs. Dyson's bill as soon as he ordered gin and ale. Kate Dyson had added another seven pounds to his credit since he'd taken to his bed but he didn't mind; her rebuff this morning was forgotten; and he joined her at their usual table ready to renew the good old days.

"How's hubby?" he inquired.

"You haven't heard?"

"Heard what, love?"

"He's been fired."

"*Fired?*" The term was unfamiliar to him.

"Dismissed—without reason. Just like that!" She snapped her fingers in his face.

Charlie could scarce imagine Dyson being sacked from anything; on the contrary, he saw Dyson as being a man who would find others at fault and cause them to lose their jobs. But he made no comment.

"He's in Sheffield right now looking for another post," Mrs. Dyson said. She studied the gin in her glass morosely. "Life'll be rough 'til he finds one."

"We've got each other." Charlie touched her sleeve.

But she merely glanced at him and swallowed back her drink. "C'mon, let's be going!"

"Go!" Charlie was dismayed. "How abaht summat t'eat? Another gin?"

"Nope." Mrs. Dyson rose with a set expression. "I've changed me mind. I want to be home when Arthur gets back."

Charlie realized there'd be no moving her and helped her with her cloak. But before they left the Halfway he purchased a large bottle of Satin in case she relented.

Outside the public house it was raining and the snow in the cul-de-sac was being turned to slush. They walked up to the junction with the main road and were in the mouth of the lane when a loud voice hailed them.

"Hulloa there! Ah've bin lookin' for tha!"

An angry tone. Charlie stopped, thinking of policemen. But he saw a burly man with long dundreary whiskers on the far side of the street. The man wore the leather apron of a quarryman and carried a heavy stick; it was Mr. Sykes.

"Oh, hello Jim," Charlie said. He didn't like the look of that stick; it was a "morgan-rattler"—loaded with lead.

"You insulted my missus!" Sykes continued, crossing the street. "Tha flaunted thine member at her!"

" 'Twas an h'accident," said Charlie, "for which I make h'apology."

"That's not what my missus say!" Sykes was both nervous and angry, a dangerous combination. "And ah wants full satisfaction!"

"I *says* I'm mortified," Charlie reasoned. "Come, Jim, I'll buy thee a yard o' ale."

But Sykes was determined to fight. "Nay, I wants thy bordeaux, not thine beer!" He approached Charlie, swinging his stick. "Now let yon harlot stand aside!"

Kate Dyson gripped Charlie's arm. "Easy, lass, easy," he murmured. To Sykes he said, "You've no cause to speak of Mistress Dyson that way, Jim! So mind thy delfer's tongue!"

But Sykes laughed sneeringly. " 'Tis known she's nowt but a ginny whore, Charles Peace! 'Appen she won't be so partial ta thysen when ah've finished beatin' off thy lugs!" His stick rose, the balls of lead rattling down the shaft.

Charlie reacted in a flash. The gin bottle in his hand flew in an arc and hit Sykes's jaw with a soggy crunch. Clogs shot off the quarryman's feet as he sprawled in the gutter; the gin bottle bounced twice and shattered.

"Bloody waste," Charlie muttered.

"Mother have mercy on us!" whispered Mrs. Dyson.

Charlie unprised her fingers and ambled up to Sykes. He

picked up the stick and then examined its owner's jaw. The latter was dislocated, but Charlie snapped it back into place with an ancient skill. "Ye'll live, Jim," he informed the groaning man. "But 'appen tha'll stow thy jaw awhile." He returned to Mrs. Dyson, stick under arm. Her eyes were wide with shock. Charlie was not surprised—no lady liked being called bad names. "Come, Kate, forget this fraction!" Linking his free arm in hers, he walked her quickly away from the cul-de-sac.

Constable Pearson arrived too late to witness the incident, but he found the injured Sykes, whom he sat on the curb.

"What's afoot, man?"

"He tra'd ta murrer me!" moaned the quarryman, holding his aching face.

"Who did?"

"Yon Peace! Ta murrer me! Isn't tha goin'ta do owt?"

Pearson considered what he might do; very little, was his conclusion—for he'd seen nothing. Moreover, quarrymen had a reputation for getting into fights. "You can take out a summons," he advised Sykes. "Go t' magistrates in the morning and have him for assault." That said, he helped Sykes to his feet, retrieved Sykes's clogs, and sent him on his way. Pearson was content not to be involved.

But when Dyson came home that afternoon, he was accosted by Rosie Sykes. She'd been waiting for him behind a rubbish dump at the end of Victoria Place.

"Yes, ma'am, what is it?" Dyson asked. He was very tired after an unsuccessful day in Sheffield.

"Charles Peace of Number 40 done laid his neifs on my Jim," he was told.

Dyson grew impatient. How could the antics of the awful Peace be of concern to him? "I'm sorry," he said, "but so what?"

"Thy lady wife bore witness, sir!" said Mrs. Sykes with relish.

"She'd been ta public house wi' Peace and all!" Mrs. Sykes had planned her line of complaint; it was high time Dyson knew a thing or two. "Drinkin' wi' him!" she added.

"Was she just?" Dyson murmured. So his wife was back on the bottle? After his humiliation at York, his lack of prospects in Sheffield, this was the final straw. "When did this occur?" he asked.

"This aft'noon, sir. Peace ferricadouzed my Jim wi' a bottle!"

But Dyson was less interested in Jim Sykes than his wife's drinking habits. "What else have you to tell me, ma'am?"

Mrs. Sykes licked her lips. "We hear quaint rumors, sir."

"Rumors? What sort of rumors?"

But Mrs. Sykes lost the nerve to tell him more and merely shook her head. Dyson waited for her to speak, but to no avail. That was the trouble with the folk in Darnall, he thought, they were all so slyly primitive.

"Well, you were in order to tell me what you have," he thanked her. He tipped his hat and left her standing by the smelly dump. He was anxious to carpet his wife, and he vowed to speak sternly to Mr. Peace on the morrow.

III

Charlie arrived back at Darnall with the dawn. He'd been over to Birley that night—burgling the home of the owner of Birley Moor colliery, a fine residence on the edge of Hackenthorpe Wood, but he'd met with a mishap; the house had awkward gables and he'd slipped to fall ten feet, hurting his foot and losing his tool bag. That, together with Kate Dyson's adamant refusal to accompany him to the garret, did not put him in the best of moods.

"So you really wants to marry that Billy?" he suddenly challenged Janey at breakfast. "Go on, lass, go on! Tha'll be pickin' coal bits outta his back for the rest of ye natural!" And he continued to diatribe against all things connected with mines and miners—pit owners with fancy houses in particular.

But he perked up when the postman called. A card had arrived from his mother. At long last she was prepared to leave Hull and settle in Sheffield.

"In the bosom of Peace," he said gleefully. He'd find the old lady a place near Dan'l and Aunt Rosie. His mother would also arrive in time for the Whitsun celebrations—*and* Janey's wedding, since that seemed inevitable.

A second knock on the door heralded the milkboy with a verbal message from Dyson. Would Mr. Peace kindly call at Number 36 this morning, at his soonest convenience.

"Summoned like a skivvy," Charlie grumbled. He didn't know what was afoot—and guessing didn't ease his suspense.

He called at ten—dressed up for Sunday in a bell-top hat—and paused outside the house to peer through the parlor window, where he found himself face to face with Dyson and quickly withdrew to ring the bell. Dyson answered the door, but there was no sign of his wife.

"Ah, come in, Peace!"

Charlie left his hat on the hall stand and followed Dyson into the front room. Dyson closed the door, positioned himself before the fireplace, and spoke loudly.

"I've a reputation for talking plain!" he roared. "I have it on good authority that you partook of strong liquor with Mrs. Dyson yesterday. How say you, Peace?"

Charlie looked up at the gigantic man; he felt he was back in the dock facing a clerk of arraigns. "Guilty, sir."

"You play base games with a young woman's frailty," Dyson went on severely. He was unwell today with an upset stomach, which was paining him badly. "I have long suspected you, Peace, for your—er—*unusual* ways," he continued. "You delight in the sound of your own voice, you play comic turns, you are a fraud and a flatterer. I daresay some silly women are fooled by your tricks. But not so my wife. D'you follow me, Peace?"

"H'indirectly, sir . . ."

"Pray don't interrupt!" Dyson's face had turned an unhealthy green and he was holding his midriff. "Not only did you soak my wife in poisonous spirit, you involved her in fisticuffs outside a tavern! Is that not right, Peace?"

"He come at us with a morgan, sir . . ."

"Again you interrupt! Have you no control over that tongue of yours? I'm not interested in the cause of the affray; the point is, it was witnessed by my wife!"

"Yes, sir."

"That won't do, will it, Peace?"

"No, sir."

"Good!" Dyson wagged a finger, long as a churchwarden. "Never, never again, Peace."

Charlie suddenly realized the interview was over. He'd been expecting the worst charge to be put—indeed, he'd been preparing some lies to meet it—but Dyson had evidently finished. He was gripping his stomach, crippled with wind, but Charlie didn't see he was ailing. Nervous reaction made him want to befriend the tall man. "I call God to witness I'll nivver trouble thine missus h'again!" he promised.

"Good—good! Now off with you, man!" said Dyson in agony.

But Charlie refused to be put out. An idea had occurred to him —a way to win over Dyson. "You and I must 'ave a romp around town," he said, confidentially. "We could have a joyous evening together in Sheffield sometime. Visit mine fambly, and go on to the Star for the girls . . ."

"*Girls?*"

"Aye," Charlie winked, "all decked out in bijou dresses 'n' garters."

"*Garters?*"

Charlie nodded. Reaching inside his Sunday suit, he drew out some pictures. All were of buxom country lasses dressed in undergarments or less, and he fanned the photographs so Dyson could see them all. "Ye could 'ave any of 'em with Mr. Goodlad's compliments, sir."

"Have them?"

" 'Appen they've nivver been with so lofty a gent," Charlie laughed.

The full horror of this proposal was now confirmed and proved too much for Dyson. "Get out of my house, you fiend!" he shouted, pushing Charlie, knocking him down. He fled the parlor, while Charlie hurriedly crammed the pictures into his jacket and slunk out of the house, forgetting his top hat.

In the street he stopped and scratched his head.

"Yon Dyson's a loon," he said to himself, very puzzled.

"Loon" or not, Charlie had the sense to stay clear of Number 36 for a spell. He convinced himself that Kate Dyson must be afraid of her husband—which didn't surprise him, considering the force of the man's shove in the parlor. He had certain plans, of course: some definite proposals for Kate Dyson—which were not discouraged by his receipt of a fresh outbreak of notes in her hand. "Send me a shilling or two and a drop—and keep very quiet," said the first. So Charlie surreptitiously sent her cash and gin in a pop bottle, and the new notes joined the old in his tin. He was content to bide time.

But another matter annoyed him still: the slanderous talk of the Sykeses—whom he knew must have spoken to Dyson with regard to the Halfway. The Sykeses must be punished, he reasoned, and his revenge took this course:

Four Sundays later, Trinity Church was crowded with the Peaces, the Sykeses, the Padmores, and others. Dyson was there —howling hymns in his bad tenor voice. Charlie and family took their pew in good time, behind Dyson and son, with the Sykeses over the aisle to the left. Charlie bowed to Rosie Sykes as he settled into his place. She looked away quickly. He was pleased to note her husband's jaw was still marked.

Reverend Littlewood mounted the pulpit midservice to deliver his sermon. His mien was brusque this morning; he didn't even give the Peaces his customary nod. And he directed his talk against domestic strife.

"If you want to fettle-to, stop leatherin' your wives and try your dukes in a prize ring!" he exhorted the men in the congregation.

"Hear, hear!" cried Charlie. " 'For wrath killeth the foolish man—and envy slayeth the silly one!' " Littlewood, however, ignored his outburst.

Charlie then sat quietly awaiting the next bout of hymns. Mrs. Padmore was in the organ loft—the "Modern Chophoffen," Charlie had dubbed her—and she squeezed out a fuzzy opening of Psalm 122. The congregation rose, Arthur Dyson their tower, and Jim Sykes had his hymnal in hand. His wife would find him the appropriate page because he couldn't read very well.

" 'O pray for the peace of Jerusalem; they shall prosper that love thee!' " yelled Dyson.

" '*Peace* be within thine walls; and plentizniz in thine palaces!' " sang Charlie, watching Jim Sykes intently.

The quarryman's wife found the psalm in her husband's book, but as she opened it several cards fluttered out. Some landed on the pew seat in front, others did aerobatics into the aisle, and Mrs. Sykes caught one in midair. She looked at it, and her mouth fell wide.

"What's this then!"

Every worshipper heard her cry, and Jim Sykes peered at the card in her hand. It was the tintype of a bob-capped maidservant, naked save for a frilly lace apron.

"You dirty dule you!" shrieked Mrs. Sykes, lashing out at him with her umbrella. She began gathering up the rest of the pictures, seizing them from inquisitive children, cursing her husband in the language of a Tee-side lighterman. She barged her family out of their pew with her large stomach, while Mrs. Padmore's bad music droned on. Bent with humiliation, the Sykeses left church amid whispers and stares.

" 'Oh, what a fearful mess!' " Charlie sang in Hannah's ear. " 'Oh, dear Lor-ord, *what* a frightful *mess!*' "

But Hannah gave him a withering look.

Service over, everyone filed out of church. Littlewood was outside on the steps, shaking hands with parishioners. But when Charlie's turn came, his hand was refused.

"Good day, Mrs. Peace . . . Janey? Willie? What a nice hat, Janey!" Littlewood rounded on Charlie. "A word with you in the vestry, Peace. . . . If you don't mind?"

Charlie sent Hannah and the children on ahead, and followed Littlewood to a side door at the rear of the church. They passed into the vestry, which smelled of starched vestments and wood polish. Littlewood studied Charlie a moment and then came to the point.

"The Madeline, Peace, where is it?"

"In the Bible Class, sir?"

"Until a week ago, yes. But not now. What have you done with it, Peace?" Littlewood was perfectly calm.

And his accusation was plain: the clock was missing, presumed stolen, and Charlie was under suspicion. Charlie blushed and the vicar took his coloring for guilt. "Don't dissemble with me, Peace!" he said severely. "Return it, and we'll threat the matter as closed."

But Charlie was livid. "Bloody-end to thy clock, sir! You do me great wrong! Who says I took yon clock? This is as foul a falsehood as ivver was said! You know I'd do nowt to harm you or Mistress Littlewood! Why, I loves you like Maddy the Whore loved Sweet Jesus!"

Littlewood had never seen Charlie so excited; the little man was wringing his hands with anxiety. "Stop blaspheming, Peace. Nobody has suggested you stole it. . . ."

"Oh, yes they has! And I blasphemes against the h'injustice!"

"I merely found it gone, and formed a certain opinion, Peace."

But Charlie shook his head angrily. "No, tha didn't! Some bugger's slipped a downright lie into thine ear! Pizened thee like Hamlet's father!"

"Calm yourself, man! Go home and forget the matter." Littlewood was beginning to give Charlie the benefit of a small doubt. He flung open the vestry door. "Please go!" he repeated when Charlie lingered.

"Please hear us out, sir?" Charlie begged.

But the vicar wouldn't listen; he refused even to look at Charlie —who went out trembling with rage, shaking his head still and muttering invective as he walked through the tombstones. Littlewood watched his departure with some consternation. Perhaps he'd done the man a injustice. In a way, he hoped he had. Better an innocent Peace than a sudden reversion to old ways. But the vicar remembered Newman's views about "reformed" criminals, and decided never again to employ Charlie at his Sunday School.

Charlie caught up with Hannah at the beginning of Britannia Road. He did consider himself grievously wronged. He didn't blame Littlewood, but he was sure someone had slandered him, and this belief touched a dormant paranoia. He didn't think it was Jim Sykes—he couldn't see a simple quarryman inventing such a lie—and his second choice was Arthur Dyson. Yes, Dyson had done it, the bugger!

"You ought not have done as tha did." Hannah's voice invaded his thoughts.

"Dyson done it!" Charlie mumbled.

"Dyson? That's rare!"

Charlie stared at her—there was a trace of humor in his wife's gray eyes. What was so funny? "Done what?" he demanded.

"Put them prints in Sykes's hymn book."

Charlie realized they weren't on the same subject. "Nay, woman, 'appen we're both talkin' rubbish!" And he went on to tell her about the Madeline clock. By the time he'd finished, Hannah looked very grave. She could see Charlie being pinned with a theft and the shadow of the workhouse.

"I can see us best out of this neighborhood," she murmured.

"Sod that! We've only just h'arrived!" Charlie protested. "Besides, me mother's coming next week!" To leave Darnall now was unthinkable. He was happy in Darnall, close to his family in Sheffield, and if his darling Janey did marry, she too would be settling down locally. Nothing would drive him from Darnall . . . Hannah was just fretting unduly again. He patted her freckly hand. "Don't be flayed, lass. Things'll calm down!"

IV

Weeks did pass calmly enough, during which Charlie moved his mother into the city, continued to supply Kate Dyson with liquor and money, and avoided Trinity Church. But at the end of April, he made up his mind to try and woo Mrs. Dyson again.

Kirkham delivered his message, and it was a simple epistle: "Cum too the Whitsing Fair. Brng W. H. only. Hav some thng portant ter say." Charlie's misspellings were deliberate and he scribbled the note with his bad hand. Kate Dyson read it with interest and burned the note in the grate. She persuaded herself that no harm could ensue from going to a fair, and she was curious to know what he meant by "something portant." She decided to make her own way with Will Henry—neither informing her husband nor traveling with Charlie's party. That would enable her to say that she'd simply run into Charlie by accident.

Whitsing Fair—a "Second Pentecost" founded by the Sheffield

Sunday School Union—was an honored occasion which took place every Whit Monday in Norfolk Park. It was traditional for the Peaces to attend en masse, and a far cry from the rough Winter Fair. There were choirs and bands, peep shows and showmen, flowers and fairy lights, and not a diddiki in sight. A Whitworth gun announced lunch, and Charlie's table for twenty was close to a sheep-shearing contest. His family ate their roast beef to the tunes of "Baccy and Ale" bands, and the fun was well under way when Kate Dyson sauntered up to their group.

"Kate! Will Henry!" Charlie jumped up to greet them.

"Mrs. Dyson, please," he was corrected. Kate Dyson's face was hidden by a veil.

"Of course," Charlie said. "Wilt thou join my fambly?"

"Nope." Mrs. Dyson was conscious of Hannah regarding her with open hostility. At the head of the Peace table was a very old lady whom she guessed to be Charlie's mother, about whom she'd heard so much. "Let's away awhile," she added. "You can tell me what you want to say." She turned about and started walking toward a mobile photographer's van. Charlie shrugged and went after her, but he beckoned Willie Ward to follow them.

"Well?" Mrs. Dyson asked when they were a safe distance from the Peaces. The photographer came up to beg some custom, but she shooed him away.

"I've been thinking, Kate . . . May I call you Kate? . . . I've been thinking about oursen'." Charlie didn't like her veil—it masked her eyes.

"Thinking what?"

Charlie endeavored to find the right words. He stammered and kicked the ground with his feet. The photographer had come up again—he was standing with his apparatus a few yards to their left —and Charlie gave him a nod out of politeness. "I love you, Kate," he managed at last. "I really think I does. I was just wond'rin' . . ."

"Wondering what?"

" . . . wonderin' if you'd care to leave thine hubby, so that we . . ."

Kate Dyson's shrill laugh cut him short. "Well, he's not thine real hubby anyroad!" Charlie argued. "You told us as how you'd got the banns up the chimney!" But Mrs. Dyson continued to laugh at him. "I'd set thee up in a shop in t'city; fill it full o' fancies!" he went on desperately. "Leave that miserly bugger, Kate! I can make thee happy!"

Kate Dyson stopped laughing. "Would you leave Hannah to marry me?"

It was a catch question, as Charlie knew, and he had only one answer. "How could I?" he said unhappily.

"Because you love her?" Another test.

"I love thee too, Kate!"

"But not enough to leave her? Is that it?"

She had him over a barrel, and he squirmed. "We could all be happy, Kate!"

Mrs. Dyson shook her head. "I don't need you anymore, Charles Peace," she said quietly. "I don't want your charity or anything. We're finished, you understand?"

Charlie gaped at her. He looked so silly that she started laughing again. But at that moment there was a terrific flash—the photograph had caught them all with a double tintype—Kate Dyson, Charlie, Will Henry, even Willie Ward grinning in the background.

"What in blazes!" she swore. "Destroy them, Charlie! I *insist* those pictures be destroyed!"

Charlie came out of his trance and obeyed. He crossed over to the photographer and bought the clumsy tintypes. He nearly ground them underfoot, but didn't; his back was to Mrs. Dyson and he slipped them under his coat. He waited by the cameras to make it seem that he was destroying the pictures, and when he turned round Kate Dyson and her son were walking rapidly away.

"Hey there, Kate!" he called after them. "Hey, Kate, come back!"

But his cries were to no avail: Mrs. Dyson's strides grew longer and more purposeful. Charlie started to run after them, but they were nearing his picnic table and he stopped. Hannah and his mother were looking at him—as were Janey and Bolsover. He stared after Mrs. Dyson; she'd almost gained the park gates. No stopping her now, he realized. She had a temper as quick as his own, she'd surely cause a scene. Again her words rang in his head —"We're finished, you understand?"—horrible, but as clear as day. She *had* finished with him—she'd scorned all his entreaties —he was of no further use to her. Women like Katherine Dyson gave a fellow short shrift once he'd served his purpose. In other words, his money and his body now bored her. This had never happened to him before; he ground his teeth at the insult. Averting his face from his family, he slowly walked in the opposite direction. And he didn't stop until he was far away from everyone —deep in the park. Here he wiped his eyes with a large bandana and noisily blew his nose. Anger was gradually replacing grief, until he was consumed by hate. "Bloody whore!" he shouted at the trees. "I'll show her yet!"

6

Parke's Law

May and June were bad months for all concerned. Dyson was unemployed and broody. He and his wife kept indoors—for Charlie had started to plague their home, loitering around the front and back, pulling faces and hissing whenever he spotted either of them. The empty Number 38 stood like a wall of bad feeling between Numbers 36 and 40.

Nor was life much better in Number 40. Janey and Willie kept clear of the house while Hannah endured Charlie's moods. Sometimes he moped, seeking solace with his pets, but he was given to bouts of rage—one of which served an indiscreet Willie with a puffy lip—and Hannah feared her husband might do something really stupid. One afternoon in late June she spoke her mind.

"Us saw tha hangin' round the Dysons," she accused him in the kitchen. They were alone—but Janey was due in any moment. "Tha'll land us in trubble!"

"Shut thy gap, woman." Charlie was slumped by the range.

"*And* we be in trubble with the Rating Office!" Hannah added, not to be put off. " 'Appen we'll find oursen ejected!"

"Bugger the rates." Charlie unwound himself and wandered around the room. But he knew the truth of her words—he hadn't paid the rates in months, he'd neglected crime, and cash was short. Moreover, Janey's wedding was nigh and he wanted all his money to give her a good day. The Rating Office could wait. He

74

strolled up to the mantel, thinking of happy newlyweds, and his eye fell upon yet another memorial verse he'd written years ago. He took it down, wishing his eyes were better. He promised himself a pair of spectacles, for his eyes had grown weak of late:

> I was so long with pain opprest, that wore my strength away,
> It made me long for endless rest, which never can decay

went the words on the memorium. Sad words—for his dead sister, driven to an early grave by a drunkard husband, but fortunately not before Charlie had thrashed the lout. He replaced the card with a sigh; well, at least Bolsover was a gentle lad. Charlie determined to do his best for the couple; they deserved the best. And tomorrow was Janey's seventeenth birthday. Charlie had her present in his waistcoat pocket—an engraved silver pencil case. He'd give it to her tonight, wrapped and tied with a blue ribbon. He'd have liked to have shown it to Kate Dyson for her approval for the silver was engraved with one of his poems—he could recite the words without consulting the case. He said aloud:

> "There is a flower, a gentle flower,
> That blooms in each shaded spot,
> And gently to the heart it speaks,
> Forget me not, Love."

"That's thy trubble!" Hannah's voice rang out from the ironing board. "Tha can'st not forget yon Dyson woman!"

Her comment was unfortunate. Charlie scowled. No, he couldn't forget Kate Dyson, however hard he tried, and mere mention of her name from someone else's lips unleashed his rage.

"I'm goin' out," he said.

Hannah heard the front door close, and knew he'd gone to play bo-peep at the Dyson home again.

It was a hot afternoon, made all the more stifling by the blasts of warm air that came up to Darnall from the industrial complex of Sheffield. Dyson was in the parlor in his shirtsleeves, reading a manual, and the bow window was open. Charlie's "Hello, there, sir!" caused him to leap from his chair. Charlie was at the window, again, grinning through the aperture. Dyson launched himself across the room and slammed the window shut. His wife heard the noise and came running from the kitchen.

"It's that damn Peace!" Dyson said hoarsely.

And Charlie was still at the window, his nose pressed flat against the pane, bright eyes scanning them both.

"Go away!" Dyson waved at him.

Charlie waved back.

"Get along with you, dammit!" Dyson tapped on the window.

Charlie tapped back—a tattoo.

"Go away—or I'll call the constabulary!" Dyson cried hysterically.

Charlie drew some words on a grimy section of the glass. Dyson cocked his head to see what he'd written. "Let me be yr friend," he read.

"Confound his impudence!" Dyson tried to wipe out the words, but Charlie responded by underlining the writing. Then he disappeared and the doorbell rang.

"Don't let him in, Arthur!" begged his wife.

Dyson shook his head. He was minded to take a broom to Charlie, but he remembered Sykes's sad injuries. Drunken Indians in Missouri had been one thing—but the man outside was inhuman. "Let's retire to the rear," he said.

They retreated to the kitchen and sat with Will Henry, virtually imprisoned in their own house, while Charlie continued to pound on the front door. "I'm very bad!" his voice came through the letter box. "But I wish to make h'amends!"

Will Henry suddenly looked up from his toys with interest.

"Nuncle Charlie!" he said happily. "Has Nuncle Charlie come to play?"

Dyson stared at his son. *Nuncle* Charlie, indeed. . . . Even his boy's accent struck him as odd. . . . Of course: he sounded just like Peace! "This is too much," Dyson swore. He strode across to a Welsh dresser, accidentally kicking over a model Pullman. He didn't notice the toy—if he had, he'd have spotted Charlie's handiwork—and he rummaged in the dresser. "Where have all my visiting cards got to?" he asked his wife. But then he found one—the last remaining—and returned to the kitchen table with a pencil. "I shall be blunt!" he announced, licking the point, and he began to write.

"What have you said?" asked his wife when he'd done.

"Very little—but enough!" Dyson smiled with satisfaction. The card was for Charlie, of course. He'd deliver it himself—but not yet, later, when this infernal hammering had stopped and Peace had gone away. Dyson waited patiently, and his wife admired his calm. She was sure whatever he'd written on that card was bound to discourage their tormentor.

II

Charlie discovered the message next morning, lying in his front garden. It was wet with rain, but it was perfectly legible.

"Charles Peace is requested not to interfere with my family" —Dyson's hand, on Dyson's card.

"Bugger that!" Charlie put the card in a pocket and returned indoors. He stretched himself out on the front room sofa, pondering. It was the word "interfere" he found objectionable; he was, in effect, being *ordered* off. Yet Dyson hadn't the grace to face him man to man. Why not? Surely not because he was afraid of him—Dyson was a good foot taller than himself. No, it must be because Dyson feared what *he* might do—lay hands on Charlie. Very well, Charlie would drive Dyson into striking him. And Charlie, like a saint, would turn the other cheek. *That* would be very canny—he'd earn Kate's respect.

So he swung his legs off the sofa, put on his billycock, and left the house in search of Dyson, who he thought had perhaps gone into the village, so he looked for him along the High Street. But there was no sign of the man. Charlie next dropped in at the Halfway, on the off chance Mrs. Dyson would be there. She wasn't —but Mrs. Norton called him over.

"That fratch ye had wi' Sykes has led ta questions," she informed him.

"Oh, aye? Who's askin', mistress?"

"Peeler Pearson of Darnall lock-up."

"What's he say then?"

"That you're responsible—and he'd like ta see tha."

"What did you tell him?"

"Nowt. Nobody talks wi' a bobby, does they?"

Charlie smiled. "Thankee, mistress." He was truly grateful for her silence, but he was worried that the local policeman was seeking him.

He returned to Britannia Road, debating what he should do about Pearson, when he suddenly spotted Arthur Dyson walking up ahead and Pearson was forgotten.

Dyson had been into Sheffield, looking for accommodations, and he didn't hear Charlie approaching. But he uttered a groan as his name was called.

"Hello, sir!"

Dyson quickened his pace, but Charlie tugged his sleeve. "Leave me be!" Dyson pulled his arm free. "Get away, you hear me!"

Charlie darted behind him. Dyson let out a cry as something nipped his ankle. "Wuff-wuff!" barked Charlie. He pinched Dyson again and the tall man stumbled and nearly fell. "Grrr-

grrr!'' Charlie tried to trip him by catching at his heels. Dyson lashed out with a haymaker, missed, and Charlie laughed. Dyson's stride lengthened into a run, faster and faster, and he ran until he'd gained his house, where, gasping for breath, he turned to face his persecutor. But Charlie hadn't followed—he was far behind, still barking and dancing like a dog on hind legs. Dyson rushed into his house, shut the door and bolted it, his face a deathly white.

From her bedroom window, five doors along, Mrs. Sykes had observed the incident with interest.

The man from the Rating Office caught Charlie on his return to Number 40, and their confrontation was unhappy. Charlie must pay his rates or face a summons.

When the official had gone, Charlie went out to his pet shed and cleaned a pair of pistols, loading one with powder and ball. He'd lost his precious pepperbox at Birley Moor and was now reduced to pin-fires, wobbly foreign guns of awkward caliber. But he'd require a revolver tonight—he had plans to "work" a house at Rotherham—and he slid the loaded weapon in his belt. He'd also lost his tool kit, but he had a bunch of skeleton keys and thought he'd confine himself to hard cash tonight. After all, plain money was what was needed to pay the rates and arrange his daughter's wedding.

He left the shed at nine, intent to catch the half-past train to Rotherham. As he passed Mrs. Sykes's cottage he saw that a group of ladies were standing beneath the gaslight, in earnest conversation. By the streetlamp, he identified Mrs. Sykes, Mrs. Padmore—and Kate Dyson. And the ladies had seen him, too: six angry eyes looked his way. Charlie walked on, nodded to the women, and made to pass them by. But Mrs. Dyson suddenly stepped out. She was flushed and reeked of gin and she poked at Charlie with her parasol.

"Why are you annoying my husband?" she demanded. "Everywhere he goes, you annoy him!" She jabbed him again with the ferule.

Charlie smiled. "I'll h'annoy you and thine husband wherivver ye go!"

"You dare!" She raised her umbrella.

Charlie turned to the other ladies. "Bear witness that she hit me!" he cried.

The door to Number 26 now opened; it was Mr. Sykes. "Hey, Jim!" Charlie called to him. "Bear witness she tried to hit me with a life preserver!" Sykes shook his head. "She did, by God!" Charlie swore. He sought to scare them all and drew his revolver. "By God, I'll blow thy bloody brains out!" He shook the gun at Mrs. Dyson. "And thy bloody husband's too!"

Sykes moved on the front path of his house. "Stand back!" Charlie warned him. "I've enuff ball to do for the lot of you!" Sykes stopped; his wife and Mrs. Padmore backed away in terror; only Kate Dyson remained unmoved, her face set and shiny under the lamp. Charlie gave her a long look and then tucked away his pistol. "I h'abominate the lot of you!" he snarled, and made off in the night. But he knew he'd overplayed his hand by presenting a weapon.

And Charlie was correct. Once Arthur Dyson heard about the production of a firearm, he took positive action. He went to the magistrates next morning, along with his wife and Pearson. According to the constable and a case called "St. George," it was an assault "to point a loaded arm, to wit, a pistol, then and there loaded with gunpowder and leaden bullet" at another. That was the decision of one Baron Parke in 1840, and who were the justices to argue with so learned a judge? A summons was duly issued in the name of Charles Peace and served by Pearson at Number 40. The constable had hoped to meet the accused, but Charlie was out, and his wife didn't know where.

Hannah put the summons on the parlor mantelpiece like a birthday card to await Charlie's return from Rotherham. When he got home that evening, his face fell, as he read the summons. He examined it from every angle and ended by tearing the document to shreds.

"That won't cause it ta disappear," Hannah observed from the doorway.

Charlie nodded and lit a pipe. Failure to present himself at court in answer to the charge would automatically lead to a warrant for his arrest. Then he'd be exposed to a general inquiry. Either way, the police would probably investigate him; he was seriously endangered. God blast his stupidity in showing a pistol! Better for him to have shot the mob all dead. For now he must quit Darnall at once—worse, leave the West Riding altogether. He'd be wise to go east—to Hull, even Hamburg. And he couldn't leave Hannah and Willie. His daughter would be safe enough—officially engaged to a local man—but his wife and stepson might be persecuted by the police. So would his family in Sheffield—they'd be pressed as to his whereabouts, even his dear old mother. Charlie allowed himself another outburst of oaths.

"Get oursen packed, Hannah love!" he added more quietly when he felt better. "I go tonight—you follow when I sends for thee." He paused. "But 'appen I'll be back soon enuff—and then there'll be the best o' bloody murder!"

7

Manchester
Rick-Rack

Jacob Bradbury had been promoted and now occupied the inspector's office at Water Lane. He sent to Darnall for Pearson and thought the constable grown fat and soft on his quiet village beat, but he wanted the latter's opinion.

"Heeley Hall again," he said, and laughed when Pearson looked surprised. "We don't give up cases on this division, remember? Now then, look at this lot." He indicated a bag and assorted hardware on his partner's desk. "They were dropped by some villain up t'no good at Birley Wood. All the drills be made by hand—a clever hand. So were these screws"—he held up a longish twist of steel—"recognize it?"

Pearson seemed unsure; he'd forgotten the details of last November's burglary.

"Same as we found at t'Hall," Bradbury reminded him. "But here's summat far more interesting!" He handed Pearson a pepperbox revolver. The cylinder was fully charged and some buckshot fell from one of the chambers. "Ring a bell?"

Pearson nodded. "Aye, sir. Didn't we dig such rubbish out of the panelwork up t'Hall?"

"Less o' the 'rubbish,' lad. You'd not find me happy facing a five-tongued squib!"

But Pearson still thought the pistol too old-fashioned to be dangerous. "Guns be on the pop'lar side these days," he commented.

"What makes you say that?"

"Just a thought, sir."

"Tell it me!"

Pearson chose his words with care. " 'Appen we've a loony out at Darnall who's been brandishin' a gun. Name of Peace. He's wanted for common assault. Poked his gun at a lady. Her hubby's gone quite barmy. I'm not surprised—rumor has it that Peace's poked more than just his pistol at his missus! But he's gone now, owing rates, and good riddance!"

Bradbury had listened carefully. "This pistol—wasn't a pepperbox by chance?"

"Nay, sir. One of them cartridge revolvers."

So Bradbury lost interest in Peace and rang a bell on his desk for tea.

Charlie boarded a train in Sheffield looking like himself, but he got off at Hull as someone else. He was now "John Ward," itinerant merchant, with a shorter beard, a brunet wig, and wearing spectacles.

First he found lodgings in the Fishy City. Inquiries at Town Hall provided him with the name and address of a Sergeant Gilbey, City Force, who had a room to let near Collier Street, in a middling part of town. Gilbey was a quiet man, with a quieter childless wife. He collected model ships—his tidy home was strewn with bottled vessels.

Gilbey and Charlie got on famously, but Charlie couldn't sit around forever helping the policeman with his hobby. Hannah and Willie were still in Sheffield, staying with Mrs. Peace, and he wanted them in Hull. When they came they would all require a "front," and to this end, he rented a chophouse in Collier Street in the name of Hannah Peace. This restaurant was a going concern—work for Hannah and Willie, revenue for him—and there was suitable accommodation above. So he soon wrote off to Hannah to join him at the shop.

She and Willie duly arrived, laden with luggage, and Charlie settled them in.

"Here, you be Mistress Peace and Son, lately deserted by the vile Charles," he told them both. "When I call, I be John Ward —perambulating vendor and mostly h'away. Follow?"

They nodded—Hannah unhappily.

Charlie frowned. "What's up West?"

"Sufficient. Tha's wanted—on warrant."

So he had assumed; but at least Jack Law wouldn't waste precious policemen scouring the East on Dyson's account. It just meant he couldn't go back to Sheffield.

"Janey?" he asked, a slight catch in his voice.

"Living with Mistress Bolsover. She and Billy plan ta wed next month." Hannah's mouth went hard. She delved into her bag. "She sent thee this, so she did. . . ." Hannah handed him the pencil case. "Janey don't want it—says it's bad luck now—says tha's ta throw it away."

Charlie looked at the case. "Miss J. A. Peace. Given to her by her beloved Father on her 17th birthday." He polished the inscription with the ball of his thumb, close to tears. Janey reminded him of his own mother—calm, gentle, very sweet—that's why she mattered so much. Her return of his present saddened him, and now he'd not even be able to give her away at her marriage. . . . "Bloody Dysons!" he muttered.

Hannah snorted. "Tha's thysen ta blame, all said. Anyroad, they're movin' away from Darnall."

"When?"

"Neither know—nor cares. 'Tis said Arthur Dyson forgives her —'tis said he's a saint!"

Charlie grunted. " 'Appen he's more in line for martyrdom."

Then he smiled—rather wolfishly. "I'm goin' h'away a few days," he said, "but not for long."

In fact, Charlie took the boat over to Hamburg. The cat-backed mate was still with Olsen and Charlie's passage was cut half-price, but he was nevertheless sick throughout the trip, and perked up only when he met Otto Senf in a bar on Davidstrasse. He had little to sell the Lübecker this time, but they discussed the European market for gold and silver over Danish beer.

"Good silver is desired in Deutschland," Otto said. "Bismarck is old, but the Kaiser ambitious. Our peoples want wealth. They see sterling 'pewter' as a good investment—cheaper than gold, and useful in *das haus*. You get me silver, *hein?* We make much money."

Charlie nodded. He needed "much money" and he promised to get Senf his "pewter." "Oh, and one small favor, Mr. Mustard," he added. He took three postcards of the Elbe from his pocket. "Post these for me. Frank 'em with a Deutscher stamp, eh? I'd ha' done it mysen, but I can't fathom thy pfennigs."

Senf took the cards. They were addressed to some people called Dyson in England. "This I will do," he said.

II

With Hannah at her restaurant, renamed the Collier Grubbery, Charlie was content to stay with the Gilbeys for the rest of the month. But he was restless.

By now his Hamburg cards would have reached the Dysons. He tried to envisage their reception—Dyson would undoubtedly give them to the police, who might assume their author had gone to sea. Charlie even considered doing just that—to erase all his memories of Mrs. Dyson. As it was, she consumed his mind. He talked with Gilbey, helped him with his models daily; he walked the waterfront and drank with whalers; he visited Hannah as an ordinary customer; but nothing worked to drive Kate from his thoughts. He only wanted to be near her—to see those violet eyes and hear her laugh. He didn't know whether he loved or hated her; she just lived in his brain and his mental anguish began to show on him physically.

"Tha's off thy food and thin as a gavelock," Hannah told him one evening, clearing away his untouched plate.

Her mention of a crowbar reminded Charlie of his undertaking to Senf. Work was what he needed to pull himself together, and he conceived a plan.

Yorkshire was vast, but his description might have been circulated even east of Doncaster. Hull didn't know him—but the city held Hannah and Gilbey, his wife and his retreat. He decided to "hit" another county altogether and settled on Lancashire. Manchester—home of King Cotton—was a likely place, a suburban sprawl for the very wealthy.

So on Monday, the last day of July, Charlie packed a grip and took a westbound train. Charlie arrived in Manchester dressed as a country parson. The bag in his hand contained nothing more sinister than a Winfield knife and a picklock, but he carried a loaded pin-fire. Hannah and Gilbey both believed him to be in Nottingham; they both would have been shocked to see him in clerical cloth.

At the station, he bought and perused a map of the city. He chose the parish of Stretford, and caught a cab to respectable Chorlton-cum-Hardy. That night, in his Temperance hotel, he selected the district of Whalley Range as a special target. But first he must spy out the land. . . .

In the morning he paid his bill and tipped the parlormaid and began to scout Chorlton. He located the police station and found it next to the local Magistrates Court. Experience had taught him that the police hung round a Petty Sessions like flies, so he went into court. He very much looked what he wasn't—the visiting vicar with a kindly, albeit twisted, face. Room was made for him in the public gallery. As he'd thought, the courtroom was crammed with blue-coats—giving evidence, looking on, forever chattering. A case was in progress and Charlie listened. A pimply young constable was accusing a nurseryman of having been drunk and disorderly. Shades of Kate Dyson. The constable added that he'd also been threatened by the defendant and his brother—having successfully summoned the latter for being drunk last month, when the brother was fined. But this defendant had an alibi, it seemed. It was all very tedious and Charlie got up to leave when the man sitting beside him became very agitated.

"He's a liar, that bobby!" the man said. "That little bobby is a bugger!"

Charlie would have agreed that most policemen were of that nature, but he remembered his cloth. "Hush, my son!" he said.

The man looked at him—a dark young man, dressed in dungarees like the man in the dock. "You don't know him, Father," he said, very Irish. "He had me foined foive shillen on account of his lies. He needs shiftin', he does. Give me a chance and I'd shift him meself!"

Ah, thought Charlie, this must be the brother. "Forgive him, my son," he urged the fiery young man.

Up on the Bench, the case was being resolved. The justices found fault with the constable's tale and the charge was dismissed.

"Well done, Billy-boy!" shouted the brother.

"Quiet!" ordered the clerk of court.

"I'll no be quiet!" insisted the other. "That dirty rick-rack's been disbelaved on his oaf"—he pointed at the constable—"will ye not have him fer perjury!"

Charlie grinned. But police were approaching to silence the brother and Charlie slipped away to avoid being involved. Outside the court, he paused to glance at the case list. "Police versus Wm. Habron" he read. Good stuff—great fun! He hoped the lying constable was in due course soundly "shifted."

Charlie wasn't much worried by the police he'd seen at court —most had been either very young or too old to block his nimble path. In the city, bobbies were a different breed: big men who walked two abreast with neddies under their arms. Out in Chorlton, they plainly parked recruits and old horses. But he was slightly alarmed by their number.

With these thoughts in mind, he sat in a ditch and checked his revolver. He'd double-charged each cylinder. The bullets were conical Eleys and the pistol itself a Liège "reporter"—hair-triggered. The noise of a shot would be considerable—enough to frighten away any young bobby with a sweetheart or hopes of a pension. But Charlie was confident he wouldn't even have to make show with his weapon.

He remained in the ditch until dark. When he came out he was no longer a parson, but a pot-hatted laborer, wearing rubber boots which rendered him noiseless as he left the ditch and climbed down a railway embankment. The tracks led to Whalley Range and he followed them into that area. He went past a field where he saw a man huddled in front of a brazier, and a dog was barking incessantly from behind some big houses so he stayed on the railway, hiding in the dip until midnight. Then he clambered up the embankment to a track that led to a turnpike called Brookes Bar. This was the main road into Manchester. It was flanked by houses, but Charlie's prey were the mansions back by the field on the Old Trafford Road. Across that field and down to the railway would be his line of retreat. He left Brookes Bar and went toward a junction called Seymour Road until he heard voices and stopped. Four people were standing by a jutting stone in the center of the junction, and two of them were uniformed policemen. Charlie almost turned back; but he hadn't been noticed, so he just pulled down his hat and waited. Three minutes passed and the burble of voices continued. Then the group dispersed—"Good nights" were said—and the people went off in different directions. One man, not a policeman, came quite close to Charlie, who drew back under the lee of some overhanging branches. When everyone had gone Charlie darted up to the junction and turned left. Here were the big houses. The first was in total darkness, but Charlie thought the dog's bark had come from this house so he chose the third mansion, climbed over the wooden gates, and landed with a crunch on the driveway. No lights shone at any window, but a gas jet hissed and fluttered by the porch. He came to his feet from a crouch and was about to step onto the front lawn when one of the shadows on the porch moved strangely. Charlie froze. It was a man—with a pointed head? A helmeted bobby! Charlie ducked back into the bushes by the gates and lay flat. Footsteps came down the drive, a heavy plod that didn't hesitate. But they passed and went to the gates. He heard the gates open and snap shut. The bobby had gone— Charlie hadn't been seen. He breathed shallowly, wondering what to do. He was no longer tempted by this house; nor could he remain long where he was; he decided to try somewhere else. He left the shrubbery and went out the gates. The street seemed deserted. He started to walk off toward Old Trafford, but he'd gone only a few paces when a voice called out sharply.

"Hey, you there!"

Charlie stopped short. That bobby—who else? And close behind him.

"Don't run—I'll blow my whistle!" Boots pounded up the pavement. Too late for Charlie to run. He spun around to face the policeman, drawing his pistol. He was startled to find himself face to face with the young constable from Chorlton Magistrates Court, truncheon in hand.

Charlie raised his revolver. "Stand back, lad!"

But the bobby seemed unafraid. "Drop that pop—or I'll do you with this!" He swung back his truncheon.

This was no time for argument. Charlie pointed his gun to the right and loosed off a shot, deliberately wide. The noise was deafening, but the bobby came on at him and Charlie fired a second shot wildly.

"Ah, you bugger!" cried the constable. He dropped his stick and clutched his breast, a jet of blood squirting between his fingers. He fell on his side in the road, still staring at Charlie with glassy eyes. Charlie looked back at him briefly. Then a police whistle sounded from Chorlton Road and Charlie took to his heels. He went through the gates of the house he'd just left, round the side of the building, across a large garden, over a wall and into a lane. Beyond lay the field. The man by the brazier was still there, squatting motionless. Charlie stooped as he ran across the field to the railway, got onto the rails, and hid in a tunnel to catch his breath. The dog was barking furiously again. Charlie started to jog down the track, revolver at ready, and he didn't stop running for two miles. Then he got off the railway, onto a highway, and paused to decide his next move. It was now unsafe for him to be abroad anywhere. Better he hide till the morning. He wandered about until he came on a workmen's shack by some hoardings and went inside it, his gun cocked, but the hut was empty. He lay down on some old sacks and bags of cement and closed his eyes to rest. He knew he must be out of this shack before daybreak, and his sleep was fitful. He feared for the bobby he'd shot. He hoped the young man was not badly injured. He even planned an anonymous letter to the chief constable expressing regret at the incident.

Thank God Hannah didn't know he was in Lancashire.

III

Sergeant Gilbey had missed Mr. Ward. The latter had brought him the model Leissz windjammer from Hamburg and he wanted his lodger to help him bottle it, but Mr. Ward was only three days "in Nottingham" and the two men soon got together.

"How's trade?" Gilbey asked. They were consuming some wine in the sergeant's "den" of an evening, surrounded by shipping.

"Not good at all, sir," said Charlie. " 'Tis 'ard to h'earn a living these days."

Gilbey nodded, brushing his whiskers. His face was so whiskery that he reminded Charlie of a griffon. "That's true, Mr. Ward. Our country lacks bottom 'n' brains. We're on the short road to anarchy, I fear. Why, people are even shooting at the Force!"

"Shooting at whom, sir?"

Gilbey crossed his untidy den and returned with a newspaper. "Just you read that, Mr. Ward. Makes one's blood boil!" He thrust the second page of the paper under Charlie's nose.

Charlie looked at the columns. The Queen was going to Balmoral. . . . No, this was what Gilbey was talking about: "MANCHESTER OUTRAGE—Murder at Stretford." Charlie's blood in fact turned to ice.

On the night of August 1, PC 1015 Nicholas Cock was shot at Chorlton-cum-Hardy. Two brothers, William and John Habron, were arrested the same night by Police Superintendent Bent, who is in charge of the case. Our Stretford Reporter states that the Habrons bore the deceased a grudge and had been heard to utter threats against him. They were arrested on the premises of their employer, Mr. Francis Deakin, and appeared the next morning at court where they were remanded in custody. Both prisoners vigorously deny the charge of willful murder. Mr. Bent declined to comment on the nature of the evidence against the two men, but it seems PC Cock did not die immediately and was able to pass certain remarks before he eventually expired at the house of Dr. John Dill, who was in attendance.

"Makes a man sick, eh?" Gilbey said as Charlie put down the paper.

Indeed, the article did make Charlie feel unwell. He read the column again until the print swam before his eyes.

"At least they've caught the bastards who did it!" said Gilbey.

Charlie glanced at him briefly. The Habron brothers? Both, as he knew, charged quite falsely. He folded the paper and stood up. He needed some air—away from this smoky parlor and Gilbey. He needed quiet to think. "I've got to go out," he murmured.

"At this hour?" It was past midnight. "I was hoping you'd help bottle my boat!" He shook the wine bottle at Charlie. It was nearly empty and ready for use: Gilbey planted only good boats in wine bottles.

"You drink it, sir," Charlie said.

He left his startled landlord and went out into the streets. He walked Hull for a long time. The night air was balmy, but he didn't notice. He was thinking of what he had read. He hadn't intended to kill that policeman—he didn't know what he'd intended. The bobby hadn't given him time to form a specific intent. The first shot he'd fired to scare, but the young fool had come on and the gun had gone off again. Hair-triggered, of course, but he must have cocked back the hammer—he couldn't remember. That would have been a matter of reflex. He'd been in a panic, with only escape on his mind, but now he was surely a murderer. . . . His thoughts turned to the Habrons. They were accused of his crime. If found guilty they'd hang. But surely they'd prove their innocence? They must have an alibi. And Cock had spoken before he died. Cock had seen his assassin—he would have described Charlie to others—and Charlie didn't fit the description of either Habron. This would come out in court. The brothers would be discharged—and by then the scent for anyone else would be cold. Charlie felt suddenly better. The quick arrest of the Habrons had probably made it so easy for him to get out of Manchester; he'd seen no bobbies at the station or on the train. But the death of Cock was a very bad business. . . .

Praise God Hannah didn't know.

8

Nathaniel
Down Below

After what had happened, Charlie thought it judicious to stay away from the West for awhile. He'd no "pewter" for Senf, but Hannah's shop was showing a good profit and he was glad he'd no cause to "work"—although he did go away for the odd night, just to allay any suspicions on the part of the good Sergeant Gilbey.

In the middle of August, Janey and Billy were married at Darnall. It was far less of an affair than Charlie had hoped; only Hannah returned for the wedding, while Willie Ward minded the chophouse and Charlie cursed the warrant that held him at bay.

But there was one small compensation—Janey and Billy were induced to honeymoon at Cleethorpes, the health resort just outside Great Grimsby, and Charlie was able to join them. His daughter was still rather cool toward him, but he didn't care; she was obviously happy with Billy. They all stayed at an expensive hotel, Charlie having burgled a house in Wooton to pay for that pleasure, and September was blessed by an Indian summer. The subject of the Dysons wasn't raised until the last day of the holiday. Charlie and his son-in-law were alone in the foyer, smoking cigars among the potted palms, waiting for the ladies to come down for dinner.

"Seen owt of Kate Dyson?" Charlie asked casually.

"Nay, Dad. We keeps out of their gate."

"Very sensible. . . . But what news of 'em?"

Billy shrugged. "Folk say they're moving to Ecclesall. Funny that."

"Why funny?"

"T'minister as married us—Mister Newman—he comes from Ecclesall. Mr. Littlewood wast away visiting, and this Newman took over at Darnall."

Charlie hadn't known this—he was intrigued. "And the Dysons be going to live in Ecclesall?" He knew that part of Sheffield very well—it was to the south of the city and less quiet than Darnall. He also knew that, as far as police jurisdiction was concerned, the district was out of Attercliffe and into the Highfield Division. "Billy-lad," he addressed his son-in-law, "I want you to do summat for us. . . . Keep yer glims open on yon Dysons and report back to me. They be h'inveterate t'wards Charlie, and 'appen they'll serve us shabbily if they can. So I want 'em watched careful." He took a card with Gilbey's address from his waistcoat and wrapped it up in a five-pound note. "Contact me by post," he said, giving it to Billy. The money did much to augment the salary of a simple collier so of course Billy was bought. Nor did he question the name "John Ward" on the card. He simply nodded and put the cash away. "Say not to either Janey, or thine mum-in-law," Charlie added.

Then those ladies appeared on the broad staircase and the family went off to dine.

II

The Dysons had been fearful of what might arrive with the post since the receipt of Charlie's three postcards. The views of the

Elbe had been harmless enough, but obscene limericks on the reverse didn't amuse Arthur Dyson one bit. He'd hidden the cards from his wife, intending to keep them for his solicitor, but Kate Dyson discovered their place when dusting the top of the dresser. She read the least rude:

> "A gladsome grand lady named Dyson,
> Used to find Peace in the back of a hansom,
> When she begged him for more, the little man swore,
> 'You may be Delilah, but I'm hardly Samson!' "

And she had smiled in spite of herself.

When the letter box rattled one October morning she let her husband go to the door and expressed relief when he returned with more ordinary mail. "All fixed then!" Dyson said, having read the letters over breakfast. He'd been hoping for compensation from the railway for months now; that wasn't forthcoming; but he'd secured the lease of a house in Ecclesall. "We'll be moving to Banner Cross Terrace on the twenty-fifth," he told his wife. "We'd best order the vans. No time like the present. What you doin' today, Kate?"

Mrs. Dyson hesitated. "I *was* going into Mansfield with Mrs. Padmore and the children," she replied. Any excuse to get away from her husband and near a public house.

"You can go this aft'noon—catch the two-fifteen train," Dyson told her. "But fix up the vans this morning."

Interestingly enough, Charlie was on that very train, disguised as a crone, in some of his mother's tattier clothing, having followed the ladies down to the station. He was up front, while the ladies occupied a rear compartment. The train was not crowded and Charlie had a third-class compartment to himself. This was just as well, for as they crossed the Notts border he started to change clothes. The more feminine garments went out the window—skirts and stays flying down the train. One shift lodged itself briefly against the window of Kate Dyson's carriage.

"Eeee, what's that!" cried Mrs. Padmore. But then it was gone.

When the train stopped at Mansfield, Charlie emerged in corduroy britches and shirt, but still sporting a pair of ladies' laced boots. He sought out the women and followed them through town. It was a warm afternoon, and the ladies called at a hostelry, the Mercian King, which advertised "Teas." Gone to earth, thought Charlie, who'd expected Kate Dyson to choose a more alcoholic establishment.

He followed the ladies into the saloon, sat at a table behind them, and ordered a glass of sherbet. They still hadn't noticed him. When Mrs. Dyson asked a waitress for soda pop Charlie laughed loudly.

"H'off the Satin, lass?"

Mrs. Dyson swiveled around and winced at the sight of him— as if confronted by the Devil. Charlie came up to her table. " 'Ello, Kate? Mistress Padmore? Will 'Enry, lad?" He nodded at the children and Mrs. Padmore. "A word with Mrs. Dyson alone, mistress, *if* you don't mind?" Mrs. Padmore was only too happy to make herself scarce and moved with the children to a nearby table. Charlie sat down opposite Mrs. Dyson. Her face was tense, but her voice was controlled when she spoke.

"You've got grit, I'll give you that. What d'you want, Mr. Peace?"

Charlie was dampened by such formality. He'd wanted to pour out his woes but he realized he'd be wasting his time. "H'only one thing I want, Kate," he replied.

"Speak up and begone."

"Drop that summons h'against hus."

Kate Dyson appeared to consider his request. "I think not," she answered. "Arthur holds that you asked for it and I agree with him."

"Please?" Charlie begged her. He could see Mrs. Padmore listening, and wished they were really alone. "Drop it and, within the hearing of God, I *swear* I'll nivver trubble you no more!"

Mrs. Dyson tossed her fine head of hair. "Go away, Mr. Peace, you weary me." She turned to Mrs. Padmore. "You may rejoin us, Jane. Mr. Peace was just leaving!"

Charlie came to his feet. "You bloody gin 'n' tatters!" he cursed her. "Begod, I'll make it warm for you! You mind for thysen, you hear?" He shook his fist at both women. Had they not been in a public place, he might have struck Mrs. Dyson. As it was, he stormed out of the tearoom without paying for his sherbet, uttering all manner of menaces.

III

It was agreed between the Dysons that if Charlie bothered either of them again the police would be immediately summoned. Otherwise, they were too busy preparing to move to concern themselves with the little man.

They took their leave of Darnall on a blustery Monday. The two-horse furniture wagonettes called in the morning and Billy Bolsover heard their iron-wheeled racket along the High Street. Their departure interested him, so he didn't go to work, but followed them to Britannia Road, hanging around Victoria Place until they were loaded. When they left the Dysons themselves caught a cab to the station. Billy decided to keep track of the vans and since he was a fit young collier, he was able to trot behind the vehicles all the way into Sheffield and along the Ecclesall Road. However, by the time they reached Banner Cross he was exhausted, and he paused to rest outside a small hotel, called the Terrace, which was on the main road, one of seven villas, modern and modest, facing some fields and a vegetable garden. The hotel was the last house, five villas down from the Dysons' new home, which was next door to a shop called Gregory's. Billy watched the vans being unloaded. The Dysons had yet to arrive. The nearest station was more than a mile away, and he assumed they'd engaged another cab. He would have time for a pie and a pint, and he went into the hotel bar. Great was his surprise when he found his father-in-law already there, supping ale with a stranger.

" 'Ello, Billy-boy!" Charlie greeted him. He bought him a beer and introduced the strange man. "This be Mr. Gregory. I've been h'apprizing the poor man of his neighbors-to-be." He waggled his beard. "A villainous couple, Mr. Greg. Dyson's a duffer, but his missus be devilish!"

Billy nodded obediently and drank his beer. He took it that Charlie had been staying in Sheffield following his recent communication to Hull. But he was mystified as to how his father-in-law had discovered the precise day of the Dysons' removal to the exact address. Billy wouldn't have known himself if he hadn't followed the vans.

When they finished their drinks they all left the hotel. Mr. Gregory returned to his shop, but Charlie went into the Dysons' new home, elbowing his way through the vanmen. Billy remained outside during the latter's inspection, and his heart sank as a hansom drew up with the Dysons and their hand luggage. Billy thought of making himself scarce, but at that moment Charlie came out of the house. He grinned at the sight of the Dysons, stepping up and raising his hat.

"Charles Peace, removeler, at thine service," he said.

Arthur Dyson was speechless. He hefted an armful of cases and marched past Charlie without saying a word. His expression was so determined that Charlie got out of his way. But Kate Dyson found her tongue soon enough.

"Why are *you* here!" she screamed, her face ashen under a bonnet.

"I'm here to h'annoy you," Charlie said reasonably, "and I'll h'annoy you wherivver you go."

"There's a warrant out for you!" She made sure the vanmen could hear. "You're wanted by the police!" Some of the men had stopped work to listen.

"I care nowt for any warrant and nowt for the bobbies," Charlie said. "Nor dost I care for thysen. But tha's not heard the last of me. . . . 'I know thy abode, and thy goin' out, and thy comin' in, and thy rage against me'!" He'd remembered a suitable quote from the Bible. Then he turned to Billy. "Come on, lad, let's leave these bad people be!" And they went off down Ecclesall Road.

Kate Dyson watched them disappear. She felt a sudden chill and went into the house. Her husband was in the hall passage, lighting a bracket lamp, and his face was grave.

"If that man shows up round here again, Kate, I swear I'll effect a citizen's arrest." The taper in his hand trembled slightly.

Kate Dyson sighed, unpinned her hat, and sat on a stool in the hall. She felt utterly despondent. Charlie had traced their new whereabouts, he'd sworn to badger them still, and she had little doubt that he'd do so. What was the use of the police or a warrant? She suddenly needed a drink.

IV

Charlie kicked his heels for a month back in Hull, resisting the urge to plague Ecclesall. It occurred to him that Dyson might have mentioned his visit to Highfield Division, a tough force to his knowledge, with a wide jurisdiction. So he forced himself to be patient, watching the ships and drinking with sailors. He drank far more than his custom, which did not pass unnoticed by Hannah.

"I'm going to Manchester tomorrow," he told her toward the end of November.

"Business?"

"Nay, to h'observe a trial. Two Paddies are being tried for snuffing a bobby."

Hannah didn't believe he was going for a trial. Of what possible interest could it be to him? She believed he was intent on a burglary spree, and his recent drinking did not ease her mind in that respect. "I'll come with you," she said, and was surprised when he accepted her offer.

They traveled together as "Mr. and Mrs. Jack Robinson" and took lodgings with a Mrs. "Dollymot" Williams in Angel Meadow, Manchester's crime quarter. For Charlie to consort with criminals when "on business" was rare, and Hannah realized he was indeed here for a trial.

The Habron case opened at the law courts on the twenty-seventh. Charlie went there alone, dressed in the bum-freezer jacket and striped trews of a law clerk, and sat with the rest of the death sentence ghouls up in the public gallery. The Habrons pleaded not guilty in terrified tones and the Crown's case began before a Red Judge and jury. The charge against them was simple: both brothers had shot Cock out of revenge; no gun had been found, but John had threatened to shoot the young constable and brother William had promised to "shunt" and "shift" him as well. Here was the motive. But when it came to the evidence of the actual shooting and death of Cock, and of the brothers' arrest, the case was less clear. Only one man had been seen near the scene of the crime, by a student called Simpson and a Constable Beanland. Simpson described him as stooped and elderly. Quite right, thought Charlie, it was himself Simpson had spotted under the trees. Beanland, however, said he saw the same man, yet averred he was young and fresh-faced—just like William. Bloody liar, thought Charlie, the copper's out to nail William. Now Cock had been found alive and been put on a cart for transport. A Constable Ewen asked Cock who had shot him. "They have done for me this time," was the alleged reply. "I do not know, they have done for me." Another bloody lie, thought Charlie: if Cock had spoken at all, and he obviously hadn't, he would have described his assailant in the singular. Cock was taken to the surgery of one Dr. Dill with some life left in him. "Leave me be!" Cock had shouted. "Frank, you are killing me!" But there was no one called Frank in the surgery. Doctor Dill had to admit that Cock had protested, "You are killing me!" when he was probing the wound. "And kill him ye did!" Charlie muttered, to the amusement of those beside him.

Then came Superintendent Bent. He dealt with the arrest of the Habrons after the murder. He'd gone to the nursery where they barracked in a hut. He said a light had gone out as he arrived. The brothers were awake in a communal bed. He arrested them for murder without naming either time or place—yet John had said, "I was in bed at the time." Charlie snorted—he could see Bent inventing that remark to ensnare John. Bent had gone on to search the hut. He found no firearm, just a half-burned candle: "It had been recently burning," he opined. He also recovered a boot from William, an ordinary rubber-soled boot, one of a thousand. But he'd discovered a footprint at Seymour Grove, near the murder, and, from the impressions he'd made, the marks of the sole corresponded exactly. Mr. Justice Lindly paid great heed to this evidence. But Bent had not finished. He'd searched William's waistcoat and found two percussion caps. Charlie was bewildered. What had caps for a muzzle-loader got to do with a cartridge pin-fire? The Crown answered that question by calling an ironmonger. A day or so prior to the murder, William had inquired after the price of a revolver and .45 cartridges. But he hadn't actually made any purchase.

"What's the point of yon rubbish?" Charlie said to a fellow observer.

"Shows the intent, I suppose," shrugged the man.

The Crown next called an "expert"—Mr. Griffiths, a Manchester gunsmith. He said that the bullet recovered from Cock was conical and fired from a breech-loader. "A number 442," he added importantly. But Charlie shook his head. He'd loaded that bullet himself—a straight .44 fired by twenty-three grains of powder to augment the bang. . . . But now the Crown's case was closing and proceedings were adjourned for the day. Shackled and crushed, the Habrons were led down the dock steps.

Back in Dollymot's sink, Charlie ate a supper of steak and onions in silence. Hannah questioned him about the trial, but he was noncommittal. "Read about it in the papers, woman."

Hannah was less interested in the case than she was in her husband's present gloom. Why was he concerned about two Irish laborers in Lancashire?

"Mrs. Dollymot says folk think they're guilty," she commented.

Charlie looked at her balefully. "They're h'innocent! Those coppers have tried to swear their lives h'away!"

And a small suspicion started in Hannah's mind.

Next day, the Habrons' defense began. They were not permitted to give evidence themselves, so nothing was said about William's query as to the price of a revolver and ammunition. They called instead certain witnesses, none of whom took the case any further, and the defendants were left without a good alibi to cover the shooting of Cock. Charlie listened to their counsel's speech with dismay, to the Crown's reliance on circumstantial evidence with alarm, and to the judge's summing-up with contempt. The latter fumbled over his words, misquoted parts of the testimony, and set much import on that footprint in the case against William.

The jury retired at about five, and remained absent for a suspenseful two hours. Charlie smoked many pipes outside the courts, talking to a sympathetic court usher, until verdicts were reached.

John Habron was found not guilty and promptly fainted. Charlie's own hopes were raised and then dashed. The jury found William guilty, but recommended mercy on account of his age. Charlie sat back on his gallery seat, covering his face with his hands. He scarcely heard the clerk of the court ask William why he shouldn't be sentenced to hang, nor the judge warn the youth that the jury's recommendation would not necessarily be followed. But he did hear the sentence of death, and William's cry of "I'm innocent!" ring out below. The charade was now over; press and people rushed around noisily. Charlie waited till the fuss had subsided before slowly walking out of the courtroom. He passed the usher at the door.

"Can tha smell summat?" Charlie asked him.

The usher sniffed the empty court. "Aye, there's a musk in the air."

Charlie nodded. "The honk of the 'posse mobilitatis'—come to see a man die," he said, and tipped the man sixpence.

Hannah and Charlie left Angel Meadow that evening—she to return to Hull, he ostensibly to visit his mother in Sheffield. At Manchester Station, the news vendors' boards were full of the results of the Habron case. "Are we going to let a boy hang?" said one, and promised a petition on William's behalf. Charlie's low spirits were lifted a fraction.

He bought Hannah her ticket and took her onto the platform for Hull. She didn't tax him about his proposed trip to Sheffield, but his intensity over the Habron trial still bothered her. While they waited for her train, she raised the subject. "Still trubbling 'bout yon Paddies?"

Charlie stared at her. "So would thee, lass, if ye knew what I knew!"

"But I don't, dost I? I know nowt." She was waiting for him to divulge his great secret, whatever that was.

"I just hear that lies have been told," he muttered.

But Hannah wasn't fooled—either Charlie was speculating wildly, or he was somehow involved in the issue. Suddenly, she didn't want to know the truth lest her husband had done something dreadful. "Well, if anyone's lying about those boys, he must be feeling a proper Nathaniel!" was her comment. Her train was approaching, huffing up the track like a black monster. She'd be glad to hop aboard and get out of Manchester.

Charlie found her a second-class carriage and kissed her good-bye. Then he slowly walked back to the booking office. Only part of his mind was on Sheffield; most of it turned over what Hannah had said. Nathaniel "down below"—lower than hellfire itself. She was right, that's just how he felt. Even if William Habron was reprieved, he'd spend the rest of his life in some prison. And Charlie had put him there. But what could he do? If he told the truth in an anonymous letter, his confession would be regarded as the work of a crank. If he gave himself up to the police, he'd just be congratulated on his courage before he was hanged. He felt impotent, totally base, and was close to hysteria. Part of his brain that was mad began to consume his whole being.

9

Every Bullet
Has Its Billet

Charlie stayed the night at his mother's, but not much was said
between old lady and son. Mrs. Peace was angry with him; she'd
heard of his insulting behavior last month; the news had soon got
around. The reaction of the police had been typical: they'd
searched her house as roughly as possible, questioned Aunt
Rosie like bullies, and placed an injunction on Dan'l's liquor
license. But she told Charlie none of this; she wanted neither his
help nor his rages; she only wanted him out of the city. And
Charlie was in too much of a state to take note of her icy reception.

Next day, he decided to harry the Dysons in a last attempt to
persuade them to withdraw the summons. He carried his gun in
case of nosy policemen, and the bundle of Kate Dyson's "notes."
As the last resort, he'd blackmail the woman into bending her
husband's will.

He took a horse tram down the Ecclesall Road to Banner
Cross, but got off a mile from the Terrace. He sought out the
Bierlow Boar, a tavern frequented by employees of the Sheffield
Coal Company—good company to waste time with while he
planned his approach of the Dysons. Drinking York ale, he chat-
ted with the colliers until something of a party began. All that was

required was a spot of music, but the public house owned no instruments.

" 'Appen us can h'improvise," Charlie told the assembly. He took a large poker from the inglenook and a ball of twine out of his pocket. He tied the string to the tip of the poker and hung it upside down. "Fetch us a whippy stick," he said, and a feather duster was quickly produced. Whacking the cane against the taunt twine, he beat out a singular oriental sound, which he varied by pinching the spring on the poker. The rhythm increased, both in speed and volume. He played "The Citizen Gallop" and "Rosa Lee," sounding like a slack banjo. He thrummed polkas and minstrel songs while others danced and sang. The taproom was as noisy as an Indiaman. Ale flowed freely in a frenzy of entertainment. And it went on until dusk, when Charlie threw down his poker to mop his face. He drank a last beer, declining pleas to play on. He felt drunk and it was time to leave. Someone had fetched a squeeze box, so nobody noticed when he slipped out of the tavern.

Charlie started off toward Banner Cross Terrace, but a small signpost prompted him to turn down a lane to Ecclesall Church. He was in search of the Reverend Newman, who had married his daughter and was friendly with Littlewood.

Newman's housekeeper answered the rectory door. Yes, Mr. Newman was back from Darnall, she said, and he was at home in his study. The woman could smell the drink on Charlie and was suspicious, but she announced his arrival. Charlie "h'apologized" for this intrusion and gave his name. Newman, being curious, bade him be seated. He could tell his visitor was drunk. "Hoive come for h'everyone's good, my good sir," said Charlie, between belches. "Hoive come t'correct a few falsehoods. Hast thou heard of the Dysons?" Newman indicated that he had. "Well, a werry rum couple they are, sir!" Charlie went on. "Kate Dyson and me've been cohabitating. As God is my judge, that is true! But she made me nettled, so I threatened her, h'although I did not h'intend what I said. But she took out a summons against me; made me wretched as a rat in a tar barrel. I just want her to drop that damn summons, so I may reside in Sheffield with the rest of my fambly. Oh, dear, what a mess, sir!"

"What's this got to do with me, Mr. Peace?" Newman interrupted.

"Why, them Dysons now be thy parishioners, sir! 'Appen you should know the truth 'bout them!"

"I know no such thing, Mr. Peace," Newman said coldly.

Charlie delved in a pocket and produced his bundle of documents. "These prove what I say!" He handed them to Newman, who gave them a cursory glance and handed them back. "You see what I mean, sir?" Charlie said.

"I'm afraid not, Mr. Peace. It seems to me that you've made yourself a rather untidy bed which you must suffer to lie upon." Newman rose from behind his desk. "Now, if you please, I'm very busy. . . ."

"But I want your h'advice, sir!" Charlie protested.

"Advice you shall have then: stay off the bottle, eschew slander, and confine your hands to your own property." Newman opened the study door. "Good night, Mr. Peace."

Charlie slowly climbed from his chair and lurched out. He was infuriated by Newman's indifference and counsel, but the vicar's skeletal features frightened him; they reminded him of a very hard judge. So he mumbled good night and took leave of the rectory, set upon confronting the Dysons.

A moon was up when he reached Banner Cross Terrace. Lights shone in both the Dysons' house and Mr. Gregory's shop. Charlie went to the latter—he thought Mr. Gregory might be sympathetic to his cause and wanted his help. But only Mrs. Gregory was behind the counter. She said her husband was out playing cribbage so Charlie left. He thought Gregory was probably at the hotel. But he didn't go in; he stood outside the hostelry on the far side of the street, waiting for Gregory to emerge. The road was deserted, but he soon heard footsteps clipping down the pavement. It was a woman. Hoping it was Kate Dyson, he accosted her.

"Evenin', missus."

But it wasn't Mrs. Dyson—just a middle-aged body in a cloak. Charlie thought of something sensible to say.

" 'Scuse us, missus, but dost tha know who lives in that house yonder?" and he pointed toward the Dyson home.

"No, I don't."

"Well, tha should know the woman's a bloody whore. If that's a hubby, tha'd do well to stitch up his fly!"

The woman backed away quickly. "You mind what you say!"

Charlie laughed. "H'only joking, missus. But would thou do us a favor? Go to yon house, and tell the lady what dwells within that a gent'lum would speak with her?"

But the woman didn't like the look of Charlie, the smell of his breath, or the peculiarity of his request. She shook her head and walked off. Charlie remained where he was, pacing up and down, until more footfalls caught his attention. It was a man this time —wearing a boater with a colorful ribbon. He came abreast with Charlie under a lamppost and Charlie was intrigued by his hat.

"Been to a party, hast thou?" he asked cheerfully. "Or to t'Winter Fair?" It had dawned on Charlie that today must be the day of the fair, the dates of which tended to vary. Had a whole year really passed since he'd taken Kate Dyson? "Dost thou know the new folk come to live h'opposite?" he asked the man.

The man said he didn't. "I live in Lane End, mister."

"Well, I know 'em!" Charlie said grimly. "And the woman's a proper h'Eliza. Look what she wrote me!" He showed the man his bundle of notes and photographs.

"I can't read, mister," the man admitted.

"Then tha'll not sully thy mind!" Charlie put the notes away. Then he shook his finger under the other's nose. "But I h'intend to make it warm for those folks before morning!"

The man blinked and hurriedly crossed over the road. Charlie watched him turn off by the fields. He looked across at the hotel: Gregory must be still at his cribbage and could be for hours. Charlie decided to forget the grocer and try his luck alone at the Dysons. He walked back to the shop. Having inspected these houses before, he knew the backs as well as the frontages. He went down an alley until he had a good view into the Dysons' back bedroom. The blind was up and a candle was flickering. Somebody's shadow crossed the room, and he was sure it was Kate Dyson, putting her son to bed. He snapped his fingers and gave a low whistle, and the candle was quickly extinguished. Interminable minutes passed and then he heard a clatter of clogs at the top of the passage, coming toward the water closet. The moon broke through the clouds and he saw it was Kate Dyson, carrying a lantern. She passed straight into the closet, locking the door behind her. Charlie waited outside the tall narrow shed. Mrs. Dyson was not very long, and she came out humming a ditty—which turned into a shriek when she saw Charlie.

"Hush now," he whispered. "Did tha not hear us calling?"

Kate Dyson shone the beam of her lamp on his face. "No, I did not!"

"You must withdraw that summons," Charlie said in his most menacing voice. "I'm tired of being hunted about. I want to come and go as I please."

She laughed harshly. " 'Tis to jail you'll be goin'!"

"I'm warning you, Kate . . ."

"Warn away, you galoot! You shook a gun in my face and you're to pay!"

He drew his revolver. "And I've still got that gun." He twisted the lanyard around his wrist. "You take care. You know me of old, and what I can do." He held his pistol up to the lamplight.

The effect upon Kate Dyson was immediate. "Help, murder!" she screamed at the top of her voice and struck out at Charlie with her lantern. He moved aside and she sprang back into the water closet, slamming and bolting the door. Charlie beat on the wood with his gun, but stopped as heavy footsteps ran up to the passage entrance. He saw the enormous figure of Arthur Dyson looming under the archway. Charlie looked toward the back wall—minded to escape that way—but he knew Dyson would be on him before he could clear it.

"Stand back!" he warned the giant.

Dyson continued toward him. "I'm taking you in, Peace." His frame blocked the narrow alley from wall to wall.

"Let me pass!" Charlie said, raising his pistol.

"Not this time, Peace!"

Charlie cocked the hammer and fired a shot well over to the left of Dyson. The passage was lit by the flash, and the bullet whacked harmlessly into the stone archway. Charlie now bolted to get past, but tonight Dyson was tough. He seized Charlie as he went by, gripping his revolver arm like a vise, trying to force the weapon from his fingers. Only the lanyard kept the gun in Charlie's hand, and he lashed out with his free fist, striking Dyson's nose with a large ring. "Goddamn you!" Dyson grunted and he pitched his weight against Charlie so that they both toppled sideways into the wall. Charlie tried to wrench free his gun hand, but then something went wrong. The hammer was ensnared in Dyson's coat and the gun went off, the bullet striking Dyson on the left side of his head. Charlie thought it a glancing wound, but Dyson went limp and fell to the ground on his back. He uttered a gurgling sound and Charlie assumed he was stunned. He hovered over the stricken man, wondering whether to help him, the pistol still smoking in his hand.

"Murder! Oh, you villain, you've shot him!" Kate Dyson's cry made him turn about sharply. She'd come out of the closet and was staring at her husband, hands to mouth in horror.

Charlie started to speak—to tell her it was only an accident, that Dyson was not badly hurt, but he heard voices from outside the alley in the Ecclesall Road and he couldn't dally. He raced out of the passage into the street, his gun still strapped to his wrist, crossed the main road, and swung over a fence into the vegetable garden which adjoined a large field. Charlie leapt over the dividing wall and failed to notice that he had dropped Kate Dyson's correspondence from his pocket. He hared across the moonlit field like a man possessed, untwining his gun and ramming it into his britches, and he didn't stop running until he got into some woods. There he paused to wrap his scarf around the lower part of his face, hiding his beard. Beyond the wood he came out in a lane well south of the city. He wanted to get back to Sheffield rather than face a hue and cry in the countryside, so he headed west until he struck a branch line of the Sheffield/Chesterfield railway. He followed the tracks to Beech Hill, a suburb. It was now ten o'clock. He found a hansom outside a public house and engaged it to take him to Spring Street, where he planned to hide a few hours with Aunt Rosie and then take a first train out of town. The killing of Constable Cock had been a serious mishap, but the shooting of Dyson was far graver. If Dyson died, Charlie knew he'd be the most wanted man in all Yorkshire.

10

Cutting
Quick Sticks

The coroner's inquest on the death of Arthur Dyson was held in
an upstairs room at Stagg Inn. Jacob Bradbury gave evidence as
to how he'd been called to Banner Cross and found the wounded
Dyson just alive in a parlor chair, groaning piteously while Surgeon Harrison gingerly probed for the bullet in his left temple,
but Dyson had soon fallen into a coma and had died. Kate
Dyson's grief had moved the inspector—until one of his constables discovered the packet of letters on the edge of the field
where Charlie had dropped them. Those letters more than puzzled Bradbury, as they did Mr. Whiteman, the coroner, for whom
they were produced at the inquest, because Kate Dyson ada-
mantly denied all knowledge of them.

"Do you mean to swear that *you* never wrote a word to Peace?"
Whiteman put to her.

"I *never* wrote to him!"

Mrs. Dyson's eyes darted from Whiteman to Bradbury to the
members of the jury. Whiteman and his jury just shrugged with
surprise, but Bradbury was sure she was lying. What then of the
rest of her evidence? he wondered: her assertion that she had
seen Peace shoot down her husband, two shots in one second,
without the slightest of struggles? Bradbury didn't know what to
believe. However, she was the sole witness to the shooting, the

jury accepted her word, and a verdict of willful murder was found against Charles Peace.

After the inquest, Bradbury approached Kate downstairs in a lounge. She looked very fetching in her black dress and veils, very pale and widowly, but she tensed as the inspector came up to her.

"A dreadful day for you, Mrs. Dyson," he said gently. "But it's all over now. May I buy you a small brandy?"

"Never touch the stuff!"

Bradbury nodded; the letters had implied otherwise, but they'd been denied. He sat down beside her and produced a Trinchinopoly cheroot. "D'you mind if I smoke?" She shook her head. "Did Peace smoke, ma'am?" he asked.

"How should I know? I hardly knew the rascal!"

"Quite so. . . . A *very* queer bird from the sound of him. . . . Writing nonsensical cards to himself. . . . Proper daft."

Mrs. Dyson eyed him through her veil. "What will become of those letters?"

"I don't know, ma'am. Why, d'you want them?"

Mrs. Dyson hesitated a fraction too long. "No, of course not!"

"May I ask what will become of yourself, ma'am?" Bradbury said.

"Is that any concern of yours, Inspector?"

"We shall require you to give evidence when we catch him, ma'am."

"*When!* That might take till Judgment Day!"

Bradbury just puffed on his cigar. "So where will you be?" he persisted.

"As it happens, I'm going back to Ohio. I shall be with my sister in Cleveland." She opened her purse and gave the inspector a small printed card.

"Not *another* card!" he laughed.

"My agents in St. Louis, Missouri," came the answer. "They will know my address."

Bradbury looked at the card—some sort of railroad agency,

presumably connected with her late husband. "I trust you shall hear from me," he said.

"I doubt that, Inspector!"

"Oh? Why so, ma'am?"

"Because a man like Peace can't be caught."

Bradbury feigned surprise. "Is that so? I'm grateful for that titbit about him. After all, *I* hardly knew the rascal, did I?"

II

Hannah was serving breakfasts when Pearson called at Collier Street. He had with him a Hull officer and both were in uniform. Their appearance was greeted by a lull in conversation among the diners. The police had misjudged the time and venue of their visit.

"Hey, you Jacks trying to spoil our grub?" one loud docker demanded.

"Aye, go round t'back way!" said another. "Like t'tradesfolk!"

Further insults were directed against Pearson until he sought refuge by going up to Hannah at the till. "You know why we're here, missus," he said quietly. "Have you seen Charlie?"

"Would I say if I had?" Hannah asked.

Pearson was prepared to divulge some information. "He's been seen in Brumm, Derby, and Doncaster. He's also been spotted in Lunnan, Bath, and Bristol. He's been seen on a train twixt Oxford and Stafford, and he's attended several assizes."

Hannah bared her teeth in the semblance of a smile. "Cutting quick sticks all over, is he? Allus did love the law courts. Tried the Lords yet?"

Pearson grew exasperated. "Listen, woman! He shot Arthur Dyson! He's a murderer!"

"Who says he did?"

"Dyson's wife."

Hannah snorted. "That slotch! 'Appen she'll nivver testify! She'll keep her gap closed after all her adultery! Where is she, anyroad?"

But Pearson wasn't going to admit the woman had gone back to America. "If you hide Charlie, you'll be harboring a criminal," he warned. He was minded to search this restaurant, for which the other constable held a warrant, but fear of present rough customers stayed his hand. He'd leave that for a day or so—and raid the premises at night with more men and a few muskets. "You've been cautioned, missus!" he added dramatically.

"Cum all t'way from Darnall ta tell us that, has thou?" Hannah came round from the till and opened the glass-fronted door. "I'll tell him tha called when ah see him; he'll be sorry ta've missed thee!"

Once the policemen had gone, Hannah took off her apron and retired to the kitchen. Willie was busy at the ovens but he quickly abandoned his cooking when his mother came in.

"Where is he?" she asked.

Willie raised his eyes heavenward. "On t'roof."

"Well, tell 'im ta cum down afore he gets smutchy. Tell 'im they've gone."

Willie grinned and went upstairs to fetch his stepfather from among the chimney stacks.

III

The Reverends Littlewood and Newman strolled together in the Trinity churchyard, a cold December wind blowing the dead leaves around their gaiters. They had discussed Charlie's visit to Newman at great length, as well as the murder and the inquest. Newman had a copy of the Sheffield *Independent* under one arm, and one thing concerned him.

"Do you think I could have stopped him that night, John?" he asked. "D'you think if I'd listened more. . . ."

"No!" Littlewood cut him short. "I've known Peace for ages. I'm surprised by his conduct, but he's a wild sort of fellow, self-willed and intractable. I only pray, for the sake of his soul, that he did not intend murder."

"What of those letters he showed me?"

Littlewood stopped by the tomb where he'd conversed with Charlie a year ago. "I believe Peace was sinning with that woman as he claimed, although it grieves me to say so," he replied.

"Mrs. Dyson refutes them all," said Newman. "Perhaps Peace lies?"

Littlewood shook his head. "No, that implies he concocted them. Had he done so, I feel his forgeries would have been somewhat more skillful. I wish, in many ways, they were bogus, for I'm sad for Hannah."

"I met her. I know what you mean," said Newman.

"A strong silent woman, who bears her cross well. We have much to learn from her loyalty."

Newman looked at his friend. "I believe that you, too, John, are loyal to Peace!"

Littlewood produced his daily ration of jujubes and popped three in his mouth. "Peace is a knave," he said, "perhaps even an assassin, yet I do like him. Deep in that rascally heart lurks a smidgen of good. I lament the fact he now faces the halter." He took Newman's arm. "But come, my dear fellow, less talk of the hangman. . . . I'll show you the most ingenious toy the wicked Peace once gave to my wife. It is the most clever of things! I really don't know how he came by it!" And he led Newman back to the vicarage.

IV

Charlie spent ten days at the Gilbeys'—in bed, shamming a bout of the flu. The sergeant was out most of the time, hunting a man called Peace, on behalf of West Riding colleagues, and Charlie was nursed by his wife.

"Oh, I am yet ill!" was his lament every morning. "Without you, Mistress Nightingale, I would surely perish!"

Gilbey would visit his ailing lodger each evening, usually with a model ship to be fixed, and always with tidings about the elusive Charles Peace.

"Hast thou caught the rogue?" Charlie asked him.

Gilbey shook his head. "Pearson and others turned over his wife's shop. They found some of his clothing—covered with soot —but naught else. I'd say he's quit Hull, wouldn't you?"

"Hmm. . . . Probably gone up to the Land of Cakes, sir. Right out of the North Counteree."

"Still, we've posted him well in the city," said Gilbey, taking a leaflet from a top tunic pocket.

Charlie reached out a frail hand and took it.

"Murder," he read, and "One Hundred Pounds Reward." The rest spoke of the murder of Dyson in his wife's presence, the inquest of December 5, and the reward being payable for such information or evidence that should lead to Peace's discovery and conviction.

"That's not much good," Charlie said. "Doesn't describe the bugger."

"I have his description," said Gilbey, and he read from his notebook: " 'Thin and small. Forty-six to fifty-six. Gray beard and whiskers. Fingers missing offen his left hand. Walks funny and speaks peculiar. A great boaster.' "

Charlie laughed—fortunately his bad hand was under the covers.

"It goes on to say," added Gilbey, "that he associates with loose women and has been to prison for burglary."

"A most h'unsavory fellow!" said Charlie—and they went on to talk about ships.

On the eleventh day Charlie rose from his bed. According to Gilbey, the hunt for Peace was dying from frustration, although Gilbey, following Mr. Ward's advice, had sent messages up to Scotland. Apparently everyone in England had either seen or been robbed by Charles Peace—including the chief executioner. Charlie thought it time to leave Hull, and that task was easy. He informed the Gilbeys that he'd lengthy business to attend in Nottingham, and that he'd be gone for some time. Mrs. Gilbey fussed about his ability to travel after so long abed, but her husband shushed her quiet.

"Without workers like Mr. Ward," he opined, "this country would go to the dogs!" He shook Charlie's hand warmly. "Your room will be waiting for you when you return!"

And Charlie promised to return. "Meantime, you catch yon Peace," he told Gilbey. "And make sure you get the reward. You bobbies are too hardly dealt by these days!"

When he left the Gilbeys Charlie contemplated a call upon Hannah. Too risky, he thought—Pearson had warned her about "harboring." It was a shame just to leave her like this, with no word of his going, but he decided to send her a postcard, via an overland circuit of post coaches, to say he'd be back one fine day.

Meanwhile, he executed another piece of daring. He booked into a small hotel as John Ward, just for a sleep, and said a Mr. Thompson, his cousin, would come for the bill that afternoon. Mr. Ward was not to be disturbed on any account.

Once in his room, Charlie got out his razor and hand mirror, and filled the washbasin. He changed the shape of his whiskers and beard, shaved the front of his head bald, and doctored the rest of his hair with black dye. He then dressed himself in a Tweedside suit and donned a Bollinger hat. He put on some spectacles and admired himself in the long mirror. He looked different and good. Almost younger. But the test was yet to come. He left his room and went out of the hotel by a back door, entering it again by the main entrance, like a man of the world. Pinging the receptionist's bell, he was pleased to find himself served by the same clerk who'd booked him in that morning as Mr. Ward.

"I've come to pay Mr. Ward's bill," he informed the man in a nasally twang.

And the clerk didn't glance at him twice, merely pricing the room and accepting his money. Charlie was well pleased with himself as he left.

11

In the Marsh

Sue Bailey considered herself a handsome woman. At thirty-five, she was yellow-haired, tall, and buxom, although inclined toward stoutness, and she had bold brown eyes with a wandering look, which did not endear her to her own sex.

But Mother Adamson, proprietress of the Bendigo, was prepared to tolerate Sue provided she got on with her chores. The Bendigo was a criminals' tavern in a back slum of Nottingham known as the Marsh. Sue had arrived there in November begging for work. Her husband had beaten and left her, she said, and her own family would have nothing to do with her. Mother Adamson neither believed nor questioned this tale. The Bendigo catered for all sorts, from deserters to the "dangerous classes," and Sue proved she could entertain the customers with song as well as launder and cook. It was her singing that introduced her to Charlie. . . .

Charlie moved in on January 5. He was just plain Mr. Thompson, always flush with money, who insisted upon a room at the top of the old Tudor house, close to the roof. All eating at the Bendigo was done downstairs in a gigantic refectory and most of the guests could afford only cow paunch, but Charlie invariably dined on the choicest roasts, washed down with a flagon of wine. This was something noted by Sue, as were Mr. Thompson's silk cravats and heavy gold chain, so one night she directed the bulk of her songs at him, perched on a stool by his side.

"Jemmily sung!" he cried when she'd finished. He poured her a glass of his wine. "You should go into h'opera. But you'd need a good manager."

"You're a theatrical person?" Sue's hopes were quickly raised.

"In a manner of speaking. I'm an h'artist myself. But what about you . . . ?"

Sue told him much of her history, some of it true. Her family were of good stock, but cruel, and her husband of just a few weeks had been a bullying swine who'd seduced her. She'd struck on hard times and nobody cared for her. Charlie listened attentively, plying her with more wine till she'd finished his bottle. He ordered more, and this was soon drunk too. She likes her tipple, he thought, as much as Kate Dyson does. She also has as many lies in her head, but not Kate's strength. Nor did Charlie believe that Sue had ever been seduced—not with those eyes and moist lips. He decided that she was a mere haybag of chatter, greedy, and not very clever, but he admired her proportions and full-blooded voice. She was certainly vivacious and he'd nothing to lose by dallying with her.

"How would you care for a night in the town?" he interrupted her flow. "I know some very nice spots where the swells do go."

This sudden invitation appeared to take Sue by surprise, and she stared at him. Charlie guessed what she was thinking—that he was old and probably criminal. But she'd also been weighing the gold in his pockets.

"I'm willing," she said.

Days passed, and Sue Bailey learned that Mr. Thompson, whom she now called John, was more than he seemed. He might be outside the law—she supposed him a fraudsman—and he might not be a theatrical manager, but he certainly had money to burn. He was also courteous and kindly, with a Regency charm in spite of his gloved hand. He took her to restaurants and music halls, hailing cabs as a matter of course, and bought her expensive clothes. He also taught her how to pile up her long tresses and apply cosmetics, like a fashionable actress.

"You should have been on the staff of the *Young Lady's Book,*" she said.

"Or a figaro—as I've ofttimes maintained," he replied.

One night, at Nottingham's premier Gaiety Bar, Sue stopped pouring out her endless trivia to ask him a question. "Are you married?"

"Well, in a manner of speaking . . . I have a wife and stepson, but we be parted, my pet."

No more was said on the subject. Sue went on to opine that if she'd ever been given singing lessons, she would certainly have succeeded on the international stage and Charlie wasn't minded to disagree with her—of late, she'd taken to squeezing his gloved hand and calling him "love." So he decided to discover just how "seducible" was Mistress Bailey, and they rounded off the meal with large brandies.

Back at the Bendigo, at the foot of the rickety staircase, Charlie invited her up to his room.

"What for?"

Charlie grinned bashfully. "Well, I confess I h'abominate chitchat at two in the morn' . . ."

"You're drunk, love!" But it was Sue who had to support herself on the banister.

"Only by your beauty, my pet," said Charlie, taking her arm.

Sue allowed herself to be led upstairs. She knew what he wanted all right—nor did his desire displease her. John Thompson was far too rich for her to endanger their friendship and besides, he was such an old fellow he'd likely fall asleep the moment his head touched the pillow. She'd pass the night untroubled by his fumblings.

But Mr. Thompson proved to be neither sleepyhead nor fumbler. In the darkness of his bedroom Sue discovered him something of a tiger. Her cries of pleasure soon caused such a racket that other lodgers beat upon their ceilings in protest. And dawn found her exhausted.

"I'll make you a proposition," Charlie said, smoking beside her.

"What's that, Jack?" She yawned happily.

"I ply a tricky trade, my pet. I need a partner. You pretend to be Mrs. John Thompson for a spell, and I'll nurture you like a h'ornamental pheasant." And to this proposal Sue sleepily agreed.

II

They stayed on at Mrs. Adamson's through spring and summer. Charlie never ventured into Yorkshire, but he raided many a Midland mansion, secure in the knowledge that Nottinghamshire concerned itself only with county crime and was not on the lookout for some obscure gunman from Yorkshire.

Living with Sue was pleasant enough. The lady was insatiable but she was inclined to drink too much, particularly when Charlie was away for nights on end. Her tipple was port wine, which tended to blotch her skin, and Charlie saw her rather earthy beauty fading within a year or so. She also had a capacity to bore and annoy him with her continuous prattle so that sometimes he'd become quite sharp with her, whereupon she'd weep profusely, and remind him of her unhappy life until he took her in his arms. He grew to love her only as he might a fretful child, and his thoughts often returned to Kate Dyson.

But if part of Charlie's heart was with a woman in America, the other part still belonged to Hannah. He'd regularly sent her cards, but he longed again to see her dismal face and hear her terse complaints. So, late in August, he burgled a house in Melton Mowbray and came away with sufficient swag to justify a short vacation.

He and Sue went to Hull together—"to see the ships and smell the sea" as Charlie put it—and booked into a hotel near Victoria Pier, with views of HMS *Southampton*, the training ship for boys. On the second morning Charlie left Sue and sought out Hannah.

He first kept watch for her on Collier Street from Anlaby Road, but he didn't want to go near the chophouse, so he engaged the services of a passing urchin to deliver a message.

Hannah was at her customary place behind the till when the lad handed her the missive and demanded his penny. "I am waiting to see you just up Anlaby Road," read the note, and she recognized Charlie's slanting scrawl. She put on her bonnet and left the shop without a word to Willie, and found a dressy Charlie waiting outside a fish bar. They went inside and sat down in a gloomy spot.

"Begod, 'tis good t'see thee, woman!" Charlie said, tears in his eyes.

"And ah can see time's not been unkind to thysen," Hannah replied impatiently. "Where's te baan, these nine long months?"

Had it really been so long? "Tempus fugit," he said. "In t'Black Country."

"'Appen that should 'ave stayed there—thy name's plastered in ev'ry shop in t'city. Tha've gumption comin' here at all!"

If Charlie hadn't known Hannah better, he'd have thought her displeased to see him.

"How's Janey then?" he inquired.

"Happier hiding under Billy's name."

Charlie was stung. "That's a wicked thing to say!"

"But the truth. The name of Peace hugs trubble like the Devil hugs a witch. You stay clear of Janey, hear?"

Charlie frowned at his wife. He'd no intention of inflicting himself on any of his family nor was he in Hull to quarrel with Hannah. "Don't nettle me," he said. He had a confession to make. "In Nottingen I met with this lady—Mrs. Sue Bailey. She's a bit of a locomotive, like mysen. And a bit of a songstress, too. H'anyway, she and me are cohabitating as Mr. and Mrs. Thompson. 'Tis safer this way for me—the bobbies be'll looking for Charlie alone, not hutched up to another. But our h'union is pure, Hannah lass. Sue's no pinch-prick—I swear that, in the hearing of God!"

He thought it best to tell this lie for Hannah's self-respect, but the look on her face told him she believed not a word of it. "You must bear with us," he went on hurriedly. "I care nowt for this Sue, she's full o' grease-paint and gin, but she gives me good cover. Dost thou follow?"

Hannah merely shrugged. A year ago she'd have met his admission with a tirade of abuse. But not now—she was too tired to protest any more. "And where's thy woman?" she asked without interest.

"Victoria Pier Hotel."

"Alone?"

Charlie nodded. "She will be from tonight. I'm minded to stop awhile with mine police sergeant."

Hannah hooted with mirthless laughter. "Ye what? Tha must be mad, man! How'll tha explain thy change of appearance?"

Charlie ran a hand over his face. That had also occurred to him. "I'll tell him I'm sufferin' a dose of 'figaro's h'itch,' " he replied. Barber's itch was common enough in sailor towns and necessitated the shaving of facial hair.

"And why dost tha want to stay with the sergeant?" asked Hannah. "Art thou minded ta thieve?"

She'd guessed the truth. " 'Appen," he admitted. "I want for t'build up a nest egg for us all."

"This Sue Bailey included?"

"Nay! Just for the three of us, woman!" Charlie shook his head. "Pretty soon, I'll be giving Sue her papers t'march." He planned to buy Sue off with a tidy sum. "Once done, I'll be goin' south and lay up in lavender. Then I'll send for thee and Willie." His hopes and intentions were true, which showed on his face, and Hannah didn't question him further. Time would tell what her husband really intended. So they talked instead of the family in general, and of the police maneuvers to catch him. It was agreed that Hannah and Sue should not meet in Hull—if ever at all—and Hannah was glad to be spared this indignity. Nor was Charlie to see much of his wife. He was to complete his "work" as quickly as possible for the sake of them all.

"Where wilt tha strike?" was Hannah's sole question on the subject of "work."

"Look in t'papers," she was told.

But if Charlie was right about the avarice of Sue, he sorely misjudged the extent of her cunning. Behind that bland Slavic face lurked a certain resolve. She had no desire to return to the murk of the Marsh or to give up her new benefactor. She was determined to cling to her new way of life like a leech. Jack Thompson, she'd decided, was a most resourceful man—he worked alone and never involved her. Not by the farthest stretch of the imagination could she be termed his accomplice so she was secure.

Therefore she pandered to his every whim and stayed on at the Victoria Hotel when he moved out to lodge "elsewhere," as he put it, and behaved like a model wife whenever required. That she pleased Charlie was evident: he called her his "pet," his "canary," and so on, and escorted her round town every day. But each evening at six o'clock sharp, he would suddenly vanish.

This was because his nights were ostensibly spent with the Gilbeys. The couple had been delighted when the "new-looking"

Mr. Ward returned to their home. They gave him his old room and commiserated on the sad loss of his hair—Gilbey scratching his own luxuriant growth and cursing the diseases of "foreigners." Charlie, in turn, had presents for both man and wife—a fine model ironclad for Gilbey—and he assured them his ailment was uncontagious. He was busy these days, he said, over in Withernsea, selling ladies' "negglidigees" from Bruges, which required him to be out from A.M. to P.M. All this hard work, he added, made him sleep sounder than usual.

"And you'll not be disturbed," Mrs. Gilbey promised.

"One h'other thing . . ." Charlie went on, looking awkward. "My room. . . ."

"Not too cold?" she cried, very anxious.

"Nay, snug as toffee! But 'tis werry high up, Mrs. G. . . . Heights give us the faints, you see? And now that the window's open for summer, I have this h'urge to jump out."

They all laughed at his vertigo, but it was decided to put him down on the ground floor, with a window at pavement level, so he'd suffer no more.

A wave of crime now hit the city. Night after night, big houses were robbed. The thief concentrated on only one neighborhood and the papers were full of the outrages. Sergeant Gilbey was relieved none of the burglaries occurred on his particular beat.

" 'Twould mean the stripes on my sleeve if they did," he confided to Charlie.

"Nivver fear," his lodger assured him. " 'Appen thy manor shalt not be disturbed."

Nor was it. Charlie figured out his friend's beat, even drew in the boundaries with a crayon on his map.

"Sarn't Singleton's in for the high-jump," Gilbey told Charlie one evening. "He's been given extra men by our superintendent, but the thieving goes on."

"It must be a gang," Charlie ventured.

Gilbey nodded. "No one man could haul off such swag."

Charlie felt inclined to agree: last night's load had caused him to strain his back, particularly heaving the sacks over the ground-floor windowsill into his room. The floor under his bed was piled up to the springs, and Charlie was resting.

"Tell us about Singleton?" he asked, mischief in mind.

Gilbey put down his ironclad. "Proper bastard, Singleton. Known and disliked him for years. Always after promotion; a right little catch-fart."

Charlie considered these confidences. He mainly disliked policemen because they were often roughs recruited from the military after years of bullying in the queen's little wars. But he hated a toady even more than a bully.

"Tell yon Singleton to use 'ounds," he advised Gilbey.

"Bloodhounds?"

"Nay, foxhounds. Borrow 'em off the local master of hunt. The pack'll soon pick up the gang's scent and wilt yoddle away till their lair be h'exposed. 'Appen the venture 'twill make or break Singlebum."

The Day of the Dog was fixed for a Saturday morning, and Gilbey kept Charlie informed. After much wrangling, the master had reluctantly lent his hounds to Singleton, who was given direct responsibility for their loss and conduct. Many voices within the City Force criticized the project, saying it was novel in their own experience, but Singleton couldn't be swayed, so desperate was his need to track down the gang. He even invited his superintendent along to bear witness to the hounds' performance.

On the Friday night Charlie stole out of the Gilbeys' and into Singleton's "manor," not to thieve, but to lay a drag scent. The latter ran around in concentric circles, through houses, churches, and schools, and finished where it began—on the banks of a canal. It took him six hours to cover four miles of genteel suburbia, and he used up three pounds of aniseed, two pounds of peppermint, and a bottle of hashish oil.

Next day, he awaited Gilbey's report. The Gilbeys' house was a long way from the field of battle, but Charlie could have sworn he heard the odd distant howl as the evening drew on. Gilbey came in at six, late for his tea, muddy and footsore, but grinning behind his beard like an Afghan.

"What happened?" Charlie asked casually.

Gilbey threw down his helmet and his shouts of wild laughter made him incomprehensible until Charlie poured him a brandy. "The buffers went mad!" he explained at last. "The whole force is out trying to round 'em up! Singleton let 'em loose as instructed. Then they went haywire—tore up gardens, dirty-pawed right through parlors, got panicky in a church, wrecked the grammar school, killed several cats, destroyed chickens, smashed the mayor's greenhouse, worried some prize racers, pissing on everything everywhere!"

"It was not a success?" Charlie asked.

More uncontrollable laughter greeted the question. "One of 'em pissed on my superintendent!" was all Gilbey could answer. "You should have seen old Singleton's face! I almost felt sorry for 'im!"

Charlie shook his head gravely. " 'Cry havoc, and let slip the dogs of war.' I wonder what went wrong?"

"That's what Singleton will have to explain! But seriously, Mr. Ward, 'twas your idea—d'you know what went wrong?"

Charlie frowned, seemingly trying hard to think. " 'Appen we should have stuck to bloodhounds," he said. "But I'm no dogster mysen." He raised his glass in a toast. "H'anyway, here's to Sarnt Singleton, and all bobbies like him, hopin' he'll come up with the right answer one day!" Gilbey lifted his own glass, still grinning, and they settled down to high tea.

Although Charlie was never to learn it, the aftermath was that Singleton lost his grand beat in the city and was removed to a constable's post in a neighboring village. Gilbey, like the rest of the Force, was pleased to see him go.

But Gilbey was very unhappy when Mr. Ward took his leave at the end of October—a sudden decision, it seemed, made on the very eve of departure. "I must h'away again, sir," was all Charlie told him.

Mr. Ward appeared to have accumulated a large quantity of baggage during his stay. Gilbey helped him fetch a cab and load up for the station. He offered to see Charlie off, but the little man said he found "farewells heartrending," and bid Gilbey goodbye on the doorstep.

Mr. and Mrs. Thompson were reunited at Hull Station and took a train to Birmingham in a first-class compartment reserved. Once the train was under way, they drew down the blinds and kissed.

"I got your note last night, Jack," Sue said, rearranging herself. "Where are we going?"

Charlie slid up a blind to watch the countryside. "We tour for a spell, pet." He lit his pipe and counted his bags on the overhead racks; there were five more in the baggage car. "To Brumm at first," he added. That city would have buyers for his line of merchandise. "Then on to Leamington, to h'enjoy the beauties of Bard County. And so on to h'Oxford, seat of learning 'n' scholarship. And then . . ." He paused, much lost in thought. He must write to Hannah from all of these places; he'd have liked to have seen her before leaving Hull. What strange premonition had driven him out of that city so suddenly?

"And then, dearest?" Sue was asking.

He looked across at her. His "wife" sat, large but prim, in her best traveling clothes, trimmed with beaver, hatted in beaver, even her gloves were fur-backed. She reminded Charlie of a generous beaver itself, bright-eyed and nosy.

"And then ta Lunnan itself," he told her.

He was supposed to rid himself of this woman, but he found her too companionable for such a drastic decision.

12

"Down ta Lunnan"

Certain marked peculiarities as to the modus operandi of the Hull burglaries caused the superintendent of that city's force to communicate with Inspector Bradbury in Sheffield. Bradbury and Pearson duly arrived, read the unhappy Singleton's reports, and heard about the disastrous exercise with hounds. Bradbury was convinced that the burglaries were attributable to Peace. Where, then, was Charlie? Bradbury and Pearson paid a call on Hannah hoping she could shed some light.

Hannah disliked Pearson, but warmed slightly to the looks of the older Bradbury.

"I'll talk with thysen," she said to the inspector, "but thine bobby can wait in t'kitchen."

So Pearson was left with Willie Ward and Bradbury taken upstairs.

"I gather your premises were searched by Pearson," the inspector said at once. "If they were left untidy, I apologize. Now, this is a silly question but I've got to ask it: Have you seen your hubby of late?"

"Yes."

"Where?"

"Here—in Hull."

"When?"

"Last month. He's gone now. Hull was too hot for him."

"You won't tell me where he's gone, of course?"

"If us knew, I wouldn't," Hannah agreed. "But I don't know."

Bradbury thought she was telling the truth, but he'd his duty to perform. "I shall have to search again," he said unhappily. "No mess—I promise."

He called for Pearson and together they searched the chop-house. They found nothing untoward, not even the large amounts of cash in the till. The restaurant was obviously doing well on its own. In the cellars Bradbury tore the sleeve of his coat on a meat hook.

"Tha's torn thy reefer, silly man!" Hannah commented when he re-emerged from below. "Cum here, ah'll fixit!"

Bradbury let himself be thrust in a chair while Hannah got to work with needle and thread. His coat had cost him two pounds. Mrs. Bradbury would be livid if she saw the tear and he was grateful to Hannah. "You're a good seamstress," he complimented her.

"Charlie taught us."

"Where did he learn?"

"On the Moor. He was the best nip-louse they had. Saved him from cuttin' peat all day."

"We aim to put him behind bars again, missus," said Bradbury sadly.

To his surprise, Hannah laughed. "Nay, thy aim's ta hang him this time!"

"Maybe he shot Dyson in self-defense?" Bradbury suggested.

"That'll not save him!"

Bradbury knew Hannah was right. Her husband was too confirmed a criminal to be given full justice—he'd no more chance of reprieve than a bushranger. Willie came in with some tea for him—expensive Indian tea. As Bradbury drank, he guessed Hannah was being supported by the missing Charlie, wherever he was, and he felt sorry for her. "Tell you one thing, missus," he said, "I don't believe your hubby ever loved Katherine Dyson, or vice versa."

Hannah shrugged. "Mak's no diff'rence."

Bradbury nodded. No point in his trying to console this woman, and he'd been here quite long enough. "Come along, Pearson," he said, putting down his cup. "We've work t'do at the station." He solemnly shook Hannah's hand, as if thanking her for some cooperation or help. He was surprised by the power of her grip, and decided her a true daughter of Sheffield.

Back at headquarters, Bradbury and Pearson reappraised the voluminous reports of the Singleton thefts. Bradbury found the account of the foxhounds very funny and he investigated how they came to be employed. He discovered their use had been recommended by a Sergeant Gilbey. As a joke? He sent for this Gilbey.

"Pearson and I head the hunt for Peace," he explained to the whiskery sergeant. "We believe Singleton's manor might have been hit by him. Now you suggested a gang was involved and advised foxhounds. Why so, Sergeant Gilbey?"

"It wasn't my idea, sir!" Gilbey said cagily.

"Oh? Whose then?"

"The notion came from a lodger of mine, sir. Mr. John Ward. It was he who suggested the dogs."

Bradbury frowned. *Ward*—now that name had a ring to it. "Tell me about Mr. Ward," he said calmly.

"He's a nice little body, sir." Gilbey told the inspector all that he knew of his ex-lodger. "Always travelin', he was, sir, up 'n' down dale. Very busy—very upright."

The small suspicion in Bradbury's mind gradually grew into a terrible realization.

"Describe Ward," he told the sergeant.

"Short, thinnish, baldy. Funny face, funny walk—was sort of crippled, sir," Gilbey said.

"Crippled?"

"Aye—left leg and hand. He always used to wear one black glove. But that didn't stop him being a fine craftsman . . ."

Bradbury waved him quiet. Now he was sure. He drew a great breath and leaned back in his chair. "Shall *I* tell you some more about Ward?" he said. "Clean-shaven now he may be, but once he was bearded, with bacca-pipe whiskers. Old scars on his neck?" Gilbey was nodding. He looked both puzzled and worried. "He has a leathery face," Bradbury continued, "with a nut-cracker jaw. He likes to talk to your wife very nicely, and his knowledge is wide. Yes, that's Mr. Ward, no mistake. Well, I have bad news for you, Sergeant. You've been harboring a serpent. Mr. Ward has a wife in this city—name of Hannah. She was maiden-named Ward and has a stepson who still carries that monicker. But her real name is Peace—wife of Charles of that ilk —who's made a Fig o' Spain at the lot of us."

"Peace!" Gilbey sat down heavily.

"The same—and I wager he's cackling with merriment too." Bradbury looked up at Pearson. "But there's no need for his jape to go outside this office, no need at all. I shall write a report for myself, pulling a rug over everything." He was anxious to protect Sergeant Gilbey's pride and reputation, was warning Pearson to do the same. "Right, you can go," he told the unfortunate Gilbey, who crept out small and crushed.

"What now, sir?" Pearson asked when Gilbey had gone.

Bradbury tapped his teeth with a pencil. "What indeed, lad? I daresay Peace will continue to ninnify us—" He suddenly laughed: this investigation was steeped in high comedy. "But I'll tell you one thing, Constable. Even if Peace has gone under, the lies and legends about the bugger will blow around like thistle-down—till we catch him."

"And will we ever do that?" Pearson wondered aloud.

Bradbury shrugged.

II

" 'I shall build a house of habitation for thee, and a place for thy dwelling forever,' " quoth Charlie optimistically to Sue on their arrival in London.

But Stangate Street, Lambeth, where they settled in, was an ill-chosen start for them. They took a one-room hovel of ancient foundation close to the market and the Thames where the cries of the costermongers rang out through the fogs night and day. The streets were filthy and the whole area reeked of sewage, and they'd set up in December, the worst month of the year for poverty, stench, and disease.

"Not as dainty as Stratford," Charlie conceded, "but we must start h'off very humble, my pretty."

In truth, he was broke. Their expensive tour of Warwick and Oxford, the hotels and fine outings, had rendered him destitute. He was again in dire need of "work."

So while Sue stayed at home, just beginning to grumble, he commenced reconnoitering the metropolis. London seemed far larger than he recalled from his Millbank and Pentonville days, but he was thorough. He went forth every day on foot, armed with a street map, like a fell walker. He spied out parts both rich and poor. And he was shocked by the horrors he saw—the beggars and prostitutes beside so much affluence.

"Lunnan be a shameful Gomorrah!" he told Sue.

But if the seamier side of the city depressed him, the city's wealthier aspects were disheartening too. Appearances, he discovered, could be misleading. Bayswater and Kensington, for example, were called Asia Minor because they housed so many retired civil servants from India, who, for all their pomp, were far from rich. Pall Mall and Victoria, on the other hand, boasted remarkable properties—but also many bobbies pounding a regular beat. He felt that Central London offered little, but by looking outward—toward endless suburbia, north and south—he thought he'd found what he wanted. Hampstead and Highgate might foster artists and thinkers—impoverished dreamers best left alone—but Blackheath and Camberwell, south of the river, had the quiet, genteel houses he found so inviting. He first robbed three houses in Camberwell, stealing enough to set up a front, and established himself as a dealer in musical instruments, becoming the agent for two large piano makers.

"Soon we'll have sufficient to form us an h'orchestra," he told Sue, and their room filled up with flutes and violins, some bought, mostly stolen.

As the cash flowed into his purse, Sue overcame her depression, but she now knew Mr. Thompson's real profession.

"Funny, I thought you were a fraudsman," she confessed one night.

"Nay, lass," he laughed, "just a collector!"

But Sue was not one to put too fine a point on the distinction. The jails were full of fraudsmen—clever burglars seldom got caught—and provided *she* remained vague about the niceties of his trade, *she* was quite uninvolved. Moreover, their purse was now bulging, and Jack said they'd be out of Lambeth by the New Year, with great expectations thereafter.

But five days before Christmas, Charlie had a daunting experience. He was up by the Holborn Viaduct, having collected some agency fees, and it was a fine Monday morning, full of festive spirit. Fleet Street and Ludgate Circus were crammed with benevolent pedestrians, muffin and chestnut men shouted their wares, bright lights dotted the viaduct. Charlie was up on the latter, treating some children to hot jacket potatoes bought from a man with a fire stall. He too felt benign, but as he turned from the brazier his smile quickly faded. Two yards away, staring straight at him, was a youngish man in ordinary clothes, whose look was intense. He seemed to know Charlie.

"Hey, you!" he called softly, stepping forward.

Charlie drew back, but the viaduct ramparts were behind him, forty feet above the Circus below.

"Hold fast!" said the man, trying to force a way through the children. "I've a warrant for thy arrest!" It was Pearson of Darnall.

Charlie gazed around frantically for a means of escape, but his path was blocked by the children. He knew nothing of London guttersnipes—but he'd just treated them famously. "You lot!" he said to them. "I've been thine friend, you be mine now!" He pointed to Pearson. "Yon fellow's mine mortal h'enemy! See him off!"

The munching urchins looked at Pearson. "You keep out of my way!" Pearson warned them. "I'm a police officer!"

He was unwise to admit his calling to the offspring of costermongers, whose hate for the police was traditional. They closed ranks around him. "Sodding copper! Dirty esclop! Bloody shunter!" and worse names were spat at him, followed by small buffets and kicks. Pearson was pushed by their sheer weight toward the brazier, where somebody tripped him. He fell over backward, toward the fire and onto the hands of the vendor, who was poking his potatoes with a pair of tongs.

"God's Hooks!" screamed the latter. "You stupid bastard!" and he hit Pearson a heavy blow on the head with the tongs. Only Pearson's thick skull and bowler hat saved him from serious injury, but his hat was crammed down over his eyes. He fell to the ground, covered with ash, while the children whooped with joy and pelted him with potatoes.

"Go at it, lads!" Charlie encouraged them and darted off down the road over the viaduct. He found some steps leading to the thoroughfare below and took them four at a time down to the

Circus, where he mixed with the Fleet Street crowds until he got
to the Embankment. He followed the Thames to Charing Cross
and entered the station, where he bought a two-penny ticket on
a workman's train to Highgate. He felt safer in the company of
laborers, who'd tear a peeler to pieces if one boarded their train,
and he deemed it wiser not to go back directly to Lambeth.

Much of the line ran underground, which terrified the miner
in Charlie, and he got off into Highgate's fresh air with enormous
relief. He decided to leave Lambeth till nightfall, so he wandered
about in the village and watched a blacksmith shoe a Clydesdale
for a while, and then crossed the Common where he noticed a big
red-brick building behind a high wall. At first he thought it an
institution, but high children's laughter told him it must be a
school. The gates were open and he went inside. A game of
football was in progress between some boys in a quad and
Charlie joined in—teaching them a few useful fouls—and was
thus engaged when a man's voice hailed him from the school
doors. A tall schoolmaster, in gown and mortarboard, stood on
the steps.

"Who are you, sir?" he addressed Charlie.

Charlie, ball under arm, bowed deeply. The grand man reminded him of Littlewood.

"No h'offence 'tended, sir," he replied, "and I h'apologize if
I've trespassed on 'allowed ground. But I was just showing these
young gent'lums a trick or two."

The schoolmaster had seen some of his skill and was interested
in the monkeylike stranger. "Are you a showman?" he asked.
Such people did call at his college.

Again Charlie bowed. "Theatricals, gymnasticals, h'etcetera!"

The schoolmaster thought for a moment. Today was the last
day of the term, his pupils were restless, and he saw a chance to
contain them. "How much do you charge?" he asked.

"I'd verily h'entertain your young gent'lums for free," said

Charlie. "And seeing as how they're proper-born lads, how about a spot o' theatricals, sir?" The schoolmaster agreed. He summoned the boys and took Charlie inside the college, along passages smelling of polish, to the school theater. Other boys idling against walls were also summoned to attend.

When all present were seated Charlie nimbly mounted the stage and disappeared into the wings. He was in his element, shaking with excitement. Out of sight, he took off his coat and put it back on inside out, so he now wore a jacket of quilted red satin. Unlacing his boots, he walked on the heels, increasing his height and straightening his posture. For the rest, he decided to rely on grimaces, and now he was ready to perform. He danced onstage and raised his hands for silence: his only props were a tea chest and a broom handle.

"I'll give you Bill Shakespeare!" he announced to the boys. "Whose words burn like lime in mine brain! Let's take Bold 'Amlet, Prince o' the Danes, h'Act Five, Scene One. Thou must h'imagine a churchyard, full of bones and bad h'omens, with two sack-'em-up men with spades. Fair h'Orphelia hast been drowned in a ditch, and she's to be put to bed wi' a shovel. Bold 'Amlet's come for to see her off—along with his good pal Horatio. Bad King Claud—a B-flat polone, who's done in his dad—comes along with Queen Gerty, who's been up to no good neither. Poor 'Amlet's feeling h'inveterate t'ward Claud, remember? He later sticks him with his sword like a pig. But right now he's gaumless —talking to skulls, one off a fella named Yorick (a jester like me) —and most of what he says is screaming fine nonsense. . . . But you'll have to h'imagine, my Lord Bishop and gent'lums, that I be h'every part in the act—from Gerty to poor Yorick's bone-dome. So here we go!"

The schoolmaster was surprised by this unusual introduction to Hamlet and flattered to be called a bishop, but the performance that followed amazed him as much as it delighted his pupils.

The boys hooted and clapped Charlie's faces and voices, and he in turn worked hard for them. Nor did he forget one word of his Shakespeare—every line of the act was correct—but it just wasn't Garrick. Deafening applause greeted the end of his Hamlet, so he gave his audience another full hour of sonnets and snatches of tragedies. When he finished he was exhausted and the boys were hoarse from laughing. The schoolmaster shook his head in wonderment as Charlie came down from the stage.

"You have singular style, Mr.—er—I don't think you mentioned your name?"

"Blondel, sir. H'Archimedes Manningtree Blondel."

"Ah, yes . . . Very interesting . . . May I ask who taught you to act, Mr. Blondel?"

Charlie hesitated. "Just twixt oursen, sir?"

"But of course."

"Mr. Henry h'Irving."

"Irving, by Jove! Are you serious!"

Charlie nodded solemnly. "I was a mere stage lad at the Lyceum when the Great Man was doing *The Bells*. Mr. 'Enry lent us some of his time, God bless him."

The master was mystified, but he knew all things were possible in the twilit world of the theater. He watched Charlie reverse his coat and rebutton his shoes. "Are you sure there's no charge, Mr. Blondel?"

Charlie shook his head vigorously. "I won't hear of it. Haply one day some of your lads shalt remember me when I'm dead 'n' gone." He consulted his watch. He'd enjoyed the afternoon, but it was time to go home. "I must depart, my Lord Bishop," he said, shaking the schoolmaster's hand. He said goodbye to the boys, who escorted him out of the school. One of them even gave him a toffee.

Back at Stangate Street, Charlie's mind was still on the policeman at Holborn. He went to a suitcase and counted his savings.

Thirty pounds. He looked at Sue, heating soup over an oil stove, a gin bottle at hand. Her expression was miserable.

"Don't fret, pet," he said. "We'll be gone from here in a few days."

She brightened visibly. "Into a big house?"

He smiled sadly. "We move because of summat that happened today," he said. "I bumped into a man who knows me of old—a bobby." He saw fear in her face. "Not a Lunnaner—a West Ridinger, I think, where they'd give one hundred pund for thy John."

Such a price on his head astounded Sue. "What was he doing in London?" she asked.

Charlie shrugged. That was one of the questions that troubled him: Was it sheer coincidence? "But he's the cause for us moving," he said. "To Greenwich, I think." He watched Sue pour herself a generous measure of gin and frowned. "You mind yon stuff, it ain't tea."

Christmas in Lambeth was dreary, and on January 2 they moved to Crane Court in Greenwich, into a house, but a place pokey and damp, and almost on top of the Thames. Charlie soon looked elsewhere and decided on a larger villa in Billingsgate Street, still in Greenwich, for fifteen pounds per annum. For the moment, he was content, though Sue still hankered for finer premises away from the river.

"And I'm bored," she complained, for he was often out.

"Find work, my pet," he advised.

"You need money to get on the stage," she said crossly.

"Then find work in a shop."

"In a shop?" Sue sounded horrified and reached for her bottle, now a constant companion. Her drinking had steadily worsened since their arrival in London, mottling her skin, giving her a livery look. Charlie wondered if he drove all his women to drink. He thought not—it had just been his misfortune to pick up several lushingtons. He smiled faintly at what Hannah might say. He

missed Hannah and wanted her down in London. He thought she'd be a good influence on Sue. But would Hannah come south? She regarded southern folk as depraved.

He decided to put her to the test by writing a letter, which was found by Sue on the hall table, ready for postage.

"What's this?" she taxed Charlie. It was noon, but her speech was already slurred.

"To my wife, pet," he said.

"Your *wife?* I thought you'd finished with her?"

"Oh, we reunite now and then. I've h'invited her here for a spell. I trust you will like her."

"Invited her *here!* But I don't *want* her here! I won't have her here! This is my house—not hers!" Sue screamed at him, her eyes wide and glazed. Charlie had anticipated this sort of reaction. But it was her noise he couldn't stand. He slapped her face hard, knocking her down, and then pulled her up on her feet. She was stunned with surprise. "Cease prattling and listen," he told her, in what he hoped was a reasoning tone. "This be thine house as thou says, but I be the lawgiver. You can swim in gold, but you must do as I say. If thou dost not, I'll clip thy fine wings, my dove. So don't nettle me." The hazel eyes burned and Sue nodded dumbly. She'd never seen this ferocity before and she was terrified. She rubbed her cheek and he let go of her arm. She seemed defeated. He was glad—he didn't like striking women. It would all be much easier when Hannah arrived. He took Sue into the parlor and sat her down. "You'll like Hannah and Willie," he went on, as if nothing had happened. "You must *larn* to like 'em! You may find old Hannah cross-grained, but remember her age. She's got a good twenty years on thysen. And remember, we must all venerate the h'old lest the Lord calls upon the bears to devour us. So do this to please Jack, pet, and you stay on as Mistress Thompson, queen of this house. Now, let there be no more h'unpleasantness, my blossom!" He bent down and kissed her red cheek, and as a treat, he opened her a bottle of claret.

While Charlie awaited some answer from Hannah, he made a few plans. Like Sue, he wanted somewhere grander than Billingsgate Street. He desired a house with a stable, so he could have his own trap, and he wanted it close to a railway. He'd a penchant for railway lines since his escape from Whalley Range. Greenwich itself was on the L. & G.R. Line, but—in deference to Sue—he looked further south. Peckham Rye was on the Chatham & Dover line, but the estate agents said nice houses were pricy. Very well, he'd make a rich haul and pay his way.

He considered robbing a merchant bank in the City, but he thought that might cause too great a hue and cry. Instead, he settled on Lord Shaftesbury's mansion in Wandsworth. He was loath to steal from a man who'd done so much for the poor, but he reasoned that Shaftesbury might make a donation, seeing how he, Charlie, was endeavoring to set up a good home. Remembering Heeley Hall, however, he approached this new expedition with care.

Shaftesbury's London residence stood back from Common Land. Charlie spent a week reconnoitering the locality, variously disguised as a coal merchant, crossing sweep, and rag 'n' bone man. He found the house itself a rambling hotchpotch of architectural styles, with porticoes and good guttering, and realized that much climbing would be required. The grounds, on the other hand, were small, with an empty mews to the rear of the mansion. He also ascertained the comings and goings of the household by watching and by the odd discreet inquiry, and he discovered that His Lordship and staff retired to the countryside at weekends, leaving the house in care of a couple of elderly basement slaves. Charlie further observed that the neighborhood bobby was no effectual limb of the law—he was a slouchy constable who imbibed on the beat and was drunk by ten at night. And it was upon a Saturday night, with benefit of smog, that Charlie struck.

He left Greenwich in a hired dog cart, jogging the pony across South London to the Common. No sweep or ragman that night, Charlie was disguised as an Italian musician on his way home from an evening's orchestration at the Alhambra music hall. To this end, he wore evening dress and a cloak, the wig on his head was black as patent leather, and he sported huge Garibaldi mustaches. Fiddle and mandolin cases in his cart also bore witness to his trade. And if he was questioned by a nosy bobby, he would make his replies in Italianate gibberish—he knew London policemen were terrified of foreigners.

He gained the Common at midnight, parked his cart in the mews, and walked around to the front of the mansion and through the open gates. Under his black cloak, he carried a violin case full of tools, a collapsible ladder, and a rope with grappling hooks. He approached the house quite boldly, for it was shrouded in thick mist, the windows were all in darkness, and the ancient servants were certain to be in bed. At the grand front door, he stopped, listened, and then flung up his grappling line, which caught on a gutter above the portico and held. Charlie sped up the rope like a cloaked fiend, found a small flat roof, pulled up his line, and hid the evidence of his climb in a drainpipe. He next crossed the roof to a window which was draped by curtains on the inside, on the first floor, and probably gave access to a landing. He taped and broke the glass soundlessly—"starred the glaze"—but then he found his way blocked by bars.

"Clever buggers," he whispered, but he knew how to deal with all but the toughest bars. Retrieving his rope from the drainpipe, he doubled it and passed a section around the central two bars. He commenced to twist the rope, harder and harder, never relaxing his strong grip, and the two bars began to bend toward each other. He twisted the rope into a large knot, leaving a gap on either side. Then he passed through his fiddle case and ladder, wrapped his cloak tight around him, and slid himself through the largest gap—doing a "snakesman."

As he'd suspected, he was on a landing, with bedrooms off it and broad stairs leading down to a marbled hall. He went down the staircase, feeling his way in the dark, holding his breath. Fluted pillars to the left of the hallway gave way to a large chamber, and here he dared light his spotlight. He was in a salon as big as a ballroom. He was taken aback by its splendor—the gilt, the crystal, the tapestries, and the portraits of Shaftesburys frowning down from the walls. The wealth belonged to the Arabian Nights—not to its present owner, friend of the "deserving poor." Charlie set out to explore, to value the best ornaments. He drew one sack then another from under his coattails and filled them to capacity. This one room alone offered him more than he could possibly carry. And what of other parts of the mansion—the dining room with its silver, the library, and so on? Charlie was consumed with frustration, suddenly wishing he'd worked with a gang to cart away so much booty. Emotionally exhausted, he snuffed out his light and sat on a Louis Quinze chair to ponder. He knew he'd already been in the house long enough, but he dared not deliver his current haul to his trap and then pay a return trip. Then two things occurred to him and he got up to start browsing again.

He left the salon, found the dining room, and relit his lamp. Plate was displayed in abundance, the finest items of which he marked underneath with a knife, scratching "C. P." to proclaim his new ownership. He explored in the library, an anteroom, a lounge, and a writing room. Then he crept upstairs to the bedrooms. He found Lord Shaftesbury's room very humble, but discovered a small old-fashioned safe in the dressing room. No keys. Charlie had a drill in his fiddle case—a "petter-cutter"—which he clamped to the keyhole. The hardened steel bit bore a hole over the lock. Through this went a "ward," a twist of steel, which opened the safe. Within, Charlie found a dead mouse, some papers of parchment, and a sharkskin box. The last contained brooches, cuff links, tiepins, and rings. Charlie discarded all of those which boasted a crest or were plainly heirlooms; the theft of a family memento, he knew, could be heartbreaking. But he pocketed the rest, including a man's signet ring set with a stone bearing the profile of Charles II. The long-nosed king seemed to sniff like Hannah as Charlie examined the ring, but Charlie recalled that the monarch had forgiven Colonel Blood for trying to steal the Crown Jewels, and thought his namesake would extend that merciful view toward himself. . . . The ring went into his waistcoat.

It was high time to leave and Charlie took his departure from the "starred" window. Once out on the portico roof, he scrambled up over the edge of a turret to find the rear of the house. The mansion was narrower than long, and soon he was overlooking the mews. The fog still swirled, blanketing sights and sounds, and Charlie had to guess his height above ground. He climbed down a tiled slope as low as he could. The slates were slippery and he trod with caution. At the rim he unfolded his ladder and positioned it against the house wall as low as his long arms permitted. He clambered over the guttering, one foot found the top rung of the ladder, and he sought a hold for his other foot. But his long cloak became tangled up underfoot and he slithered off the steep tiles and fell with a "Bugger me!"

He landed atop some spear-headed railings, one of which embedded its blade in his thigh. The pain was more of bruising than wounding, and he tugged free his leg without a whimper. Blood soaked down his trousers. He almost dropped his sacks of swag and the violin case, but he guessed he'd only a flesh wound. He reached the cobbled mews, hopped about raging silently, staunching the hole in his leg with spit and a handkerchief, and retrieved his paraphernalia. The ladder he almost abandoned—"Bloody-end to that!" was his view of his handiwork, but sense told him not to leave it around: he had a second call to pay upon Lord Shaftesbury, and if tonight's "modus" had proved untoward, he might repeat the procedure step by step.

Charlie found his pony almost comatose on dope he'd given the creature. But testing laudanum on a pony hadn't appealed to Charlie, so the dosage was minimal, and the beast picked up its senses and speed soon after heading east of the Common.

"Would Sue be as square-rigged as thysen," Charlie grumbled to his pony. His mistress was likely flushed-drunk in bed: she never waited up for her benefactor. "But 'appen she'll like what us earned," he added, twirling his false mustaches. "Sufficient for a nice treat for old Hannah when she cum south!"

And the next weekend, Charlie duly paid a second visit to Wandsworth. He collected those pieces he'd been unable to transport the previous Sunday morn—those bearing his initials. And he encountered no difficulties. It was obvious that his Lord-ship had summoned the police, for two bobbies pounded the beat, but no other security surrounded the big house. Charlie assumed Shaftesbury too involved in political matters to care very much for his property: he'd left matters to his minions and the Commissioner of Police—neither of whom blazoned that effi-ciency Charlie thought worthy of their pay.

"No wonder us poor public got no confidences in t'police!" he groused later to Sue, as they inspected his takings. "But y'know, these nobs live werry nice!" He examined again the Charles II ring. "I h'admire a man wi' good taste!" He was content. His thigh had healed well and a new home was obtainable.

At the end of January, Charlie's letter to Hull was unexpectedly answered. Hannah turned up on the doorstep with Willie in tow and pots and pans and portmanteaux at her feet.

"Bloody 'eck!" said Charlie, paying off the cab. "I wasn't h'ex-pectin' you just to h'arrive!"

"But ah allus cum when ah'm sent for," replied his gaunt wife. She pushed past him into the hall and inspected the house. "Ah see tha's been busy," she observed, noticing Lord Shaftesbury's property littering the parlor. She sniffed the air. "And I can smell tha's still got thy woman. Where is she?"

Charlie called up the stairs for Sue, who'd been in the bedroom at her gin and toiletry for a good hour. She came down as if dressed for the lord mayor's banquet—in a ball gown of white silk and tulle, with puffings and gigots, and paper flowers in her hair. Hannah was stunned by the spectacle.

Charlie coughed nervously. "This is—er—Sue Bailey, and this be—er—'Annah, my missus," he introduced them.

Sue ran forward with outstretched hands. "Mrs. Thompson!"

"Peace!" snapped Hannah, dodging her.

She stopped with surprise. "Of course I come in peace, Mrs. Thompson! Jack has told me so much about you!"

"Has he just?" She looked Sue up and down with distaste. "'Appen he's not told thee the lot."

Willie was grinning at the sight of the women, but Charlie thought it time to intervene—even if caution had to be thrown to the winds. "Ahem! Now see here, you two! 'Tis my fault we've this pickle, so let me h'explain. . . ." He turned to Sue. "You'd best be told—my real name is Peace—Charles Peace—and Hannah's my true wife. Yon pimply bugger be Willie, my stepson. Both of 'em now carry the name of Ward, and nivver must the name of Peace be mentioned again. Understand?" Sue nodded, dazed and obedient. "Good!" He crossed to the mantelpiece, muttering "Bloody wimmin!" as he passed Willie, and turned up the lamps. "Now then!" he addressed them again, his back to the fire, very much in command. "We must larn to live together like 'ighly civilized 'umans. You, Sue, continue as Mrs. John Thompson. You two, Hannah and Willie, continue as Mistress and Master Ward. We shalt live together in peace—without feuding or fratching—and I'll make it hot for the one that causes h'any trubble!" This threat was directed chiefly at Sue, who was looking unhappily at her feet. Charlie turned to stare at his wife more anxiously. "How say you, Hannah?"

Hannah shrugged. " 'Appen I'll stay."

"So shall I!" cried Sue, not to be outdone.

Hannah glared at her. Painted slut, she thought. She wants me to leave and to have Charlie all to herself. She looked at Charlie. Dirty devil, she thought, he wants her, too, but with me to spy on her. So be it: she'd stay to plague the life of Sue Bailey. "Hast thou a spare room for Willie and mysen?" she asked.

"Of course!" Charlie rubbed his hands. "And we're not stopping in this sty very long. We're h'off to Peckham as soon as maybe. To live like gentlefolk. 'Tis my solemn pledge to keep you in luxary!" He sought and found a suitable quotation. " 'And Solomon overlaid the house within with pure gold'!"

Hannah was unimpressed. "Show us our room," she said crisply, one hard eye on Sue.

III

With two ladies more or less settled in, Charlie's mind now turned to disguise. If the man on the viaduct had recognized him with his beard trimmed, that meant his less hairy description was in circulation. But he was good with make-up and set about another physical transformation. On Sunday, he disappeared into the spare bedroom with Hannah, armed with a razor and odd pots from the chemist. His beard came off completely and more hair was shaved from the crown of his head—what remained was dyed white. He then worked on himself with the juice from the rind of the walnut, a dark brown stain which he liberally applied to his face, neck, and hands. He labored the stain right into the skin, testing it occasionally with a damp cloth until it ceased to come off. That done, he admired himself in a mirror. His features looked flatter, distinctly Negroid, and the nut-brown face contrasted sharply with his white hair.

"Begod, 'tis the return of the h'Ethiopian Wonder!" he said to Hannah.

When Sue saw the new Mr. Thompson, she was dismayed.

"But you look sixty or seventy!" she cried. "You *can't* go around looking like that."

"Oh, yes he can," countered Hannah, "and tha'll go along with him."

She eyed Sue with contempt. Willie was howling with laughter at the sight of his stepfather, and Charlie was grinning.

"I think I look 'ighly distinguished," he said. "Rather like an h'explorer just back from h'Africa." He posed in front of the parlor mirror and pulled a few faces.

"You look like a nigger to me," Sue protested.

It took her three weeks to get used to the extraordinary disguise, during which time Charlie practiced certain airs to go with his face. He aimed at eccentricity, dressed like a dandy in outlandish clothes, and sported huge hats. But the atmosphere at Billingsgate Street did not improve between the two female occupants. Try as he did, Charlie couldn't pull down the hostility. The women seldom spoke to each other, but their respective complaints were passed on via Willie.

"Mum says she's takin' ta snuffing," he said, showing Charlie snuff on an antimacassar, or, "Sue says Mum's hid her gin in t'closet."

"Oh, what a bother!" groaned Charlie, and visited the estate agents again.

Messrs. Grundy and Figg of Penge had a suitable house, they said. It was large, capable of division, and right on the railway.

"I'll have it, Sweet Jesus, I'll have it!" cried their dark-skinned customer. Two small snags, said the agents: the house was twenty pounds a year and the landlord was Samuel Smith.

"I'll pay thirty and Old Nick can be landlord!" said Charlie.

The agents smiled. They were sorry, they said, but Mr. Smith was a builder and a Mason; the property was in desirable Evelina Road; Mr. Smith would be anxious about letting his house to someone with Mr. Thompson's complexion.

"I'm no darkie!" Charlie protested. "I'll h'invite yon Sam'l Smith to dine with me!"

Mr. Smith accepted this invitation. He was fed off gold plate, filled with the choicest wines, and kept amused by Mr. Thompson's stories of the Dark Continent. He was also impressed when his host offered six months' rent in advance, and at the end of the evening a contract was signed.

Mr. Smith thought Mrs. Thompson looked ravishing, although she was rather heavily scented and her husband obviously earned enough to run a couple of servants, since Hannah and Willie had waited diligently at table.

"What d'you do for a livelihood, Mr. Thompson?" Smith asked over coffee.

Charlie smiled mysteriously. "I h'invent things," he said.

"Really? How very clever. You must meet Mr. Brion in Peckham—he's another inventor."

Charlie promised to make his acquaintance. Business completed, he and Sue saw Smith off in his cab, both waving cordially.

"Bloody little crook!" Charlie muttered as they turned back into the house. "Come on in, pet. 'Tis getting parky."

They shut the front door. Hannah was waiting in the hall—still in her apron—and her face worked furiously. She'd heard Charlie's term of endearment for Sue and it angered her. She drew him aside.

"I'll not play thy skivvy!" she rasped. "And ah'll stop here no longer!" She threw off her apron.

Charlie saw her point. It had been Sue's idea for Hannah and Willie to pose as servants. He should have known better than to permit such a thing. "There's a house with rooms free down the road," he told Hannah. "You and Willie can stay there till we move."

To his relief, Hannah relented and grunted assent. He was hoping things might improve at Evelina Road—with a large house for Hannah to manage, while Sue just sat about like a pretty stick of furniture. He also reckoned he'd have to be very busy at nights to maintain their high standard of living. But at least he'd have the days to himself, and he'd certainly look up the inventor called Brion.

13

At the House
of Nobs

Number 5 East Terrace, Evelina Road, was all that Charlie could
have wished. The villa, a two-story house above a large basement,
was semi-detached, being the last in the terrace. It had eight main
rooms and an attic. A back door led into a long rear garden, with
fruit trees and potting sheds, which ended on the embankment
of the Chatham Line railway. A stable and gate in the right-hand
wall gave access into the adjoining street.

Hannah and Willie were supposed to be lodgers, so Charlie
gave them two upstairs rooms and the kitchen. Sue and he had
all the front rooms, as befitted master and mistress.

"We shall buy some very fine meublements," he promised Sue
and vans duly arrived with Indian carpets, a suite of walnut furniture, and a small upright piano. "You ladies see to the house,
while I see to the jardin," Charlie said. Spring was in the air and
he began planting bulbs, refurbished the stable, and purchased
a young pony called Tommy. The garden and sheds were his
private domain and he sawed a hole in the end fence to give
access to the railway. He trained Tommy to pull a rubber-
wheeled trap and to tread very quietly.

News of the Thompsons' arrival traveled fast in the neighborhood. Mr. Smith said they were "Good folk," and so it seemed

when Charlie and Sue attended St. Atholine's Church on the very first Sunday. The choir was a small pride of Peckham, and Sue added her fine voice to the hymns. Mr. Long was the organist, as well as the local milk roundsman, and he made an effort to befriend the new couple. "I shall be pleased to deliver your milk, sir," Long told Charlie after service. Then he introduced the Thompsons to Ben Driblett, a Phillips Road chemist, who transpired to be a neighbor of the illustrious Brion. Charlie expressed interest. "Then, by jingo, you must meet Mr. Brion," said Driblett. He consulted his wife. "Come to tea this afternoon!" He did not extend this invitation to Long, who was only a milkman; people knew their position in Peckham.

A large Sunday roast sent Charlie to sleep in the afternoon and he dozed on till four, when he leapt from the sofa yelling for Sue, afraid they'd be late at the Dribletts. But he found her ready and waiting in the hall, and they flung out of the house without further ado. (Some neighbors, who spent their leisure hours spying through curtains, were surprised by the apparent vitality of old Mr. Thompson.)

The Dribletts lived above their shop in Phillips Road. They welcomed the Thompsons and took them into their "best room." The Brions had already arrived.

Forsey Brion was a man in his forties, huge of head but diminutive in body. His wife, Alice, was equally short, but plump as a bird and sparkly. Brion himself was far from a cheery soul; he lived for fortune and fame, and any run of bad luck made him lugubrious. He shook Charlie's hand suspiciously. Smith had mentioned a few things of this stranger—including his perpetual suntan.

"I hear you're something of a traveler?" Brion said over tea. His manner was stiff; his voice squeaky.

"H'Africa in the main, sir. Savage place, h'Africa." Charlie looked round to give Sue a grin, but she was busy at a cake trolley with Mrs. Brion.

"Which part of Africa?" asked Brion, slightly more interested.

"Zanzibary, sir. In the footsteps of Burton and Speke."

Brion's face fell a fraction. "Oh, yes? Ah, my province is further north—the Sahara in fact."

"You have been there, sir?"

Brion shook his great head so violently his thin neck seemed in peril. "No, not exactly. You see, I'm engaged on a scheme to fertile the desert. Cut canals and flood it from the Atlantic. The sun will then dry up the salt and leave the wasteland a Garden of Eden. Only a theory, of course. . . ." Brion didn't add that his project had been thoroughly rejected by the powers that be.

"Forsey has a model of his idea up at Mansion House!" Driblett cut in.

"H'indeed?" said Charlie. "I should werry much care to see it, sir."

"Would you really?" Brion was pleased.

"Yes! Certainly. When can we go, sir? Tomorrow—Tuesday—Wednesday?"

Brion hadn't reckoned on such enthusiasm; he even managed the ghost of a smile. "Tomorrow would be fine, Mr. Thompson. We could go up in the morning and lunch in the city. I could then give you a detailed exposition of my hopes and frustrations."

Charlie nodded. "And I can present my petition in the h'afternoon, sir."

"What petition is that?"

"Hast thou not seen the papers, sir? I plan to petition the House of Nobs to decry the slaughterous war of the Turks. They be biffing the Russkies most 'orribly, the h'infidel swine. I h'abominate the Turks, sir. They have the Winchester, you know?"

Brion did not. "The Winchester?"

"Beastly gun, h'invented by an h'American shirtmaker. You load it on Sunday and fire it all week."

Brion was impressed. Not only was Mr. Thompson an expert

on firearms, but also a man with social conscience. He decided
he would accompany Mr. Thompson when he called at the House
of Commons. He felt a friendship of mutual advantage was born.
Wresting himself out of his customary gloom, he chatted to
Charlie on mechanics and sciences for the rest of the afternoon.

Next day, true to plan, the two men set off for the city. At
Mansion House, Charlie inspected Brion's handiwork. The
model, which occupied a great table in an upstairs room, was
crude, with Africa shaped like a banana. But Charlie made the
right noises, while Brion expounded his theories in an interminable drone, a monologue that lasted till lunch.

They sought food in Fleet Street. Charlie slightly resented
having to pay for Brion's refreshments, but after lunch they
looked for an omnibus to take them to Westminster, Charlie's
petition enclosed in a large buff envelope. However, fate diverted
their path when they passed a newsvendor and Charlie bought
the *Gazette*. Its headline announced the start of an important
criminal case: three police officers were due to appear at Bow
Street Court that very afternoon, charged with corruption.
Charlie was intrigued; he'd never countenanced a bobby in the
dock and the prospect was pleasing to him. Moreover, the paper
said the case was celebrated—the hearing would be well attended
—and it was advisable for the public to obtain tickets from Great
Scotland Yard if they desired a seat in the gallery.

"Let's go!" Charlie suggested. "We could 'op over to the Factory, pick up a couple o' tickets, and be at court by two!"

Brion was much less interested in crime, but he was persuaded,
and together they went up to Whitehall. There were throngs of
people loitering outside the Yard, but Charlie and Brion gained
access and were directed to a superintendent's office on the first
floor. Here they had to pay three shillings and wait in a corridor
while tickets were fetched. Charlie found himself examining a

green-baize notice board screwed to the wall. It posted bills of REWARD and WANTED covering the country. One poster, older than most, caught his immediate attention.

"Charles Frederick Peace," he read, and suppressed a desire to flee the building. "Wanted for Murder—£100 Reward." It went on to describe him in some detail, showing a picture taken in 1864, when he'd had thick brown hair and Anglican whiskers. The poster's sharp eyes stared down on him mockingly. He was transfixed by the portrait, and started when someone touched his sleeve, but it was only Brion, a tall police officer beside him.

"What an 'orrible face!" Charlie said, indicating the poster with his stick. "Have you caught that scamp yet?"

The policeman shook his head. He remembered the latest report on Peace—that he'd been spotted in London some months ago and then vanished again. Gone back north, it was thought. "I'm sure he'll be found, sir," he said comfortingly.

"Such scoundrels should not be at large," Charlie added. "You must h'instruct your h'officers to be more vigilant!"

The policeman watched the critical old gentleman leave, but he didn't care: Peace was no longer London's concern.

Outside the Yard, Charlie and Brion caught a cab to Bow Street. The paper was right—the courtroom was packed—but they found seats and saw the crooked detectives sent to the Old Bailey for trial.

" 'Tis a scandal!" Charlie said. "If you can't trust the Jacks, who can one trust? A shameful h'affair!"

They then took the four o'clock train back to the Rye, and discussed the Saharan venture during the journey. Charlie didn't think Brion's plan would come to much, but the seawater—together with his concern about the Russo-Turkish war—had given him an idea, which he now put to Brion.

" 'Tis the navies of Britain and Kaiserland that'll soon rule the world," he prophesied. "But the ships be all iron nowadays, costing mill'ons of punds, and when one founders, oh, how the sea nobs tear their hair! But suppose we've an h'ironclad resting on the seabed, Mr. Brion, why just leave it there? Why not raise it up again?"

"How, Mr. Thompson?"

"By pumping gasses and h'air into the 'ull, sir. Wouldn't that cause the vessel to rise to the surface? 'Appen I'm talkin' baldydash, Mr. Brion, but what say you?"

Brion didn't answer at once. He considered Charlie's notion very carefully, his amazing head cocked to one side. When at last he spoke, his zeal surprised Charlie. "Of course it should work! I must congratulate you, Mr. Thompson! My, what a wonderful thought! Have you any other plans? Tell me more!"

Charlie laughed. "Hold hard, sir . . . I've h'only just dreamt of it."

"But we must get to work!" Brion insisted, the Sahara forgotten. "Let us decide upon our respective roles immediately!" And the two men agreed that Charlie should experiment with models in a tank in the garden, while Brion, who was better at paperwork, would prepare all the plans. Brion wanted Charlie to come back to his house straightaway, to discuss the matter further, but Charlie pleaded a headache. He suffered, he said, from sleepless nights. . . . Not to be put off, Brion went into Driblett's for a vial of laudanum, despite Charlie's protests that he never took drugs. The chemist was behind his counter. He opined that the best cure for Charlie—for every ill that he knew of—was a dose of Epsom salts, and he gave Charlie some free of charge.

"Well, if I'm not h'allowed to pay, sir, at least take this!" Charlie said, handing Driblett a large Havana.

The chemist loved a good cigar, his wife was out, so he lit up in the shop. "A perfect smoke, Mr. Thompson," he said. "Where *do* you obtain your cigars?"

"I steal 'em," came the candid reply.

They laughed—even Brion. "Then steal some for me!" Driblett cackled.

"Certainly," Charlie replied, and made a mental note to do just that when he next burgled a rich house.

But it had been a long day. Charlie really did want his bed—with Sue in it, for preference. He'd have to be up again soon after midnight; a few hours' sleep was essential. So he said goodbye to Driblett and Brion, and headed off home with his salts. He'd give those to Sue, to purge her puffy liver, and he hoped she hadn't rendered herself insensible during the course of the day.

II

Spring turned slowly into summer. While Hannah ran Number 5 with quiet efficiency, Willie loafed around, which suited him admirably. Sue, on the other hand, socialized with various neighbors, including the Longs and Alice Brion. But she continued her drinking and snuffing until she began to look bloated. She was jealous of Hannah and frightened of Charlie and she thought Willie Ward a treacherous imbecile—especially when he started following her to the Hollydale Arms and other public houses, sometimes on his mother's instructions, other times out of spite. She complained to Charlie, of course, but he merely laughed. He was too wrapped up with his innumerable hobbies to care, and he'd just buy her a new dress, or steal her some jewelry, by way of recompense. He now had a new zoo—acrobatic pigeons, guinea pigs, cats and dogs, and parrots which chanted anti-Turkish jingles. Too he had taken in Mr. Long's milk pony and had trained it as well, and had started a veterinary service to doctor sick pets in the area. Then, after the livestock, came Charlie's soirees. Musical evenings were held on Wednesdays and Fridays, with Sue at the piano and singing, and Charlie on fifteen odd instruments. A typical soiree started at seven and ended promptly at ten, when Charlie hinted it was time for his medicine and bed.

"I'm very h'infirm," he would say. "I nivver know when I'll be facing my Maker."

And to bed he then went—for a spell, after which he'd creep from the house, around midnight, usually disguised and always carrying a revolver. He struck out for suburbia either on foot along the railway or with Tommy and trap. Sometimes, he used Mr. Long's pony, but he gave that up when the milkman complained of its dozy state in the mornings. Charlie rampaged throughout the whole of southeast London till dawn, when he returned to catch up on sleep. So many were his burglaries that a question was raised in Parliament, accusing the police of inefficiency. Number 5 became a treasury of spoils, while Hannah grew worried, but Sue turned a drunken blind-eye.

Nor did Charlie forsake Forsey Brion. He floated, sank, and raised a model warship in the garden tank by means of a hydraulic pump. This ship—made of brass and tin, and loosely based on the *Hashemy*—was also taken down to Peckham Pond, where Charlie permitted children to scuttle his toy—much to the disapproval of Brion, who thought their "work" should be taken more seriously. But Charlie loved his pose of affable eccentricity, and encouraged that view by devising other nonsenses.

"I'm h'unhappy about the lot of our firemen," he told neighbors, and fashioned a helmet, on the line of a deep-sea diver's, to supply air under smoky conditions; and, "Our railways are downright disgusting!" he said, producing a scrubbing brush through which water could be flushed; and, "All these burglaries are a sign of the times!" he agreed with the newspapers, reporting his own night ventures, and advised friends on how to lock up their homes.

Hannah observed him with growing alarm. He was overacting,

she thought, and also he was failing to dispose of enough stolen goods. Moreover, Hannah was convinced they were harboring a Judas—Sue Bailey.

"If she keeps a-drinkin', 'appen she'll shoot off her mouth," she warned Charlie.

"Nay, woman! She likes the brass too much! She'd do naught to harm us!" And he couldn't be persuaded otherwise.

At the end of May, the Brion-Thompson experiments reached final fruition. It was time to place the boat before the public. But how? It was Brion who came up with the answer.

"Samuel Plimsoll's our man," he said. Charlie hadn't heard of the gentleman, but was quickly enlightened. "He's called 'the Sailor's Friend,'" Brion went on. "An M.P.—and England's expert on mercantile matters." It seemed that Plimsoll had recently secured a statute to outlaw coffin ships despite much opposition. He was a fierce West Countryman with definite ideas. Charlie agreed that Plimsoll must be interested in their invention.

"H'off to the House of Nobs then," he said, and sought out his Turkish petition.

They lobbied the Commons for weeks before they got to see Plimsoll. An appointment was arranged for a Friday afternoon, and they arrived at Westminster punctually—Brion bearing the model ship and plans, Charlie carrying an enormous fish tank of water, specially dyed blue to look like the sea. They were taken along corridors by a nervous secretary to Plimsoll's parliamentary office. The Sailor's Friend sat behind a desk littered with important bundles of paper, all neatly handwritten, the results of hard work.

"'Ere's the tank!" said Charlie, pushing the papers aside. Plimsoll frowned as the tank was heaved onto his desk, some of the water slopping over the brim. Brion stood beside Charlie and began to outline the scheme, but he was so excited and spoke so quickly that the effect of what he said sounded gibberish. Plimsoll grew impatient and his secretary more nervous so Charlie decided to intervene.

"What you want is a practical demo! Well, milord, kindly h'observe!" He snatched the model from Brion and plunged it into the tank. Having sunk the ship, he took the rubber tubes running out of its hull and put the ends in his mouth. He then took a deep breath—his biggest since his flight from Banner Cross—and blew until he went scarlet. Veins stood out on his brow, but nothing happened. He blew even harder. The water in the tank began to burble and the ship rocked a fraction. Still harder he blew, and the vessel rose a few inches. Then it suddenly shot forward, swift as a shark, and the sharp prow collided with the end of the tank. There followed a loud crack, the glass starred and broke, and the entire tank fell to pieces. Water rushed in a small tidal wave over Plimsoll's precious opinions, upsetting an inkwell to add to the deluge. Charlie leapt back in alarm, cannoning into Brion, who fell against a bookcase. More glass was shattered, books thundered to the floor, and the secretary uttered a small whimper.

"My papers!" roared Plimsoll.

"Oh, *what* a mess," said Charlie.

Plimsoll rounded on him. "Get out of my office, you idiot!" He picked up the boat and threw it at Charlie. "Get out! Go on! Get out!" He was almost in tears as he tried to gather up his ruined manuscripts.

His secretary seized Charlie's arm and backed away to the door. Brion followed, apologizing, tripping over his own feet, while Plimsoll continued to shout at them.

Outside in the passage, the secretary tendered some unfriendly advice: "Please go away, gentlemen, and *never* come back."

But Charlie had regained his dignity. " 'Twas an h'accident, sir! And I still have this. . . ." He produced his Turkish petition. "I'd like to present it!"

The secretary barely looked at the envelope. "Send it by post, whatever it is," he said. "But *not* to my master, understand?" And he abruptly turned back into Plimpsoll's office and shut the door.

Charlie was outraged and complained about his treatment all the way out of the Commons, his voice ringing loudly, and kept up the ranting into Westminster Place. " 'Tis bloody h'infamous!"

Brion was apprehensive lest they be arrested for public mischief and hurried Charlie along the Embankment.

"We'll sell out to the Heinies h'instead!" Charlie threatened.

Brion thought this might be treason; he urged his companion to be quiet.

"Why bloody should I? I'd done well to have rammed those pipes up yon bugger's breech!" Charlie's language grew coarser and Brion was deeply shocked by this new side to Mr. Thompson. He'd never seen such a tantrum; he became convinced that Mr. Thompson was unstable; and it occurred to Brion he'd do well to have their project patented in only one name—his name—as soon as possible.

III

Following the disaster at the Commons, tragedy struck. The pony Tommy caught a chill and died, despite much nursing, and Charlie moped for days. But he pulled himself together, to find a sudden coldness had developed toward himself on the part of Forsey Brion. The latter was still working on their invention, yet shunned Charlie both at Evelina Road and the pond, for which Brion had designed his own, rather clumsy, model ship. Charlie sensed treachery and acted accordingly. Before Brion could sneak off to the Patent Office and enter *his* design, he read of it in the *Patent Gazette*.

"No. 2635. Henry Forsey Brion and John Thompson, for an

invention for raising sunken vessels by the displacement of water within the vessels by air and gasses." Brion was furious and complained of Mr. Thompson's awkward ways to Sue when she called upon Alice.

"Oh, I know," agreed Sue, but cautiously. "Jack *is* temperamental."

Having lost Tommy, Charlie was being obliged to burgle on foot—during short summer nights when he had to move fast—and he wore himself down. He slept longer than usual in the day, quietly walking the Common in the afternoon, wondering what he might do to cure the atmosphere at Evelina Road. He still loved Hannah of course, but he'd grown to depend upon the carnal pleasures of Sue. Moreover, for the first time in his life, he was really living like a prosperous citizen. If his home broke up he'd lose everything.

Summer dragged on into autumn. Charlie tried to keep the peace within Number 5—but it was an uneasy peace. Sue had added laudanum and nicotine to her drinking, while Hannah watched and waited in silence. Willie, whose brain seemed affected by the hot weather, fell to talking to himself and behaving childishly.

Then storms ended the summer and nights came more quickly. Charlie shook off his indolence, the burglaries began again, and his victims complained to the press. After one very busy week, the last one in September, Charlie confided some news to Hannah: police patrols appeared to have been tripled. "Forest Hill and Penge are swarming with the buggers!" he said. "I'd best look toward Blackheath for a spell."

" 'Appen tha should pack it in!" Hannah advised.

But he didn't—he couldn't—in case Sue's presents had to stop and she left him. A short while ago, she had actually become peevish when he'd been unable to afford an astrakhan coat she wanted. So he mapped and robbed Blackheath in a series of raids, footslogging the railway night after night. And it was during this purge, when he was sleeping by day, that events exploded at home.

Sue went out after breakfast one day, leaving Hannah down in the kitchen. Willie saw Sue leave and followed her because he wanted to borrow some money for a paper kite he'd spied in a toy shop. Hannah had already refused him, Charlie was abed, so Willie looked toward Sue. He tracked her to the Hollydale Arms, watched her go into a Ladies' Bar, and hung about till she emerged at midday. She was tottering slightly and didn't notice Willie at her heels as she went into Kimberley Road. She was intent upon visiting Mrs. Long, whom she found cleaning the doorstep. The ladies began to converse and Willie moved closer, hiding behind a dung cart.

"And how's Mr. Thompson?" he heard Mrs. Long say.

Sue hiccupped and leaned against the front fence. "He's a brute to me!" she said tipsily. "But not as bad as his wife!"

Mrs. Long looked up from her kneeling position. "His what?" she asked with surprise.

Sue giggled. "Shouldn'a said that, should I?" She swayed to and fro and then shook her head. "But I don't care! I could tell you things to make your hair stand on end! Why, d'you know what Jack does . . . ?" But her voice trailed away as she spotted Willie peering over the cart. She went pale and chewed on her lip. Willie's hostile stare was unnerving and she quickly left the fence to walk unsteadily away. Mrs. Long looked after her, mystified.

Sue hadn't gone very far when Willie trotted up to her.

"Can'st tha give us sixpence, missus?"

Sue stopped. Willie was grinning at her; perhaps he hadn't heard what she'd said to Mrs. Long. "Yes, of course," she replied without thinking. Willie put out a grubby hand. Sue frowned. What did he want? Oh yes, sixpence; very well, she'd give the little oaf a shilling. She looked inside her bag and into her purse. But she hadn't a farthing—she'd spent all her money at the Hollydale. "Sorry, Willie," she smiled at the expectant boy. "No money, I'm afraid."

Willie's mouth fell. He looked cross. "Tha promised!" he said.

"I'm sorry." Sue showed him her purse.

Willie turned red. "Then why put thy mouth where thy money ain't?"

"I've *said* I'm sorry, you silly!"

It was the last word that did it. "Tha's playin' games with us 'cos ah'm gaumless!" Willie accused. He began to sob with rage —now he'd never get that kite. He didn't like Sue; his mother said she was wicked; and his mum was right. He drew back from Sue and ran headlong for home, bent on revenge. He'd tell Mother about the shabby trick he'd been played. *She*'d tell Charlie, and he'd chuck the bad woman out of the house. Then they'd be back together like the old days, and his mum would start smiling again.

"Come back! Willie, come back!" He heard Sue calling after him, but not even a king's ransom would stop him now.

Hannah was duly informed of everything her son had seen and heard. She gave Willie his sixpence and sent him off to the shops. Charlie was still asleep; he would be till five or six; and Hannah had no intention of waking him. She'd talk to Sue Bailey herself.

She waited in the hallway until Sue returned. Then Hannah pounced and hauled her physically into the parlor. She wore a frightening smile and a pair of Charlie's spectacles on the end of her nose, like a schoolmarm.

"Sit ye down!" she said, shoving Sue hard into a chair.

"Whatever Willie's told you is lies!" Sue protested at once.

"Willie's too stupid ta lie. Now, what was tha sayin' t'Mrs. Long?"

"And what right have *you* to question me?" Only alcohol gave Sue some courage.

"You'd better tell me than have Charlie flay it out of you," said Hannah.

Sue thought she was being threatened with a skinning. Her courage failed her, she began to tremble, and Hannah seized her advantage. "Ah'll tell thee summat, and ah'll say it but once," she said grimly. "You think Jack's just a thief—but he's summat else besides. He's Charlie Peace he is, wanted for shooting a man up North. He's in queer with ev'ry bobby in England. He's wanted for murder. Murder. Tha heard that. Should he get took, he'll nap the winder for sure. But 'appen he won't get took. He's safe at moment. 'Tis when he's unsafe he starts shooting guns. Hast thou noticed how many there be in this house? Aye, there's three in thy bed of sin alone! Now if Charlie—and damn the name Jack! —if Charlie gets ta hear of you and Mother Long, 'appen he'll shoot thee dead. I know, you see? You may know a fella named Jack Thompson, but *I* know Charlie Peace!"

It was the longest harangue Hannah had ever delivered, and she was justly rewarded. Sue Bailey fell off her chair. In her terrified state, she looked obese, even ugly. Now she knew why £100 was offered for her lover; she'd been sleeping with a murderer. That explained his fantastic disguises. "Lord have mercy," she whispered.

Hannah smiled. "Happen—but Charlie won't."

Sue commenced to weep. "He'd surely not murder *me?*"

"He surely would."

"But you won't tell him about Mrs. Long?" She grew frantic. "Please God, no! I'll go away, Mrs. Peace! I'll go now!"

Hannah laughed bitterly. She'd dearly love the woman gone from the house. But it was too late. "Nay, you're stoppin' here, lass—where I can watch thee. Whether I tells Charlie or not 'pends much on thysen. But you stay away from the Longs! You mind thy mouth! And lay off Tom Gin! Dost thou read me?"

Sue understood very well. Hannah gave her a handkerchief, on which she mopped her eyes and blew her nose. Hannah knew she had broken Sue Bailey. Evelina Road was now her spider's web, with Hannah the mate of the spider. Once it was safer, Hannah vowed to drive this soppy woman out with a broom. Until then, let her suffer all manner of terrors.

14

Rozzer Robinson's Rumble

Charlie was anxious to patch up his differences with Brion. He arranged a fine dinner party for Wednesday, October 9, inviting the Dribletts and the Brions. Hannah and Sue, who had become most submissive much to Hannah's satisfaction, polished the silverware while Charlie roasted a suckling pig.

The guests came at six. Brion was curious to discover the motive for his invitation, and Charlie quickly enlightened him. As soon as Brion arrived Charlie took him into his study, where a desk was strewn with various drawings and documents.

"You're still my partner, sir," he said, "and I propose to give thee fifty percent of *all* my h'inventions." These included his fireman's helm and carriage brush, with which Brion had had nothing to do. But both were commercially viable, so the other was happy to add his signature to an agreement, and some of his hostility toward Charlie dissolved.

Dinner was a prolonged affair, with much wine, and it finished with a treat from Morocco—a pineapple. Afterward, they all gathered in the parlor for music. While Charlie banjoed and fiddled, Sue sang and Hannah pounded the piano (she made every tune sound like a funeral dirge). The party ended at ten and the guests wended their way home under the influence of port. Nobody, save Hannah, had noticed how little their host had drunk this evening.

When everyone had gone and lamps were extinguished, Charlie strolled out into the garden. Hannah joined him on the lawn, where he was smoking his last "peace pipe."

"Very dark sky," he observed.

"Whereto?" she inquired.

"Blackheath—St. John's Park."

"Have a heed!"

Charlie turned to her. His wife looked monstrous in a long silk gown—shaped like a letter box from shoulder to ankle. He laughed and went into a potting shed, Hannah behind him. He changed his smoking jacket for an old tweed coat by the light of a spirit lamp he used for melting down plate. He went to his workbench, which had neat racks of tools, and filled his pockets with gimlets and bits and a small jemmy. Then followed a procedure more complex. From a drawer, he took out his pin-fire, checked the cylinders, and began to strap the weapon to his right wrist. Hannah helped him. He grinned at her, but she didn't return his smile.

"Too much port? Gassy tummy?" he teased. He was in a cheerful mood. He looked at other implements on the bench, pointing to a collapsible ladder. "Bloody useless!" he said. "I contrived it for porticoes, but the bugger dropped me on the railings one night! That sod Brion can 'ave it!" He picked up a clasp knife. "Now this h'ain't so bad. . . . Got it from an Ikey over Dulwich road—some sort o' shipwright, judging from the junk he had." And he slipped the knife inside his coat. Then he blew out the light and they left the shed.

A sliver of moon was showing, but the clouds were still very black. Hannah paused—full of misgivings. There was mischief in the air: visions of Sheffield, the Dysons, and coffins flitted through her mind. "Don't go, Charlie," she said quietly.

"Why, bless you, lass!" Charlie was touched by her worry; old Hannah seldom did more than lift an eyebrow when he "went out."

II

The spate of burglaries south of the Thames had put the police of R Division on their mettle. Tonight, no less than three officers patrolled St. John's Park—Constables Girling and Robinson, under the direction of Police Sergeant Brown. All three were bored; Girling—recently crossed in love—was also bad-tempered. It had rained around midnight, and the elms in the avenue dripped on the officers. They had different beats, but they would meet up every half-hour by the junction though there was nothing to report and it was dull work indeed.

Robinson went off down the small road behind St. John's Park at about two. He was at the back of some large detached houses. He could see over the fence into their gardens. It was quite chilly, and he longed for his tour of duty to end. There would be tea and biscuits back at Greenwich Station, and then glorious bed. Suddenly he stopped in his tracks. Was that a light flickering at the ground-floor window of Number 2 St. John's Park? He supposed the light came from the dining or drawing room. It now moved across a bay window. Robinson ran up the road to fetch Girling.

"I've rumbled onto something in Number Two," he said.

Together they ran back to the fence. The light had disappeared. Girling was about to grouse at his colleague when it came on again. Both officers just watched for a while, and were startled when their sergeant came up to them. He'd seen their huddle and now saw the light. Brown was quicker to act than his constables. "Right, we've got us some villainy!" he said. "You two stop 'ere while I 'op round the front. I'll knock up the 'ouse and frighten our friend. If he comes out the back, you 'ead 'im orf!" And he tiptoed away on size-ten boots.

Robinson and Girling weren't long in waiting before they heard bells ringing. One of the dining-room windows immediately slid up and a figure leapt into the garden.

"I'll get 'im!" said Robinson, vaulting the fence. Girling left him to hurry up the road lest their quarry tried to escape through the garden next door.

Robinson, meanwhile, headed straight for the man, who darted across the lawn, saw Robinson, and doubled back to the house. Robinson chased him, running as fast as he could, until he was only a few yards behind. Got you now! he thought, preparing to launch himself in a tackle. But the man stopped dead and turned. Robinson saw the wink of metal in his hand and checked himself. The man had a weapon.

"Keep back! Keep back—or, by God, I'll shoot!"

Robinson thought he was bluffing. Was it really a gun? "Don't be a mutt!" he said with a laugh. Three flashes followed in rapid succession, and bullets buzzed past his head. Bloody 'ell! he thought, lashing out with a fist. He expected to miss, but the blow caught the man full in the face. The gun blazed again and a fourth bullet whined over the constable's head, hitting a window with a tinkle of glass.

"You bugger, I'll settle you!" swore the man. He fired twice again. Robinson flung up an arm to protect himself, and a sharp pain tore through his tricep. I've been shot! he thought, and flung himself at his assailant in terror. He was far bigger than the gunman and bore him to the ground. A fierce fight ensued, with Robinson trying to get the gun, but hard as he tugged, it wouldn't come free, so he gripped the man's wrist and battered him about the head with his own revolver. "You bugger!" howled the man. "I'll settle you this time!" He writhed under Robinson, who drew his truncheon as an extra weapon. The man was on his back, trying to reach inside his coat. Robinson feared another pistol and turned the man over on his face, pinioning his neck with a knee and doubling up the gun hand. By now, Girling and Brown had arrived. The sergeant saw the gun and tried to strike it from the man's hand with his truncheon and, when this failed, bent down to tear it free from its fastenings. Their prisoner at last ceased to struggle. Handcuffs were snapped onto his wrists and he was hauled to his feet. Girling had his truncheon out at the ready.

"I've been shot," Robinson panted, one finger on the hole in his sleeve.

"I h'only did it to frighten!" the prisoner muttered, hopping about.

Brown steadied him. "You get back to the station," he told Robinson. He turned to Girling. "Search him!"

Girling was very rough in going through the prisoner's pockets. He kneed him several times until the man fell limp with a moan. Girling relaxed his grip for a second—deliberately. His prisoner tried to break away, just as he'd hoped, and he belabored the man with his truncheon until Brown shouted for him to stop. The prisoner slumped on the grass groaning piteously.

"You could 'ave snuffed 'im!" Brown accused Girling.

"So what, Sarge? 'E nearly did for Ted, didn't 'e?"

But Brown decided to take control himself. Young bobbies like Girling got silly when one of their number was injured—and villains sometimes got killed. Understandable, of course, but it got politicians excited. "Come on, you!" he said to the prisoner. He helped him up and manacled him to his own wrist.

"I h'only shot to frighten," the man said again, and was led shuffling away.

At Greenwich Police Station, they stripped Charlie naked and examined his bruised body and clothing. Sergeant Brown and

Inspectors Body and Donney were present. They were curious about the old scars on that muscular frame, as well as the whiteness of skin when compared with the prisoner's face.

Brown was especially interested in a clasp knife they had found in his jacket. " 'Moss Isaacs, Herne Hill, Dulwich,' " he quoted from the handle's inscription. "That you?"

No reply.

"What's your name then?" asked Body.

"Find out!"

"We will. . . . Where d'ye live?"

"Go ta 'Alifax!"

"Halifax? Don't give us that one! C'mon, where you from?"

No reply.

So Charlie was ordered to dress and formally charged with attempted murder, burglary, and other offenses. He was then fed boiled eggs and locked up. He ate one egg, despite his battered face, and people came to peer at him through the cell bars. "Is he a Negro?" asked a voice. "No, he's from Halifax," answered another. Robinson came also, his arm in a sling, cheerful now because his friends had called him a hero. Even Charlie brightened when he saw him.

"How's thy h'arm, young fella?"

"None the better for you!"

Charlie heaved himself off his straw palliasse and came up to the bars. "I'm sorry," he mumbled. "May God forgive us what I've done. I nivver h'intended to slay thee!"

"So you say now!"

Charlie shook his head sorrowfully. "God, what a pickle . . . But why did thy colleague lamm us so hard?" He touched his face gingerly. " 'Twas no need for that—I suffer a fistula!"

Robinson smiled. His catch certainly looked an old fellow, but he hadn't arrested a villain so tough in eight years of service. "You're a one!" he said.

At nine, Charlie was taken before the magistrate for a formal remand into custody. His appearance was so decrepit that there was a buzz in court when the police outlined the facts of his arrest.

"And he refuses to name himself," Brown told the Bench.

The magistrate got around that problem by immediately allocating the prisoner a solicitor, Mr. Beard, who was to be paid initially out of police court funds, though they were slim.

Beard was local and trustworthy—a scruffy lawyer in a frock coat, the collar of which was dusty with dandruff from his white balding head. Beard preferred matrimonials to crime, but he saw Charlie back in his cell after the hearing.

"I must have your name," he insisted. "At the moment you've simply been recorded as 'X—of negro-type.'"

Charlie tried to laugh, but his cracked lips bled. "John Ward," he said.

Beard wrote the name down, together with some preliminary instructions, on the reverse of the charge sheet. His new client said he'd been poaching in Blackheath—after pigeons, at two in the morning, with a revolver—which Beard didn't believe.

"That'll do," he interrupted the story. "I'll come and see you again at Newgate."

"Newgate!" cried Charlie. "That's an 'orrible place. I'm not going there! I shall complain!"

Alone in his dungeon, Charlie thought as deeply as his aching permitted. Girling's handiwork had taken its toll, but Charlie still had most of his wits about him. He'd already examined the cell for means of escape, but had found that impossible. Greenwich was all brick and iron as opposed to a drystone Yorkshire lock-up. So he next thought about Hannah. He must get word to her as quickly as possible. But how—without divulging his true identity? The answer seemed unattainable till dinner time, then Charlie's good fortune came with an unpalatable meal. An inebriate—undergoing a day's detention working in the cells—served him bread and stew.

"H'imagine the malt ten shillen could buy!" Charlie tempted him.

The drunk stuck a blue nose through the bars. " 'Alf a quid, mister?"

Charlie approached him. The man stank like a brewery. "Go to Five East Terrace, h'Evelina Road, Peckham—and ask for Hannah. Tell her to cut quick sticks. Got it? She'll pay thee thy money."

The drunk was a trusting soul and short of cash. He nodded eagerly, promised to go when they released him at four, and ambled off back to the charge room. Charlie sat on a stool and tried to eat, but his jaw muscles had swollen and he pushed his plate aside. Then he returned to his bunk and closed his eyes. Would the drunk keep his word or inform the police of his mission? Charlie thought the former—half a sovereign was too much to lose. He turned his thoughts to himself; he was now certainly astride a losing streak. He'd have to think up some defense to the charges for his lawyer. He cursed Robinson's courage. Bloody bobby, he should have shot him dead with the first round instead of trying to scare him away.

15

Traitress Sue

Panic followed the delivery of Charlie's message to Hannah. She and Willie wasted no time, packing up as much as they could carry and ordering a cab to take them to the station, intending to seek refuge in Yorkshire. But Sue Bailey caught them on her return from the Hollydale, just moments before their departure.

"What's happening? Where's Jack?" she asked in alarm.

"He got took!" Hannah said brusquely, helping Willie load a box into the hansom.

It took a moment for Sue to appreciate Hannah's meaning, then she had hysterics. "What's to become of me?" she cried, wringing her hands.

"Tha's big enuff ta fend for thysen," said Hannah.

"But where are you going? Can I come too?" begged Sue.

" 'Appen not!" was Hannah's reply, and that was that.

Once Hannah and Willie had gone, Sue wandered around Number 5, trying to pull herself together. She couldn't stay here, she reasoned, but where could she go? She had the friendly Dribletts and Longs—even the Brions—perhaps they would take her in. Her final choice fell upon Brion, Jack's co-inventor, and she hurried round to Phillips Road, rehearsing the role she would play. Her loud knocking brought Forsey Brion to the door, just as he and Alice were about to have dinner.

"Let me in, for pity's sake!" Sue cried. "I've been betrayed!" And she executed a passable swoon.

"Well, I'll be licked," said Brion, supporting her into the front room, where Alice hopped about like a hen while Brion fetched brandy for Sue.

"He's deserted me," Sue said after a long gulp of liquor. "He's a bigamist! He was already married to that Hannah Ward!"

Alice started to giggle and Brion shushed her. "When did this happen?" he asked, amazed. His wife was less surprised—she reckoned Sue's drinking had driven Mr. Thompson away.

"They all upped and left at teatime," Sue lied. "They waited until I was out, and then tricked me!"

"Where they bound for?" asked Brion.

Sue shook her head, finished her brandy, and held out the glass for a refill. Brion filled the glass with a frown. He was puzzled by Mr. Thompson's sudden leaving, but he knew Thompson was extremely erratic. Then Brion remembered their mutual invention and grew more concerned. Supposing Thompson had made off with the patent, intent upon completing and selling the project all for himself? Such things did happen in the field of inventions. That agreement last night might have been part of the ruse —designed to allay Brion's suspicions. The more Brion thought of it, the more sure he was that it was he who'd been tricked. He handed Sue her fresh glass.

"You must stay with us, Mrs. Thompson," he said, much to Alice's surprise. "Stay as long as you like." He wanted Sue in his home; she might be the victim of bigamy, but control over even a bogus wife was better than nothing. Thompson might contact her and reveal his whereabouts. "We shall get to the bottom of this," he assured her. "I believe we've all been had by a bounder!"

Sue expressed her thanks and settled down to her brandy. So far so good.

Days passed, but there was no sign of the occupants of Number

5. Sue visited the house often—taking away odd items of value until she'd accumulated quite a nice little nest egg. She also found paper money under a mattress, which she rapidly pocketed, but she remained very apprehensive as to what lay over the horizon.

Then on a Wednesday, Forsey Brion appeared at breakfast carrying a letter in front of him as if it was contaminated.

"What's that?" asked Alice.

"Came in the post. Addressed to me, but doesn't make sense." He held up the letter and Sue started when she saw it was headed NEWGATE PRISON. Brion sat down, read the missive to himself and then some of its contents aloud. " 'My dear sir, Mr. Brion. I don't know how to write to you. I'm nearly mad to think I've got into this fearful mess, all with giving myself up to drinking. My family have broken up and gone I don't know where. I beg you to come and see me' . . ." He paused. "Then it's signed 'John Ward' and says I can call any weekday and 'inquire for John Ward for trial.' What can it mean?"

Alice shrugged, but Sue knew exactly what the letter meant—Charles Peace had written from Newgate and was asking Brion to visit him. She avoided looking at Brion, but her face had flushed crimson.

"Who's John Ward?" asked Alice.

"Who indeed!" said her husband.

"Will you see him?" Alice asked.

Brion made no reply. He put the letter carefully back into its envelope and stirred his tea thoughtfully. Odd things were happening of late, he reflected. Well, he'd go to Newgate—today—and meet the author of this mysterious epistle: maybe "John Ward" had something of import to say. . . . "I'll go this morning," he said, and buttered himself a muffin.

II

Charlie had no muffins at Newgate. That grim prison lived up to the stories he'd heard. Great granite walls enclosed a warren of small, airless cells, each equipped with a bed, prie-dieu, and Bible. The prison was a man-made echo chamber, filled with the sounds of rattling keys and clanging doors. The warders were noisy and brisk while their charges only clanked chains and shuffled. Some—like Charlie—awaited their trials in the adjoining Central Criminal Court; others were already condemned to tread Dead Man's Walk to the scaffold; total despair prevailed everywhere.

But Charlie hadn't abandoned all hope. Beard had called, and they'd discussed his case from the worst viewpoint.

"I'll get the bolt for the burglary," Charlie accepted. "A twelve-stretch at least." He'd hesitated. "Unless they bellowse us?"

But Beard had explained that transportation was no longer in vogue—the colonies didn't want England's scum anymore. "That leaves the main charge," he'd added unhappily. Both men were silent—both knew a conviction for attempted murder carried a maximum of life imprisonment. And life meant life—"For the rest of your natural life" went the judge's formula. No ticket of leave was available; a man rotted in jail till he actually died. Charlie ground his teeth at the prospect.

" 'Appen we'll have to fight that bill," he'd told Beard.

The solicitor had nodded. Contest the charge on the basis of accident. His client insisted that he hadn't intended to kill Robinson, though five shots had been fired. "You'll need a good barrister," he'd informed Charlie. "Have you money?"

Charlie said he had. He didn't want a bad "dock-brief" barrister. "Get us summat better than an h'Old Bailey rope-walker," he'd urged Beard. "I'll dig up the brass."

"I'll instruct Mr. Williams," Beard had promised, thinking of a name among the ranks of competent counsel.

When Beard went, Charlie's thoughts had been of cash. He had at least fifty pounds back in Peckham, together with furniture to raise more. But he was still John Ward to Beard and the prison authorities. What he needed was an outside contact to lay hands on his money. Hannah had gone—he hoped—and Sue should be kept out of the affair for her own good. He'd wracked his brains for someone to tell, and his choice had fallen upon Brion. He'd written Brion a letter, couched in strange terms to confuse censorship. He'd hoped Brion would respond and be trustworthy because of their recent agreement.

"H'officer, come quick, I'm dying!" he'd begun shouting through the Judas hole, and he'd kept up the racket until a warder had come. Paper and pencil had been provided, and the letter to Brion had been carried off to the Governor. Charlie had wondered how Brion would react to find his old co-inventor in prison.

Brion duly arrived at Newgate and rang the big bell. As soon as he'd declared himself, he was taken before the Governor and Chief Warder Mapleson. Brion denied all knowledge of a "John Ward," so he was taken to the Monkey Cage to confront him. In this grated visiting room sat Charlie, in his own clothes, the jacket torn after his struggle with Robinson, and streaked with grime and dried mud. Charlie's tan had also faded over the last few days, and for a second Brion didn't recognize him. When he did, he let out a cry of surprise.

"Know him, sir?" asked Mapleson.

"But it's Jack Thompson!"

"Sadly mortified," mumbled Charlie, coming to his feet.

"But what is he doing here?" Brion looked at the Governor.

"He shot a police officer," the latter replied.

"A cruel h'accusation," said Charlie. "Let us h'explain, sirs . . . I'd been h'imbibing in a public house, shame on me, and I hopped into someone's garden for a quick jimmy-widdle, when low and behold, I was suddenly set upon. I didn't know 'twas a bobby! I thought I was being h'attacked by a footpad!"

"He had a pistol," the Governor commented.

"Of course I did!" Charlie snapped. "I allus carry a pop nowadays in case some Rusky spy tries to steal our h'invention! Mr. Brion, tell 'em about our h'invention! Tell 'em I'm not a housebreaker!"

But Brion didn't know what to tell anybody. His confusion was absolute. The Governor came to his rescue. "Mr. Brion, I suggest you get in touch with the Greenwich Police, and give them full particulars of what you know about this man."

Brion nodded absentmindedly. He was desperate to get back to reality and hurriedly turned to leave.

"Mr. Brion! In God's name hear us out!" Charlie called to him.

But Brion ignored this entreaty; and Chief Warder Mapleson grinned at the Governor; the meeting of these two strange men had served to enliven an otherwise routine prison day.

Inspectors Body and Donney, with a swarm of constables, moved swiftly on Brion's information. They raided 5 East Terrace next day on a warrant, leaving its contents, which varied from revolvers to chamber pots, in orderly messes. Most of the property was unidentifiable, but Body discovered one item of interest—a silver pencil case, celebrating the seventeenth birthday of a "Miss J. A. Peace." Body read the poem tooled on the lid.

"Very touching," he said. "Dirty dog, that Ward, stealing from a young lady." He put it away in his gladstone bag and sought out Donney in the garden sheds.

"Bloomin' animals everywhere!" said his colleague. "What a pong! We'll have to shift them off to some home!" The birds and beasts were removed from the sheds and placed squawking in the Black Maria.

"What now?" Body asked Donney, the search over.

"See Mrs. Sue Thompson at Brion's. Shake the ghost into her until she squeals."

Brion had promised to have Sue available at lunchtime. He kept her at his house with divers excuses without hinting at a visit from the police. This had been Body's idea, and the inspectors' arrival shook Sue to the core—as they had hoped it would.

"A serious word with you, ma'am," Body said to her in Brion's parlor. "We're minded to charge you as an accomplice to larceny. We know all about Thompson, you see. We found burglarous tools and the proceeds of theft at your house. As his wife, you were aware of his trade?"

Sweat formed through the powder on Sue's upper lip. "I wasn't! And I'm *not* his wife!"

"Yes, you are," Brion said fiercely.

Sue rounded on him. "That's what you think . . . But I'm not! My name's Bailey—I just lived with him!"

"In sin, was it?" said Donney.

"Yes—yes! You see, Hannah was his real wife!"

The Ward woman, thought Donney. "And where is she now?"

"Sheffield, I think—Jack said he was from there!"

Body nudged Donney. "Ward said he was from Halifax."

"No, he's from Hull!" said Sue. She moistened her lips and tasted salty cosmetics. She'd risk telling the truth, she decided. "And his *real* name's Charles Peace."

Body and Donney looked at each other. The former opened his gladstone and took out the pencil case. "This speaks of Peace," he murmured to Donney.

"Hmm!" said the other. "Peace is it! Then what do we call the fellow on the file?" They had to have a name on the file before it was sent up to the Treasury Solicitor. "Shall we stick with Ward?"

"Or Thompson," suggested Brion.

"I tell you he's Charles Peace!" said Sue.

Both inspectors would have dearly liked to charge her, but it now looked as if she could be an important witness. "What else can you tell us?" Body asked.

Sue hesitated. She feared arrest, but she needn't fear Charlie anymore: he was safe at Newgate, he'd pulled the house over all their heads by his misdoings. Nor could Hannah get at her from Sheffield. *And* there was that £100 reward. . . .

"Go on, miss," Donney urged. "No use shielding the likes of *him* for the sake of sentiment."

"I'm not the sentimental sort!" she said haughtily. "He's wanted for murder in Yorkshire, that much I do know! I'd have gone to the authorities before, only I was threatened. I've been living these last weeks in mortal terror!" She shrugged as if her broad shoulders were relieved of a great weight. Ignoring Brion's look of disbelief, she spoke on. "Hannah said he'd once shot a man—that he'd shoot me too, if I ever breathed a word. He himself told me there was a reward for his capture."

Brion was quick off the mark. "A reward? How much?"

Sue turned to him; she didn't like the gleam in his eyes. "One hundred pounds," she said unwillingly.

"Good God! Whom did he shoot?"

"I don't know."

"Then we must find out!" Brion was beside himself. "It's of paramount importance that we know!" He reasoned that, since he had led the police to Peckham, any reward in the offing was his. "I'm proud to think we've brought him to justice!" he told Body.

Body shook his head. The Ward case was growing out of all

proportion; he wanted written statements from Brion and Sue. He looked at them in turn: Brion and Sue facing each other like a couple of toms over a dustbin. Body anticipated a good deal of conflict between the two claimants for any reward.

III

Montagu Williams, a man in his forties who aspired to becoming a Metropolitan Magistrate, had little time for either his client or specious defenses. He was briefed following Charlie's committal to the Old Bailey from Greenwich, visiting him at Newgate. He was quick to reject any denial of guilt of burglary; stolen property had been recovered from Charlie's person, more being stacked up in the house at St. John's Park ready for removal. He also turned down Charlie's tales of night poaching, a bursting bladder, and Russian spies. They had to concentrate upon the main charge, he said, all the others were trivial in comparison.

"Besides," Williams added, "we don't want to antagonize Hawkins by flanneling."

The name of this judge caused Charlie to think of his menagerie. He turned to Beard. "Bugger 'Awkins, what's become of my h'animals?"

"The police have them."

Charlie grunted. "Well, I hopes they treat 'em kindly!"

But he began to worry less about his livestock and more about himself on November 19, the following Monday. His trial was heard in Court One—a gloomy chamber, heavily columned, and very stuffy. Mr. Justice Hawkins had an aversion to open windows. His court was normally reserved for capital cases, but not only was Charlie reserved for Hawkins, he was already something of a cause célèbre. He was arraigned at ten o'clock as both John Ward and Charles Peace, which did little to ease his mind, and sat between two big warders in the massive dock, trying to look old and penitent. His trial lasted less than a working day, and, try as he did, Williams failed to shake the evidence of Robinson, Girling, and Brown. After awhile, Williams seemed to give up any detailed cross-examination, upset by Hawkins's impatient pencil tapping, and Charlie grew restless.

"Bloody rotten h'advocate I got!" he commented to his warders.

They adjourned for different kinds of lunch: Hawkins had venison, and Charlie a plate of "Bum-Charter"—prison bread steeped in gravy.

At one o'clock, they reassembled. The Crown's case was quickly finished, and the law said Charlie couldn't go into the witness box, so Williams made a speech to a sour-faced jury. He placed all blame for his client's unhappy position on that troublesome pin-fire revolver.

"We know pistols have a propensity to misfire," he said. "Might not Ward, engaged as he was in a tangle with Robinson, have tugged the trigger inadvertently?"

"What, five times!" Hawkins interrupted.

Williams frowned, as did Charlie, but was determined to continue. "By 'inadvertently,' members of the jury, I mean, of course, 'without advert' "—Williams was floundering—"But what do I mean then by 'advert'?"

"Buggered if I know," Charlie muttered.

Charlie was hoping Hawkins might pity him and think his crime out of character, but had heard it said this judge was quite merciless.

When Williams had finished his confusing address, Hawkins commenced his summing up. He sounded bored as he reminded the jury of the facts. Nor did he appear to think much of Williams's submissions with regard to the gun. Indeed, he gave a little demonstration up on the Bench for the jury's benefit—

cocking and releasing the hammer as if that required superhuman effort, belittling the defense of accident.

"Yon gander's got h'arthritics!" Charlie shouted. "This will nivver do!"

But Hawkins either didn't hear or didn't care; he was hypnotizing the jury in soothing tones. "Why was this deadly weapon strapped to the prisoner's wrist? Why did he tell Robinson, 'I'll settle you this time'? Why did he fire a shot directly at Robinson's head? Aren't these the factors that point to his guilt or innocence?"

It was a quick summing up—too quick, thought Charlie—but, having repeated something about a "burden of proof," Hawkins finished by asking the jurymen if they seriously desired to retire. Twelve stern faces shook their heads. They talked among themselves for about three minutes—two of which involved the appointment of a foreman—and told the court their verdict.

"Guilty!"

Charlie was brought immediately to his feet for judgment. He was about to protest, but the clerk of arraigns began asking him whether he had anything to say before sentence. Charlie looked around. Everyone in court seemed to be expecting him to speak —even Hawkins, who was regarding him with hooded eyes. Charlie resolved to make a moving appeal.

"Yes, I've this to say, milord!" he began strongly. "I've not been fairly dealt with! If I'd h'intended to kill, I could easily have done it! I didn't fire five shots—only four! If your lordship wilt look at yon pistol, tha'll see it goes h'off easily! I really didn't know 'twas loaded!" He stopped; he realized he was contradicting the evidence; and Hawkins was shaking his head. So he adopted a plea stacked with religion. "I hope, milord, you'll have mercy upon me! I'm so base and bad I'm neither fit to live nor die! I've disgraced mysen; I've disgraced my friends! I'm not fit to live among mankind—nor h'am I fit to meet my Maker!" His voice broke, he hung his head, he banged his hands on the dock rail. He tried to weep, but tears refused to come, so he found his voice again. "They've painted my case blacker than what it really is! I hope tha'll take that h'into consideration, and not pass a sentence that'll have us die in prison? There, I'll have no chance to prepare to meet my God! Give us a chance to regain my freedom?" He sank to his knees, but was forced to get up again because he couldn't see over the dock. He found Hawkins smiling. How dare he smile. . . . "Even *you*, milord, dost h'expect mercy at the hands of your Great and Merciful God!" he added. "Oh, milord, have mercy upon a miserable man! I'll try to become a good 'un! Good enuff to meet my God—my Great Judge —and receive the Great Reward at His Hands for True Repentance!" He paused to catch his breath. "I'll say no more, milord, but have mercy upon us!"

This tirade was received in utter silence. Charlie lay slumped across the dock rail, but one brown eye roamed the courtroom to study others' reactions. Many looked startled; most embarrassed. Then spoke Hawkins's thin voice.

"Let him stand up properly!"

Charlie was supported by the warders. The void between dock and Bench seemed narrower, Hawkins's features nearer, a face younger than Charlie had supposed—and rather like one of his parrots.

"John Ward," said the judge. "The jury have found you guilty of having fired this pistol five times at a constable with intent to murder him. You are an accomplished burglar—armed in a manner that shows you were determined to resort to foul means. Thank God, the constable's life was spared. I should fail in my public duty if I did not pass the extreme sentence—which is, that you be kept in penal servitude for the rest of your natural life. Take him down!"

Hands took Charlie's elbows, guiding him out of the dock and down narrow steps to the casemates below. His case was over and, out of the theater, he quickly recovered.

"A lifer! 'Tis scandalous! There'll be a petition!" he promised his jailers.

IV

Now Charlie had other worries. The use of his name in the indictment meant that all were fully aware of his true identity— that Sue or someone had talked—and that Hannah stood at risk. Montagu Williams he never saw again, but he raised the subject of Hannah with Beard.

"What's h'up North?" he demanded.

"I can't say," his solicitor replied. Nor did he know; he was given to understand that the Metropolitan Police had certainly been in touch with Sheffield, but no more. He expressed the desire to be released as Charlie's solicitor, but undertook to find a suitable alternative.

"Forsake me, would you?" Charlie grumbled, but he dispensed with his services with no further comment since he was highly dissatisfied with his lawyer's recent efforts on his behalf.

Time passed, but Charlie was not removed from Newgate. He'd anticipated his rapid incarceration at either Pentonville or some other "long-term" prison. Instead, he was kept in his same old cell and continued to wear the clothes in which he was arrested. Something was afoot, and he predicted low trickery. Then one chilly morning his fears were justified to the full.

The Governor and Mapleson came to his cell at ten. Charlie was told to mind his mouth and follow them.

"Whitherto?" he demanded, but received no reply. Serious and silent, the Governor's contingent took him out of the central wing into a small enclosed yard. Prisoners were already exercising around the high-walled perimeter, some chained, the majority wearing the "broad-arrow" convict uniform. Charlie was directed to join the line. This he found suspicious as he was usually exercised alone, as a high-security risk, after teatime. The Governor moved away to a private door in the far corner. While Charlie mingled with the shuffling band, this door opened to admit five people, who stood by the Governor. Three wore a police mackintosh cape, but two looked odd in plain clothes—a youngish man and a middle-aged woman. The sight of a female brought the convict line to a halt.

"And stay still! No moving—talking—anything!" commanded Mapleson's voice.

Charlie blinked at the newcomers, trying to focus. He squinted, so hard did he look. Then he recognized the civilians—the man in the boater and that woman he'd accosted on Ecclesall Road long ago. Fear tore at his bowels. He was on an identification parade, and the slippery devils hadn't warned him. But he should have guessed. . . . He studied the three policemen. Who were they? One seemed vaguely familiar, but not the others. They'd finished talking to the Governor and began to approach the U of prisoners. Charlie was in the middle of the right-hand tongue— those near him were taller, darker, fairer, younger, and bore no resemblance to him. He tried to hide by stepping back, but he couldn't disappear into a thick stone wall, and he only made himself all the more obvious by breaking the line.

The woman came first, flanked by the unknown policemen. Behind her marched the constable with the homey face, the laborer from the Winter Fair bringing up the rear. Charlie hunched his shoulders, pulled up his collar, and contorted his features. His jaw cracked with the effort; he bared his teeth, screwed up his eyes, and flared his nostrils. He still had some dye on his face and hoped this would confuse. But it didn't. Mrs. Sarah Colgreaves of Dobbin Hill, Ecclesall, stopped and pointed him out to her escorts. She was quickly hurried off, and her position taken up by the constable.

"Good morning, Peace!" he said, very affable.

The laborer—a Charles Brassington—was next. He seemed more uncertain than the others, but then he nodded to the Governor, who looked relieved and led him away. The witnesses passed through the corner door and the parade was over. Mapleson beckoned for Charlie to leave the line and join him in the center of the yard.

"What was that all h'about?" Charlie asked him.

"Seems you're a popular man, Peace."

"Ward, sir! My name is Ward!"

The chief warder stared at him. Names meant very little to Mapleson; he far preferred numbers. "Then on your way, Ward," he said, roughly pushing Charlie toward Central Wing and the cells.

Charlie realized it was futile to continue pretending he was anyone other than himself. That night, in his bed, he decided to abandon all such pretext. Two people, specters from Banner Cross, had been sent down from Sheffield to identify him. Neither had witnessed Dyson's death, but Charlie couldn't tell what they might say. He knew that only Kate Dyson had been upon the dread scene. And she'd long since departed for America. Without her—and the Crown would have to do without her—what was the case against him? Only his presence at Ecclesall on the relevant night. Why, she herself might have done the actual shooting! So he determined to calumniate the woman as much as possible. He'd cast aspersions she could never deny. Doubts would be raised as to his own culpability.

He rang the bell and asked for paper and pen—ink, because of the vital nature of his letter and its recipient. His request was granted, and he used the shelf of the prie-dieu as a desk. He wrote in a studied illiterate hand, smiling at some of his spelling, and he addressed the letter to "the Right Honerbul, Secretary of State." He said Kate Dyson had "as now hepstonded to amarcketer," that she'd never been Dyson's wedded wife, but Charlie's lover, in which respect she'd written him a "greate" number of "noates." These, together with some "Porthrates" must be in the hands of the police. He urged that they not be destroyed. He added that Kate Dyson had "tracten" the life of her husband and that Dyson, in turn, had "tracten" both her life and Charlie's—with a "Paire of Pistels."

The letter was sanded and Charlie sat back, feeling better. He suffered no qualms about the lies in the letter: Kate Dyson must have told as many at her husband's inquest. If the police still had her notes and the photographs, a long shadow would be thrown across the Banner Cross incident. The Home Secretary would order a thorough inquiry into the turbid background of the case. Some folk in Darnall would confirm the true relationship of himself and Kate Dyson. An old triangle of husband, wife, and lover would be born. And if the authorities became satisfied that Mrs. Dyson had lied at the inquest, where could they expect to find the truth about anything? The Crown's dubitation *must* resolve in his favor.

"I feel mentally h'enfranchised!" he told the warder who monitored his letter.

16

Little White Lies

When the Sheffield *Independent* announced Hannah's arrest, the Reverend Littlewood took himself straight into Sheffield. He wasn't a man to interfere with law and order, but he cornered Bradbury in his office at Water Lane Station.

"Monstrous!" he cried, looking decidedly dangerous. "This smacks of persecution!" The inspector happened to agree, and calmly bade the vicar be seated. He'd heard of Littlewood from Pearson, and he warmed to the large man. "None of my doing, sir," he explained. "A Metropolitan officer came up to charge her. But her warrant was backed for bail and she's been released, care of her daughter, till her case comes up in the New Year."

"Poor woman," said Littlewood quietly. "Isn't it sufficient they've at last caught her man?"

Bradbury nodded. His own chief constable wouldn't have arrested her—nor would any West Riding jury convict the wife of a thief for receiving. "She'll get off," he said optimistically, although he wasn't so sure about a jury of Southerners.

"Who put London onto her?" Littlewood asked.

Bradbury gave a short laugh. "Ah, there's some treachery! A woman calling herself Bailey—one of Peace's paramours. 'Tis said she's after the reward." The papers had already named her "Traitress Sue" and, since his identification, more had been written about Peace than any other criminal Bradbury could recall. " 'Twas her who put the finger on Peace," he added.

"And what of him? Has he been charged?"

"Not yet. I'm due at Pentonville Prison tomorrow."

"You'll charge him even without Mrs. Dyson?" Littlewood sounded surprised.

"*With* her, I hope. But we've got to get her back from the States."

"You're going to America!" Littlewood made it seem like a trip to the moon.

Bradbury shook his head. "Not I, sir." That was another man's brother. "Our Inspector Walsh leaves for New York come Christmastide. 'Tis up to him to persuade her." Bradbury had been honest with Chief Constable Jackson, expressing his private opinion of Kate Dyson. His chief had deemed it wiser to send the younger Irishman in his stead. And Bradbury had advised Walsh to hold on hard to his britches.

"And do you think she'll return?" Littlewood asked.

"No. . . . But we're under pressure to get her. . . . Peace has set the Home Office buzzing." Bradbury shouted through the open door of his office for a pot of police station tea. He knew something of Littlewood's association with Charlie and was curious. "Off the record, sir, how well did you know Charlie Peace?"

Littlewood decided he trusted the inspector, and so told him some of the history of their relationship, including the better aspects of Charlie's character. When he had finished, Bradbury was silent for a while, digesting the tale over highly stewed tea. Then he spoke. "This bird he gave you, sir. . . . D'you think I might look at it?" Littlewood's description of the mechanical toy rang a belfry of bells.

A look of horror crossed Littlewood's face. "You don't think it's stolen?"

Bradbury was sure it was—but he saw no cause to alarm the good vicar. "Happen not, sir. . . . But anything's possible with Peace. . . ."

Charlie was allocated to "the Vile" pending developments in Yorkshire. Pentonville was aptly nicknamed: it was one of the grimmest prisons in England. Built as a "model" in 1840, it embodied the "Silent System." Strict separation was enforced among the inmates, with "industrial employment and moral training forever under the Eyes of the Lord"—such as picking oakum, stitching mailbags, or turning a pointless crank in solitary. Here a felon might reflect upon his debt to society undisturbed and for the remainder of his days. Suicide and insanity were common.

But Charlie was luckier. As a potential escapee, if not meat for the gallows, the authorities confined him to a large cell and watched him vigilantly. He was fed infirmary food, given writing materials, and permitted visits. One of the first was from Inspector Donney of Greenwich.

"We've arrested your missus," said the officer.

"You wicked buggers! Where is she?"

"Out on her own recognizance."

Charlie sighed with relief; the thought of Hannah in a London jail would have broken him. He thought of something else. "How much to see her free, sir?"

"I didn't hear that, Ward."

"Then why're you here?"

"We want to know where you fence your booty." R Division was determined to find Charlie's contacts. Sue Bailey had suggested a few likely places—including Petticoat Lane—but to no avail. "You've nothing to lose by telling us."

"Aye, but what 'ave us to gain? Wilt thou drop all charges against my 'Annah?"

"I can make no bargains." This was true—the assistant commissioner had made that plain.

"Then I'll tell thee nowt!"

"But I could speak up for your wife at her trial," Donney hinted.

Charlie studied him. No, he didn't trust this bobby, he decided; he had the face of a welcher.

"Try the Jews," he suggested.

"We have. Whitchapel's never heard of you."

"Try Rotterdam."

"*Where?* You're having me on! How did you get the stuff across!"

"By h'unterwasser vessel.... Ask Brion.... He helped h'invent it." Charlie started to laugh.

But Donney wasn't amused. "Damn your games, Ward! You'll not hear from me again!"

"But thy commissioner will, sir. You mark my words!"

Donney felt tempted to mark more than Charlie's words. He stormed out of Pentonville, none the wiser and bitterly disappointed.

That afternoon, Charlie played cards with his warders, cheating when he could, and regaling them with stories. He was thus engaged when a key grated in the cell door. Chief Warder Crosgrove, six-foot-two and fifteen stone, made his first grand entry.

"Uppity-up!" Crosgrove had parade-ground lungs and everyone leapt to attention, even Charlie. Behind Crosgrove appeared a smaller man in a reefer jacket of some age. "This is Inspector Bradbury!" Crosgrove bellowed. "He's 'ere to charge you with 'omicide!"

Thus Bradbury and Charlie came face to face for the first time. The inspector drew a flimsy sheet of paper from inside his coat. "Charles Frederick Peace? I formally charge you with the willful murder of Arthur Dyson, at Sheffield, on the night of November 29, 1876." He rattled off the words and put away the paper. "You needn't say owt, but if you do, 'twill be writ down and given in evidence."

Charlie followed his advice and said nothing. Bradbury was

staring at him curiously—at his scrunchy features, whitish hair, and crooked frame.

"Have you got a good lawyer?" he asked.

Charlie shook his head.

"Then' get Clegg of Sheffield. He's more gaum than most." Bradbury nodded to Charlie and turned to the chief. "Any problems?"

"Not in *my* happy prison! *My* lags tow the line!"

Looking at Crosgrove, Bradbury was sure that they did. He gave Charlie a final glance and left the cell, Crosgrove shouting for the occupants to "Stand easy!" before slamming the door.

"Who in 'ell was that?" Charlie asked his frightened warders.

" 'The Corncrake,' " he was told. "The only thing in the Vile that ain't silent!"

Charlie smiled. But he had work to do. He left the warders to their cards, and wrote two letters—the first to the Commissioner of Police, as he'd promised Donney. It was a long letter in his worst hand, declaring Hannah's innocence of his own past misdeeds. He said that Sue Bailey was more guilty a party, confident that she'd not be harmed since she'd obviously become an informant. His second letter was to Hannah herself, at Janey's address in Darnall. It was a simple message, telling her that he was still alive, but urging her to contact this Mr. Clegg of Sheffield, begging her to raise funds to meet his legal costs. Charlie was grateful to the mysterious Inspector Bradbury for the lawyer's name, and found it odd that he should have been given help by a total stranger.

II

Inspector Tom Walsh, who'd been sent to get Kate Dyson, being Irish and in the Crown's service, had a morbid terror of Fenians. He saw them everywhere from the moment he docked in New York, on the train across Pennsylvania, and their image abated only when he'd crossed into Ohio.

Dyson's St. Louis agents had put his wife at her sister's home in Cleveland. Cleveland, so Walsh understood, was a port on a lake, and that was about the sum of his knowledge of the American continent. He discovered a Christmas in Cleveland even colder than the ones he'd known in Yorkshire, with icy winds off the Erie freezing the Cuyahoga Valley. Walsh in his thin English clothes shuddered with cold.

Cleveland, though cold, seemed a boomtown. The harbor yards were busy with lumber, iron ore, and coal. A newish viaduct, of immense proportions, spanned the city vale, and Superior Street shone with more lights than a carnival. Walsh had envisaged the States a primitive place of backwoodsmen and sought to console his confusion with bourbon in a hotel off Public Square. He drank till he'd recovered his nerve and decided to face Mrs. Dyson as quickly as possible. He now wished Bradbury had made this odd trip, and regretted that personal ambition which had caused him to volunteer.

He sought out Kate's address on Boxing Day, tramping around acres of parkland in a pair of borrowed galoshes. Kate's sister answered his call, inspected his warrant card with sharp Irish eyes, then ushered him into an outlandish parlor and told to wait. He feasted his eyes on the rich furnishings—someone had money, he reasoned, but supposing this house was full of Fenians living on friendly "donations"? He'd have his throat slit for a traitor.

Then Kate Dyson appeared—elegant in a red tunic and skirt. She smiled, put him at his ease, and he thought her a beautiful woman. According to Bradbury, this lady had tumbled with Peace, but Walsh found that impossible to believe. A uniformed maid came in with hot chocolate laced with liquor. And Bradbury had said that this woman drank. But where was the sin in just toddying a cup of cocoa? They talked of England for a time, and neither hurried on to the subject of Peace, though Walsh knew she'd been warned of his visit. But at the end of a pause he raised the matter at hand.

"Peace is caught, ma'am. He's in custody for your late hubby's murder."

He was amazed when Kate Dyson giggled. "You sure did take your time!"

"He tried to murder a police officer in London," Walsh explained. "One thing led to another. .... He was a professional burglar, you know?"

"No, I didn't. . . . But nothing surprises me. . . . He was blacker than any villain his precious Shakespeare ever conceived!"

She spoke with a hatred which heartened Walsh. "Shot down your dear husband before your own eyes, I understand?" he reminded her. "Ghastly!"

Mrs. Dyson shut those eyes—wonderful eyes, Walsh had noticed. "So he did! I saw it all!"

"You're the only one who did, ma'am."

The eyes opened. "Meaning?"

The inspector put down his cup. "Meaning you must come back with me, ma'am—or Peace escapes. You wouldn't want that, would you?" His voice was at its melodious best—an enticer of many confessions from fools. "Awful, should he go free. But he will—without you to put an end to his smirking!"

"Smirking, is he!" Kate Dyson reddened. Walsh was cunning with words.

"What d'ye want me to do, Mr. Walsh?"

"Return and shut off his smile. . . . He thinks you'll never come back. . . . He's even libeled you to the Home Secretary." Jackson had ordered a copy of the letter from Charlie to be shown to Mrs. Dyson. He now produced it, unwillingly on his part, and placed it before her. He watched her closely as it was read, observing her expressions, which ranged from outrage to disgust. He judged it right to speak first when she'd finished. "All lies of course, ma'am. Nobody believes one word of it."

"Of course!" Kate Dyson looked as if she'd gladly have torn up the document. But she then peered into the fireplace as if the glowing coals held omens. "Where are those letters he said I wrote him?" she asked softly.

"With my chief constable."

"Will Peace have right of access?"

Walsh hesitated. He decided upon what he thought was the whitest of lies. "He has no rights at all, ma'am. He's already a convict."

At that moment, the parlor door opened and a young boy ran in. He was about nine years of age—and he stood still next to his mother.

"Willie, this is Mr. Walsh from England. We're right busy now, dear!" he was told.

The boy didn't move; he looked from one adult to the other. Walsh feared children almost as much as rebellious fellow countrymen, and smiled nervously.

"Skip off, Willie!" said Mrs. Dyson. "You hear me now?"

But Willie pointed a finger at Walsh. "You from Darnall?" he demanded.

"Well, from that part of the world, young sir!"

The child smiled. "Then you must know Nuncle Charlie. Pleased to meet you!" He sprang forward to shake Walsh's hand. "How's Nuncle Charlie, mister?"

Walsh was saved by Kate Dyson—who rose and led Willie out of the room, lecturing him upon good manners and idle inquisitiveness.

"I'm sorry," she said on return.

Walsh, who was on his toes, bowed graciously. "Just tell him the truth, ma'am. . . . Tell him how his so-called uncle was a thief and a killer. . . . That'll cure the lad's silly notions!" He sat down, lowering his rear just as Kate Dyson did, and gave her his most sympathetic smile. "Peace made your son fatherless—have you thought of that? Come back and let the son know his dad was avenged!"

Mrs. Dyson succumbed completely. She wept—but not before she'd found her handkerchief—and Walsh rushed to console her. He held her hand, muttered cajolements, and even stroked her fine head of hair. "Come back—come back!" he kept saying, until he sounded like the old Skye ballad.

"Can't I just write an affidavit?" she sobbed.

Walsh's hand left her raven locks. "I'm afraid not—your evidence must be oral."

"Will I be questioned—accused?"

"Accused of what, ma'am?"

"Misconduct!" Kate Dyson sat upright and pushed the inspector's hands away. "Maybe I will! But I don't care! I've done nothing to be ashamed of!"

"Nobody who matters says you have."

She nodded. "That letter you showed me—will anyone make use of it?"

"I doubt it. Peace's lies only compound his crime."

"Then I'll come!"

"You're sure?"

"If I have to walk all the way on my head!"

Walsh relaxed; he'd achieved Bradbury's impossible. A real lady, Mrs. Dyson; quite angelic. . . . He'd fix her a saloon passage on the *Britannic* from New York to Cork. She might be a few years his senior, but he fancied a voyage in her company.

III

Hannah was tried at the Old Bailey on the January 14 before Mr. Commissioner Kerr, who withdrew her case from the jury at the close of the prosecution. He ordered her discharge, ironically, on backstage advice from Mr. Justice Hawkins.

Once freed, Hannah went straight to Pentonville to see Charlie. Their reunion took place in his cell, after Hannah's large shopping basket had been thoroughly searched for picklocks and files. Charlie hugged her until she told him to stop being "soppy."

"So Scotch Kerr gave thee the let-out!" Charlie was delighted with the news.

But Hannah considered her own adventures unimportant. She delved into her basket and stabbed Charlie with a rolled-up newspaper. "Trubble," she sniffed. "Feast thine eyes."

Charlie did. The paper was the Sheffield *Telegraph*, dated the seventh. A news extra reported the arrival of Kate Dyson in Ireland, "for the trial of Charles Peace, the notorious burglar."

"That's not nice," he muttered.

"Nowt's nice nowadays," agreed his wife. "But I've got thee thine lawyer."

"Jemmily done. . . . What's Mr. Clegg say then, lass?"

"He hopes ta see thee afore the magistrates hearing."

Charlie nodded. He wanted to see his new solicitor as soon as possible. He had to give him good instructions to flush Mrs. Dyson out into the open. "And what's become of Sue Bailey?" he asked.

Hannah frowned. "Why not ask after thine daughter?"

"Janey? Not sick is she?" There was panic in Charlie's voice.

"Only as a mother-ta-be."

"With child? Sweet Jesus! When's it due?"

Hannah shrugged. " 'Bout the same time as tha's due to pass on."

Charlie laughed uneasily. "Begod, you're a Jonah!" But he was very excited by the thought of a grandchild. "I'll nap no winder till I see the little 'un!" he vowed.

"Then stop fussin' about the likes of Sue Bailey," Hannah said crossly. "Now, tellus what messages ta pass ta Clegg?" And for the rest of her visiting time Charlie gave Hannah some basic instructions.

When she had gone to catch her train back to Sheffield, Charlie lay on his bunk, stricken with remorse. He thanked God for Hannah's acquittal, but trembled to think how close he'd brought her to prison. She'd looked very haggard this afternoon, and much older. She'd stuck by him through thick and thin for twenty years, but he'd treated her badly. She was as loyal as he'd been callously selfish. How could he ever atone to her for what he'd done?

Two days passed. Charlie was up early on both of them, shaved and washed by seven, expecting the arrival of Clegg. But nobody came to him. He made inquiries of his warders, even the Governor, and received unhelpful replies until he grew desperate. He felt deserted and lost in the labyrinthine passages of Pentonville, as if the great outside denied his very existence. Then, on the night of the sixteenth, he received a visit from Chief Warder Crosgrove with some unexpected news.

"They must be rushin' your case, Ward," he announced. "You're to be fetched up to Sheffield tomorrow at sparrow-fart! And *I'll* be feeling your collar all the way. So no monkey business!" He twirled his mustaches, like the sergeant-major he once used to be.

Charlie could only stare back in shock. Before the Sheffield magistrates in the morning? And he hadn't even seen his lawyer yet!

"We take the six A.M. from King's Cross," Crosgrove boomed. "We'll be riding a *very* special car—first class for you, Ward. But don't think that means you won't be fettered, because you will, all the way, with fifty weight of iron!" He saluted the junior warders in the cell, pointed to the disorderly state of the table, and marched out.

It snowed over London that night. The whole of England was in the grip of foul weather and Charlie shivered in the Black Maria as it rattled along to King's Cross. Crosgrove sat on the opposite bench, huge in a blue greatcoat, from which protruded the hilt of a cutlass. A second warder sat beside Charlie, and he and Charlie were joined together by handcuffs. Charlie hadn't caught his name, but the fellow had a face like wax, so he mentally called him "Aguecheek." Those fetters Crosgrove had mentioned lay in a heap on the floor.

It was still dark when they arrived at the station, but the Sheffield Express was fired and ready to leave. Charlie was marched up to the front, near the great hissing engine, and to a carriage marked "S." The rest of the train was empty apart from third class; few gentlefolk traveled at this unholy hour. "S" carriage was opened and Charlie led inside. The blinds were pulled down by Crosgrove while Aguecheek manacled the prisoner's legs. Crosgrove next checked the windows and doors, for this train had no corridor, and even inspected the communication-cord handle. He then lit a fat cigar.

"This is a Ladies' Non-Smoker," Charlie said, indicating a sign. "Put that beastly weed out, sir."

"Quiet, you!" Crosgrove laid a hand on his cutlass, sat down on the plush seat, and put both feet up on the upholstery.

Charlie slipped on his spectacles and examined the chief. He loathed the man's bullying manner—which embraced both convicts and warders. Very well, he'd lead Crosgrove a merry dance —all the way to Sheffield. . . .

" 'Appen I want t'use the toilet," Charlie said, just as the express pulled out of King's Cross.

"You can't!"

" 'Appen I must, sir. . . . I've contracted the Vile's Revenge from thy rotten food!"

Crosgrove scowled. The Revenge was a frequent complaint. He got up and worriedly studied a route map screwed to the wall. "Well, you'll have to hold it till Biggleswade!" he said.

Charlie looked at the map for himself. The train was destined to halt at seven stations before Sheffield. Right-O, he thought, at every one he would insist on using the lavatory.

And that's what he did—doubling up and howling whenever they drew into a station, from Biggleswade to Worksop, forcing his guardians to unshackle him, seek out a platform convenience, and reboard the train before it departed. Twice they almost missed the express, and Crosgrove was snarling by the time they rolled into Sheffield.

Charlie was handed over to a score of constabulary from the Highfield Division and bundled into a nondescript van. And the police weren't the only ones to greet his arrival—the station was crammed with onlookers, pressmen, even Town Hall officials.

"He's quite a celebrity," Pearson explained to Crosgrove.

"He's the bloody-end!" said the chief, hoping his charge was off his hands for good. "I only hopes Marwood strings 'im up slow!"

The van took Charlie to the Stipendiary's Court at the Town Hall. It was nearly ten o'clock, at which hour his case was due to be called. Charlie was taken to cells under the courtroom.

William Clegg, a son of Sheffield, saturnine and cynical for his twenty-nine years, was there to welcome his famous client. He met Charlie in the passage outside the cells with only minutes to spare.

"Mr. Peace?" He shook Charlie's hand. "We're up before Welby any second—which is ridiculous! I shall ask for an adjournment! I'm blind as a bat at the moment!"

Charlie liked this straight talk and forgave Clegg his youth. He also liked the way his solicitor identified himself in the cause as "we." "Have we got them damned letters?" he asked.

Clegg shook an untidy head of brown hair. "Only the papers from the inquest—and copies, to boot, mostly illegible!" Clegg showed him a bundle of documents, and Charlie detected Hannah's scribble on several. God bless her, for what she was doing for him. . . . But Clegg was speaking again. "Mr. Pollard appears for the Treasury. He told me he aims to call Katherine Dyson. Also, a man called Brassington and a woman named Colgreaves. They gave evidence at the inquest, but I gather they also picked you out at Newgate?"

"So they did, sir. But us looked darker 'n' different then. 'Appen they was sneaked into the O.B. for to h'identify us on the sly!"

"Jacob Bradbury's in charge of your case," Clegg continued. "It was he who charged you. A good man, Bradbury; he's the one to help us with regard to those letters you speak of."

"We must get hold of same!" Charlie swore.

"Yes, they are clearly of import." Hannah had mentioned them to the solicitor.

"H'inconceivably so, sir! They be in Kate Dyson's hand!"

"Saying?"

"Showing we weren't just h'acquaintances, sir. She and me was cohabitating."

"You were actually intimate together?"

"Till her chimney smoked!"

Clegg smiled. "Mrs. Peace says she also drank rather heavily?"

"Oceans, sir. She was gay as a goose in a gutter on drink!" Charlie sighed and leaned against the wall. He was very worried. "Thou must get thine dawls on those letters, sir," he repeated. "Justice wilt h'evade us till thou dost."

Clegg nodded. He wanted time to examine every one of them. "Why did you keep those bits of correspondence?" he asked out of interest.

Charlie shrugged. "I tend to collect things, sir."

Clegg chuckled. He'd heard of the Reverend Littlewood's peculiar bird. But at that moment Constable Pearson appeared at
the end of the corridor. "You're on!" he called, and Charlie
recognized him again.

"I trust thy tail weren't scorched too bad that day on the viaduct?" he said. Pearson didn't reply; he took Charlie's arm and
began to lead him to the foot of the steps up to the dock. This
time there'd be no escape for Charles Peace.

Clegg meanwhile approached the courtroom via a witness
room. Several people, police and civilian, sat along benches. One
was a tall woman, dressed in black with a veiled hat. He couldn't
see her face properly, but he guessed this was Kate Dyson, here
for the kill.

The courtroom itself was crowded. The chairs on the Bench
were empty, but the clerk was already in his place below, beside
old Mr. Robinson, the court's taker of depositions, who it was
said seldom recorded evidence accurately.

Pollard had taken up position in the solicitors' row, surrounded by papers tied with red tape, and Clegg joined him. He
didn't much care for the London advocate, so prim and secretive,
and wondered why the Treasury hadn't instructed a local man to
act as its agent in such a regional case.

To one side of the Bench was an area reserved for the chief
constable, Bradbury, some town dignitaries, and the better class
of journalist. Clegg nodded good mornings and sat down. He
knew Mr. Welby was the single magistrate today—Sheffield's stipendiary—but observed that his big chair was flanked by smaller
ones. This meant he was sitting with lay justices, anxious to be
seen at so newsworthy a case, even if they were not to be heard.
Clegg also knew that Welby would probably consult their advice
out of courtesy, and that wasn't much to his liking. He foresaw
a hearing fraught with difficulties.

"All stand!"

Upon the court officer's call, Welby and the justices made their entry like so many penguins, bowing in every direction. Pollard returned their bows like a jackknife.

"Put up Peace, alias Ward!" said the clerk.

When Charlie's capped head appeared over the top of the dock a hubbub ensued. Heads craned to catch sight of the man in convict dress, and there was a murmur of surprise when he removed his cap and bared a bald brown head with silvery hair. He looked less like a murderer than some scullion off a Bombay liner.

Meanwhile Charlie's eyes quickly darted around the court. He saw no sign of Hannah or any other member of his family. He blinked at Clegg and fastened his gaze upon the row of officialdom, from Welby to a journalist beside Jackson. Then he fixed his look on the clerk, who was speaking to the magistrate.

"This defendant has been already committed on a coroner's warrant," the clerk was explaining. "On December 8, 1876, a jury discovered him guilty of murder."

Welby leaned over the Bench. "Yes, but we are to reconsider that verdict."

This was pure formality. Charlie sat down next to the dock officer, and Pollard came to his feet.

"I believe application will be made for an adjournment," he said, looking at Clegg, and shaking his head with disapproval.

Clegg rose. "That is so, sir." He was highly regarded in Welby's court, and his request was made abundantly clear—he needed time to take good instructions from his client, who was accused of the gravest of crimes, and who might have witnesses to call on his behalf. His plea embraced the justices as well as Welby.

Argument followed. Pollard promised only to call witnesses already heard at the original inquest, no more. Clegg insisted he still needed proper time to prepare the defense. Welby hesitated, sought the justices' opinion—as Clegg had feared—and ruled against an adjournment. From the dock, Charlie groaned, flung his cap at his feet, and emitted a stream of complaints. He now believed his tribunal highly partial, most un-Yorkshire, and resolved to interject as he thought fit. His interruptions were not long in starting.

"The prisoner escaped justice two years ago," Pollard began, "but that didn't stop his career of crime. Last year, he was captured. . . ."

"I object!" said Clegg.

"So do I!" Charlie said.

"But he *was* taken into custody," Pollard protested. "I simply said he was engaged in another offense."

"Give a dog a bad name!" said Charlie.

"I still object," said Clegg.

"But he's here in convict dress," cried Pollard, pointing at Charlie.

"That's werry rough on t'skin!" Charlie added, and was told to be quiet by the dock officer.

Welby consulted his justices. "Let us put that fact from our minds," he decided. "We must go back to November, '76."

But Charlie frowned; he thought the court would continue to bear his present conviction well in mind.

"I'll call Katherine Dyson," Pollard was saying.

Mrs. Dyson walked into the courtroom slowly and erect. From beneath her veil she could see all eyes on her, but that black net hid her own expression, even her look of surprise when she glanced at the dock and saw Charlie, whom she could barely recognize. She went into the witness box and was handed a Bible to take the oath.

"Wilt thou be kind enuff to take off thy veil? And thou hast not kissed the Book!" The voice came from the dock and Kate Dyson turned to it. Dear God, that rasping tone! At least that hadn't changed. . . . She saw glaring eyes, and her heart skipped a beat. But she carefully raised her veil to be sworn. That done, Pollard rose to question her. She gave him her name and the address of her present lodgings. But her mind was still on Charlie: she could feel his stare upon her back, and she actually shivered.

"D'you know the prisoner?" Pollard asked her.

She nodded, remembering the touch of his hands on her flesh. "For a long time," she said—in another lifetime. She knew she must relax and answer all questions calmly, as Walsh had told her to aboard the *Britannic,* so she concentrated hard on her questions. She was being asked about Darnall. Yes, her husband had asked Peace to leave them alone, but he'd refused and threatened to blow out her brains. So she'd taken out a summons which, unanswered, became a warrant. Yes, she'd seen Peace at Banner Cross—he'd been there when she and her husband arrived, saying he was there "to annoy" them. She'd seen him next on November 29, skulking outside the water closet with a gun. She'd screamed when he threatened her, and her husband had come running. He'd pursued Peace down the passage, but the other had turned and shot him twice. She'd seen it all. . . .

"And what became of the prisoner?" Pollard asked.

"He went across the road. He stood in the middle for a moment"—Kate Dyson paused—"thinking whether to fire again or not."

Clegg leapt to his feet. "You must not say that!"

She eyed him coldly. He must be Charlie's mouthpiece. And *why* shouldn't she say it? True, she couldn't really recall whether Charlie had stopped in the road. But wasn't it likely? He was a murderer, after all. Then Pollard asked her another question.

"In what position did your husband fall?"

She hadn't actually seen Arthur fall. But this was a silly question with an obvious answer. "He fell on his back," she replied.

"And have you seen the prisoner since?"

"Not before this morning." Except in nightmares.

Pollard handed her up a visiting card, with her husband's full name engraved upon it. "Charles Peace is requested not to interfere with my family," she read his handwriting. "Did your husband give that to the prisoner?" Pollard asked.

She nodded. "Threw it into his yard." Or had it been tossed into the front garden? What did it matter now. . . . But what of the many cards *she* had written? She looked down at Pollard, but he didn't seem to have them and he was sitting down. Had Charlie's lawyer? She looked at him, all set for a harsh interrogation. But Clegg surprised her. "I ask that the cross-examination of this witness be adjourned," he addressed the Bench.

And this request was granted. The clerk told Kate Dyson she might go—that her deposition wasn't yet complete, so it would be read over for her signature at the next hearing. She lowered her veil again, looked briefly at Walsh, and left the courtroom without so much as a glance at the man in the dock.

During Mrs. Dyson's evidence, Charlie hadn't moved a muscle. He was transfixed by her presence; he'd absorbed very little of what she'd said; but once she was out of court, the spell was broken.

"I'm a bit of a liar mysen," he muttered to the dock officer.

Mrs. Gregory, the grocer's wife, was the Crown's next witness. She told the court of bangs and screams in the alley where Dyson died. Charlie found her story unobjectionable, but he suddenly noticed the man next to the chief constable, apparently sketching.

"Ho there!" Charlie shouted at Chief Constable Jackson. "Yon bugger's taking my portrait!"

Everyone was startled. Jackson looked at the offender's notepad, but he saw no drawing, only a confusion of shorthand. "He's only taking notes," he informed the magistrate. Charlie shrugged, but he was far from convinced this was true.

Then Sarah Colgreaves was called. She was asked about Banner Cross.

"I met the prisoner at half-past seven," she said. "He asked me if I knew who lived in the second house up. I told him no. He asked me to deliver a message—to say an elderly man wished to speak to the woman of the house. He called her a 'bloody whore.' I said, 'Go yourself!' " And she looked at Charlie with strong disapproval.

"Psst!" Charlie attracted Clegg, who approached the dock. "Ask yon bundle if she ivver saw us on trial at the O. B."

Clegg nodded and returned to his pew. Pollard was already on the question of identification.

"You saw him at Newgate?"

"Yes."

Clegg took over. "Did you see him *before* Newgate, ma'am?"

Mrs. Colgreaves became confused. "Yes?"

"In the Central Criminal Court?"

"No-oo."

Charlie decided to put the question himself. "A day afore you saw us at Newgate, missus?" But she shook her head at him; she'd never been inside any Lunnan law court.

"How did you identify Peace in prison?" Clegg pressed her.

"By his looks—his face and stature."

"Did you notice the color of his face?"

"A little—yes."

Charlie leaned forward. "Was I like this, missus?" he shouted, and he pulled that terrible face.

Welby and Pollard stared at him in horror. "You'd better not interrupt," the magistrate warned.

Charlie stopped grimacing. "Beg pardon, sir, but my life is at stake! I'm going to vindicate my character as best I can! If thou dost not want us to speak, then gag my mouth, because when I hear a person perjuring hersen, I'll speak!" He became calmer and lowered his voice. "At the time this lady saw us in Newgate, I'd disfiggered my face—so as to deceive all the jenny darbies in Lunnan. And I say I was disfiggered when she saw me."

Welby shrugged, not really understanding what was in issue. But Clegg silenced Charlie with a wave. He questioned Mrs. Colgreaves, but she was positive that the same Charlie had been on the Ecclesall Road.

Nor did the case for any defense improve with the next witness —Brassington. Pollard took him through his evidence very smugly. Not only did the laborer recognize Charlie, but swore he was the man who'd shown him photographs outside Banner Cross. And worse was yet to come.

"He told me he'd make it warm for the strangers before morning," he went on. "He said he'd shoot them both."

This was too much for Charlie; he'd told the man no such thing. "You villain!" he screamed at Brassington. "God reward you! He will!"

It was Pollard's turn to feel annoyance; Brassington was a vital witness for the Crown. "Did you take a good look at him?" he asked the man.

"Not very great notice."

Which was not the answer Pollard wanted. "Where next did you see him?"

"In London."

"Where in London?"

"In Newgate."

"Where in Newgate?"

"At the Town Hall."

Brassington wasn't an intellectual giant, but his reply threw Pollard completely.

"What? A building like this?" he snapped. "Or out in a yard or where?" He was leading the witness, but he didn't care.

"Yes, they were walking aboot in a yard," Brassington remembered.

"So there were others with him? How many? Several?"

Brassington nodded happily.

"All walking around in this yard," Pollard repeated for him. "Was that in the *prison* at Newgate?"

Charlie was up in a flash. "Stow that!" he cried. "Why dost thou put the word Newgate on his tongue? He didn't say Newgate, he said 'Town Hall'! You deliberately put Newgate in yon dafty's mouth!" He turned to the magistrate. "I'm going to have fair play, sir! I've seen a great deal of h'injustice done in courts, but I'll have none of it here!" He shook his fist at Pollard. "He said he saw us in t'Town Hall, then *you* says he saw us at Newgate!"

Welby sought to restore order. "It's not worthwhile going into that," he told Charlie.

"Oh, yes it is! 'Tis worthwhile to me! I'm not a dog, and my life is at stake! I'll h'interrupt if you don't do us justice!"

Pollard was reminded of Charlie's earlier reference to gagging, and the idea appealed to him. "If the prisoner doesn't conduct himself properly, you can order his removal," he told Welby.

But the magistrate had also considered this. "We have great power," he replied, "but it is not always wise to exercise it." By which he meant that there were too many pressmen in court.

Charlie, however, was overcome with a presage of doom. He was sure Welby was siding with the Crown in all matters, so he lounged back in the dock and let Pollard get on with doing his worst. He didn't blame Clegg for one moment—the young man was in an unenviable position. He'd get nowhere by questioning any Crown witness; each was undoubtedly well rehearsed in advance by Pollard with his flash Lunnan ways. Charlie was aroused only when the enigmatic Bradbury, his unknown prosecutor, was being cross-examined with regard to the letters.

Yes, the inspector admitted, documents had been found in a field near Banner Cross, one a picture of Mrs. Dyson taken with Peace, and all the correspondence was in the hands of the chief constable. He had no doubt that everything would be made available to Clegg.

Charlie saw Pollard speak to his lawyer.

But Pollard shook his head—quite a good actor, thought Charlie—and stood to address the magistrate. "That is my case," he said with a bow.

"Mine hasn't started," Clegg added, rising. He asked Welby again for an adjournment, and leave was formally given. The hearing was adjourned to the twenty-second.

"Bravo!" Charlie acknowledged his lawyer before he was led down in handcuffs. His last sight of Clegg was of him in earnest discussion with Pollard and Bradbury, with another inspector hovering nearby. Charlie allowed himself a sweet fantasy—that the men were striking a bargain, whereby the charge would be dropped against Charlie provided Mrs. Dyson's letters might be burned. But it was only a flash of a fantasy, he conceded. Whatever use Clegg made of the letters, the outcome of Charlie's case would be the same: he was as dead as cold mutton.

And Clegg was shortly to heighten this pessimism when he saw Charlie in a cell and disclosed the bald facts of what had been exchanged with the Crown: Kate Dyson was denying every word of her hand on any of the past correspondence, refuting the inference that she'd been Charlie's lover.

"And Pollard certainly believes her," said Clegg.

Charlie shuffled uneasily. "I can't h'abide a man who'll prate against reason," he said. "What did that funny h'inspector say, sir?"

"Bradbury? He made no comment—but I formed the impression that he's more on our side."

"Then 'ave him speak same! Welby'll listen to him!"

Clegg shook his head. "An opinion alone—even Bradbury's—is inadmissible as evidence."

"Then let our witnesses say so!" Charlie said. "There's Kirkham, the milkboy. He was a go-betwixt for Kate and mysen. And there's Goodlad—the Star's ivory-tinkler—he'll h'endorse what I say. And what of good folk in Darnall? Rosie Sykes and Jane Padmore?"

"The last two are bound over for the Crown," Clegg replied. Pollard had ensnared a multitude of possible witnesses, and they'd given statements to the police, which made it difficult for the defense to interview them lest they be accused of interference. But Clegg still had one hope. "Of course, they will be available for cross-examination by your barrister at the trial, which is even better for us. Nor can the Crown deny us the chance of questioning them—their names are on the back of the indictment." Pollard had already shown Clegg a draft copy of this document. The Treasury advocate was also proud of the wordage, and Clegg doubted whether he'd permit any change in the details.

"Why not 'ave 'em next time round?" Charlie demanded.

Clegg had no straight answer. The weavings and dealings of the legal profession were often hard to explain to the layman. "I think I've engaged a good barrister," he said instead. "Frank Lockwood—a true fighter on the way up."

"Young, I hope?" asked Charlie, largely to compliment Clegg.

"In his thirties—but"—Clegg paused to smile—"he's an insidious drawer of portraits."

Charlie laughed. "Nivver heed, good sir! 'Appen I'll give him a motley o'faces! When dost I meet Mr. Lockwood?"

"Later." Clegg produced large sheets of lawyer's paper and pens from his bag. Charlie had asked another difficult question, for Frank Lockwood was an expensive hire. Clegg thought he'd consult Hannah Peace before telling Charlie the possible fee. But Clegg was determined on Lockwood.

"What about Kate Dyson next week?" Charlie asked. "Wilt this Lockwood get shut of her?"

"No—she's my task still." Indeed Clegg wished he had the barrister. "I shall endeavor to discredit her, of course." He looked at Charlie. "If only we can get her to admit she was your —er—close friend, Mr. Peace."

Charlie shook his head.

17

Death Only Wars
on the Quick

Charlie was sent back to London with a grumbling Crosgrove. But this time Charlie was as quiet as Aguecheek throughout the journey, staring out of the carriage window. A large early moon lit up the snowy countryside between Sheffield and Worksop—terrain familiar to Charlie—and the sight of it gnawed his heart. He was thinking of Clegg's last remark. Would Kate Dyson ever concede their relationship? Not for an entire distillery. . . . And even if she did, what difference would that make to his fate? None whatsoever; the Crown would then say he'd murdered Dyson to get hold of his wife, and they'd hang him on a rope of morality. Charlie shut his eyes, enjoyed the warmth of the carriage, and listened to the clickety-clack of the wheels. He put the train's speed at around forty—not as fast as this morning's express. Charlie loved trains, with their hoots and steam and rocky motion and into his melancholy mind sprang the germ of an idea. At first he rejected it as another mad fancy, but it kept on returning until he couldn't dismiss it. He opened his eyes and shifted in his seat, causing his chains to rattle.

"Not again!" said Crosgrove, on the opposite seat.

But Charlie shook his head with a smile. No, he didn't need a lavatory. Not yet—not this time.

Over the weekend and throughout the following week, Charlie remained strangely composed and remote. He had no visitors, but played dominoes with his warders and wrote a great deal. He scribbled the fullest instructions for Clegg in his best hand; he wrote to Hannah at Darnall, telling her to be of good cheer, sending his love to Janey and family; and he actually wrote to Sue Bailey. His letter to Sue was short. He said he was sorry if he'd ever caused her distress; that he forgave her betrayal of Hannah; and begged her to help raise him some money. He knew she must have obtained some valuables from 5 East Terrace, and he asked her to sell a few on behalf of his defense. He addressed this letter care of Inspector Donney at Greenwich, who presumably was still in touch with Sue. Charlie resisted a temptation to write to Kate Dyson; the look she'd given him in court was one of pure hate— or had it been fear?

Charlie also asked his warders for needle and thread, with which he was observed to mend a tear in his convict jacket. The warders knew most men liked to look smart in court, so they made no comment.

Then came the twenty-second, a Wednesday, and one of the coldest days since '76. Crosgrove roused Charlie at five for the trip to King's Cross. They traveled in the same van as before with Aguecheek, and Charlie proved troublesome from the outset.

"Oh, my dear sirs!" he groaned in the van. "I've got the Revenge back h'again!" He clutched his stomach and was rushed to a lavatory as soon as they reached King's Cross. He locked himself in and refused to come out for an unconscionable time, while an irate Crosgrove hammered on the door with his cutlass and Aguecheek was obliged to hold up the express. He handcuffed Charlie when at last he came out, savagely twisting the screws, dragging him along the platform to the reserved compartment. Crosgrove, meanwhile, had obtained a large stock of paper bags from the railway staff. He had no intention of allowing his charge off the train at any stop this time, whatever his condition.

The huge engine drew out of King's Cross eight minutes late and picked up speed when they reached Barnet Junction. Charlie fell quiet, biding his time. His stomach rumbled convincingly because he'd taken no breakfast that morning, though he now wished he had. But he had to play his part well. And he let the curtain rise just beyond Biggleswade.

"Oh, my bladder's afire!" he suddenly cried.

Crosgrove sprang to his feet. He opened a window and handed Charlie a bag while the latter danced a jig around the carriage. Charlie turned, pretended to use the bag, and then hurled it out the window. Crosgrove made a noise of disgust, thrust Charlie back in his seat, and slammed shut the window.

"You can bloomin' well boil your bladder till we reach Sheffield," he said.

Charlie stared at him sulkily. "You asks the h'impossible," he muttered. "But I'll do mine best."

He in fact did his very worst from then on—demanding a bag every ten minutes and the same procedure was repeated. He also asked to be let off the train when it stopped, but Crosgrove refused. The latter was minded to give his charge a good hiding, but knew he couldn't very well produce him looking battered at Sheffield. Nor did he really want a brawl in the carriage—and he knew Peace's fame as a fighter.

Charlie meantime had been weighing up certain chances since they'd pulled out of Grantham. A wintry dawn was breaking over Lincolnshire; soon they'd be crossing Notts for the West Riding. He watched his two warders and gently tested his handcuffs. The steel bracelets were very tight and he held up his hands in supplication.

"They're nipping like Billy-O!" he complained.

But Crosgrove just grunted, a fresh paper bag ready in his hand.

The skies became brighter. More snow had fallen up north and the Notts-Yorks border was deep with drifts. They halted at Worksop. The next station would be Shireoaks, a few miles from Kiveton Park, and not far from Darnall. Charlie slumped forward and moaned.

"Not again!" said Crosgrove. He rose and flung up the window wide. An icy blast came into the carriage. "Stay close by him!" he ordered Aguecheek. Charlie used the bag and moved to the window, Aguecheek holding the chain of his handcuffs. The bag flew out the window and Charlie turned around slowly. Aguecheek moved aside to let him pass. Then—quick as a flash—Charlie spun about and dived headlong out the window. Aguecheek's fingers were torn from the handcuffs, but the young warder was quicker than Charlie had supposed: he grabbed Charlie's foot by the boot just as it was about to disappear, holding on with both hands. Chaos ensued. Most of Charlie was now outside the carriage, his body being buffeted against the side of the train. He twisted and wriggled to free his foot, but Aguecheek hung on like a bulldog.

"Don't let him go!" shouted Crosgrove, who was unable to help because Aguecheek was blocking the aisle. It didn't occur to the chief to hold on to Aguecheek; instead he pulled the communication-cord handle. He tugged it many times to no avail—the cable which ran along the top of the train was faulty, and the express pounded on. Outside the train, Charlie struggled upside down while chips from the track whipped up and stung his face, which was already blackened with soot. Then he espied a knob on the side of the coach where it curved under to the thundering wheels and strained till he reached it. That gave him leverage and he pulled with all his might while Aguecheek still gripped his boot. Charlie twisted around to look up at the youth, who was himself hanging out of the train. The boy's strength was incredible but he couldn't hold on indefinitely. Charlie began to swing his body like a pendulum and felt his foot start to slide out of the boot. He jerked hard, the cheap prison laces gave way, and he fell free—carried backward by the slipstream. He bounced off the steps of another carriage and thought he'd broken his back, but the impact shot him clear of the train and its wheels. He was spinning away. He hunched himself into a ball, shut his eyes, and protected his head with manacled hands, but this didn't save him: he hit the sidings headfirst. There were hard cinders under the snow and his scalp was ripped open. The blow rendered him semi-unconscious and he lay where he fell without moving. When he opened an eye he saw a signal box and some fools who were waving at him. The express had now passed by completely. He heaved himself up on an elbow. Pain shot down his spine. He gritted his teeth and tried to stand, but couldn't. He fell back heavily, tried again and again, but his legs wouldn't function and his back was in agony. Then he heard the pad of running feet. He glanced over his shoulder; Crosgrove and Aguecheek were trotting toward him, and the train had stopped five hundred yards away, with passengers looking out of the windows.

"Bloody 'ell," was his comment as the warders discovered him.

"You're under arrest!" said Aguecheek, paler than ever, another pair of handcuffs in hand.

"Easy, lad, easy," said Crosgrove, who could see that Charlie was badly hurt, and bent down to examine his injuries. "What a silly dolt you are, Mr. Peace," he said, his voice unusually soft. "Can you see as well as you cuss?" He was peering into Charlie's eyes for signs of concussion. Charlie nodded. "Quite a jump you made," the chief went on conversationally. "Saw a man do that once off a train in the Crimea. Deserter, of course; we shot 'im as soon as he'd mended."

"I wish you'd shoot *me!*" Charlie groaned.

Crosgrove laughed. "No, it's the 'angman for you, matey."

By now some railwaymen had come up to the group, both from the train and the signal box. Crosgrove briefly explained the situation.

"Well, you'll have to put your prisoner on the next train through," said the express guard. "I'm not 'aving a dead man on my train."

"He's not dead! And he's due at court by ten!"

"Well, the beaks'll 'ave to wait. My train won't carry suicides, mister. You can put him on the nine-eighteen slow-coach—that's due any minim." And the guard refused to be persuaded otherwise, leaving Charlie and his warders on the track as whistles were blown and the express went off down the line.

It was a long, cold wait before the 9:18 local-run arrived to be stopped by the signalmen. Charlie was hoisted aboard the baggage wagon and wrapped in a blanket. By now he was shuddering with cold. The blood had congealed on his wound, but any movement caused pain and he was sure several ribs must be buckled.

"Why not hang me now and have done with it!" he said to Crosgrove.

"Why did you jump?" Aguecheek spoke for the very first time.

Charlie looked at him blearily. Then he reached gingerly into a pocket and handed the warder a small scrap of paper. Both Crosgrove and Aguecheek examined it. "Bury me at Darnall" were the words written—pinpricked into the paper by needle and smudged over with prison dirt. "I thought to get shut of mysen," Charlie said, "to slip further trubble and distress." He leaned back in his blanket and tried to sleep as the local-run set off for Sheffield. But the baggage van swung about mercilessly, jarring his every nerve, and rest was impossible. Poor little swine, thought Crosgrove, placing the suicide note in his tunic.

II

News of Charlie's leap from the train arrived at Sheffield with the express. The tale quickly became twisted; some said Charlie had escaped and some said he was dead. It was the latter version which reached the ears of Kate Dyson, while she waited in the Town Hall witness room.

"Do leas a anama!" she said, crossing herself.

Bradbury had come in and heard her. "What's that, ma'am?"

"I was praying for his soul, black that it was," she replied. She was hiding her face behind her veil but she was glad Charlie was dead; the saga was at last at an end.

Then Jackson appeared with the truth. "He's alive and being brought in on a freight," he informed both of them.

Kate Dyson paled and felt guilty for the thoughts she had held. "I will annoy you wherever you go"—Charlie's words rang terribly true. "So I'll have to go back into the witness box?" she asked Jackson.

He nodded. "Once he's fit."

So there was still a chance he might die? Mrs. Dyson walked to the window and looked out. The street was full of people—like the people who'd followed her remorselessly around Sheffield, pointing and whispering. She knew they were calling her a harlot and likened her to that other woman of Charlie's. They probably longed to watch her destroyed in court by that snappy young defense lawyer. She glanced sideways at Jackson, who was talking to Bradbury. How she loathed them. But she'd withstand any manner of questioning by Clegg. She had "calmacht," as her sister would say. . . .

"I shall stay in England till I see justice done," she told Jackson. And then she'd leave this accursed island forever.

Charlie was taken from Sheffield station on a stretcher to Water Lane, more dead than alive. At the police station he was housed in a cell and seen by a doctor, who patched up his head, roughly and badly, in a huge linen bandage.

"Begod, I'm as flayed as Mary Bateman!" Charlie mumbled. "Give us a drink!"

Crosgrove disappeared and came back with some milk, into

which the doctor put brandy. "I want whiskey!" Charlie protested, adding, "Help, murder!" when he was forcibly fed. "I want justice! I want Mr. Clegg!" he continued to grumble, laid out on a mattress, spitting out the taste of the brandy. Then Crosgrove showed the doctor the suicide note, and they were looking at it when Clegg arrived from the Town Hall. The solicitor read the note and heard the facts with mounting concern.

"Why did you do it?" he asked Charlie.

"I'm not fit to live!"

"You're not fit for court anyway," agreed his lawyer. "The Stipendiary's adjourned everything till Friday. You're to be kept here until then."

"Thank God for that," said Crosgrove, his duties at last finished.

Clegg turned to the doctor. "But will he be fit for Friday?" he asked.

"Fit for any kind of disposal," said the doctor.

"Disposal!" Charlie sat up in bed. "I'll not be disposed of! This is an h'outrage!" Clegg wanted words with his client alone and asked Crosgrove and the doctor to leave. Then he spoke strongly to Charlie. "What's your game?" Charlie struggled out of bed and limped over to the cell door. He peeped through the Judas hole to ensure no one was eavesdropping. The dark passage outside was deserted. "No game, sir," he said, returning to bed. "No fight for thine life is a game. I dove off yon train with my brain full h'engaged. 'Appen I'd killed mysen, then that was that. But I h'aimed to h'injure myself."

"But why!"

"If we can hold up proceedings for a couple o' months, I reckon Kate Dyson wilt clear off to h'America."

Clegg was shocked. "And you'd harm yourself to that end?"

"Take a bath if that helped! Where's that bloody woman, anyroad?"

"Still in town." Clegg had seen her that morning, and talking with Pollard, which he considered unethical.

"Oh, aye? Who pays her bills?"

"The Treasury."

"In return for her lies!" Charlie frowned. "But my witnesses shalt contradict her damn fibs!"

Clegg was staring at the brick floor; now he looked up unhappily. "I've some bad news, Mr. Peace. None of yours will come forward—not the milkboy, not Mrs. Norton, no one."

"What about Denny Goodlad from the Star?"

"He has a record; he's frightened. I can get them to court, of course, but they will not testify."

"Warned off by the bobbies, eh?" Charlie rubbed his eyes. He was very tired. "What a mess! 'Appen I'll have to refuse to go to court mysen."

"What d'you mean?"

"I'll stop here and not move. . . . And I'll darken the glims of anyone that h'endeavors to shunt us!" And with that he rolled over to face the wall, declining to talk further with Clegg. The solicitor eventually felt obliged to leave his client and report his obstinacy to officialdom.

After much debate, it was decided to conduct the rest of Charlie's committal in the passage outside his cell. Welby refused any postponement; Chief Constable Jackson wanted Charlie for the February assize; and Pollard lectured them all about persons "mute of malice."

So at eight o'clock in the morning the police got busy in the passage, dragging in a great table and chairs. The corridor was without gas, and candles were fetched. All this bustle disturbed Charlie in his cell.

"What the bloody 'ell's happening?" he called through the door. But nobody answered him.

Just before ten, the court personnel arrived. Welby took his place at the head of the table, flanked by his justices, while Pollard and Clegg were to face one another about halfway down. One place remained empty—a low armchair for the prisoner. Soon all was ready, and on the dot of the hour Charlie was brought from his cell. He was sat in his chair, draped in a blanket, with a policeman on either side. The whole scene was ghostly by candlelight and not at all to Charlie's liking.

"What's this—a séance?" he asked.

Welby's voice answered him from a long way off. "The inquiry is to be proceeded with." Old Robinson was writing behind him.

Charlie shook his bandaged head. "I'm h'unable to bear it! I oughtn't be here!"

"You must do your best. You're represented, and the inquiry must finish today."

Charlie looked for Clegg. "I'm werry cold, sir. Have 'em put summat more round my shoulders!" Another blanket was found. Charlie lifted it over his head so he looked like a bad-tempered nun. "I'm h'unable to go on!" he insisted.

"You must take it for what it is," said Welby severely.

" 'Tis a bloody shambles!"

But Charlie fell silent as Kate Dyson was ushered into the passage. She was told to stand next to Welby and to give the rest of her testimony. Pollard, as a matter of tactics, questioned her first with regard to the letters.

"Have you seen these before?"

She was handed them. "Yes—at the coroner's inquest." She stared at Charlie fearlessly.

"Do you know the handwriting?"

She flicked through the bundle. "No . . ." Her answer was casual.

"I want the milkman called!" Charlie cried.

Both Pollard and Mrs. Dyson ignored him. "Were any written by your authority?" Pollard went on.

"I know nothing of them," she said.

Pollard smiled and sat down. Clegg got to his feet slowly, coughed, and asked for the letters, from which he selected a photograph. It was of Kate Dyson and Charlie at Whitsing. He had an usher pass Mrs. Dyson the picture. "Whose photograph is this?" he said.

"His and mine," she replied. "It was taken at Sheffield Fair."

Charlie grunted and showed his approval by putting his feet up on the table.

"You mustn't do that!" he was told by the magistrate, and he obediently lowered them.

"Had you been to more than one fair with him?" Clegg asked Mrs. Dyson.

"No."

"Not to what is called the Winter Fair?"

"No!" And a definite shake of the head.

Clegg looked at Charlie's instructions and tried another line of attack. "When were you married, Mrs. Dyson?"

"I can't remember the date." She looked surprised.

"Don't remember? Well, what year was it?"

"I can't tell you that. But I can find out. . . ."

"Have you a marriage certificate?"

"Yes—with my agent in Missouri. I left it over there for safety."

"Safety?" Clegg shook his instructions at her. "I must suggest that. . . ."

"Yes, what are you suggesting?" Welby interrupted. "How can any of this be relevant? Let's get on with proper evidence!"

"It is a question of her credibility," Clegg insisted.

"She'd the banns up the chimley!" Charlie said. "Dyson nivver married her because she's of the Venerable h'Aunt!"

Clegg scowled at him; he was having enough trouble from Welby without Charlie's comments. "You were very intimate with Peace," he returned to Kate Dyson. "Have you not been to places of amusement with him?"

"Not to places of amusement."

"To public houses?"

"Not along with him; but he has followed me into them when I was with my husband." Mrs. Dyson smiled wistfully at her big lie.

"Have you not been to the Halfway House and had drinks put down to Peace?"

"Not to my knowledge."

"Have you ever met the pianist at the Star Music Hall?"

Mrs. Dyson shook her head and Goodlad was brought into the area for inspection. "I've never seen him before," she added. Goodlad was led away.

"Do you know the Marquis of Waterford in Russell Street?" Clegg continued.

"No."

So the hideous Cragg was fetched into the passage. Kate Dyson gazed upon that mutilated face for a second. "I never remember seeing him before," she said.

Clegg grew exasperated. "You've been to several public houses with Peace and had drink?"

"I've had a bottle of soda water or pop," came the reply.

Charlie roared with laughter until one of the policemen beside him shook his shoulder. Charlie was about to remonstrate with the man, but then thought it wiser to hearken to Clegg, who was asking about the July summons.

"Before you took out this summons, had you any quarrel at all?"

Kate Dyson stiffened. "He was a constant source of annoyance," she snapped. "He'd listen at the door, jump over the wall, and be very disagreeable indeed!"

Charlie was furious; he tried to rise from his chair, but collapsed. The police doctor was summoned, took his pulse, and again declared him fit for "disposal." But Charlie did have his way in one matter—a stool was produced for his feet, and it arrived in the corridor at the same time as Kirkham, the milkboy. Clegg had the youth presented before Mrs. Dyson immediately.

"Do you know him?" Welby asked her.

"He delivered the milk with his father."

"But you gave him notes for Peace?" Clegg put to her.

"No, no notes."

Clegg continued to examine her with regard to the letters, but Welby grew restless.

"What does it all lead to, Mr. Clegg?" he asked in a bored tone.

"To this, sir. . . . She has sworn that she didn't write any of these letters, and I'm in a position to prove that she did. . . ."

"But she distinctly denies it!" said Welby.

"And *I* demand justice be done!" Charlie moaned.

Welby rounded on him. "Don't *you* start now!" He addressed Clegg again. "I rule that sufficient has been asked about those letters. I stop them now. You can prosecute her for perjury, if you wish. I have given my decision. You will please proceed with the case."

"I object to proceed," Clegg replied bravely.

"Hear, hear!" Charlie encouraged him. But the issue was nevertheless dead as far as this court was concerned.

Clegg nagged Kate Dyson on life in Darnall for another ten minutes, and her replies got him nowhere.

"Did you ever borrow money from the prisoner?" for example.

"I never did!"

So Clegg moved on to the issue of the murder itself, the most dangerous ground he had to cover. Mrs. Dyson said she and her husband had left Darnall because they were frightened of Charlie. And that she had been told by Mrs. Padmore that he'd prowled around at night in female attire. She also said that she'd received threatening letters from him, including the postcards from Germany. Clegg skipped over these (which he'd never seen) and came to the night of the shooting.

"Did you see the prisoner from a bedroom that night?"

She denied it.

"When you were coming out of the closet, did he say he'd let you have the notes back if you got your husband to stay proceedings against him?"

"No, sir."

"Your husband came up just then. Did he try to get hold of the prisoner?"

"He wasn't close enough!"

"But didn't you see the prisoner on the ground? Wasn't there a struggle between your husband and him?"

"No!"

"Will you swear they weren't struggling?"

"They weren't close enough!" She was adamant, and this point was vital.

Clegg shook his head; Charlie had described a fierce fight between himself and the tall Dyson. Clegg looked toward Charlie, but the latter was staring at Mrs. Dyson. Clegg thought he saw Charlie mouth something. "What's that?" he asked of him.

"I said, 'Go on, lass, thou art getting along nicely'!" Charlie repeated, his face frozen with hurt.

"Oh?" Clegg could think of no more to say. He sat down, hoping that Frank Lockwood would make up for his own inadequacies.

Mrs. Dyson's deposition was read back to her in full by Robinson. The shorthand writer spoke in sonorous tones, misquoting and mixing up questions and answers endlessly. Charlie groaned noisily with his head on the edge of the table. Then he started to sing, a dreadful sound, to the tune of "Villikhens and His Dinah":

> "Death met a coachman, driving his coach,
> So slow that his fare grew rapidly sick,

But he let him pass on in this tedious way,
For Death h'only wars on the quick!"

Robinson's reading stumbled all the more, and Welby ordered Charlie's escorts to quiet their charge. They pulled Charlie upright, muttering threats, but he thrust them away and pulled a blanket right over his head, hiding underneath, but he continued to shout snatches of song:

"That woman's not one to foster,
Once her hubby had thought he had lost her,
'Til he spied on the grass—the marks of her arse,
And the knees of poor Charlie who'd crossed her!"

The blanket was wrenched from his head, and he then lolled about, baying like a wolf, adding to the eeriness of the cell passage. And when he looked again, Kate Dyson had gone.

Pearson was called as a witness to formally identify Peace. He also spoke of the aborted attempts to trace the prisoner in Hull but Holborn Viaduct was oddly forgotten.

Charlie didn't mind. He felt drunk with fatigue and he believed Clegg would soon call witnesses on his behalf. . . . No, he wouldn't! Charlie remembered; the buggers were refusing to testify; the Crown had paid them off. . . .

"Can't ye call mine witnesses?" he shouted at Welby. "What's the bloody use of witnesses h'unless they're bloody well called?"

Welby didn't like all this bad language, but the proceedings were now almost over and he quietly told Charlie he could call his witnesses, but did he first want to make a statement himself?

"Simply say 'Not Guilty,' " Clegg advised his client.

Charlie saw Robinson's pen poised to write what he said. "I'm not bloody guilty! And I say justice hasn't been done to me! I want to prove I'm h'innocent—so why don't you let me call my witnesses? I'll tell you why, because us hasn't the brass ta pay for 'em!"

This outrageous suggestion was duly recorded by Robinson as 'I have not the money to pay the expenses.' Robinson left Welby and came closer to Charlie, book in hand, to get down what else he might say.

"I have lots of witnesses to prove that bad, base woman has thrattened my life!" Charlie went on. He was feeling muzzy and sick, and spoke anything that came to mind. "I feel werry bad, but she's ofttimes thrattened to kill me—and her hubby. She's pointed pistols and things at us! All I ivver pointed at her was mine pissle!"

Welby had had enough of this nonsense. "Sign your statement," he ordered.

Robinson handed Charlie his deposition book and pen.

"I'll try, but I can't see," Charlie muttered. His head was spinning, but he managed to write his name. Then he rested his head on his arm, barely listening to Welby's next words.

"You are committed to take your trial at Leeds Assizes," said the magistrate.

Charlie lifted his head. "Can I sit before a fire a bit, sir? I feel werry bad!"

He was certainly shivering. "He complains of being cold," Clegg told Welby.

"Aye, werry cold!" Charlie agreed. "You can put me in irons, but give us a fire!"

But Chief Constable Jackson envisaged some trick. Having been committed, Charlie was now entirely his responsibility, so he spoke out. "The cells are warm enough," he assured Welby. "It's this corridor which is so drafty, sir."

Clegg thought this was probably true. "You'll be warm in your cell," he told Charlie.

A gray face looked up at him. "I want to see you, Mr. Clegg."

"Of course!" Clegg nodded to his client's escorts, who carefully drew him out of the armchair and assisted him, two on each elbow, down toward his cell door. Clegg watched him go. Never in the solicitor's life had he attended so bizarre a hearing, or represented so extraordinary a client.

"Quite a performance," he commented to Robinson after Charlie had been resettled in his cell.

The other smiled slightly. "I've excluded most of the swearing," he said, tapping his book. Robinson had an orderly mind; he also knew that Welby would not like a demonstrable record of such pandemonium occurring in his court. That would look very bad.

III

Kate Dyson reckoned she'd done well in withstanding Clegg's many questions, and Mr. Pollard endorsed this view when they took tea together in Bradbury's office. The inspector was also present, as was Walsh, but made no comment.

"What happens next?" Mrs. Dyson asked, her face shining with success.

"His trial will open on February fourth before Mr. Justice Lopes," Pollard replied. He knew Lopes would brook no nonsense from Peace. "Campbell Foster will prosecute," he added. "He'll take you through your evidence just as I did. You have nothing to fear, madam."

"But you'll then have to face Frank Lockwood," Bradbury put in.

Pollard snorted. Lockwood wasn't even a Silk—just a run-of-the-mill brash Northerner as far as he was concerned, and Pollard loathed Northerners. "I doubt Peace will be able to afford Lockwood," he said. "I hear he's quite pricy."

But Bradbury knew a fair deal about the barrister. "He'll take the case," he replied. "I'd wager my pension on that, sir." He believed Lockwood would defend Charlie for free, if necessary:

Lockwood wasn't one to be timorous about defending the notorious. He glanced at Kate Dyson, and saw some of the complacency had gone from her expression. "Lockwood will tax you about those letters you didn't write," he warned, "as well as about that struggle your husband didn't have with Charles Peace."

"And I shall continue to tell the truth!" she replied.

"Good." Bradbury smiled at her. "Because we don't want Peace just convicted of manslaughter if it was really murder, do we?"

"It was murder all right," Pollard interrupted. "And Peace has run his last race."

Next day, Charlie was taken to Wakefield by an afternoon train. Nine prison officers were employed to carry his stretcher, to which his wrists and ankles were fastened by handcuffs. A large crowd saw him off from the station, and another crowd greeted his arrival at Wakefield.

The old House of Correction looked the same from the outside, but the interior of the jail had been modernized. Charlie no longer saw the rooftops over which he'd once tried to escape, nor the treadmill sheds or brick-making kilns, but he nevertheless felt his life had turned full circle, that he was back where his convict life had begun, and he wondered if this prison would be his last place of confinement.

"Dost thou have a scaffold?" he asked the nearest warder.

The other laughed. "Not since '66, lad!"

And Charlie realized he was only in transit.

He was given a cell on the ground floor. Someone had chalked "Category A" on the ironbound door, extra bars had been fitted to the window, and Charlie had to smile. Did they seriously consider him to be a security risk? In his present condition he couldn't walk two paces, let alone run. But at least he'd have the company of many warders.

That night he wrote a letter to Sue Bailey, again asking her to raise funds and send cash to Clegg. "I'm very ill from the effects of the jump from the train," he wrote. "I tried to kill myself to slip all further trouble, and to be buried in Darnall." He paused before finishing the letter. How could he touch Sue's greedy heart? "I remain your ever true lover till death," he added, hoping Hannah would never read this epistle. He'd write to Hannah, too—but later, for he thought she'd be allowed to visit him soon. He then worried about Janey. Would his daughter suffer much giving birth? Hannah had had her child without difficulty, but then his wife was husky. His own mother nearly died having him. . . . But enough of these mawkish thoughts! He completed Sue's letter and invited his warders to outcheat him at cards.

Hannah didn't materialize over the weekend, but a letter from her arrived on the Monday. Her hand was as indecipherable as Charlie's could be deliberately bad, but he knew her scrawl and read her tidings. These were hard: she'd seen and talked to his witnesses, but all seemed to suffer lapses of memory, even Cragg and Mother Norton, and nothing could induce them to give evidence. Charlie was upset—but not surprised.

What did surprise him, however, was a second letter that morning. It was an answer from Sue. She said she was still living with the Brions, that she had no money, that she was being jeered at in London streets and hounded by newspapers. She *could* raise some money, she added, if only he would confess all his crimes to her in writing, which she would then sell to the press. In this way they both would benefit, and she would find it in her heart to forgive him the distress he had caused her.

"Well, I'll be buggered!" Charlie said with a laugh. But he had to admire Sue's nerve. He immediately penned a letter to Hannah, informing her of Sue's refusal to assist him. "She says she has nothing to make money for me," he wrote, "but I know she has plenty of things." He didn't tell his wife about Sue's suggested "confession"—he could scarcely believe her proposal himself, and wondered if Forsey Brion might have played a hand in that idea. Perhaps that scatty inventor had created a "Truth Machine" to extract admissions of guilt? Charlie could imagine that pumpkinhead waggling over such a device. . . .

Charlie didn't stay long at Wakefield. Far away in London, the Home Office was in receipt of another communication from one Susan Bailey, alias Thompson, ratified by Mr. Brion, gentleman. They said they both had the interests of justice at heart. They feared that the "machiavellian" Peace might escape justice by taking poison and urged the Home Secretary to incarcerate the prisoner in the Tower of London. The Home Office considered this advice carefully, but thought the Tower rather remote—if not too lordly—a place for a commoner. They did, however, direct that Charlie be moved immediately to Armley Gaol, Leeds. They also ordered that a special cell be constructed for him there —one which made any physical contact with visitors impossible.

"What's h'up? What's this?" Charlie asked on arrival at Armley. This prison was strange to him—a veritable fortress on a hill, overlooking back-to-back slums. The stonework, medievally carved, was black with soot; the windows slicked with oil fallen from an industrial sky. "This is an h'abominable place!" Charlie observed as he was lifted from the police van. The gates were being closed behind, but he caught sight of some waste ground beyond. "What's that place?" he asked a warder, for it was oddly sinister.

"Gallow's Field," he was told.

"Aha, so you have a scaffold?"

He received no answer, but was carried up a broad stairway into the main building. The prison Governor came out of an office on the left, together with a chaplain, and interrupted the procession.

"My name is Captain Smith," said the Governor, "and this is Mr. Cookson."

Charlie looked from one to the other and settled his eyes on

Cookson. "Dost thou know the Revvy Littlewood, sir?" he asked. "Good man, John L., and I wish he was here."

Governor and chaplain accompanied the party down a ground-floor passage. They at last arrived at a double cell, divided into two parts by stout bars. A military cot stood in the middle of the floor of the right-hand section, near a table screwed to the floor. Charlie sat on the bed, stared about him, and then stretched himself out with a groan.

" 'Tis a death cell, and I'm not yet condemned!" he accused the Governor.

"No, it's not! You've been allotted the best room at Armley!" The Governor had received specific orders from the Secretary of the Prison Commission not to upset his charge.

"And what dost thou keep h'over there?" Charlie gesticulated toward the barred-off area. "Songbirds to lull mine savage breast?" He laughed, and began coughing. His lungs were in a terrible state.

Then the chaplain spoke. "Do you want to see this Mr. Littlewood? I'm sure this can be arranged, Peace."

Charlie nodded, pulled the pillow under his head, and hugged himself. " 'Appen I'll see him when ready. Meantime, I'd crave some warmth, sir. . . . Mine teeth are chattering an ape's paternoster!"

So a stove was fetched, kindled, and lit. The Governor instructed his warders never to let Charlie near the thing—"the convict is most artful and cunning," went the words of the Prison Secretary. *Convict?* The state seemed very sure about the result of the trial. . . . "No visitors, I fear, until after the assizes," he informed Charlie. "Save for your lawyers—and this parson you mention."

"Parsons come later and less expensive than lawyers," Charlie said. " 'Tis palpably plain, sir, that I'm already served out by the Crown. But should mine missus come here, pray let her come visit? She'll bark at the moon if thou doesn't!" His plea was calm but pathetic.

And the Governor was moved. The Home Office thought poison could be passed in a kiss and Mr. Secretary Cross forbade any contact with family—of which Peace had apparently legions. Very well, he decided, no actual contact. . . . But Hannah Peace might see him from the far side of the bars whenever she wanted.

"I hear you," he said. "I shall do what I can, Peace."

Captain Smith and Cookson then left. Neither spoke until they gained the cobbled yard.

"A madman," said Cookson.

"Or a badman," said the Governor.

"Bound to hang?"

"Until dead."

"A certainty?"

"So I hear."

"And who are these women he's fouled?"

"Money-grabbers—drunkards—insults to their own sex!"

"You're a hard man, Captain."

"Not toward Peace. . . . I hear he expounds Shakespeare. . . . I, too, read the poet; Peace is almost a Richard the Third."

"I've not read that bloodthirsty tale, I confess."

" 'I have set my life upon a cast, and I will stand the hazard of the die. . . .' Rather Peace-ey, don't y'think?"

"I don't know, Captain. . . ." Cookson was only sure Charles Peace would sometime want a Reverend Littlewood—to his own, rather painful, exclusion. Cookson liked to prepare the souls of men about to die all by himself. . . .

18
The Harrowing of Hell

Charlie's trial was to be heard at Leeds's new Town Hall. He found himself moved yet again, into an improvised cell in the bowels of that magnificent building on February 3. Here Clegg introduced him to Lockwood, a vigorous young man with bad-tempered eyes, and for three hours the trio held conference. Charlie liked Lockwood's brisk manner, and the barrister said only two defense points really mattered. "We must discredit Mrs. Dyson; make the jury believe she really was your lover in spite of all her denials," he said. "Then we must create the possibility that Dyson was shot during a struggle. If we can do that, the jury may find his death an accident, and so judge you guilty of manslaughter alone." He glanced again at Kate Dyson's depositions at the inquest and committal proceedings. "Mrs. Dyson says there was no struggle between you and her husband, but if we can show she's a liar in respect of her relationship with you, the jury may doubt her word, and it's her word alone, that you and Dyson did not come to grips. You follow me, Peace?"

Charlie nodded. He could place trust in Lockwood, but what about his jury? "Will I get a fair trial, sir?" he asked.

Lockwood knew precisely what bothered his client. The newspapers were full of his case. They were following every development from the time he'd first been charged with murder. Lockwood drew a mass of papers from his briefcase. They ranged from local "rags" to *The Times*, from the *News of the World* to the Sheffield *Independent*.

"It is most bothersome," Lockwood said, sorting through the papers, "but your case has attracted much adverse publicity, and jurors tend to be empaneled from the more literate sector of the community." He looked at Clegg. "Let us just confine ourselves to the lordly *Times*," and he began to read from copies in an angry monotone. "On January fourteenth, they announce that Mrs. Dyson is being interviewed by the Treasury Solicitor with a view to giving evidence against you. No harm in that—but they add: 'There is every possibility Peace will be brought to Sheffield by a Writ of Habeas Corpus and, after examination before a Stipendiary Magistrate, will be sent to Leeds Assizes.'"

"So I have," said Charlie.

"Aye, but they prejudge that your case would not be dismissed by the magistrate. They assume you have a case to answer before even a word of testimony is heard."

"Wicked buggers!" agreed Charlie, understanding.

"And next day," continued Lockwood, "we have the trial of your wife for receiving property stolen by you reported in full. So by January fifteenth, everyone knows you're a burglar by trade. And on the eighteenth, we are treated to a full column describing your first appearance before the Sheffield magistrate. Again, there's no harm in that—but the paper adds, by way of comment: 'The case has excited great interest throughout the country, not only in consequence of the escape of the murderer, but owing to his daring burglaries in different parts of the kingdom since 1876,' and your trial before Judge Hawkins is reported in the fullest way."

"Miserable men!" Charlie muttered.

"Aye, maybe . . . But *you* are to blame for the next edition, I fear." Lockwood turned to the paper of January 23. " 'Escape and Recapture of the Prisoner Peace,' " he read out the headlines. " 'The Notorious burglar, Charles Peace, who is charged with the murder of Mr. Arthur Dyson two years ago, has added another to the wonderful episodes of his eventful life. Peace becomes more notorious than ever.' "

" 'Tis scandalous!" Charlie said. "Not to call me 'Mr.' 'Happen the bastards call piss-pipe bloody Dyson 'Mr.' So why not us? I'm entitled to be called 'Mr.' too!"

Charlie was red with rage and Lockwood had to laugh. Then he read from *The Times* of January 25. "Here you are given four and a half columns. Most of them deal with the rest of your committal, but things take a merry turn after that. They say you gave a 'statement' to some 'friend' as to your ability 'to dodge every detective in existence' by a 'peculiar contortion of your features' and 'forcing the blood into the face until you look like a Mulatto.' Your 'friend' adds that your criminal career stretched to the cities of Hull, Manchester, and Nottingham. Some 'friend,' Peace."

"Sweet Sue," murmured Charlie. "On t'grind for gin. . . ."

"Well, *someone's* done a lot of talking," said Lockwood. His information was that it was Sue Bailey—still calling herself Mrs. Thompson—but there were also others "who knew the infamous Peace" selling their yarns for shillings. He picked out some issues of *The Times* covering the last days of January. "They report your removal to Wakefield. And here we have an article on your 'career of crime' full of 'startling facts,' purporting to come from a statement you yourself made following your committal. Tell me, have you made such a statement?"

Charlie shook his head. He'd dearly like to, but the authorities were too vigilant.

"Good. But 'tis said you plan to auction two violins for payment of my—er—services?" Lockwood looked at Clegg, who shrugged.

"Happen old Hannah will," Charlie told them both. Perhaps his wife had such a sale in mind.

Embarrassed, Lockwood now picked out a *Times* for February 1. "This edition states that your Mrs. Thompson has made some 'extraordinary disclosures.' . . ."

"H'extraordinary woman, Sue," said Charlie.

"She speaks of guns you owned—tools you burgled with—plunder you obtained?"

"I h'ofttimes plundered our Sue, sir!" grinned Charlie.

"And today's edition," said Lockwood, tight-lipped at his client's unconcern, "gives us some 'extracts' from her promised 'disclosures.' She says: 'I believe that at different times he received sentences of twenty-one years penal servitude, but his very good conduct reduced his terms. . . .'"

"Sue's conduct was werry good h'under t'blankets," said Charlie.

Clegg laughed, but Lockwood scowled at the solicitor. "Mrs. Thompson said more. She further claims you once robbed the home of a clergyman who'd befriended you. Not very nice, Peace?"

Charlie's smile vanished. For a moment he hated Sue Bailey. But then he recalled that he'd never told her about his trouble with Littlewood over that silly school clock. No, this was Sue being malicious, probably under the influence of gin and the prompting of newsmen. His grin returned. " 'Appen I wunce worked Lambeth Palace of Bishops, sirs," he said with a wink, pausing to let the scandalous admission sink in. "But us left h'empty-handed—all them h'episcopal croziers transpired to be made o' base metals. Nay, 'tis mine Sweet Sue just fibbing—and that lass would say owt for t'brass!"

Lockwood put down his chosen copies of *The Times.* "Well, it's still undesirable publicity, Peace."

Charlie looked briefly at other newspapers; they all printed stories even more crimson. They troubled the barrister, too; the masses, stupid as they were, believed the words of the commonest journal; anything printed carried the stamp of officialdom.

"I'll trouble you no more," Lockwood told Charlie. He rose and stretched while Clegg gathered up all the newspapers. "I shall simply urge your jury to cast prejudice aside—to approach their verdict with an open mind. I shall address them on this aspect in the strongest of terms!" And he silently cursed the freedom of the press.

" 'Tis sad I'm h'unable to address 'em mysen," Charlie grumbled.

"No, you mustn't!" The one thing Lockwood didn't want was a repetition of Charlie's behavior at the lower court. "Not one word from you, fellow!"

Charlie grudgingly promised to be quiet.

When Lockwood and his solicitor had gone, Charlie sat at his cell table in silence. He ate no supper, and even refused to throw dice with his warders. He knew Lockwood was clever, but he wondered if the barrister was oversimplifying his case. Clegg had failed before the magistrate, and Charles Brassington had sworn that Charlie had threatened to shoot both Dysons. Charlie thought a jury would see the laborer as a witness with no ax to grind.

Sleep didn't come easily that night with his worries and because the authorities at Armley insisted upon lamps burning full-wick all the time, and no exception was made at Town Hall. Charlie was haggard by dawn, when it was time to get dressed in his convict garb and to be shaved by a warder.

Clegg came to see him at nine. He said Lockwood was robing and was too busy to see him at the moment, so Charlie discussed with Clegg how Brassington must be attacked. Charlie was consumed with fear of this witness, whose tale was pure perjury, as bad as Kate Dyson's, and yet Brassington had no motive to lie. Charlie thought Mr. Pollard must have fed falsehoods to Brassington until the dense fellow truly believed them. He was sure this sort of thing happened in courts.

Just before ten, a platoon of dock officers and police arrived to escort him up to the courtroom, which was brighter than the one in the Old Bailey. Tall windows gave Charlie a glimpse of the sky and a large bird that flew across. Charlie saw it from the dock steps and envied its freedom. Then, on the hour, loud raps heralded the entry of the judge, and within seconds Charlie heard his name being called. The clerk of assize was demanding he be "put to the bar"; and his warders brought him up into the oak dock, where he was made to stand while the indictment was put to him. He saw Mr. Justice Lopes, black-bearded and red-robed, high on the Bench. At least eight other people sat with him, one wearing the chain of a mayor.

The clerk was asking Charlie if he be guilty.

"H'innocent!" he replied, in what he hoped was a clear voice.

He spied Lockwood in counsel's row, talking to a man in a shiny black robe. Charlie rightly guessed this was the Queen's Counsel who appeared for the prosecution. The clerk was ordering a jury to be fetched, and nineteen men were herded into the jury box. Charlie knew he had seven "challenges" for which he need not show cause--hence the nineteen men, but he left any challenging to Lockwood, who made none.

John Littlewood sat in the well of the courtroom where the High Sheriff had kindly ordered a place be provided him. The vicar found courts stuffily tedious, but not this trial in progress. He was watching Kate Dyson. He thought she'd aged a great deal since he'd last seen her, but she was still handsome and stylish. Charlie's lawyer had failed to either frighten or annoy her in cross-examination and she was giving her evidence in a monologue, saying "I don't remember" rather than falling into possible traps. She coolly denied all the letters attributed to her.

Littlewood believed she was lying and perhaps the judge did too —he frowned a great deal. Littlewood looked at Bradbury, who was beside the exhibits table nearby. The inspector was also scowling at the woman, but not so Walsh behind him; the latter was grinning quite openly. The vicar thought it improper to smirk at allegations of adultery.

Mrs. Dyson was being questioned about the night of the murder and Lockwood was testing her cautiously. She agreed that her husband had fallen onto his back when shot, but not in the course of a struggle; Dyson had never grasped hold of Peace, and she'd seen the incident throughout its entirety. Lockwood's was a thankless task, and not made any easier by a question from the Bench.

"How long between the first shot and the second?" asked the judge.

"They were in succession," Kate Dyson answered.

If that be true, thought Littlewood, then Peace fired his gun in either rage or panic; and, if that be right, his act was murder.

Jacob Bradbury was curious to see how Brassington would fare under the plush pageantry of assizes. The laborer, cap in hand, had turned ghastly white when examined by the Crown, but Campbell Foster led him gently through his evidence and he didn't falter. When he'd finished, he turned to leave the witness box and had to be brought back for Lockwood's questions.

"Without looking at the dock, do you recognize the man you met that night solely on account of his clothes?"

"He 'ad dark clothes on," mumbled Brassington.

"Did you notice his clothes more than his face?"

"I didn't take much notice of him at all!"

"Then how d'you know it was November twenty-ninth?"

"I expect it was."

"Did they tell you it was the twenty-ninth?"

Brassington made no answer.

"How did you find out then?"

"I looked at the paper!"

"Can you read?"

"No . . ."

"Then that wouldn't help you. . . . How did you know it was the twenty-ninth?"

"Someone told us."

Good God, thought Bradbury; one of his constables must have done so.

"Who was it?" Lockwood asked.

"I don't know. I only know what others say. I've heard other folks say it."

"What others? Come on, man, think!" But Lockwood could obtain no answer. Brassington twisted his cap in his fingers, stared at the ceiling, at his boots, anywhere except at his questioner. Lockwood dug deeper. "You gave evidence before the coroner? Then before the magistrate? Yes. . . . Now, did anyone read your previous evidence to you?"

Brassington smiled brightly. "Yes, Mr. Pollard!"

"And did Mr. Pollard read it to you and say, 'This is what you're going to say'?" Brassington's eyes narrowed, he tugged his short nose, but he wouldn't reply.

What in blazes had the Treasury Solicitor been up to? wondered Bradbury. He held Pollard responsible for this breach of regulations and vowed never to trust a Southern lawyer again.

Lockwood then taxed dim Brassington on the words "I'll shoot them," put down to Peace. The barrister was endeavoring to distinguish that plain threat from his client's admitted expression, "I'll make it warm for them."

"Is it that you thought he meant 'shoot' by saying he'd make it 'warm'?"

But Brassington was stubborn. "Nay, he said he'd shoot them!"

Bradbury looked at the jury for their reaction. Brassington was the worst witness in the inspector's varied field of remembrance. But the jurymen sat like dummies, their foreman chewing, another probing his ear with a pencil. It occurred to Bradbury that, should he one day transgress the law he sought to uphold, he would not care to be judged by a dozen of his "peers" picked at random.

Hannah was aloft in the public gallery, alone and utterly miserable. She could spot the bald head of her husband twenty feet below. He sat hunched in a hopeless attitude, elbows on knees, and she wanted to go to him. She'd endured Kate Dyson's prevarications without comment to her fellow spectators. She didn't want to address any of them—she thought they watched like jackals, mouths agape, as they observed the downfall of another human being. The judge looked mild enough; he often fiddled with his beard, which seemed out of place under a wig. But his aspect during the evidence of Kate Dyson had been less indulgent, as if he'd secret knowledge the woman was a vixen. As to the matter of Dyson's death, his Lordship had written more, and grimaced less often. Hannah put his age at around fifty, which she deemed young for a judge. He came from Cornwall or Devon, she'd heard, where plain folk still worshipped smugglers and tended to commit more hellworthy acts with animals. . . .

Her thoughts were interrupted by Campbell Foster's declaration that he intended to prove Charlie had uttered threats against the Dysons in Darnall. Lockwood objected, saying such evidence was "too remote," but the judge held otherwise.

Rosie Sykes was called—Hannah hoped she'd delivered her baby well—and spoke of Charlie's vow to blow out the brains of the Dysons. Jim Sykes followed his wife, and he supported her evidence as to the threats.

"You bloody villain!" Charlie's voice echoed across the court. "Thou art a devil!"

Sykes quailed under these words, and the jury stared at the dock, some looking alarmed by Charlie's outburst.

During the rest of the Crown's case, Hannah's eyes lost their focus. I'm getting old, she mused, and 'appen I'll soon die a widow. . . .

Right at the back of the public gallery sat a man with an outsize head. Hannah hadn't noticed him, or she might have created a scene. Forsey Brion had come up for the trial. Both his wife Alice and Sue had sent him, in case that reward became mentioned. Brion couldn't see much of the trial's actors, or hear their scripts well until Frank Lockwood's closing speech to the jury, which was delivered in ringing Riding tones.

"Mr. Campbell Foster has alluded to rumors circulated with regard to Peace," he told the jury. "Aye, these rumors have not been limited to this town, but from one end of the country to t'other. There has been a merciless cry for blood!" He was referring to the press. "Never in my experience has there been such an attempt to determine the guilt of this man. People have terribly forgotten their duty. They haven't hesitated, for the sake of the paltry pence they could snatch from the public, to prejudice this man's life."

"Hear, hear!" came Charlies voice from the dock.

Brion didn't agree with either Lockwood or the voice: he thought the newspapers only too right in revealing the many misdoings of Peace and he had sold this opinion to one local paper for sixty-five shillings.

"You've had your ears filled with reports," Lockwood continued. "Won't you be careful when you come to consider your verdict? See that any bias is thoroughly eliminated! There's not a fact in the life of this man they haven't raked up. His life may have been wicked, but you must remember that, if his life has been wicked, he is at least fitted to be hurried into the presence of God."

"I'm not fit to die!" cried the voice.

Oh, yes you are, thought Brion.

And so it went on . . . for a good half hour by the round clock above the coat-of-arms over the Bench. Brion's mind wandered back to the reward money and his fear that Sue Bailey would get it. (His wife had said the woman was secretly petitioning the Home Secretary, and the Brions allowed her to stay in their house only to scotch such perfidy.) But now Lockwood was finishing his address.

"I don't care what the prisoner's life has been; I ask you to spare it because, the worse it has been, the less fitted is he now to die."

"I'm not fit to die!" agreed that gravelly voice.

Brion had suddenly spotted Hannah and he slipped from the gallery like a sneak thief, quite terrified, anxious to find a safe place in the Town Hall where he could hide until a verdict was reached, though he'd have to lie to the women in London about missing the judge's summing up of the case.

Lopes reminded the jury of the evidence with a voice lost in his beard. He was quick because it was late—nearly seven—and the court lamps were temperamental. He avoided passing a personal opinion of Mrs. Dyson, of her possible intrigue with Charlie, and left it to the jury to determine the value of the letters. But the inference was that he thought them irrelevant and he sent the jury away to their retiring room with last mutters as to "their duty to the community at large."

The foreman-elect was one Crabtree, with another, Craik, a jealous contender for that honor. The two Cs took over their remaining ten jurors in no uncertain terms from the outset. Crabtree was an avid reader of the *Police Gazette* and other "blood and thunders"; there was nothing about Charlie he didn't know. Craik, on the other hand, knew all about burglary because his own house had been recently "turned over" by some navvies, who'd vandalized what they'd not stolen. "My missus was sick when she saw it!" he told them all.

"But they was Irish, not Peace," said Number 5, called Lee.

Craik glared at him; Lee was obviously Jewish; Craik's father had once told him the Yids ate Christian babies at Christmas. Damn Jews and damn Lee.

"Well, Peace's guilty all right," said Crabtree. "The *Gazette*'s doing a phrenological design of his head. And look at his aliases —Ward, Parker, Thompson and Mann. . . . The *Gazette* has published them all!"

"Actually my name's Mann," said Number 8, apologetically.

Eleven nasty faces stared at him; Mann's decision no longer counted.

"Will he swing 'n chains?" asked Number 10, an ancient called Nettleton. The old fellow had been born in Regency times; nobody understood his jargon; he too was to be forgotten.

"So we agree he's guilty?" Craik asked the remaining ten.

Lee shrugged; he wasn't certain, but he feared to contradict the two Cs.

"I'll say 'Guilty,' " Crabtree reassumed his position as forman.

"They swung 'im on hemp from a gibbet," said Nettleton.

"What's that?" Crabtree demanded.

"Yon fella I saw turned off. And he was sort of 'wound up' and then let go. . . ." A childhood memory sparkled in his rheumy eyes.

"Yes, but they doth it more snappish now!" Crabtree retorted.

"And I had his boots when they got kicked off," Nettleton added proudly.

The jury returned after a decent twelve minutes. The judge kept them waiting a further five, and then Charlie was put back "to the bar."

"Guilty!" Crabtree answered the clerk.

Somebody was heard to utter a stifled cry in the public gallery, but all faces were turned toward Charlie.

"Have you anything to say why the court should not pass sentence according to law?"

Charlie was seen to look toward Lockwood and smile. " 'Tis no use saying owt," he replied faintly.

Mr. Justice Lopes took up his pen, but didn't write. He passed the death sentence without any comment and said "hanged by the neck" very quickly, as if it was a technical term. Charlie smiled again.

Then the warders touched his sleeve and took him below. He stumbled once, and they supported him in case he was going to faint but he shook off their hands.

"I've h'only heard them words said once before," he told them. "And then said to another h'innocent man."

II

Armley was shrouded in mist when they brought Charlie back in irons. The jail had a condemned cell, but the Governor still feared a suicide attempt and ordered him to be returned to the first-floor adaption, which had another advantage: it was nearer the gallows.

Charlie was morose, but he settled in quietly and decided to be easy on his warders, young fellows most of them, who looked very anxious.

"Get out thine cards and bid farewell to thy pay!" he told them. They were happy to oblige.

Charlie Peace seemed to have shrunk during the day in court; his movements were slower, his tongue quieter; and the warders felt a sudden compassion for him. "Some say tha'll take thine own life!" one said nervously.

Charlie shuffled the cards, fanned them, and slid an ace up his sleeve. "Who says so, lad?"

"Lunnaners."

Charlie chuckled. "Nivver heed 'bout Lunnaners—I'm back in Yorkshire!" But he thought hard while they played faro—so hard he neglected to sharp his ace—and he lost. "Today's not mine winning day," he commented, and added, "I hear my missus was at h'assize?"

They looked embarrassed; they'd heard that the prisoner's wife had fled court in tears after sentence.

"Daft woman!" Charlie said. "Ye'd have thought she'd at least tried to spring us!" He joked to spare the men's feelings. And when the card game was over, he had a test for them. "I'll give you lads a prodig'us problem, and the one that gives me the *right* h'answer gets a reward. But the *right* answer mind? He'll get my ring in our Governor's custody. How say you?"

The warders agreed; the ring was reputed to be a white-brass knuckleduster.

"So 'appen there was a bad 'un onetime," Charlie began. "He shot a man, but h'evaded Jack Law. That was all right, 'cept another man paid for the crime by being sentenced to hang. The bad 'un said nowt. Was he right? Would you hold thine tongue or speak up?"

The others discussed the issue among themselves, and reached a common agreement. "We'd say nowt," said their spokesman.

Charlie nodded. The answer he'd hoped for—but the wrong one. "That bad 'un's in 'ell," he said quietly, "and that ring goes to my barrister as keepsake."

Two long days passed, during which Charlie was silent. He played cards, always losing, forgetting to cheat, and even neglected to curse. For the rest of the time, he paced the stone floor,

Bible in hand, mouthing tracts till his guardians feared for his sanity.

"Would you like Mr. Cookson?" he was asked.

"Who? No, I've mine own pastor. . . . But I'd like my blazers and summat to write on. . . ."

His spectacles were found, and he wrote two letters, both religious and vague. "I think I shall have to die in a fortnight from now," he wrote Hannah, without really knowing the date set for his execution. "I'm yet very ill," he finished, for his lungs rattled like those of a silicotic. He also wrote to Billy Bolsover, telling his son-in-law not to take revenge on the Sykeses for their perjury, since he "felt no imbetterness against no Person in this world." He nonetheless advised Billy to shun the Sykeses' company—and included a "Prayer," which he hoped would join other mementos on Peace mantelpieces.

His health didn't improve and he demanded whiskey, which he was given by the tumblerful and which he shared with his warders. He decided it was better in some ways to be "condemned" than "in durance vile."

He perked up on the seventh, when he had a letter from London. "It's from a Miss Bailey," the Governor told him, handing Charlie her letter.

"Well, God bless her!" Charlie smiled while he read it. "She wants to see us! Says she must—or she'll die!" He looked up from his bed. "Can I see her, sir?"

The Governor hesitated; he thought of poison, but remembered that it was "the Traitress" who had given them that very warning. "I suppose so," he agreed.

"I'll write her straightways!" Charlie sprang from his bed like a youngster, his health restored. He penned Sue a short answer, insisting she come, but asking her not to communicate his letter to the press.

"You really want to see her?" the Governor said when he'd

finished. Charlie's affection for someone so disloyal amazed him.

"Aye, sir . . . I h'enjoyed her companionship for nigh on two years. Bit o' a peg-puff, is Sue, but I was part of her downfall. Dreadful snuffer, too—snuffs half an h'ounce per day—and she drinks like Kate Dyson. She'd do well to put herself in an h'asylumm for drunkards. 'Appen I can talk her into doing just that —make a good woman of her, like Maddy the Whore."

The Governor frowned. He still didn't understand, but he'd some bad news to impart. "Your—er—execution has been fixed," he said, looking at the floor, "for the twenty-fifth of this month."

A short silence followed; the warders also stared at their feet; but then Charlie slapped his thighs. "Who does it, sir?"

"Mr. Marwood."

"Us had us two ferines called Ketch and Calcraft," Charlie said reflectively, "but nivver a Marwood."

"He's quick—experienced—" said the Governor.

"Tell 'im to grease the rope, sir."

The Governor looked up uneasily. "You know about hangings, Peace?"

"No, but I'm good on ropery."

The Governor shivered. "Yes, well I'll leave you now, and have your letter sent off. . . . D'you need anything else, Peace?"

"More whiskey, sir!"

Charlie woke with a hangover, but his fuddled mind recalled the Governor's news. He was to be hanged in fifteen days' time, and Sue was allowed to visit. The Governor hadn't mentioned any possible reprieve—not that Charlie expected further endeavors on his behalf. But he did receive a small consolation. One of his warders handed him a copy of London's *Times*. It was days old, but his trial was covered. In the paper Kate Dyson's denials of their association were described as "feeble."

"Nowt feeble about the lass 'twixt blankets," Charlie told his cellmates. "She was a proper pinch-prick!"

Their laughter was overheard by Chaplain Cookson, come to visit the condemned. Cookson had heard about the whiskey, and voiced his disapproval, but *humor* in the death cell was beyond his ken. Nor was his reception very happy.

"Not you, sir, I want Littlewood!" Charlie told him.

"I thought you'd wish to discuss your soul?" said the chaplain. "You *do* believe in God?"

Charlie nodded. "I believe in God and the Devil, sir. . . . But I fear neither."

Cookson was shocked. "Don't you fear for your soul?"

"Aye, at the moment. But I'll soon be 'arrowed."

Cookson shook his head. "I fail to comprehend you, Peace." He assumed more whiskey had been consumed and left with his outrage.

That afternoon, the Governor and chief warder came.

"Some of your family are here," Charlie was told. "You may see them, but keep your distance." The chief drew a line in chalk a good three feet from the bars dividing Charlie's cell. "You're not to step beyond this mark."

"But how can I kiss them?"

"You can't," said the Governor, who still feared a vial of poison might be passed in a kiss.

Charlie muttered angrily, but waited expectantly to see who'd come. It was Hannah, looking ferocious in flannel, who first came into the far end of the cell. She was followed by Willie Ward, Bolsover, and Janey—with a babe in arms. Charlie was about to run to them, but remembered the line. He dared not cross it lest further visits be stopped.

"Us can't come closer!" he explained with frustration. "The buggers won't allow!" He blew Janey a kiss. "Hold up thine child, darling, so its grampy can see it!" The baby was raised to the bars. "God bless its little soul!" Tears smarted in Charlie's eyes and he wiped his nose on a sleeve. "And how are you all, my pets?"

Hannah stepped up to the bars, her expression terrible. "Thine mother's dead," she said bluntly.

"Oh, my God!" Charlie felt for a chair. He found one screwed to the floor, but tore it loose and sat, ignoring a shout from the warders. "Did she know all?" he asked, his voice breaking.

His wife nodded. "But that didn't kill her. Her heart died a long while back. Forget her, and look to thysen; tha'll be seeing her in heaven soon enuff."

"Less I'm bound for a diff'rent place, lass!" Charlie almost smiled. But Hannah was right: he'd little time to mope, and his mother must have been a good ninety. He talked awhile to Janey and his son-in-law, who said they planned to leave Darnall and try their luck across the seas. Then Willie promised never to abandon his mother, nor marry while she lived, and Charlie's mind was set at rest. He asked the children to leave, so he could speak with Hannah privately. But his warders were still within earshot, and he addressed her in the vaguest terms.

"Recall h'Angel Meadow in '76? Aye, there was two brothers done. 'Appen I should have stood in their place. One went free, but t'other must still be making breakwaters. I could speak up and fake his slangs?"

Hannah understood what he said; an old suspicion was confirmed; he had shot that bobby at Whalley Range. And now he was asking her whether he should confess. She thought he should—but one dire thought stopped her saying so. "Suppose there's a reprieve in offing over present trubble," she said, thinking of how some newspapers were attacking Mrs. Dyson's evidence. "If there is, and tha tell owt about Manchester, won't it get chucked from window?"

Charlie shrugged. "I lay odds there'll be no mercy, h'anyroad."

"Still, think on it," Hannah warned him. " 'Twould be a pretty mess if there was. And tha's not cut out for martyrdom, Charles Peace!"

She was advising him to hold his tongue. He was surprised; he'd thought his wife would have insisted otherwise; her old spirit was crumbling. But Charlie had made up his mind; he wanted to make a grand gesture before quitting this world; so he changed the subject.

"Sue wrote us," he said. "She wants to visit."

"Not while I'm alive!"

"Come, woman. She can do no harm."

Hannah stamped her clogs. He'd been unwise to mention Sue —for whom Hannah's hatred had become implacable over the last few months. "If she comes, tha'll see nowt more of me!" she swore. "Nor Janey, neither!"

And Charlie knew she meant her threat. "As you will," he mumbled. "I'll have Captain Smith keep her out." He saw Hannah was about to leave. "Nay, lass, stay awhile!" he begged.

But his wife gave him an infernal look. "I'm going because tha's made us vexed! I'll cum back anon!" And she strode out of the cell to find Janey.

None of them returned that day, and Charlie brooded over the Bible. A whole week passed, and nobody came, and he grew frantic. Was he to be deserted?

III

Sue Bailey arrived in Leeds during that week. Having sold jewelry from 5 East Terrace to good profit, she traveled first class, and her clothes and luggage were expensive. Forsey Brion had suggested she undertake the journey because he was sure that Charlie had stowed a mass of stolen property somewhere in

Peckham, and if Sue could only get Charlie to disclose its where-abouts, Brion and she would share any award paid for its recovery. (The Home Office were still being enigmatic about the £100 reward.)

Sue had several brandies on the train, and she made a fuss at the station because she couldn't hire a cab. Her language was unladylike until a hansom agreed to take her to Armley and as she climbed inside she failed to notice a little wherry, containing two people, being lashed up in pursuit of her.

The cart followed the cab to the prison gates. Sue paid off her hire, but asked the driver to wait. She approached the wicket door and pulled the big bell. A grille opened and a man's face appeared. She told him her name and the purpose of her visit, but he said she couldn't enter without written leave. She commenced to argue, shouting at the gate officer, and the door was shut in her face. She screamed with rage and beat on the gate with her parasol, but the door remained firmly closed. She turned to walk back to her cab—and found it gone. She looked around in alarm; her bags had been dumped on the cobbles; and then she saw the wherry. Willie Ward was at the reins, but Hannah was approaching, cart whip in hand.

"You!" shrieked Sue, falling back with fright.

And Hannah was fast upon her, the crop raised, and she brought it down a stinging blow across Sue Bailey's ear. Sue dropped to her knees, howling and cringing, her hands raised to protect herself. But Hannah didn't strike again; she just spat on her contemptuously. "Get up, you brazen hussy," she ordered.

Sue obeyed, but quivering. "Please don't hit me!"

Hannah lowered the whip. "He'll not see you," she said. "Nor will tha try ta see him. Yonder is his grave now; you should know, you dug it for him."

"But he asked me to see him!" Sue whined, producing Charlie's letter.

"That was yesterweek. He's changed his mind."

"I don't believe you!"

"Then believe this: if us catches you here again, I'll beat tha blind!" Hannah lifted her crop and Sue ran to gather up her luggage, and fled onto Execution Field. She ran down the hill as fast as her thick legs could carry her, staggering under the weight of her bags and losing a shoe in the mud, but she didn't stop running till she gained the town below. So great was her terror that she was now quite sober, but she wept as she started the long trudge back into the city.

That night Sue was still in Leeds only because she'd missed the last train to London. Topped up with brandy, in cheap lodgings, she penned Charlie a last letter.

"My own dear Jack," it began. "What do you mean by turning against me? I who have cared for you! Why am I to suffer this? Have I deserved it? John, darling, I must see you again. I implore you upon my knees to see me!" Sue's ear still buzzed from the whiplash, but she finished the missive as lovingly as she could. "Please let us meet for one final kiss, your dearest most affectionate Sue."

Brion would be pleased she'd written this letter, but Sue only hoped it would pain Hannah.

IV

Littlewood came to Armley on Saturday, in response to a letter from Charlie—who said he had a "great message" for the people of Darnall. The vicar was relieved to be summoned; he'd come to believe himself forgotten by the little man.

When he arrived at the prison, he was drawn aside by Cookson. "No contact is allowed," the chaplain said snidely. "Even you must talk to him without touching." The Governor was away and Cookson made mean use of that fact.

"And how *is* Peace?" Littlewood asked.

"Canting from dawn to dusk. Shameful humbug!"

Littlewood laughed. "Of course it is! But you should be grateful he's canting, not cussin'!"

He found Charlie parading his cell with candle and Bible, intoning like a friar, doubling up when he coughed. They couldn't shake hands and the warders refused to "pike off," as Charlie requested.

"Then get Mr. Littlewood paper and pen!" he roared at them.

This they did, together with a table and chair. Their curiosity was aroused, but Charlie told them to "shut their lugs" and stay at the far end of his cell. He then came as close to the bars as he dared. But Littlewood spoke first.

"Well, Peace, what a fine pickle we're in! Did you know I attended your trial?"

"I did not, sir. And I'd not be in this pickle if my witnesses had testinessed!" He paused, fingers to lips. " 'I have spoken unto them, but they have not heard; I called unto them, but they have not h'answered!' " And he rolled his eyes heavenward. One of the warders tittered. "Shut thy gap, you bugger!" Charlie snarled at him.

"Very good, Peace," said Littlewood. "Jeremiah, is it not? Now then, what great message have you for me?"

Charlie cleared his throat. "Well, sir . . . about that school clock you say us stole . . . I nivver did—nivver touched it!"

Littlewood sighed: had he been brought here just to hear that again? As it was, he accepted Charlie was innocent of that particular theft, and he thought it apt to reply with another Bible quote. " 'You are clean and without transgression, Peace, I'm sorry I putteth thine feet in the stocks!' "

Charlie grinned. "Werry good, sir—Book o' Job!" He grew serious. "Us wanted to see you to h'unburdon mine mind, sir. I know I'm to die next Tuesday, and I want to take from my conscience summat that weighs heavy. If I could h'undo what I've done, I'd suffer my body cut to pieces by the h'inch." He made Littlewood sit at the table. "Jot down what I say, sir, for I mayn't repeat it."

The vicar feared a religious tirade and hesitated. But Charlie seemed so anxious, he eventually dipped the pen in the inkwell. "Not too fast, Peace. . . ."

Charlie nodded; he chose his words carefully, a bit of an eye on the warders. "I was in Manchester in '76—to work some houses. I went to a quarter called Whalley Range. I passed two bobbies on t'road. One later made a grab at us. My blood was up —being so disturbed. I told him to stand off, or I'd fire. He wouldn't—he had his staff and was about to strike me. These Manchester bobbies are terrible obstinate! I'd no time to lose. I fired wide at him—but the daft bugger came on. I then fired a second time; the ball struck him in the breast and he fell. My great mistake has allus been this, sir; in all my career I've used ball. I did wrong—I ought to have used blank—then I'd nivver have taken a life. But I didn't h'intend to murder him. I've fired hundreds of barrels at folk to frighten 'em—with threats that I'd shoot 'em—but I made it a rule not to take life. . . ."

"God save us!" Littlewood interrupted. He'd given up writing; he was simply listening in a daze.

"H'anyroad," Charlie went on. "I got clear—which was all I wanted. Some time later, us saw in t'papers that certain men had got took for the murder. I h'attended their trial for two days, and heard the youngest get sentenced to death. This was afterwards reduced unto servitude. . . ." He stopped to stare at his confessor. "Tha'll say I'm a hardened wretch? But what could I do? Had us done h'otherwise, I should have been hanged!"

Littlewood nodded.

"But," Charlie said, "I've nowt now to gain from secrecy. I deem it right to clear this young man!" He coughed violently and drank some water; whiskey seemed inappropriate at the moment. "Now, sir, dost thou wish to hear about my shooting Mr. Dyson?"

Littlewood wasn't sure what he wanted to hear—but he was given Charlie's version of the Banner Cross killing in detail.

"I nivver h'intended for to murder that long pipe o' piss!" Charlie finished the narrative.

Littlewood shook his head. "I haven't recorded much of this," he admitted. "You'll have to say it all over again."

"That I will, sir."

"And I'm not a Roman priest, you know? You haven't my vow of silence?"

Charlie smiled. "I know that—but I want the world to know, and your help, sir."

"Help?"

"To stop folk niggling my fambly. They've done nowt—they had no more to do with mine felonies than the greatest stranger in t'land!"

"People in Darnall are kindly," Littlewood assured him. "Now, what about your confession?"

"'Tis God's truth!"

"I daresay. . . . But will others think so? The authorities may believe you're just trying to get a man out of prison. Another one of your pranks. They distrust you, Peace. And you can't blame them—you've hoodwinked the law far too long."

Charlie saw his point. Nor did he think jackass law quick to admit a dreadful miscarriage of their precious justice. He remembered the trial judge—a fool who'd set so much store on a footprint. If that gander still strode the Bench, he'd likely repeat his silly views. Charlie stared at Littlewood. Here was an upright man who knew him. "Surely the buggers will take thine word, sir?"

But the vicar shook his gray head. "Why should they? I'm just an old country parson to them—'strong in arm and thick in the head,' as they say." Littlewood flicked at the papers before him.

"No, if you seriously wish to force their hand, you'll have to write and sign a confession yourself. Then send it direct to the Home Secretary." He smiled. *"He* daren't hide such a document—to do so would be ammunition for his political enemies." The smile vanished. "And if you save this man, Peace, I do believe your own death will be easier. . . ."

Charlie agreed—and thought there was nothing "thick" about Littlewood, either. Just talking to him had made the prospect of death far more bearable. Now he taxed him as a good man of the cloth.

"Dost thou believe God be merciful, sir?"

"Certainly."

"Even to the likes of mysen?"

"Especially so!"

"Then who's in hell?"

"Perhaps hell is empty. . . . Save for poor Judas. . . ."

Charlie disagreed; he was enjoying this discussion far more than his confessions. " 'Appen not even the h'Iscariot," he said. "I've mine own theory about the Hot Place, sir. . . . Bear with us, and I'll tell it thee! When the Ikeys cruxified Jesus, he was took down dead from the cross in body. Aye, but what happened to His Spirit? My legend says It went down to hell—to fetch out the Good Thief. And whilst It was there in the Oven, he found Judas and other bad buggers. They started yowelling as how they also deserved h'anuther chance. So Gentle Jesus hauled 'em all up to Heaven, saying now they was harrowed—purified—and fit to lodge in the Sweet Place. This wast called the 'Harrowing of Hell.' . . . Hast thou heard of same, sir?"

Littlewood had not, but thought it a very nice story. He decided to repeat it to Newman when next he saw him—though he envisaged his friend's long face when told of its author. "D'you think you're being 'harrowed' here in Armley?" he asked.

"I most solemnly do, sir. I'm flayed to death by the thought of

Old Hobb. Besides, 'tis said Paganini's down below, and us hates competition on t'fiddle."

Both men laughed. But time was passing, and Littlewood had much to do. "Let us be serious, Peace. Now, repeat to me everything you've said of Manchester and Banner Cross, and *slowly* this time!"

Charlie did so, speaking in a soft monotone, pausing whenever the vicar indicated. "I feel penitant for all my crimes," he finished, "and I shall h'endeavor to die bravely. That's it—no more, sir." He was looking worried.

"What is it, Peace?" Littlewood exercised his stiff fingers.

"Dyson and that bobby must both be in Paradise. 'Appen they'll give us a hard time should I show up there!"

"I'm sure they'll flap their wings in your face. . . . Now then, Peace, what else can I do for you?"

Charlie thought for a moment. "Preach a sermon next Sunday to the good folk of Darnall. Tell 'em to abhor a bloody life such as mine, but tell 'em I died game. And wilt thou now pray with me, sir?"

Littlewood nodded. "But no more stupid quotes from the Testaments!"

They got to their knees, Charlie's cracking with rheumatism, and even two of the warders knelt down.

"Let's start with the highest hope," Charlie suggested. So they prayed for his actual deliverance from the scaffold, and ended with the plea that the hangman be quick. "They say Marwood's good?" Charlie interjected.

"They also say you and he once met on a train," murmured Littlewood.

"I nivver did! But I once had a polecat called Calcraft!"

"Shut up, Peace. . . . Now let's pray for your family."

Charlie clasped his hands together. "O Lord, make old Hannah more beautiful! O Lord, make poor Willie less gaumless—

put a brain in his head or else still his tongue! O Lord, guard darling Janey and mine grandbrat! O Lord, send Kate Dyson to hellfire!"

"We'll leave out the last one," said Littlewood. "Now, pray for yourself again, Peace."

Charlie closed his eyes. "O Lord, make this stone floor less buggery on mine knees! O Lord, let them give us malt whiskey on the day of h'execution! O Lord, h'intercede so there'll be no such day h'anyroad! Let us out of here, Lord, and I'll mission for Thysen in cannibal countries! Or, Lord, give us a reprieve, and I'll mission for Thee in prison till I make my h'escape. . . ."

Littlewood interrupted. "Peace, you're rambling. Get up, and say the rest of your prayers on your chair."

Warders helped Charlie be seated, and for the next ten minutes he continued to pray. But his prayers probably confused the Almighty; they certainly irritated His earthly representative.

"I've discovered a truth about you," Littlewood said finally. "You treat life as some kind of jest. Have you never considered the mischief you've caused?"

Charlie hung his head. "Aye, sir. I'm unfit for h'anything. . . ." He perked up. "But I will be on Tuesday, sir! I'll be truly gallusworthy!" And he beamed at the vicar.

"D'you want me there?" asked Littlewood.

"No, sir. But I'd like you to be with old Hannah?"

"I will." Littlewood rose and gathered up Charlie's confession. The two men looked at each other through the bars. It was time to say goodbye. Charlie suddenly had an idea.

"Hey, you!" he called one of the warders over. He took the man's left hand and told him to thrust his right between the bars for Littlewood to hold. In this way he shook hands with the vicar.

"Fare thee well, sir. I pray we may meet in the Sweet Place."

Littlewood smiled, but he felt very sad.

V

Charlie's next visitor felt no such emotion when he came to Armley on Sunday. Forsey Brion had traveled up from London most reluctantly—he believed barbarism started somewhere north of Watford Junction—but he felt his trip was imperative. Sue had failed dismally on her mission and Brion felt it needed a man to deal with Charles Peace; also Brion had much to demand of the fellow before justice took its due course.

The Governor was back, and he allowed Brion to see Charlie when the strange-headed Lunnaner spoke of being "his best friend and fellow inventor." And Charlie was pleased to see Brion—to see anyone in his last few days—although he was surprised by the visit. But Brion was as starchy as ever.

"By jingo, it's cold in this place!" he complained, pulling his tweed cape around him. He also wore an outsize deerstalker hat, which he wouldn't remove. "All well in Peckham?" Charlie asked.

Brion's eyes stopped roving the grim cell and settled on its chief occupant. "No—that's why I've come, Mr.—er—Peace. The neighborhood has become most discourteous toward my wife and myself, as well as to Miss Bailey. They still seem to think we had something to do with your—umm—'enterprises.' . . . It's really intolerable!"

Charlie laughed loud. He could well imagine the whisperings in Phillip and Evilina roads. "What can I do to stop thine trubble?" he inquired.

"Well, you could help prove our innocence by writing a letter?"

" 'Appen? What sort of letter?"

"Just stating that we knew nothing of your—er—businesses.

. . . Perhaps disclosing where you hid some of your—umm— spoils?"

Charlie laughed again. "There's no h'Ali-Baba's cave, sir! I'm just worth a few hundred pund—and that's mostly gone to Messrs. Lockwood and Clegg. But I'll write thee thine letter concerning my bizniz." He sat at his table and took up a quill. He spoke aloud the words he was writing. " 'I do truly say that neither you nor h'any other friend did know h'anything of what I was doing, for I allus represented mysen as an h'independent man. I'm werry sorry to think people round Peckham Rye should h'affect an innocent man's character by connecting it with one of the worst men this world ivver produced.' " He smiled at the last words—perhaps Brion would sell this letter to the highest bidder. He signed the document and asked a warder to hand it to Brion.

"Much obliged," said Brion, tucking it away. "There remains the question of our inventions, Mr. Peace?"

"All thine, Mr. Brion."

"I fear I've lost your original agreement," the other said. This wasn't true—the Patent Office had merely refused to recognize it. "Could you make them a gift?"

Charlie sighed and dipped his pen again. He quickly drew up a deed formally bequeathing, free of cost, all his inventions to Brion. The other examined it carefully for legal flaws. "Yes, that'll do," he said at last, and the deed followed the letter. He consulted his watch. "My, it's past six! I must away if I'm to catch my train!"

"So much for thy visit," Charlie muttered. "Good day to you, sir." He now felt sickened by Brion's behavior and wanted him gone. And Brion was about to leave when a loud hammering was heard. Charlie got up and peered through his cell's small window into the courtyard beyond. This was a central yard in the prison, but the glass panes were so thick he could see nothing.

"What's that din?" Brion asked.

"My scaffold," said Charlie. And when he turned from the window, he found Brion had left.

VI

The new week began with an onslaught of bitter frosts. Snow followed, with winds that howled around the keeps of the prison. Perched on its hill, Armley Gaol belonged to a dark world outside reality, and Charlie appreciated the drama of it all.

"Old Macbeth would 'ave loved this pile," he told his warders. "H'any ghosts?" The warders looked scared, but shook their heads. Charlie shuffled the cards. " 'Appen I'll haunt it then!" He cackled with laughter, uttering low moans in keeping with the wind outside and one of the warders turned up the gaslights.

At midday Hannah arrived for the last time. With her came Willie, Janey, and Bolsover. The chief warder was also present, in Charlie's section of cell.

"You can approach the bars, Peace," he said, although the Governor had given no such leave.

Charlie went straight to Hannah and took both her hands. He kissed her brow, mouth, and cheek, and she collapsed with a sob. Willie held her up, and Charlie stroked her worn face. "Tha's been a good 'un, old woman," he said softly. "And I've nivver weally loved no one but thee."

"I know that!" she whispered, and fell back from the bars, hiding her grief in a handkerchief.

Charlie went next to his daughter. He put his arms through the bars and gently held his grandchild. The infant's eyes were open, a dark hazel like his own, and he stared into them for a long time. Then he handed back the bundle to Janey. "Don't tell him owt about his granddad," he advised her. "Let him hear myths he'll nivver believe." He beckoned and Janey came closer. He kissed her twice and tasted a tear, which he smoothed from her cheek. It was his daughter's turn to break down and retreat, and he was left with the boys. He shook both their hands and embraced Willie. Bolsover was stiff and pale, but now Willie began weeping.

"Right, that's enuff!" Charlie shouted at them all. "I'll not have thee blubbing on account o' us! Pull thyselns together!"

His family made an effort and they talked softly about different subjects in turn. But this spasmodic conversation was interrupted by a renewal of yesterday's hammering.

"Mine gallus," Charlie lightly observed.

The chief warder heard him. "Nonsense, Peace! It's a new shed being erected."

Charlie shook his head. "That's deal, sir. I know the sound of deal being worked, and they nivver have deal in prison for owt else but scaffolds." He looked back at Hannah. "Nivver heed, woman! 'Appen I'd like to see mine own coffin 'n' grave. I look upon the scaffold as a shortcut to Heaven."

"Don't speak so," she said.

"It doesn't matter. I'll be thrown in mine grave like a dog, but h'only mine body wilt be there. My soul will be Above." Charlie delighted in such talk. He left the bars and went to his cell table, where he painstakingly began to scribble on a prison card. He smiled as he worked. In three minutes he'd finished and he brought the card over to Hannah. "Put it with the others," he told her.

She looked at the card. It was a Funeral Memoriam, etched in black ink.

> In Memory of Charles Peace
> who was executed in Armley Prison
> Tuesday, February 25, 1879
> Aged 47.
> For that I don but never intended.

Hannah stared at it and then at her husband. It was typical, she thought: even on the eve of his death, the man made black comedy. But she'd take it as asked, and stand it up on the mantelpiece with the ones to his father, sister, and son. And she'd dust it, reread it occasionally, and remember him as he looked now— happily mischievous—for the rest of her days.

"Rest in peace, Charlie," she sniffed, dabbing her eyes again.

VII

The blizzards stopped that night, but not so the wind. The nerves of Charlie's warders were stretched taut, but their charge remained serene. The Governor called just before midnight, with a half-gill of whiskey.

"Mr. Cookson would very much like to see you," he urged Charlie. The chaplain lurked in his quarters waiting, very hurt for still not being summoned. "Spare his feelings, Peace."

Charlie shrugged. "Werry well, sir—send him to us." He poured himself a small measure of liquor and a bigger one for a warder. "What time tomorrow, sir?" he asked.

"Eight o'clock."

"Marwood here?"

The Governor nodded. The hangman had been testing his ropes and the trap all evening.

"I'd like to see him afore I *formally* meet him," Charlie said. "Shake his hand and so on?"

It was an unusual request, but the Governor wasn't a man bound by strict rules at times like these. "I shall ask him," he replied. "I'm sure he'll do as you ask." He'd found William Marwood a friendly fellow.

Charlie endured Cookson until two o'clock—"blue o'clock in the morning"—and then tried to sleep. He hadn't been given the malt whiskey he'd wanted, but the spirit he'd drunk was warming, and he fell into a fitful slumber and didn't dream at all.

At six, he was shaken awake by the warder with whom he'd shared the whiskey, and that man was red-eyed with fatigue. A hot breakfast was already on the cell table, but Charlie washed his face and hands before eating. He regretted not having a bone for his teeth, but made do with a toothbrush. He looked out the cell window. It was still dark and the panes frosty. Then he sat down to a large plate of bacon and eggs.

"Bloody rotten bacon this!" was his comment.

Having eaten, he smoked a pipe of strong shag and was soon convulsed by coughs, and slapped on the back by the warders. "I wonder if Marwood wilt cure this o' mine!" he muttered when he could speak. He abandoned his pipe and retired to the lavatory in one corner of the cell. He closed the door, but couldn't lock it, and sat a long time ruminating.

"Have you done in there?" came a voice from outside, rather anxiously.

"You're in one hell of a hurry!" Charlie shouted back. "Who's getting hanged, you or me?" And he was left to his own devices.

Marwood came before the fatal hour, looming tall in the door, straps in his hand. He was as nattily dressed as an undertaker, but his face was all smiles.

"Good morrow, Peace," he said, as if to an old friend.

Charlie shook his hand, which was ice-cold and bony. "I'm glad to see you, sir. Us wanted to speak with you before the big rush." He hesitated, searching for the right words. "I know I've been base 'n' bad, sir, but tha'll not punish us h'unduly?" He hoped his tone was more cheerful than pleading.

"Of course not, my good fellow!" Marwood appeared shocked by the suggestion. "You'll suffer no pain by my hand!"

"And be quick, sir?" Now a whine had crept into Charlie's

voice, and he hated it. "Calcraft wasn't quick. . . ." he growled.

"Calcraft!" Marwood now looked horrified. "Calcraft came from a family of slow-worms. He throttled a man, I *execute* him!"

"Then I'm ready," said Charlie, standing very still. Others had entered the cell—the chief warder, the Governor, and Cookson wearing a surplice. Marwood pinioned Charlie's arms to his body. "That's werry tight, sir," Charlie commented.

"The tighter the better," said Marwood. He slipped his fingers under the main strap and led Charlie out of the cell, the Governor heading the procession behind.

The passage from cell to courtyard was short and dimly lit, but they walked out into the break of a gray new day. The yard was small, stone-flagged, and slippery. Marwood guided Charlie toward a far wall, saying "Careful now!" and "Here we go!" as if helping a child on its first walk. Charlie saw the scaffold, a tall deal gallows, the bottom of which was hung with black sheeting. A noose swung in the breeze from the crossbeam. He also saw a small crowd of men gathered at the foot of the scaffold.

"What's that?" he asked.

"Your press, I fear," said the Governor.

Good, thought Charlie; he had a few words for them. . . .

They reached the gallows and hands helped Charlie up the steps onto a flat platform. Cookson was with them, intoning the burial service, but his voice had to contend with the wind. Charlie was then positioned on the trap, which had great hinges and was flush with the floor. Marks for his feet had been drawn and he obediently stood on them. "God have mercy upon me," he mumbled. Marwood was adjusting the rope. He then drew out a white hood to cover his head, and Charlie remembered the newspapermen. "Hold hard!" he cried, all of a panic. "I want to speak!" Marwood paused. "You gentlemen reporters," Charlie called down to the press. "Say that my last respects are to my children and their dear mother! I hope no paper wilt disgrace itself by taunting or jeering them! Have mercy upon them!" And he prayed they leave his family alone.

Marwood now pulled the hood over his head and put the rope around his neck.

"It fits bloody tight!" he heard Charlie's muffled voice say.

"Then lift up your chin," Marwood said.

Charlie obliged, but the rope was drawn even tighter. It was black and suffocating inside the hood; he could scarcely breathe, and he strained slightly at the bonds around his upper body and legs. Be brave now, he thought, he'd be piked off any second. . . . "Goodbye and God Bless!" he shouted. . . . And then he was falling. A terrible pain jarred his neck. . . .

Marwood stared down the void, hand still on the trap lever. He'd given the little man a good nine feet, and knew he was dead. Talkative sort of client, he thought.

VIII

Kate Dyson stood on a Mersey landing stage. Her portmanteaux had already been shipped aboard the *Honorius,* but she was waiting for Inspector Walsh to arrive. He'd promised to see her off to America in person, and bring the last of her witness expenses in dollars. But he was late; her packet was due to sail in an hour; and she tapped one foot impatiently on the quay.

Then she spied a man weaving through the dockhands toward her. He wore a silk hat and a reefer, and she assumed it was Walsh. But it wasn't—it was Bradbury.

"Aft'noon, ma'am," he said, raising his topper. "Mr. Walsh couldn't come, so I came in his stead." Kate Dyson found his smile infuriating.

"I asked for Walsh!" she snapped.

"Oh, did you just? I didn't know that!" Bradbury had been

fully aware of her request. He took out a bag of coin. "Your money, ma'am." He gave it to her. "D'you want to count it?" She shook her head, so he obtained her signature in his notebook. "Well, that's that, I suppose," he added. "I trust you'll have a good trip."

"Yes." She was about to turn away.

"Bye the bye, they hanged him last week!" Bradbury said.

"I know—I read it in the papers." She wouldn't look at him, but stared out over the river. She'd given her own account of Charles Peace to one newspaper for a handsome sum.

"I expect you're glad it's all over," said Bradbury. "They say he met his end well."

"Nothing about that fiend was 'well,' sir!"

Bradbury considered her retort. "Oh, I don't know, ma'am," he said slowly. "He got a lot out of life."

"And now he's dead!"

"Aye, but my bet is that his name'll live on. . . ."

"What d'you mean?"

A steamer was passing, hooting its horns, and Bradbury waited until it had gone.

"As a creature of interest—unlike us," he answered. "As a sort of folk hero; as a ghost. . . ."

"*Ghost?*" Kate Dyson at last looked at him, one hand to her pretty mouth; the effect of that word had been electric.

"Yes," he smiled, "as a ghost. It seems he can't leave us in peace—or can't find such himself. He's already been seen and heard at Armley, disturbing folks' sleep with his prattle. I suppose his specter's abroad because he still thinks lies hanged him." He studied Mrs. Dyson's expression closely. Her eyes held all the fears of the superstitious, and he thought his journey to Liverpool had not been in vain. "But don't worry, ma'am!" he said with a laugh. "I've never heard of a ghost swimming an ocean!" And politely doffing his hat, he left her.

Kate Dyson watched the inspector walk off the quay and disappear on the waterfront. Bradbury was right—his words filled her with terror. A crane squeaked noisily and she started. It was only a crane, she saw, but the grind of its cogs made a strange sound —uncannily like the sob of a violin.

Addendum

1. A great deal has been written about Peace. His trials can be found in *The Trials of Charles Peace,* edited by W. Teignmouth Shore for the Notable British Trials series, 1926. A more readable account of the truer aspects of his life is *King of the Lags,* by David Ward, and a shorter version appears in H. B. Irving's *A Book of Remarkable Criminals.* A *History of Peace* was ghosted for Sue Bailey after his death, but is probably one falsehood from beginning to end—as is *Charley Peace, or the Adventures of a Notorious Burglar,* an illustrated nonsense published in 1880. There are also reams of tall stories sold to the newspapers in the last quarter of the nineteenth century.

2. Sue Bailey eventually did get her £100 from the Home Office —but Brion got nothing. Miss Bailey also managed to get on the low stage for a while, simply exhibiting herself as the mistress of Peace, until drink drove her to the gutter and death. Willie Ward's career on the boards was even shorter—a one-night stand in Barnsley, where he incoherently answered questions about his stepfather, and played a banjo so badly the latter must have turned in his lime pit. Old Hannah lived on until 1891.

3. Of Charlie himself, this much can be said. He was well self-educated, and an accomplished musician, craftsman, and actor. Had *he* tried the stage, his career might have been different. His success as a burglar developed only in the last few years of his life, but his passion for large ladies was his downfall. He was both

incredibly ugly and exceptionally strong; it was said he could carry a twenty-score pig on his back for a mile. He was a "great boaster," but some of his boasts were true, and he's not entirely responsible for all the myths that sprang up about him. Even a famous barrister involved him in one unlikely story.

4. The formidable Katherine Dyson became lost in America. There can be no doubt that she was the author of those letters to Charlie, and that she carried on with him for a while. Whether her lover's ghost pursued her to Cleveland isn't known—but it certainly haunted Armley Prison for years.

5. Some of the words and expressions in this book are old-fashioned, slang, or plain dialect. Here follows a short interpretation of those unexplained in the story.

Glossary

West Riding Yorkshire

Allus: always
Baan: been
Capt: puzzled
Danelagh: east coast Yorkshireman
Dawl: a fist or hand
Delf: a quarry
Dule: a devil
Flayed: frightened—although Mary Bateman was an old witch who was flayed after death, her tanned skin being preserved at Wakefield.
Fratch: to quarrel
Gallus: a gallows
Gaumless: stupid
Gumption: common sense
Halifax: hell
Menseful: respectable
Owt and nowt: anything, nothing
Te: you
Tha: you
Toogy: little
Walsh after: to desire

The Rest

Air and exercise: a flogging
Bendigo: a hat—after Bendigo Thompson, the boxer

Bellowsed: transported

B-flat polone: a fat crook

Blanket hornpipe: sexual intercourse

Dutchman: a German (insulting, on the basis that the Dutch are Germans with their brains kicked out)

Fake one's slangs: to get free, to file through fetters

Ferricadouzer: a knock-down punch

Flute: a pistol

Get the bolt: be sentenced to penal servitude

Have the banns up the chimney: live in sin

Immensikoff: a large fur overcoat

Jenny Darbies: policemen—from gendarmes

Knee-trembler: sexual intercourse in a standing position with some back-alley harlot

Look goats and monkeys: look lecherously

Make her chimney smoke: induce an orgasm

Meublements: furniture—from meubles

Nathaniel Down Below: lower than hell itself

Peg-puff: an older woman dressed as young

Pewter: silver

Pop: a pistol

Put to bed with a shovel: to bury

Rosin: a fiddler—from Rosin the Bow

Shake a ghost into: to frighten greatly

Squib: a pistol

Steak off the horn: hard meat, a tough fellow

Wash a negress: to try the impossible